THE ENGLISH WAY OF DEATH

THE HISTORY COLLECTION EDITION

BBC

DOCTOR WHO

THE ENGLISH
WAY OF DEATH
GARETH ROBERTS

BBC
BOOKS

1 2 3 4 5 6 7 8 9 10

BBC Books, an imprint of Ebury Publishing
20 Vauxhall Bridge Road, London SW1V 2SA

BBC Books is part of the Penguin Random House group of companies whose
addresses can be found at global.penguinrandomhouse.com

 Penguin
Random House
UK

This book is published to accompany the television series entitled *Doctor Who*,
broadcast on BBC One. *Doctor Who* is a BBC Wales production.
Executive producers: Steven Moffat and Brian Minchin

This edition published in 2015 by BBC Books, an imprint of Ebury Publishing.
First published in 1996 by Virgin Publishing Ltd.

www.eburypublishing.co.uk

A CIP catalogue record for this book is available from the British Library

ISBN 978 1 849 90908 2

Editorial director: Albert DePetrillo
Series consultant: Justin Richards
Project editor: Steve Tribe
Cover design: Two Associates © Woodlands Books Ltd, 2015
Production: Alex Goddard

Printed and bound in the USA

INTRODUCTION

I was very recently invited to write an episode of a TV series that will be making its way to your screens late in 2015. The head writer/executive producer – or 'showrunner' if you like, though nobody actually working in British television ever calls it that – outlined the job to me and concluded by saying that he was mainly commissioning new writers but wanted somebody more experienced in the mix. I wondered who that more experienced person was and then suddenly realised he was talking about *me*.

'But I'm young!' I found myself desperately wanting to scream. 'I'm new, I'm fresh! At least, I used to be young. I was once *very* young. Doesn't that count?'

Disciples of *Doctor Who* have always been on unusually familiar terms with the writers of 'their' show. When I was very young – not so very long ago, I want to scream – these writers were avuncular, seemingly rather formal types with names like Robert, Terrance, Malcolm, Philip and Barry. On the rare occasions they were glimpsed in public, or seen on the rear dust jackets of hardback *Doctor Who* novelisations, they were immaculately suited and tied. A polo neck was as casual as they would ever get, though neat beards were an option. They lived in North London and were married with daughters called things like Hilary or Felicity. They had usually also worked on

Crossroads, *Public Eye* or *The Man in Room 17*, and in their elevated minds a commission for *Doctor Who* was just any other job. The more exotic of them had yachts and were thus uncontactable for rewrites. They seemed almost god-like in their remoteness, their calm professionalism and their casual masculinity. These were men who sat in book-lined rooms, who typed with both hairy hands, stopping only to puff at their pipes.

When I first started writing professionally, I think I half-expected that some mysterious process would transform me over the years into one of these creatures. The writing world of the 1990s and 2000s seemed so different, though. The writers I came into contact with were, like me, nervy, hyper-sensitive characters, jostling for position and simultaneously conceited and wracked with suffocating self-doubt. We wore jeans and T-shirts and drank perhaps a little too much. The most established and successful of us were often the most irrational and jittery.

It was only when I came into contact with that previous generation that I realised that, outward appearances aside, they were exactly the same as us, and had suffered exactly the same fumbled triumphs and terrifying reverses. It strikes me that as a writer you are never quite the right age – you fear you are either too fresh and naive, or that you're past it. One of the other writers working on the new project mentioned above was, I discover from a quick Googling, born in 1990. I shudder and shake when I discover this, much the same way as my elders once used to boggle in disbelief at me when I told them I was born on the day Robert Kennedy was shot.

So it's both intensely flattering and intensely nerve-jangling to find myself with a career long enough to warrant inclusion in reprints and boxed sets. *The English Way of Death* is now twenty years old. It can smoke cigarettes, get married and join the army. I wrote it on the flickering green screen of an Amstrad word processor, at a time when the internet was just another strange thing Paul Cornell did in his garage. But, looking back, what do I see in it now?

The Virgin *New Adventures* were a bold move, transposing the Doctor from the family-friendly television series into a range of proper science-fiction novels for young adults. This was a canny and very clever switch on the part of editor Peter Darvill-Evans, who reasoned correctly that there was a comparatively large readership waiting for a more grown-up, more experimental take on *Doctor Who*. I began my writing career trying, rather fitfully, to slot into that risk-taking range.

But I had a problem. I discovered that, for me, the trappings of teatime family TV drama – the jokes and the madness, the frequent mismatches of style and content – weren't trappings at all. They were the very heart and soul of *Doctor Who*, the things that kept me watching and kept me happy. I knew that my books were going to be read by, at most, about thirty thousand hardcore *Who* disciples, but I couldn't help pretending there was a massive mainstream audience of millions out there, waiting to be entertained, and so I wrote for them. And the strangest thing happened – a lot of the readers really seemed to like that.

When it comes to *The English Way of Death* in particular, I recall that I'd recently rewatched Channel 4's 1980s adaptation of E.F. Benson's *Mapp and Lucia* novels, and caught up with the earlier Lucia novels set in London. I thought it would be fun to smash these genteel comedies of manners into *Doctor Who* and see what happened. As it turned out, with the terribly English team of the Fourth Doctor, Romana and K-9 it wasn't such a clash as you might at first think. The story thematically revolves around two halves of an alien entity coming together, which is very *Doctor Who*, but I had fun contrasting that with the romantic affairs of the guest characters, which isn't. Or wasn't back then.

But mainly, looking back at the days when this was written, I see a different me – with a lot less money but with a lot more creative freedom (the loss of which is inevitable if you move into the more team-based, closely controlled world of television). And, frankly, a lot more hair.

It's a shame these new editions don't come adorned with black-and-white dust jacket portraits of the authors. I think I could carry off a polo neck well enough to fool a new, younger generation of *Who* disciples into thinking I was a proper, manly, typewriter-savvy, professional writer. Till they read this bit, at least.

Gareth Roberts
September 2014

PROLOGUE
THE EPISODE OF THE
IMPOSSIBLE BATHING-HUT

There was a loud clanking and jolting of machinery. The engine bellowed like a wounded elephant. Finally, with a furious hiss of steam and a succession of jerks that sent luggage flying from racks and knocked those standing in the third-class carriage from their feet, the train pulled itself away painfully from the dinginess of London Bridge station.

Seated in one of the smaller first-class compartments were Hepworth Stackhouse and his valet, Orlick. Stackhouse was florid in face, with a barrel-shaped frame held firm by a corset and tightly buttoned waistcoat. His heavy red jowls shook as the train, after an enthusiastic start, slowed to a crawl, and a cemetery and a row of factories slid past his window seat in silent mockery. He cursed the railway company, he cursed his ailment, but the largest share of his spleen he reserved for Dr Hicks for insisting on this expedition in the first place. Heading away from the capital, even for a few days, was contrary to Stackhouse's every instinct, and the thought of the business carrying on without him was enough to bring a mild flutter to his stomach. The younger men in the office were capable – he'd hand-picked them – still, they were only young chaps, prone to every distraction and fribble. For success in industry, a man needs a heart of iron and a mind of quicksilver. Stackhouse knew he had both; they were family traits, and the firm bore the family name. But the blood of his subordinates was thinner stuff. Pulling his attention from the trundle of the cortège with a despairing shake of the head he said, 'Orlick. My newspaper.'

The valet's thick eyebrows twitched. 'Dr Hicks prescribed a complete rest, sir.'

Stackhouse groaned. 'Shall even my staff be turned against me? Disgraceful. The paper, man!'

It was provided, and Stackhouse turned with a speed born of long experience to the financial pages. Illogically, he felt a flash of discomfort that Stackhouse Confectioneries Ltd was continuing to do rather well in his absence. This was countered by the pleasure afforded him simply from the sight of the precisely arranged tiers of figures. In the last week, from the confinement of his bed, all work banned on Hicks's orders, he had wondered if the world of commerce would still exist on his return. It seemed to him that one was unlikely to last long without the other, whatever the proclamations of medical opinion.

Superficially contented, he turned back to the news pages and read in silence. There was a small crumb of comfort to be had in the situation; at least Orlick had secured them an empty compartment, away from the mass of holidaymakers weighing down the other vans. He was not a talkative man and disliked strangers on principle, feeling that he already knew too many people and loathed nearly all of them. Taking the car would have been much better but it had chosen the same moment as him to break down.

He was still contemplating the silence when the door from the corridor slid open a fraction and a bright-eyed head poked through. 'May I join you?' it enquired in a register both squeaky and, thought Stackhouse, somewhat unmanly.

Ill-tempered and uncivil to his business colleagues, Stackhouse had nonetheless been raised a gentleman and was too much an adherent to form to object to the request, and he nodded his assent. The door was pushed back fully and the newcomer entered, loaded down with two large suitcases which he proceeded to swing up on the rack. Stackhouse surveyed him. The man was about his own age, say 47, and wore summer clothes: a gaily patterned sweater; a turquoise scarf thrown over his shoulder at an artistic angle; and a pair of indecently bell-bottomed trousers. Accessorised to this emasculated ensemble were a gold-plated wristwatch and a thin moustache, and his hair was grey and cut close in small curls. He settled in the facing seat with a series of sighs and squeaks, a black canvas bag balanced on his knees. There was something unsettling, squirrel-like, about the way his thin pale fingers plucked at the crease of his trousers. It made Stackhouse want to swat him as one swats a fly.

'Oh dear, oh dear, I thought perhaps I wasn't going to make it,' he said, still catching his breath. 'Heavens above, what a mad dash! How I ran!' Stackhouse grunted. The stranger twittered on. '*Bradshaw* might as well be a wall of hieroglyphs to me. All those stations, all those times, and so hard to follow the line across the page. So I find myself running like an escaped convict half across London.' He blew out his cheeks and fanned himself. 'Goodness me.' His eyes narrowed as they settled on his fellow passenger's face, and his brow furrowed. It was an arrangement of the features with which Stackhouse was too familiar. 'I say,' said the stranger, 'have we met?'

'I'm sure we haven't,' said Stackhouse, returning to his newspaper.

'Are you certain?' The stranger tapped his chin. 'I know your face.'

'I'm sure you do not.'

'Half a moment.' The stranger clapped his hands together. 'I think I have it.' His squirrel face came closer. 'Throw back your head, smile and wink.'

'I shall do no such thing,' said Stackhouse, who was considering sending Orlick to fetch an official of the railway.

'Yes, I thought so.' The stranger rummaged in his canvas bag, brought out a brightly coloured tin and pointed to the lid, upon which a familiar ruddy face threw back its head, smiled and winked. 'Stackhouse's biscuits, 103 varieties,' said the stranger. 'I'm right, aren't I? It is "you", isn't it?'

'It is, in point of fact, my late father,' replied Stackhouse, the courtesy slipping from his voice. 'Now would you kindly let me alone.'

But the stranger, like so many of his kind, was not to be diverted. He took a biscuit from the tin and held it up between thumb and forefinger as if it were a gold sovereign. 'The Zanzibar cracknel. These are my particular favourites. Second only to the almond dessert crunch, or perhaps the apricot and ginger swirl. You must feel very proud, Mr Stackhouse.' When the other did not reply he continued, 'Your produce in the home of every cultured person. "No hamper is complete without one."' He nibbled at a corner. 'Superb. Well, goodness. Do you know, I never thought I'd be taking the pleasure with their proprietor.' He waved the tin over. 'I don't suppose you'd…?'

'No, I would not,' Stackhouse replied. It was not only the stranger's overfamiliarity that caused him to reject the offer; he had grown up around sweets and desserts and biscuits and found them tiresome. The tightness of his own girdle was the result of good red meat washed down with plenty of dark port.

The stranger finished the biscuit and flexed his delicate fingers. 'Heavenly. Quite heavenly.' His face took on a dreamy expression and he offered a hand. 'Closed.'

'I beg your pardon?'

'Closed.'

'What is?'

'I am.' He leant forward and shook Stackhouse by the hand. 'Percival Closed, esquire. I'm not in business myself.'

'Really?' Stackhouse said brusquely. The truth was his annoyance was waning and being replaced by a sense of intrigue. Definitely the fellow was a fool, and yet a far from ordinary one.

It was usual for Stackhouse to be halted in the street by passers-by eager to thank him for bringing such exquisitely processed sugar into their lives – they did not suspect how small was his involvement in the production process – but never had the greeting been made with this lack of civility or respect. There was a queer air of inaccuracy about the man. Briefly Stackhouse wondered if he might be a foreigner, but rejected the idea. The squirrel's foibles, accent and demeanour were English enough.

The train started to pick up speed, and Closed nodded with childlike approval as they passed through a handful of minor stations and the villas of Croydon, regimented and new, became more interspersed with intervals of green. It was as if these ordinary sights were thrilling and strange to him. Stackhouse made a show of reading his newspaper, but his eyes kept flicking of their own accord back up to his fellow traveller.

After a few minutes, Closed started to riffle through his bag, and at length produced a pair of knitting needles and some balls of wool. 'My vice,' he told Stackhouse. 'Puts me at ease, you know.' He began to knit, dividing his attention between the clacking needles and the window, which now provided a pleasing view of fields segmented by hedgerow. A herd of cows lay on their sides in the sunlight, looking like a set of knocked-down skittles, and confirming Stackhouse's prejudices about the country and its inhabitants.

'Have you business in Brighton?' Closed asked suddenly.

The abruptness of the enquiry caught Stackhouse unprepared. 'I'm not going to Brighton,' he replied.

'Fancy,' said Closed. 'Neither am I.' He looked up from his knitting, although the needles continued to move with mechanical unerringness, and studied Stackhouse again. 'You're an awfully ruddy chap, aren't you?' he observed gauchely. 'I'd lay odds that you and I are heading not only in the same direction but to the very same place.' When Stackhouse did not reply he nodded and tittered. 'Nutchurch, eh?'

Stackhouse and Orlick exchanged an uneasy glance. 'You are correct, sir,' Stackhouse told Closed. 'Although I don't see what business it may be of yours.'

Closed ignored the remark. 'Tricky liver, is it? Heart giving you trouble? Or diabetes? I suppose in your profession you would be at risk. Temptation on all sides.'

'None of those things,' Stackhouse said. 'My physician has advised me to take a short rest, that is all.' He gave his newspaper a definite rustle, licked his thumb and turned a page. 'A lot of nonsense, in my opinion. Never felt finer.' He kept his eyes away from Orlick, who had been waiting at table two weeks previously and seen him turn from red to blue and crash into a bowl of beef consommé.

Closed shook his head. 'One must attend to one's health, Mr Stackhouse.' He sighed and looked up at the ceiling. 'And you'll find Nutchurch such a charming place. Remote, unspoiled. Quite a haven, in fact. And to stroll along the beach, taking in the brine – such a delight!'

To Stackhouse's ordered mind it seemed incorrect to take pleasure in lack of activity, and Closed personified all his doubts about the treatment prescribed by Dr Hicks. He might go to be invigorated and return as feeble and lacking in fire.

He watched as Closed returned his attention fully to his knitting, sighing and muttering like a loon, and prayed for the journey to pass swiftly.

The final stage of the journey to Nutchurch was accomplished by changing at Worthing for a train on the branch-line, and the connection was spectacularly late. Amongst the group of passengers assembled on the platform, Stackhouse became steadily more aggrieved by the insouciance of the railway company's employees. Several times Orlick was sent to make complaints and on each occasion he returned to convey a vague assurance that all possible efforts were being made to arrange the connecting service. Stackhouse's only further communication with Closed at this stage came when the latter pointed to the slot machine vending squares of the firm's butterscotch and muttered, 'You must feel so proud.'

Eventually they were ushered away from the crowds and into the almost empty first-class waiting room. It was as he sat there, pretending to read his paper, his face turning redder and redder as the minutes crept by, that Stackhouse noticed something particularly strange, something that was to alter his destiny.

Closed had retreated to his knitting, and was sitting back on one of the well-polished wooden boards with a peaceful expression. At a loss for mental stimulation, Stackhouse ran his eyes around the room, over the sonorously ticking clock, over the stoic faces of their fellow sufferers, and over the other man's luggage – the two heavy suitcases and the canvas bag.

Inside the bag, nestling on top of a neatly folded cardigan, was the most curious object Stackhouse had seen in his life. Just looking at it gave him a peculiar thrill, as if it was something his eyes were not supposed to look upon. It was roughly tubular in shape and dull grey in colour, although it seemed not to be made of metal but from some other, unfamiliar, substance. Its centre bulged and formed a sort of disc, into which were set several small, variously coloured switches and buttons. What made Stackhouse shudder (and he was a man not used to frights) was a sensation that the object and Closed were one of a piece, and that this elevated Closed's status from oddity to conundrum. Something of his feelings must have shown on his face, because Closed reached forward and drew the bag closer to him, concealing what lay within.

A mix of thoughts passed through Stackhouse's brain. His dominant reaction to the sight, he was ashamed to admit, was a cold kind of fear. The unaccustomed sensation brought out in him a determination to sort out the mystery and put things back in their proper place. He felt as if his collapse, this railway madness and the presence of Closed were all part of a scheme on the part of fate to confound him. He considered asking Closed about the thing in the bag straight-out, but manners held him back. And then the train pulled up at the branch-line platform and the moment was lost.

'Oh, thank goodness, at long last, and about time, too!' said Closed. He returned his knitting to the bag and hoisted up his luggage.

Nutchurch came into sight between the curve of the high cliffs that formed its wide bay. The flashing light of the afternoon sun was reflected off the sea, which was still and a deep luscious blue. The beach was fringed by a line of modest guesthouses, behind which was the village. It consisted of three identically sized and parallel streets, arranged with the tidy typicality of such places. At the far side was a small Victorian church. The streets in their turn gave onto fields rising at a gentle angle, where sheep grazed under the alert eyes of a darting collie. It was precisely this kind of pastoral scene that Dr Hicks had prescribed to lift Stackhouse's spirits, and that in fact sickened him to the heart.

The track diverged from the hills and the train passed over a short bridge and slid home, an hour late. The station at Nutchurch was small and well tended, the gravel path of the approach raked perfectly level and hedged with rhododendrons. The street beyond, with its cobbler, druggist and grain store, outside which a horse was snuffling at a trough, was startlingly backward. Such a place had no right to exist in the modern world, thought Stackhouse. It was as much out of its place as Closed, and the traffic that passed by appeared rather presumptuous, like a guest turning up early at a party. In spite of the decision he had made not to enjoy himself, and the lingering feeling of strangeness from what he had seen in Closed's bag, Stackhouse felt his natural instincts, buried under years of self-denial, react favourably to the clean air, the beating sun and the clear sky with its wisps of cirrus.

From among the small crowd of arrivals, Closed nipped forward to the first taxi at the rank. As the driver saw to his luggage, he turned to Stackhouse and waved. 'Nice to have met you. I just know you will enjoy yourself.' He made a strange sign, forming a circle between his thumb and forefinger. 'And keep on making those delicious Zanzibar cracknels! England couldn't manage without them! I know I certainly couldn't!' He climbed aboard the taxi and it was gone with a splutter of exhaust.

Orlick had hailed another car and stowed their luggage. He edged closer to Stackhouse and indicated the waiting vehicle. 'Sir? Sir, we are loaded up and ready to move on.'

Stackhouse stared after the departing Closed. The taxi carrying the mystifying stranger turned a corner and was lost from view.

'Sir?' Orlick said again.

'All right, all right, don't fuss.' Stackhouse waddled over to the waiting taxi. He felt sure he would see Closed again. In a place of this size a second encounter was almost unavoidable.

And so Stackhouse was settled as comfortably as his temperament allowed at Belle Vue, the resort's premier guesthouse; or as Stackhouse came to reflect, merely its least unattractive. As was his habit, he found much to fault: it took an age for a bath to be run; the corners of his room were fluff-infested; and the towel rail was cool to the touch. Worse, the village of Nutchurch was not quite the retreat Hicks had described. It seemed that in recent years the vitalising effects of its brine had been more widely advertised, and in consequence the place was beginning to take the overspill from the larger towns along the coast and a fair number of day-trippers making their way down on the train. Stackhouse shunned the indolent crowds thronging the beach. Several idiots had already recognised him and shouted encouragements, and there was too much flesh on display for his liking – almost enough to put him off the spartan lunches packed by his landlady. Instead he took strolls along the low sand hills that debouched from the beach on the left side. There were fewer bathers here, and the wind seemed to blow the brine in with more force, which he supposed might do him some good.

Three days in Nutchurch had cleared his chest and sinuses a great deal, and a suppleness unknown since boyhood had returned to his limbs. These results he kept private. He would return to London and wag a finger at Hicks and complain about the wasted trip, and that would be very satisfying, very satisfying indeed. The prospect cheered him and his pace through the sand quickened. Orlick followed, clasping to his chest a small hamper that contained a snack of cold sliced meats and a bottle of chilled fruit juice. If he noticed a new spring in his master's step he had the good sense not to remark on it.

Stackhouse's gaze took in the fields, the uninspiring spire of the little church, the guzzling crowds and their sticky-faced offspring. He looked over the slight ridge upon which he stood down to the shoreline, which at this distance, about a mile from the beach, had thinned to a narrow strip of shale and pebbles. The cries of wheeling seagulls added to the drowsy atmosphere.

Then the spell was broken. Nipping his way along the shore in sandaled feet was Closed. He was wearing an old-fashioned red-striped bathing suit, all of a piece, and was carrying his canvas bag. The sun flashed on an exposed circle of scalp at the back of his head as he hopped with a definite air between the larger stones. The look of innocence had been replaced by a frown of great concentration and fixed purpose. Stackhouse's mind, which had been left to idle in the last three days of agonised inertia, sprang to attention. He crept closer to the edge of the ridge so as not to lose sight of the stranger, and congratulated himself. Whatever the state of his health, his instinct for smelling a fraud was unbowed. There was certainly more to Closed than first appearance suggested.

His sudden movement sent a trickle of stones skittering down, alerting Closed, whose ears pricked up, more in the manner of a fox than a squirrel. Stackhouse backed away slightly, confident he would not be seen, and after a moment Closed went on.

Stackhouse pondered. On the one hand, he felt sure he was on the brink of uncovering a matter of large import, on the other he worried he might be according Closed a deal more significance than he deserved. If the man turned out to be nothing more than a crank, Stackhouse's actions in pursuing him along the coastline would be difficult to explain away. Yet there *was* something odd about the chap, he knew it, and his glimpse of the thing in the bag had served to strengthen his suspicion to a level from which it could not be reined in. Still, his investigation would have to remain a private fancy until he could be sure of a result.

He turned to his valet. 'Orlick. I wish for some peace. You will return to Belle Vue and await me. I will be back by six.'

'Dr Hicks said that you were to be accompanied at all times, sir.'

'Blast Dr Hicks!' Stackhouse said as loud as he dared. 'I will be alone! I have been without a nursemaid for the past forty-five years, I do not need one now!' He could feel the colour returning to his cheeks.

Orlick bowed his worried head. 'As you wish, sir. Shall I leave the hamper for sir?'

'No, no, as I have said, I shall return for my dinner.' He looked nervously over his shoulder, just in time to see Closed's striped outfit obscured from his view by a line of tall grass. 'Run along, man, right away.'

Orlick withdrew, unable to conceal the distress from his face. As he moved off he looked back several times at his master. The man was a regular old maid. Stackhouse waited until Orlick was a distant black dot among the crowds, then turned about and made up for lost time, putting the full measure of his recovery to good use as he cantered along the ridge, peering between the grass for signs of Closed's passing.

The red stripes came back into sight a couple of minutes later. Closed was standing, with the bag between his feet, smack in the middle of a tiny cove. The cliff face forming the cove's inner wall was about twenty feet high, and it was at the top that Stackhouse settled on his haunches, slightly winded. Closed was facing the sea, hands on his hips, his ribcage expanding and contracting in an assured rhythm. Stackhouse felt a moment of doubt. Had he really hurried along the hilltop just to watch this silly ass taking the air? His imagination had misled him, certainly, and he started to feel like a precious fool. There was nothing remotely out of the ordinary about the scene below him; Closed was merely an eccentric, and his own behaviour was the sole mystery. Perhaps, as Hicks had predicted, the nervous strain of his work was starting to play tricks on his brain.

Then he noticed the bathing-hut.

It stood a few feet in front and slightly to the right of Closed, although still well beyond the reach of the tide. It was a small brick building, five feet square, without external signs or markings. On the side facing the cove's wall was a wooden door, fitted with a brass knob. It was every inch a representative of its kind, with nothing of note in its appearance. Its singular oddness lay in its location. Why, wondered Stackhouse, would anybody choose to build a bathing-hut here, three-quarters of a mile from the beach, on an area strewn with large rocks and pebbles? It affronted reason, and the worries Stackhouse held for his mental state evaporated instantly. In the same way he knew when it was right to swoop on a competitor or when it was better to feign lack of interest and let the opposition destroy themselves, he felt that the answers to his questions were at hand.

He watched as Closed consulted his wristwatch. He examined his own; it was twenty past four. Closed continued to look out to sea. Stackhouse pictured a network of spies passing secret messages in and out of the country by boat. He saw himself uncovering the plot, being fêted in the press and kneeling before the monarch, all the while affecting a studied nonchalance and deploring all the fuss. He'd simply been doing his duty, king and country and all that.

He was brought back to the present by Closed, who had taken the grey tube from his bag and was fiddling with the buttons in its bulging mid-section with his long fingers. Again Stackhouse felt sick as he looked upon the thing. It was some kind of wireless, by Jove, guiding the boat in so that the papers could be exchanged. A peculiar sound, a sort of hum rising steadily in pitch, came from the grey tube, growing louder and covering the distant glee of the holidaymakers and the gentle rustle of the wind as it brushed the tall grass of the sand hills. Stackhouse was forced to plug his ears with his fingers. Down in the cove, Closed seemed unaffected.

The pressure on Stackhouse's skull built up, and tears streamed from his eyes. A gust of stinging sand was blown into his face. He bit his tongue, tasting blood, and fell back as if punched by an invisible fist. Through stinging tears he saw the sky, a beautiful improbable blue.

The sky wobbled. A distinct pulse shook the heavens, an unnatural wink that curved down in less than a second. At that exact moment the hum reached its limit and howled its last.

Stackhouse could not say how many minutes he remained lying in the grass, his aching head pressed face down against the long, sweet-smelling blades. But when his strength returned enough for him to lift himself, and his woozy senses refocused on the cove below, he saw something that capped the events of the day.

The door of the bathing-hut was half open, and stepping out was a slender middle-aged woman of average height dressed in a smart beige jacket and skirt suitable for an evening function in town. She was looking around with a sort of childish wonder, uncannily similar to that which Closed had displayed on the

13

train. Closed himself was stepping forward to greet her as one might welcome an aunt at a railway station. They were talking, but their words were lost to Stackhouse's still ringing ears. Closed offered his arm to the lady and they walked off together towards the village, he gesturing around and about and she shaking her head in apparent wonderment.

The door of the bathing-hut slammed shut as they walked off.

His curiosity further drawn, Stackhouse pondered his next move. He was torn between following Closed and his new lady friend and investigating the bathing-hut. Finally the latter option triumphed. It was like some elaborate conjuring trick, a magic cabinet. But a trick is performed to bewilder an audience, and Stackhouse had been an unwitting spectator. What if a secret tunnel led from beneath the sea to the hut? That fitted the facts as he had seen them.

Stackhouse walked on, his mind whirling with the excitement of the adventure, until he came to a rough dirt path that led down from the cliffs. His determination overcame his caution and he shuffled down. The pebbles on the shore were awkward to cross in his flat-soled shoes, but he persevered despite the discomfort and came upon the cove where the hut stood, four-square and undeniably real.

The door was fastened securely. He grasped the knob but the door would not rattle in its frame. There was no sign of a hinge or, for that matter, a keyhole. It was resolutely shut.

Stackhouse walked around the hut, shaking his head and rubbing the back of his neck. There was nothing to be done except call the police and let them have a crack at it. He might feel an idiot at first, going to the constabulary with a story of this character, but duty was duty.

As he came around to the door again, having made a circuit of the hut, he became aware of a strong odour. Something like rotting vegetables. It overpowered the clear tang of the brine in a few moments.

He looked from side to side, seeking the source of the smell. Could be one of those blessed trawlers, Italian or Greek.

Thick smoke was pouring from the foot of the door in great green designs. What happened next was so quick that Stackhouse had no time to do anything about it. The foul-smelling smoke invaded his lungs, and somehow it seemed to make a conscious attempt to asphyxiate him, as a living creature might. He screamed and his legs gave way. His big red head thudded against the wooden door, but the blow was not enough to overwhelm him. Horrified, he remained conscious as the substance, which now seemed more like a gas than smoke, first blinded him and then enveloped him in its scorching embrace. It forced itself through his pores and through the thick hairs at his nostrils.

His right side, nearest to the door, felt as if it were burning away. Then it went cold and numb, lifeless.

His left arm floundered, the thick red fingers circling in a desperate summons for aid he knew would not come.

'Orlick!' he spluttered. 'Orl—'

The smoke sealed his mouth.

It ran through his bloodstream, tainting every cell. He lost sensation in his left side. The world around him faded out.

He heard his heart stop, mid-beat. His body temperature plummeted and his blood froze. All civilisation, every trace of personality and individuality was stripped away, and he became a creature compounded entirely of animal terror.

A monstrous intelligence gripped his mind. The last thing Stackhouse heard was its voice, a thick and distorted gurgle that oozed with malignance and an unutterable hatred.

Know the will of Zodaal!'

Part One

1
LET'S ALL GO
DOWN THE STRAND

Through the space-time vortex, the region of the multi-universal domain in which time and space have no meaning, there spun a craft disguised as a sturdy blue police telephone box. A blue beacon on its roof flashed as it tumbled by, ignoring a trillion possible points of egress and heading along a particular channel. This was the TARDIS: vastly bigger inside than out, and the property of the erratic Time Lord who called himself the Doctor, his more tidy-minded companion Romana, and their dog-shaped computer K-9.

Romana entered the control room of the TARDIS, rested and refreshed after the recent strains on her abilities, when she, the Doctor and K-9 had been pitted against the undead villainess Xais. She was looking forward to finding out where the TARDIS would take them next. Recently the Doctor had fitted the navigation panel with a Randomiser in order to throw another of their enemies, the vengeful Black Guardian, off their trail. So far the strategy seemed to be working, although the destinations selected by the Randomiser were no less perilous than those chosen by the Doctor. It was a dangerous universe. At present the Doctor was absent from the control room. Romana assumed that he was somewhere deep inside the TARDIS, in all likelihood consumed by one of his sudden crazes.

'Good morning, K-9,' she greeted the robot dog, who was

ensconced beneath the console, his probe extended and his tail wagging. He was absorbing information from the TARDIS's data bank – his favourite occupation whenever he could find the time.

'Greeting reciprocated, Mistress.' He retracted his probe and turned to face her. 'All TARDIS systems are functioning at thirty-nine per cent efficiency.'

Romana stopped dead. 'What? Thirty-nine per cent?' She dashed to examine the console read-outs.

'No cause for concern, Mistress,' K-9 assured her. 'Thirty-nine per cent is the highest mean efficiency grading attained by the TARDIS in the last seventeen years relative time.'

Romana's shoulders slumped. 'Please don't tell me things like that, K-9.' She cast a glance over the panels, which confirmed that the flight functions of the craft were being performed unusually smoothly. Still, she couldn't resist reaching over to recalibrate the triple-vector zigzag plotter, which had been misset by the Doctor. As she did so, she noticed that the Randomiser was inert. The bank of flashing lights built into its glass front had all gone out.

She flicked the activator control next to the Randomiser but nothing happened. 'Strange. K-9, carry out a fault locator search on the Randomiser links.'

K-9's ear sensors swivelled like miniature radar dishes as he obeyed the order. Finally he reported, 'Links functioning normally, Mistress.'

Romana flicked the activator again. 'But that's impossible.' She took a closer look at the surrounding instruments on the navigation panel, and noted that a precisely composed string of spatiotemporal co-ordinates had been laid in to the flight computer. 'According to these readings we're on a fixed course!'

K-9 said, 'Inference is that Randomiser has been bypassed, Mistress.'

Despite the warmth of the control room, Romana shivered.

'The Black Guardian.' She made for the inner door. 'I'll fetch the Doctor.'

K-9 ticked and whirred, as if caught by conflicting loyalties. 'Expedition unnecessary. The Randomiser was bypassed by the Doctor Master.'

Romana turned back, appalled. 'He's done what?'

'Bypassed the Randomiser, Mistress.'

Romana hurried back to the console and compared the co-ordinates of their destination to the corresponding entry in the TARDIS data bank. As the match flashed up on the small screen her hearts sank. 'Twentieth-century Earth again,' she said despondently.

'An exact course has been set for the Strand, London WC2 in the Earth year 1930 Anno Domini,' K-9 added.

Romana slammed a fist down on the console. 'But why?'

'Doctor Master specified a mission of great urgency,' said K-9, 'and requested that you refrain from interfering with the controls.'

'He's done enough interfering of his own. I'd better find him. You stay here.' She opened the inner door – and almost collided with the Doctor, dressed in his shirtsleeves, who burst through carrying a stack of dusty hardbacked books.

'Watch where you're going,' he said sternly. Romana sighed. The Doctor was the only person she had ever met that couldn't even walk through a door naturalistically. He strode over to the far side of the console, knelt and set the books down, then dusted his hands and gave a short, satisfied laugh. His bulging eyes were filled with a manic zeal that she found far from reassuring. He nodded absently to his dog. 'Morning, K-9.'

'Good morning, Master. TARDIS systems are functioning at thirty-nine per cent efficiency.'

His eyes widened and he gave a broad smile. 'That good, eh?' He patted the edge of the console. 'Well done, old girl.' That said, he picked up one of the books, smeared the dust from its cover with a shirt cuff, and started to read.

Romana was infuriated. 'Doctor, the Randomiser.'

'Eh? The what?' He looked up guiltily. 'Ah, yes. The Randomiser.'

She crossed the room and knelt to meet his eye level. 'Well?'

'Well what?'

'Why are we going to Earth?'

The Doctor shrugged. 'I thought you liked Earth.'

'Opinion shouldn't come into it. What about the Black Guardian?'

The Doctor leant closer. 'Romana, if you were my deadliest opponent, and had sworn to put an end to my miserable existence, where's the first place you'd think of looking for me?'

She sighed again. 'Earth in the twentieth century,' she said perfunctorily.

'Exactly. And obviously that's the place I'd do my level best to keep away from. Therefore it's probably the safest place for us to go.' Apparently satisfied with the logic of this statement he nodded as if to close the debate and went back to his book.

Romana wasn't prepared to let the subject drop. 'Doctor, we're not talking about a small-time gangster. The Black Guardian just happens to be the embodiment of all evil in the entire universe. He's not going to fall for the oldest trick in the book.'

The Doctor chuckled. 'Why isn't he? He may well be very evil, but that doesn't necessarily make him very clever. In my experience the two things don't go together at all.' He looked upward, contemplating. 'Besides, we'll be arriving during the season, and nobody got up like that would be admitted anywhere.'

Romana gave up, and decided to try to push her fears to the back of her mind. She stood. 'Can't you take anything seriously? And what's this mission of yours that's so important?'

He put down the book and picked up another. 'What mission?'

'You told K-9 you had an urgent mission.'

He couldn't catch her eye. 'Did I? I don't think I did.'

K-9 motored forward, apparently keen as ever to set the record straight. 'Your exact words were "If that girl asks you any questions, K-9, tell her I'm doing something terribly urgent, and don't let her touch anything."'

Romana arched an eyebrow.

The Doctor stood, rather sheepishly. 'It is urgent, actually,' he said. 'Well, quite urgent.'

The eyebrow arched even further.

'Oh all right, then. Slightly urgent.'

'Really?'

'Yes.' He handed her one of the books. 'They're overdue. Should have gone back to the public library on Shoe Lane on June the fifth 1930. I've been meaning to return them, but as I spend most of my time in the future the fines would have been shocking. So I thought I'd pop back and save myself the trouble.'

Romana nodded. 'And that's what you class as an urgent mission?'

He snatched the book back. 'Yes. Smaller problems like this should be nipped in the bud. It may not seem like much, but think of the consequences. One overdue library book today, the collapse of the universe by the end of the week. It's probably how the Black Guardian got started.' He fiddled with a few of the console controls. 'And what about my responsibility to my fellow borrowers, eh?'

Romana looked along the spines of the pile of books. 'Oh yes, I'm sure there'll be a great clamour for *Febrile Diseases* and *Swine Judging For Beginners.*'

The Doctor gave her a long, hard stare. 'It pays to have a wide range of interests,' he said.

Romana joined him at the console. 'Of course, this trip to Earth wouldn't have anything to do with it being your favourite planet?'

'Of course not. It won't take a couple of hours to sort out,

23

anyway.' He looked her up and down; she was still dressed in the clothes of a Victorian street urchin. 'I'd change my outfit if I were you. If you go outside dressed like that in this time period you'll be clapped in an orphanage.'

'Estimated time of arrival on Earth, twenty-five minutes, Master,' K-9 piped up.

'I'll be in the wardrobe room, then,' said Romana, conceding defeat. As she left the control room through the inner door that led to the TARDIS's enormous store of garments from every corner of the cosmos, she was forced to admit to herself that some of the Doctor's enthusiasm was beginning to affect her. For all her protests, she found she was rather looking forward to landing on Earth.

Mrs Felicia Chater stood before the large mirror in the drawing room of her new home, her left foot clasped tightly in her right hand and her left index finger up her right nostril. She held the position for fifteen seconds (the book specified twenty, but she was tired), then untangled herself and breathed serenely. Her posture exuded health. She was a petite woman and carried her forty-two years extremely well; only the slight tightness of the skin at the corners of her mouth gave signs of advancing age, and from a short distance she was often taken for a much younger woman. Her honey-blonde hair was cut to a fashionable bell, and she took advantage of her youthful looks by dressing in free-moving skirts that emphasised the balletic grace of her motion.

The book of Tibetan exercises lay open on the escritoire at her side. She turned the page and winced at the diagram of the next position in the sequence. One was requested to sit on the floor and bring one's knees up to one's forehead. For the loose-limbed model in the picture this appeared rather easy, but Felicia doubted her tenacity after this long and disagreeably humid day. Decisively she closed the book and returned it to its place on the lowest shelf of her bookcase, which had been transported to

London, along with all her other furniture and effects. No mean draughtswoman, she had plotted out a ground plan of her new residence, with precise notation on the positioning of all objects, and presented it to the removal firm. The move itself had been most distressing. She, her spaniel Rufusa, and her maid Tebbutt had followed the removal vans in the fly, Felicia half convinced that at any moment the back doors would fly open, disgorging her goods and chattels into a heap at the roadside. Stressful manoeuvres followed their arrival in London, and Felicia had to sit down at the sight of the Bloomenfeld piano being hoisted through the upper window. But nothing appeared to have been as much as scratched; her plan had been followed to the letter, and now the empty vans had set off on the return journey to the Cotswolds and the village of Shillinghurst.

Dear Shillinghurst. Felicia allowed bittersweet memories to wash over her for a moment. She had spent most of her adult life in the village, her natural air of authority elevating her to near-royal status within its bounds, and the clear air and unspoilt countryside had seemed the perfect setting for her work as a novelist, there being so few distractions. As time passed, however, this became less and less true. Felicia came to know all of Shillinghurst and its business, and when, seated at her desk before the large bow-window of her Tudor home, she had begun to pay less attention to the novel in hand and more to the goings-on in the high street below, she saw it was time to move on. Dear though her many friends were, she suspected they were wising to her tricks, and her influence was being thwarted as a result. Certainly, it was time to start afresh.

There was a further, and equally pressing, consideration behind the move. Felicia's husband, a tiresome fellow who had dealt in oil stock, and whom she had barely noticed after a couple of years of marriage, had committed the ultimate tiresome act of dying. Her initial relief at her freedom was short-lived. Felicia was too much of a realist to equate marriage with

25

love or any other silly passionate emotion, but Mr Chater's death left a vacuum in her life that she desperately wanted filled. She missed the company. It was, she came to realise, so much more convenient to be married. It means there is always somebody in the house for one to complain to. Moping around on one's own was simply humdrum.

After a year spent in mourning – an unutterable bore but form was form – Felicia had set about finding an estate agent in London, and had secured herself the white, stuccoed, double-fronted Belgravia townhouse in which she was now doing her Tibetan exercises. Now the move had been made and she was installed, once more a citizen of the town of her nativity, and wondering if the idea had been such a very good one after all.

London was so big. The dirt and the smell she could live with; it was the vastness of the place that unsettled her. In Shillinghurst she had reigned supreme; in the metropolis it would be more difficult to exert such a majestic influence.

Tebbutt knocked and entered. Her pleasantly cragged face was an assuring constant in Felicia's life. 'Colonel Radlett has telephoned, madam.'

Felicia's ears pricked up. That was jolly quick. 'The Colonel? On the telephone?'

'I'm afraid he had to ring off, madam. He was speaking from the course at Sunningdale and was being called back to his game. He said to pass on his welcome.'

Felicia grinned, her mind ticking over. 'Oh, how kind.'

'And to say that he will be visiting you tonight at six, madam,' Tebbutt concluded. 'If it's not convenient you can return his call, he said.'

Felicia was momentarily taken aback. 'Oh no, it's perfectly convenient. Too wonderful, in fact.' The Colonel, a man some twelve years her senior, had taken a summer let in Shillinghurst for four years running and had become acquainted with the Chaters. He was not a good-natured man; in fact Felicia had privately considered him pompous and boring. However, in her galling new surroundings the prospect of a familiar face was heartening. Also, the Colonel, who had never married, was one of the names on Felicia's frighteningly brief mental short-list of possible husband replacements.

There was not the vaguest chance of them being happy together, but Felicia was enough of a realist to know that happiness has little enough to do with marriage, either.

It was now almost half past three. 'I shall rest in my room until the Colonel's arrival. We shall take a light evening meal.' She considered. 'Grilled roe, I think.'

'Very well, madam.' Tebbutt left the drawing room.

Alone again, Felicia giggled and clasped her chin in one hand. It pleased her to think that she had been in London a matter of hours and gentlemen were already calling (although it was only the Colonel). Perhaps a proposal was in the offing tonight, even.

As she climbed the stairs to her bedroom, the Colonel filled Felicia's mind. Yes, the man was bluff and rather too hearty and slightly too old, and his reminiscences of India were tedious; but he was lively, in good condition for his years, and moreover he was the sort of man Felicia knew she could control. Any threat of independence on his part she would handle with ease. The match could well prove satisfactory.

She took off the plimsolls she wore for her exercises and let herself fall on the stiff, starched sheets of her bed. The pillows, three deep, had been plumped in the way only Tebbutt knew how, lending a pleasing sense of continuity to her surroundings. She stretched and let the strains of the day melt away.

Five seconds later her rest was ruined. A high-pitched ululating whistle, continual and nerve-incising, came through the wall of the house.

Percy Closed was a happy man. He sat back in the throne-like chair, basking in sensual pleasure. He had a daiquiri in one hand, a Cuban cigar in the other, the aftertaste of dressed crab on his tongue, and the room around him was filled with the very best company. At least that was his opinion of them today; he had cursed each of the Circle more than once over the last few years. But on this extra-fine afternoon in early June, with the sun streaming in through the large window and the prospect of a dazzling summer ahead, they seemed content for once to listen to all of his funny stories and to laugh riotously at all the correct points. As he looked from face to face, Percy congratulated himself on his training technique. Each of his charges appeared entirely congruous. What an achievement!

He lurched to the conclusion of his latest tale. 'And so I said, "Madam, as there appears to be a poodle poised on the top of your own head, look no further!"' His audience shrieked. Percy felt a surge of delight at their appreciation of his wit and cleverness.

Harriet Kipps, the hostess of the party, flapped her wrist to get his attention as the laughter bubbled away on the smoke-filled air. Percy found it hard to believe that she had joined the Circle barely a year before, so complete was the transformation in her manner. Her thin, bird-like features were now complemented by a pair of round silver spectacles. Totally unnecessary, yes, but the sort of detail he liked to employ to ensure verisimilitude. 'Percy, sweet one,' she said, plainly squiffy, 'your tales are marvellous, but I often wonder just how much seasoning you are adding to the pot, yes?'

There was a good-natured burble from the others. Godfrey Wyse, one of the stalwart members of the Circle, now a very old chap with a shining pink face, said, 'Harriet, the tale is in the telling, and nobody relates a story better than our Mr Closed.' The rumble of assent that followed this remark filled Percy with a warm glow.

Davina Chipperton, who had travelled from Devon to attend the June party, extended one of her plump arms and patted

Percy on the knee. 'And now,' she said, 'I feel sure the time has come for him to give us a little tune.'

'Oh yes, do!' cried the company.

Percy drained his glass and set it down, signalling with his cigarette that, oh no, he simply couldn't, they couldn't possibly want to waste time on one of his piffling recitals.

'But you simply must, Percival,' Davina pleaded, summoning up a doleful expression. 'These gatherings would be incomplete without you in your rightful place at the stops.' She leant forward. 'And besides, you wicked thing, look what I can see!' She pointed in triumph to Percy's canvas bag, from which protruded the corners of several sheets of music.

Percy grinned bashfully, all a part of the ritual. 'Go on!' cried the company. Harriet put on a mock-stern face and gestured to the grand piano in the corner of the room.

'How much you demand of me,' said Percy at last, and took the music from his bag. 'Now, what shall we have?' he asked as he lifted his tails like a concert pianist and settled before the keys.

'"Twinkle Twinkle Twinkle"!' cried Godfrey Wyse.

'No, no, it has to be "The Love Parade"!' shouted Davina Chipperton.

Harriet Kipps put up a hand. 'How about "Moonstruck"?' she suggested. 'That's a jolly one.'

Percy nodded and brandished the correct score. '"Moonstruck" it is!' There was a cheer and with a minor flourish he began to play and sing. For show's sake Percy kept his eyes on the music, although he was familiar enough with both score and words to have performed in pitch blackness had such a feat been required. The company sighed and giggled at the verse, and began to clap in time when he reached the chorus.

'I'm such a silly when the moon comes out!

I hardly seem to know what I'm about!

Skipping! Hopping! Never never stopping—'

Then Percy's afternoon, by all expectations so secure, was

shattered. From his bag there issued a high-pitched ululating whistle, continual and nerve-incising. The effect on the company was astonishing. It was as if a breathtaking illusion had been exposed as a shabby trick, and there was something in the sudden quietude of the June gathering reminiscent of children at a party when their parents arrive to take them home. That blooming whistle, thought Percy. The trouble was, in this fantastical world it sounded so damned ordinary.

Harriet was the first to speak. 'Oh dear. Whatever can be the matter?'

Godfrey Wyse passed the bag to Percy, and he hunted beneath his knitting and brought out the transceiver, which he carried constantly. The small red light on top was winking steadily.

'I say. Is there anything wrong?' asked Godfrey Wyse.

'No no,' Percy said hurriedly, cursing the timing of the incident. He muffled the whistle by pressing the delay button on the device and tossed it casually back into the bag as though he considered the matter of no importance. 'Just the Bureau fussing, I expect.' He looked around him. 'Now, where were we?'

He was not to be allowed to resume his performance. The faces of the Circle sagged with disappointment, and lines of anxiety creased their brows. 'Hadn't you better go back to your house and answer them?' asked Harriet.

Percy mounted a last attempt to restore the carefree ambience. 'Not a bit of it! They can whistle all they like, I assure you it'll be nothing at all.'

'Hang on, old chap,' said Wyse. 'That gadget of yours is only for use in an emergency, I understood? I mean to say, we're not expecting –' he winked and nudged the air with his elbow – 'another member, are we?'

'There's nobody due until November,' Percy conceded. A ripple of consternation passed around at his words. He held up his hands, palms outward, and tried to look honest. 'Don't worry, please, any of you. We shouldn't let them spoil our day.'

Harriet nodded. 'Dear Percy is right as ever, friends,' she told her fellow members. 'We all know the frightful worriers they are back—' She stopped herself, because this, England, was their home, wasn't it? 'Back there.' She rang for her staff. 'So. More drinks, everyone?'

Percy was pleased to see a slight stir in the spirits of the Circle as another tray of cocktails was passed around. He glanced resentfully at the bag. Through the thick canvas the red light blinked. What did the Bureau want now? And right in the middle of his song, too. Well, whatever it was, he wasn't going to rush back home on their account. He enjoyed these gatherings more than he could say and was not a man to pass his pleasures by.

He took another daiquiri from the tray and moved to join Harriet. The throng had broken up into small, nervously conversing groups of two or three.

'There really is nothing wrong, is there?' Harriet asked him, her tone artificially bright.

'Of course there isn't,' he replied. He indicated the picture above her fireplace. 'Now that's a new addition, is it not? Simply charming. So much more difficult nowadays to find such treasures. That reminds me, I was at an auction about two weeks ago when I…'

The Doctor had found a creaking brown leather bag in a locker and was loading it with his library books. 'That's Romana's trouble, you see, K-9,' he said, putting the last one away. 'She's very tense, finds it difficult to unwind. It's very important to relax fully once in a while, take a holiday.'

K-9 buzzed and clicked. 'My study of the TARDIS flight log suggests that your attempt to take a holiday on Earth will result in mortal peril and violent action, Master.'

The Doctor blew out his cheeks. 'What? Rubbish.' He listened to make sure Romana was not on her way back and whispered, 'What are the odds?'

'Mortal peril: ninety-seven per cent. Violent action: ninety-eight per cent,' replied K-9.

'Pah.' The Doctor stood and examined the console, which indicated that the flight to Earth was almost over. 'It just goes to show one shouldn't rely on statistics. This is going to be different, K-9. London in the day we'll be arriving is an island of tranquillity. No invading aliens, no scheming masterminds.'

'Ninety-six per cent probability of inaccuracy of your prognostication, Master,' advised K-9, but he went unheeded, his words drowned out by an unearthly trumpeting coming from the centre column. The transparent mechanism in the middle of the console stopped rising and falling. The TARDIS had landed.

Romana entered the control room. 'Ah, there you are. Just in time. I…' The Doctor trailed off. Romana had changed into a jacket, a waistcoat adorned with a fetching noughts and crosses pattern, and a pair of copiously baggy trousers that flapped above suede shoes. A striped scarf was wrapped about her neck. Her long blonde hair fell incongruously over her back, making her appearance even more striking than usual.

'Well, you told me to change,' she said. 'Do you like it?'

'Like it?' The Doctor nodded enthusiastically. 'I love it.'

Romana seemed pleased. 'K-9?'

The dog wolf-whistled his approval.

'Good,' said Romana, and reached for the scanner control.

The Doctor caught her hand. 'Wait a moment. Do you realise you're wearing male clothing?'

'Oh. Is that a problem?'

'Well, on the whole, no. I mean, you may be asked to play a round of golf or come rowing or something, but I suppose you'll carry it off. You seem to be rather good at everything.'

Romana smiled. 'And after all, we're only going to be staying a few hours, aren't we, Doctor?'

The Doctor waved his hand effusively, 'Oh, minutes.'

The shutters covering the scanner parted to reveal a narrow, well-kept court enclosed between tall grey buildings. Fortunately there was nobody about, and so their arrival had most likely gone unnoticed. The sunlight, reflecting off the windows of the neighbouring buildings, was pleasing but painful to the eye.

The Doctor checked the console panel that contained the external sensor displays. 'Lovely day for it. Eighty in the shade, very warm for June.' He looked down at K-9. 'You'll have to stay behind and mind the shop, K-9.'

The dog's tail drooped. 'Query this decision, Master.'

'We can't have you startling the natives, it's a level four civilisation out there.' He knelt and patted K-9 on the head. 'And we won't be long.'

'Estimate that you will require my assistance within twenty-four Earth hours, Master,' said K-9.

'Nonsense,' said the Doctor. 'I managed for five hundred years before you came along, K-9, with barely a scrape.' He took his tin dog whistle from his pocket. 'In fact, I'm quite prepared to leave this behind.'

'Advise against, Master,' said K-9. But the Doctor had already thrown the whistle onto the console.

Further comment from K-9 was lost under a high-pitched ululating whistle that burst without warning from a speaker on the far side of the console. The Doctor lunged forward, flicked a button and the noise stopped.

'What was that?' asked Romana.

'Nothing, nothing,' said the Doctor. He closed the shutters on the scanner and reached for the door lever.

Romana caught his hand. 'Nothing?'

'Nothing important.' He threw the lever and the double doors swung open with a low hum. Then he jammed his hat on his head, put on his long, oatmeal-coloured coat, looped his trailing scarf around his neck, hefted up his leather bag by its fraying straps and swung it across his shoulder. 'If I paid attention to every rattle the TARDIS makes I'd never get anywhere.'

'Wait a moment,' called Romana. She had hurried round to the far side of the console and was checking an instrument reading. 'That noise. It's a transmission being made on a spatiotemporal frequency.'

'How interesting,' said the Doctor, sounding abjectly bored. He nodded to the door. 'Let's go, shall we?'

'A level four civilisation, you said? Nobody in this time period can have access to receivers operating on extra-temporaneous wavelengths.' Romana pressed a few more buttons and her face was lit by a red glow from the console display. 'Doctor, according to these sensors there's a minor release of time-warmed chronon particles in the external atmosphere.'

'Oh dear,' he said flatly and stalked out.

The Doctor stood in the doorway of the TARDIS for a moment, breathing deeply on the polluted air and listening to the sounds of the passing traffic. Apart from the TARDIS the small street in which they had materialised was empty. He looked around the sun-drenched buildings, trying to get his bearings.

Romana stepped from the TARDIS. 'That suggests there's a primitive unshielded time corridor not far away,' she said urgently.

The Doctor walked to the end of the street and pointed around the corner. The adjoining road gave onto a wide street, along which open-topped double decker buses painted claret lumbered in either direction, their sides plastered with advertisements for soaps and gravy and chocolate, crowded with sweltering passengers, most of whom had slipped off their jackets and loosened their ties. 'There we are,' he said proudly. 'Spot on, well, nearly. Aldwych. I'd hoped to be nearer the Fleet Street end, but that's very good indeed for the TARDIS.'

'Doctor,' Romana said severely. 'The consequences of time pollution could be catastrophic.'

He walked off to the left, pointing to either side with his

fingers. 'That way the Waldorf, Trafalgar Square, Charing Cross Road. That way the Savoy, the High Court, St Paul's.'

Romana followed him along the curving pavement, and took hold of his scarf as they were swallowed up in the crowd. 'We must follow that signal to its source, Doctor.'

He stopped and faced her. 'We? If you're so keen, why don't you follow it? I'm not going to let time-warmed chronon particles spoil my afternoon.'

Romana sighed. 'What shall I follow it with?'

The Doctor searched in his pockets and handed her a small cube-shaped object. 'Try this.'

'It's a transmission locator.'

'Well, of course it's a transmission locator. I was hardly going to give you a divining rod, was I?' He pointed out three settings on its face. 'These are the controls for the space-time frequency.'

Romana switched on the locator, and it emitted the continual whistle they had heard back in the control room. Hurriedly she turned down the volume knob. Above the tuner button of the device was a dial similar to that of a compass, and as she swept the locator from side to side the needle kicked to her right, in the direction of the place the Doctor had called Trafalgar Square. 'The signal's quite strong. The source must be only a few miles away.'

'Yes, fascinating,' said the Doctor rather childishly, and he set off in the opposite direction. Before crossing the road he turned and said, 'Don't get lost, will you? Meet you back here.' Without a backward glance, his bag slung over his shoulder, he moved off through the crowds with his long powerful strides.

From here it was only a matter of minutes to Shoe Lane and the library. As he walked along, dwarfed by the steel columns and bronze horses fronting Australia House, the Doctor shook his head and tutted. Trust Romana to find something like that to worry about. There again, it would probably keep her out of his hair for a couple of hours.

He emerged into the Strand and looked down past the High Court into Fleet Street and the dome of St Paul's rising above Ludgate Circus. An iron railway bridge was suspended above the trilbied heads of the crowd, many of them newspapermen scurrying back to their offices, enormous cameras slung about their necks.

The Doctor thought for a moment, convincing himself that Romana was probably going to be occupied long enough for him to take a slight detour and make the most of his day off. 'British Museum, Doctor?' he pondered, oblivious to the attention he was attracting from passers-by. 'No? No.' Something less cerebral, then. 'Ah! Now there used to be a Joe Lyons' somewhere around here, didn't there?'

That was more like it. He turned about on the heels of his boots and quickened his step.

On his way back to the party from the bathroom, Percy's attention was caught by something in the hall umbrella stand. At first his mind, befuddled by the drink and conversation, and put out by the sounding of the signal, assumed that what he'd seen couldn't be what he thought he'd seen. When he stepped closer to check, he felt slightly disappointed. He hadn't expected this of Harriet. She'd settled in so well.

A varied sheaf of umbrellas was hooked on the stand. Between the handles was a small metal box, clipped to the rack by a twisted coil of wire. Percy reached out and removed the object.

The drawing room door opened and the babble of conversation, which had started to pick up again, spilled out. Harriet stood in the doorway, shaking a finger at Percy. 'Ah, there you are, you naughty boy. Davina and I have been talking, and we've decided that you simply must—' She caught sight of what was in his hand and dried up. 'Ah. I see you've uncovered my little secret.'

Percy affected a schoolmasterish air. 'You know this is against all the rules, Harriet.'

Her face fell. 'Oh, of course I know.'

'If you'd wanted to use it you could have stayed back there.' He turned it over in his hand. It felt clammy and unnatural in his grip. 'I shall have to confiscate and destroy it, you know.'

'One fiddling flying-box?' She bit her lip. 'Oh, Percy, it can't make all that much of a difference, now can it? I've only been using it once in a blue moon, and naturally only by night. There's no harm done.' She reached forward and rested a hand on his shoulder. 'London is so charming from the air.'

He brushed her away but maintained his kindly manner. 'That is as may be. The fact remains, you have broken your contract. I'm bound to dock your allowance for this, Harriet.' He edged closer to her and whispered in her ear, 'The people here may appear cultured, my dear. Don't forget, they are savages. Soon enough they are going to split the atom and treat it like a toy.' He held up the box. 'Imagine what might happen if a gizmo of this kind ended up in their hands. There could be a disaster.'

'Steady on, dear, you're dribbling down your shirt,' she said, pushing him back gently.

Percy harrumphed. The trouble was he found it so damned hard to tick people off. He wasn't going to dock a penny from Harriet's allowance because she was his friend, and on top of that a woman, and that sort of thing just wasn't done. 'Anyway,' he said finally, tucking away the box in his pocket, 'none of the others need know of this. Shall we rejoin the party?'

Harriet pushed her glasses up her nose. 'I'd bet that many of them have smuggled things in just like I have. They're better at covering them up, that's all.'

'Nonsense,' said Percy, choosing to forget the other indiscretions he'd uncovered in the doings of the Circle. Goodness, once he'd even caught old Godfrey Wyse trying to sell Third Eye songs down Denmark Street.

Davina Chipperton poked her head through the door. 'Come along, you rotten pair!' she called. 'We were beginning to wonder if you'd made a tryst and had slipped off into the garden.'

Percy allowed himself to be dragged back into the drawing room, where tea was now being served. He reached eagerly for the biscuit tin and his fingers flexed anxiously when he saw that the Zanzibar cracknels had already been lifted away. Instead he plumped for a gypsy cream. 'I met old Stackhouse, you know,' he said, tapping the side of the tin from which the laughing red-faced bewhiskered figure winked up at them. 'On a train.'

'Oh, Percy, you've told us that story a hundred times,' said Davina. 'You were taking the train to Nutchurch to pick up dear Harriet, and Stackhouse was a red-faced buffoon with a sour temper and a nose like a mulberry.'

'He was snappy and rude and so you got on with your knitting just to put him out,' Harriet finished for her.

'Oh,' said Percy, munching on his biscuit. 'S'pose I must have told you, then.' He took a cup of tea automatically from the tray, but was yearning for something stiffer to help him cope with this trying day.

'From what I hear,' put in Godfrey Wyse, 'old Stackhouse's health has not been improved by the Nutchurch brine.'

'Oh really?' said everyone, and turned their heads Wyse-wards. Percy felt put out. He didn't like it when people knew more about the subjects of his stories than he did.

'Yes,' said Wyse. 'The word at the Athenaeum is that the fellow's gone quite potty. Handed over the running of the firm to his son, dismissed nearly all of his staff, and shut himself up at that great house of his in Blackheath.' He lit and puffed on a cigar, emulating Percy. 'Passed it in my car once, a veritable Notre Dame of a place.'

The Circle cooed their interest. Percy strove desperately to think of a way to recapture their attention. Once old Wyse got started it was hard to shut him up. A risqué remark would do the trick. 'Well, as long as his biscuits remain the same, the fellow can take off all of his clothes and swing through the trees, for all I should care!'

Everyone tittered. Rejuvenated, Percy set down his tea cup and cast his eyes over Harriet's drinks trolley. He reached for a gin bottle. 'It's far too early in the day to take tea,' he said happily, and everyone laughed again.

Felicia strode up and down her bedroom, cursing London, her neighbour, and herself for ever entertaining the thought of moving. The whistling tone had been sounding for over an hour now, and her temples were pounding from the repetition of its wailing note. The benefit gained from her Tibetan exercises had been overcome by the tensions brought on by this interruption. What could be the source of the row? To her ears it began to sound somewhat unearthly, although she knew it was most likely to be the squeal from an untuned wireless that had somehow switched itself on. Rufusa had started to bark in alarm, but now lay curled up in a corner of the room, her eyes wide, in mourning for the lark song of Shillinghurst.

Felicia heard the front door close as Tebbutt returned. Eagerly she looked out through her bedroom door. 'Well?'

'I've knocked and knocked, Mrs Chater, but there's simply no answer,' replied the distraught maid. 'It's coming from next door, but there can't be anybody at home.'

Felicia pressed a hand to her temples and swallowed. The whistle, more of a drone now, continued to wreak its depressing effect. 'I think I shall be driven quite mad if that keeps up, Tebbutt. I feel as if my head were being sliced apart.'

'I tried the tradesman's entrance as well, madam,' said Tebbutt unhelpfully. 'All the curtains are drawn and I can't see in.'

Felicia nodded. 'Tebbutt, call Mr Nutbeam at the estate agency and ask him about our neighbour. If the property is a vacant one, we may have to call in the police and have the door broken down.' She breathed deeply, recalling the words of the lama. 'This really is most vexing.' She glared at Tebbutt as if she was at fault. Such glares usually worked to galvanise staff.

Tebbutt nodded and hurried away. The whistle carried on without respite. It had been going on for so long now that Felicia, whose artistic nature led her to exaggeration, saw it in her mind's eye as a never-ending spiral, as if there had not in all the history of the universe been so much as a moment of silence. She opened her mouth in a soundless scream, fell onto her bed and enclosed her head in the soft folds of her pillow.

Rufusa, whining, jumped up beside her.

The heat was stifling. From the window of the cab, the woman who now called herself Julia Orlostro watched as groups of children ran and laughed and called to each other over the green expanse of Blackheath, with all of London spread out in the vale beyond. Kites billowed colourfully against the cloudless sky; grey-skirted nannies observed and guided the games. It was impossible for Julia to take any pleasure from this scene. Her faith in the goodness of people and the value of life had been extinguished long ago.

Her hair was raven black, and she styled it back from her high forehead. Her outfit was fashionable without being frivolous, covering her legs and bosom. This was not out of consideration to her age. In her early forties, Julia remained a stunningly attractive woman, and could have worn the more daring styles of the day with confidence. Two considerations prevented this. Firstly, in her occupation it was necessary to be taken seriously; secondly, she had a pressing need not to draw attention to herself, and any peculiarity of dress would have made recognition more likely. Her singular beauty was difficult to conceal. Still, the fuss in the newspapers had died away two years ago and the English had short memories.

The cab passed along the short main street of the suburb and travelled on a distance of about half a mile. The properties on either side of the road became more ornate and widely spaced. At last her destination came in sight. Julia paid and thanked the driver, trying to keep the trace of her Italian accent from her voice.

She was left on the roadside, with nobody else in sight. The house she had been summoned to was set back from the road, its moderately sized grounds concealed in large part from passing eyes by a line of lofty poplars. Julia slipped through the iron gates, her black-gloved hand resting for a while on the wrought escutcheon of the Stackhouse family.

Beyond the gates the grounds were in disrepair. The harsh sunlight picked out every rotted fruit, every overgrown flowerbed and thriving weed as she made her way up to the massive front door of this once sumptuous abode. There was a pond to the west side of the building, now clogged with emerald slime.

The shadow of the house passed over Julia as she walked on. There was something about its grey bulk that caused her, the strongest and most unflinching of women, to pause and pass a hand over her brow. On this sweltering day the house was an apparition from a darker season. No light or sign of life could be seen through its dirt-streaked windows, and thick creepers of beetroot-coloured ivy spread like the fingers of a monster over the porch. There was none of the fastidious concern for outward appearance so beloved of this nation's ruling classes.

Before she reached the front door it opened slowly.

The first thing Julia noticed was a faint odour. She had expected the smells of dust and damp and decay, but this was different, pungent, like vegetables rotting in a street market. The next thing she noticed was the grossly distorted shape of the manservant standing framed in the doorway. The man might have been handsome, long ago. Now he resembled nothing so much as a walking cadaver. The top half of his body was twisted at an obscene angle beneath his liveried topcoat. Worse still was his face. The colourless skin was pale and stretched tight back over his skull, causing his cheekbones to protrude alarmingly. Beneath beetling brows his eyes, their pupils dilated to malevolent points, stared directly at her. He spoke in a surprisingly clear voice. 'Miss Orlostro?'

'That is I.' Julia advanced to the threshold, determined to suppress her feelings of alarm. She faced the ghoul squarely and said, 'And you are?'

He moved back, allowing her to enter the hall. 'I am Orlick, Mr Stackhouse's valet.' His blank eyes swept over her again, but there was nothing usual in the motion. Julia felt that Orlick was not interested in her as a man might be, rather that he was studying her as if she were a member of a newly discovered animal species. He lifted an arm and indicated across the hall without separating his fingers. 'This way, please, miss.'

Julia looked around quickly. The house was as bleak inside as out. The curtains and drapes on the front-facing windows had been closed, but had started to rot, allowing shafts of sunlight to pierce the gloom. The parquet flooring was cracked in places, and the walls were bare and infected with patches of mould. The odour of rot was everywhere, and Julia covered her nose with her handkerchief as she followed the shuffling Orlick to the stairs. The atmosphere of decay, particularly on this blazing day, seemed odd and unreal. It was as if an unnatural force, powerful but slow, had worked its way into the house and accelerated the processes of decline.

'Mr Stackhouse will see you now,' said Orlick, his booted feet landing with a clump as he ascended the uncarpeted staircase.

'Forgive me,' said Julia, deciding to be direct, 'but you are unwell. Won't your master allow you rest?'

'Merely a mild bout of the Spanish flu,' said Orlick without looking back. 'It will soon pass.'

Julia examined the blank walls and peeling paper. 'Mr

Stackhouse seems to have few of the comforts that an Englishman cherishes.'

'He has sold almost everything,' said Orlick, wheezing as if the effort of climbing the steps was too much for him. 'It was necessary. Soon you will understand all.'

The implication of his words was apparent, and Julia fell silent. The journey upward continued, with the oppressive atmosphere increasing as the light grew dimmer and the odour stronger. There was nobody else within the walls, none of the small army of domestics it would require to run a residence of this size. Tired of the blank passageways and landings of the house, Julia looked again at Orlick. His grey hair was thin and wispy and fell over his dust-covered shoulders. It was then she noticed something else about him, something that threatened to break her resolve and send her fleeing back out into the daylight. She swallowed hard. In these last few minutes she had come closer to unreasoning fear than at any point in her career.

Orlick's body was wreathed in a thin mist, light green in colour, a kind of gas. The substance seemed to cling to him, shifting and rearranging itself constantly around his twisted form like an aura.

At last they emerged onto the top landing, a short dark passage that ended in a heavy oak door that stood slightly ajar. Orlick stepped aside, and gestured her forward again. 'Mr Stackhouse awaits you, miss.'

Julia advanced, her heart beating furiously. She was caught between terror and intense curiosity. What lay in wait behind the door? What sort of man was Stackhouse to run his estate down like this?

She passed through the door. The attic room beyond was small, about ten feet square. A round window similar to a porthole was set into its slanting roof, admitting a strong circular beam of sunlight which served only to emphasise the surrounding darkness. Caught in the beam was more of the green mist, which Julia now realised was the source of the appalling smell. The walls of the room were, as she might have expected, bare, and there were only two items of furniture. The first was a small wooden table upon which rested a filled crystal decanter, two glasses and a newspaper. The second furnishing was a high-backed velvet-lined chair, swathed in mist. Julia had long ago dismissed religious faith from her life, but as she rested eyes on the occupant of the chair, a powerful primal foreboding tugged at her stomach, warning of devils and unfathomably alien evil.

That the creature in the chair had once been a man she had no doubt. From a distance it might have looked like a man, clad as it was in the outer vestments of an English gentleman. But as it lifted its glowing green eyes to meet hers, and its heavy jowls cracked in a sickening rictus smile, Julia knew that she was in the presence of something inhuman.

'Miss Orlostro,' it said in a strangely inflected voice. 'You answered our call. That is good.' It raised a hand and waved Orlick forward. The valet stepped up and poured out a drink, which he then handed to Julia. 'I am Stackhouse,' the inhuman continued. 'Let us discuss our business.'

2
TEA IS INTERRUPTED

On this sticky and preternaturally warm afternoon the Lyons teashop in Fleet Street, on the ground floor of Temple Bar House, contained an assortment of weary shoppers and harried office and hotel staff snatching a quick break from their work. The Doctor bustled in, his leather bag still slung over his shoulder, and apparently unaware, in his thick woollen coat, of the extreme temperature. He found himself an empty table and spent the next couple of minutes perusing the menu. The gentle susurration of conversation and the clink of china and cutlery, overlaid with the aroma of freshly brewed tea, should have been conducive to achieving his desired state of rest, but his mind was elsewhere. Absently he observed one of the waitresses, immaculate in the white apron tied around her black uniform, flicking a cloth at a wasp that was zizzing around the pink-icing cakes displayed in the shop window. It simply wasn't fair. Trouble seemed to follow him around. He looked at his fellow customers and grunted. They seemed to be enjoying themselves. So would he. He decided to forget the time pollution – for a few hours anyway.

Something else was distracting him. He sensed a vague threat in the air, as if this peaceful scene was separated by only a thin margin of safety from an unexpected threat. Over the centuries his sensitivity to lurking evil had been honed to an almost instinctive level, but what he felt now was altogether different. Most frustrating of all, the impression was familiar. He struggled to place it, in vain. His memory really was appallingly cluttered.

A waitress approached and he ordered a pot of tea and a plate of scones. The wasp had been successfully evicted and he turned his attentions to his bag and the books it contained. He couldn't remember when or why he'd taken them out in the first place.

The first book he picked from the bag had a blue jacket. Big white letters on the front proclaimed *Physics Is Fun*. The Doctor snorted and flicked it open. 'Well, that's a blatant lie to begin with,' he muttered.

The waitress appeared with his tea. 'There you are, sir.'

The Doctor held up a finger. 'Can you feel something?' he asked, opening his eyes wide in what he hoped was a welcoming expression.

'Beg pardon, sir?' asked the girl.

'Something in the air. A sort of vibration.' He poured out the tea. 'I'm sure I've felt it somewhere before.'

'No, sir, really, sir,' said the waitress, who was starting to look alarmed.

The Doctor clicked his fingers. 'I've got it! Okushiri, 1720… or it might have been Krakatoa, 1883. Or Peru, 1910?' He smiled up at the waitress. 'They make superb rock cakes in Peru.'

She smiled and withdrew. The Doctor buttered a scone and went back to his book. His fears were groundless, then. The seismic disturbances he'd experienced on those trips were unlikely to happen in England. It was probably the heat getting to him.

'Approach,' said the figure in the chair. Julia stepped forward and took the glass of brandy from Orlick. Like his manservant, Stackhouse's body was twisted beneath his clothing. His heavily jowled face, framed by whiskers, was grey and corpse-like, and only his shimmering green eyes showed signs of vitality. His voice was deep and sounded forced, as if his vocal chords were bellows being used again after decades of neglect. He was the last person Julia would have wanted as an employer, but the rewards he had promised were too great to ignore.

She gulped at the brandy, bringing the glass up and down in a swift and casual motion to show that she was not afraid, or at least that she was prepared to conceal her fear. The remaining glass stood unclaimed on the antique table. She indicated it. 'You're not joining me?'

'I have no need of liquid sustenance,' Stackhouse replied gutturally. 'This body's required moisture quotient is maintained by a layer of condensation in my primary form.'

The words meant nothing to Julia. She began to worry for Stackhouse's sanity as well as his health. 'For Orlick, then?'

'Orlick has no need of liquid sustenance.'

'Then who?'

Another figure emerged from the pitch blackness behind Stackhouse's chair. Julia cursed herself for not noticing him before, and her thoughts turned briefly to the pistol concealed in her jacket. He stepped into the light – a shabby-looking man in his late thirties, with an ill-fitting suit accentuating his thin, feeble frame. His tongue flicked nervously over his colourless lips in the same tempo that his small brown eyes darted from side to side, giving him the appearance of a weasel. His greasy black hair was combed over one side of his head and dandruff speckled his lapels. He extended a white hand. 'Woodrow,' he said. 'Alfred Woodrow, of Messrs Woodrow, Woodrow and Spence.' His delivery was sibilant and his handshake weak. Julia's heart leapt when she realised that he was introducing himself as a solicitor, and for a moment she feared that her summons from Stackhouse had been part of a blackmail plot. Then she looked again at Woodrow and her temper cooled. Everything in his appearance suggested corruption. His relationship to the law, she felt sure, was an unconventional one.

'Mr Woodrow,' said Stackhouse, 'is acting as my representative at present. It was he who suggested contacting you, with a view to offering you employment.'

That answered one of Julia's questions. She addressed Woodrow. 'How did you know where to find me?'

He smiled. 'I have a friend who owed me a favour. A friend of a friend of yours.' He picked up his drink. 'The crossing from Amsterdam was comfortable?'

'Perfectly.' She turned back to Stackhouse. 'Your telegram specified a significant payment.'

Stackhouse's shoulders shifted in what she took to be a shrug. 'Money is unimportant, merely a means to an end. If you complete your task I will honour the offer.'

'Eight hundred thousand pounds?'

'That is right.' Stackhouse raised an arm and waved Woodrow forward. 'Explain. We must move swiftly, time is short.'

Woodrow nodded and handed Julia the newspaper from the table. 'Turn to the picture page.'

Julia did as he had instructed, noting as she did so that this was *The Times* dated 20 February of the present year. The largest photograph showed an extraordinary figure: a short man dressed in a white suit, with a shock of wild hair and a shaggy grey beard. His eyes were enlarged by a pair of thick-lensed spectacles that were balanced on top of a carrot-shaped nose. There was a rose in his lapel. What lent especial singularity to his appearance was the box-shaped hat he wore.

'This is the first stage of your mission,' said Woodrow. 'Study this man well. There must be no errors.'

Julia looked up. 'Who is he?'

'His name is Porteous,' said Woodrow. 'He was a professor of physics at Edinburgh University, and has been here in London for a few weeks.'

Julia nodded. 'You want him dead?'

Stackhouse raised his head. 'No,' he said, with surprising

force. 'You must not kill him. He is needed alive.' His fingers clutched at the arms of the chair. 'I need him alive. The intuitive centres of his brain must be preserved.'

'Mr Stackhouse has arranged to meet Porteous this afternoon at a location in Central London,' said Woodrow. 'You are to keep the appointment and convey him to this address.' He handed her a small white card. 'Porteous may resist. You must persuade him.'

She frowned. 'And that is all? For eight hundred thousand pounds?'

'It is only the first stage of the task,' replied Woodrow. He leant closer and whispered, 'I will explain everything later. If you are wise you will do as instructed.' For a moment she glimpsed the suppressed terror behind his confidence. Raising his voice he said, 'You are familiar with London?'

'You should know that. I lived here for three years.'

Stackhouse spoke again. 'You accept the offer?'

'Yes,' said Julia without hesitation. The reward was only part of the reason for her acceptance; fear of Stackhouse and intrigue as to the nature of his scheme also played a part. 'Where will I find Porteous?'

The signal tracer led Romana out of Aldwych and onto the Strand. The street grid of the city, she realised gloomily, was entirely illogical. It was really no wonder that Earth was the Doctor's favourite planet. She turned back and examined the graceful curve of Aldwych, and recalled briefly the covered cloisters and high towers of the Capitol on Gallifrey, laid out with devastating symmetry and order, heavy and grandiose and dull. Erratic they may be, she thought, but at least the people of Earth knew they were alive.

The problem was that following the trace on foot through the winding and unfamiliar architecture of London would waste hours. She stopped to examine the locator. Beneath its screen was a row of tuning controls. If she took a rough reading from this proximity and calculated from that a suitable route using the public transport system her task would be made a lot easier. The locator's triangulator estimated that the signal source was some miles away south-east.

Romana was familiar with the primitive underground railway networks of Earth. In a capital city, stations would be spaced close together, so all she needed to do was follow the street until she came to one. She congratulated herself on her reasoning, and set off along the Strand towards the area the Doctor had indicated as Trafalgar Square.

Sensitive by nature, Felicia was on the point of ordering Tebbutt to call the removal firm and arrange for transport back to Shillinghurst. The fearful whistle continued. She felt like a prisoner undergoing torture, and was stamping her feet on the carpet of her room at the injustice of it all.

Tebbutt reappeared.

'Yes?' Felicia snapped.

'I checked with Mr Nutbeam, madam.'

'Yes?' Felicia snapped again, closing her eyes and pinching the bridge of her nose to emphasise just how much she was suffering.

'The house next door belongs to a Mr Closed, he says. Quite a quiet fellow, usually no trouble.'

'Hah!' Felicia waved in the general direction of the squeal. 'It is too much for me to bear. I shall present this Closed with my medical bill. This is abominable. My sinuses –' she pinched her nose harder for emphasis – 'my poor sinuses are throbbing. The agony!' She glared at Tebbutt again. 'And what is Mr Nutbeam planning to do about this dreadful screech?'

'He says there isn't much he can do, madam, and that you'd be very unwise to have the door broken down or a window smashed as Mr Closed could then accuse malicious damage.' Tebbutt swallowed.

'I, malicious damage?' Felicia smote herself on the chest. 'I cannot think; I cannot sleep; my head is pounding. The damage is being done to me! Why should I be victimised?'

'Goodbye, my dears,' called Davina Chipperton from her car, 'and many thanks again, Harriet. Simply wonderful afternoon!' She waved her fat fingers at Percy, who stood in the doorway of the house. 'Farewell, sweet Percival! Until next month, *'Wiedersehen!'* There was a protracted flurry of waves and cries and then she was gone. Most of the Circle had already departed. Only Percy and Godfrey Wyse remained – Godfrey because he was almost always the first to arrive and the last to leave any function, and Percy because he was feeling tired and unwell, in a merry sort of way.

Percy blinked in the bright sunlight and noticed that his hand was resting on one of the pillars of Harriet's porch. Why was that? He removed the hand, lost his balance, and would have cartwheeled over if Godfrey Wyse had not hurried to his aid and propped him up. 'Think you've put away a bit more than you should have, Percy, old fellow,' he said, laughing.

'Not a bit of it.' Percy brushed him away but his efforts to remain upright unsupported were ill-starred and he cannoned back into the door. Suddenly he found himself longing for his big comfortable bed. 'I'm perfectly… Er, er, I've lost the word…' His view of the residential Mayfair street wobbled uncertainly.

Harriet reached over and straightened his collar. 'Naughty boy. How are we going to get you back home?'

'I can give you a lift,' Wyse said obligingly.

Percy waved the offer away. 'Thanks, old man, but I'm quite all right, really.' He patted Wyse on the shoulder then turned to Harriet. 'I suppose I'd better be going, then.'

There was a concerned look in her eye. 'You're worried about something, aren't you, dear? You always drink like a fish when you're worried about something. It's that signal, isn't it?'

'Ah, curse the blasted signal,' said Percy, steadying himself. Harriet was correct, of course. Its unexpected sounding had thrown his world into confusion. He looked across the street, at the commissionaire of a hotel dressed in top hat and purple greatcoat, and felt a strong sense of unfamiliarity. 'Can we truly say we belong here?' he babbled. 'Any of us?' He nodded to Harriet and Godfrey, picked up his bag, and staggered away.

'I say,' he heard Godfrey call from behind him, 'Percy, are you going to be safe getting home in your state?'

Percy refused to answer. Of course he would be safe. He waved over his shoulder. 'Charming afternoon, so pleased to join you. Until July, then.'

It was now half past five. The Doctor, on his third pot of tea and his umpteenth scone, sat upright at his table, stirring, buttering and reading. He took little notice of anything in *Physics Is Fun*. It really was embarrassingly elementary, and he couldn't think what had occasioned him to withdraw it from the library in the first place. His earlier protests to Romana had been a sham; the selection of books could have been made by another person. In fact, he thought ruefully as he dabbed his knife at a blob of apricot conserve, they probably had been.

Keeping up a front was getting more difficult as the afternoon wore on. It was perfectly all right to go storming away in a huff to prove a point, he reflected, but only if one has been genuinely driven to the point of huffing. Much as he might have wished for it during his adventures, relaxation just didn't become him. Frankly, he was bored, and the matter of the time pollution was starting to push itself back to the front of his mind. Instinctively he scrabbled in his pockets for his dog whistle. It wasn't there. Another consequence of the huff. Well, he couldn't be expected to be right about everything. He wasn't a miracle worker. He'd just have to go back to the TARDIS to fetch K-9. There was no time to be lost fussing about.

He was about to depart when he heard a distinctive voice from the other side of the shop. 'I'm telling you, girl,' the voice was saying in a broad Scottish accent, 'that lettuce is rusty.'

The Doctor looked across at the speaker. He was a short man in his middle fifties with wild, white hair and a bushy beard. He was dressed in a white suit, displayed a pink rose in his tophole, and an extraordinary box-shaped hat was jammed on top of his head. His anomalous aspect wasn't all that marked him out, however. Hadn't he seen the chap's face before? For the second time in a matter of hours the Doctor was consumed by a vague jog to his memory that he couldn't pin down. How irritating it all was.

The strange little man looked up at the waitress who was attending on him. 'Don't tell me it's fresh, it's rusty!'

'We've never had a complaint before, sir,' said the waitress.

'Lass,' said the little man, 'have you ever grown a lettuce?'

'No, sir,' said the waitress with all the patience of her kind.

'Well, I have.' He slammed a palm down on the table and held up his plate of salad. 'And I know a rusty lettuce when I see one.'

'I'll see what I can do, sir.' The waitress nodded and moved away.

The Doctor scratched his head. He could have sworn the man's face was one he'd seen recently; not just in the last century or so, but in the last couple of weeks. That was extremely unlikely. Logically, thought the Doctor, he had to be somebody he'd seen earlier today. That was impossible, too. He'd come here straight from Aldwych without stopping to talk to anybody. And the hat was very distinctive – not the sort of fashion one might forget easily.

'What's your problem?' the man snapped across the room.

'I'm terribly sorry,' said the Doctor. He decided to adopt the indirect approach and find out what he could. 'Your hat is intriguing.'

'There's nothing wrong with my hat,' the little man snapped, frowning. He narrowed his eyes and looked the Doctor up and down. 'Are you the biscuit man?'

The Doctor shook his head. 'I don't think so.' He intended to ask for clarification, but his enquiry was forestalled when the door of the tea shop swung open and a tall, dark-haired, expensively dressed woman walked in. There was a faint olive colouring to her skin. Probably a Sicilian, thought the Doctor. Her eyes, jet black and fierce, swept around the few remaining customers and settled on the bearded man. She was a most unlikely customer for a Lyons tea shop.

She crossed to his table, walking with the casual elegance of the Continental. 'I have been sent to collect you,' she said.

The little man hooked his fingers in the pockets of his waistcoat. 'You have, have you? Where's the great man himself? His telegram said he was going to meet me right here.' He stood up and stuck out his bearded chin. 'I hope this isn't going to be a waste of my time.'

'Please come with me,' the woman said calmly, indicating the door. 'My employer is waiting. He is anxious to meet you.'

'Well, I'm not so keen on a man that breaks his engagements. He can whistle.' The little man turned away.

The woman produced a small silver revolver from inside her jacket. 'You are coming with me.'

The remaining customers, who had been following the altercation with the sort of amusement reserved by the English for the antics of foreigners, reacted to the sight by screaming, leaping to their feet and backing away. There was a general clatter of overturning chairs and smashing crockery.

'Now,' said the woman, gesturing to the door. 'Outside. And not one word from the rest of you. None of you move.'

The bearded man flushed. 'Wait a minute, lady, what the hell do you—'

'I said be quiet!' She gestured with the gun. 'Out!'

The man stood and shuffled out, grumbling behind his beard.

The Doctor, alone of the tea drinkers, was unafraid of guns. He waited until the woman passed before his table, then kicked it over and lunged for the weapon. Her lightning response startled him; she brought the gun around and fired at point-blank range. The Doctor ducked and threw himself backwards and into a dessert trolley, which he brought crashing down on top of him. There was more of a commotion, and he heard the bell over the door ring as the kidnapper and her victim went out.

A waitress knelt beside him. 'Oh, sir! Oh, sir!'

The Doctor looked down at his white shirt front, where a patch of dark red was expanding. 'Oh dear,' he said.

'Fetch a doctor!' somebody called.

'No need!' the Doctor cried, dipping a finger into the redness and dabbing it on his tongue. 'She missed. Shocking waste of raspberry pavlova.' He stood, brushed off the splattered remains of assorted cakes from his front, and realised that he was the cynosure of all eyes in the shop. 'Tell me, did any of you recognise—' He broke off and smote himself on the forehead, leaving a streak of lemon pie. 'Of course!'

He leapt for his upturned table, picked up *Physics Is Fun* from where it had fallen and searched its pages frantically. He stopped at a particular photograph and tapped it with a long finger. 'Aha! I knew I'd seen him somewhere before!' He read from the caption beneath the photograph, '"Professor Heath Porteous, formerly of Edinburgh University, seen demonstrating what he calls his advanced electrical barograph. Professor Porteous was perhaps the world's leading authority in physical geography and has lectured extensively around the world, but was dismissed after making wild claims about the Earth's crust." How interesting!' The Doctor squinted at the photograph and noted a familiar box shape on Porteous's head. 'Wonder why he wears that hat? Still, none of my business. I'd better get after them, hadn't I?'

He dropped the book, tossed a five-pound note to the waitress, cried 'Keep the change!' and made for the door of the tea shop.

Through the glass he could see the rush hour crowds. The heat remained intense and their faces were basted with sweat, and the Doctor couldn't help but wish for rain. Rain was what defined the national character. Most of the best days he'd spent on Earth had been murky, at least.

He didn't reach the door.

The thing that stopped him began with a faint rushing noise in his eardrums. This increased in volume, becoming first a rumble, then a deafening drum roll, then a thunderous roar. Dimly the Doctor was aware of more screams, from inside the teashop and outside in the street, but his eyes were streaming and he had sunk to his knees.

Then it came. A ripple passed through the room, strong enough to overturn the few standing tables and upset the stands in the window. The remaining slices of cake flew through the air. The Doctor himself was thrown against a wall, head first.

London shook.

3

THE INFERNAL VAPOUR

Colonel Radlett's green Hispano-Suiza, its chassis robust and well polished, its engine positively roaring its good health, was moving through the streets of Victoria. On this beautiful day the Colonel had taken off the lid and he made an inspiring figure at the wheel, upright and straight backed, his sharp blue eyes fixed ahead. He had played a splendid game, in particular around the fourteenth hole, leaving old Binky Mulliner stranded in the sand. Ha! It felt good to be positively roaring along on a day such as this, your heart full of the summer, your blood pumping through your veins, with a sporting triumph behind you and a social triumph ahead.

It was the thought of his imminent appointment with Mrs Chater that gave the Colonel slight pause. Truth was, he'd never been a ladies' man. From young adulthood he had been under the impression that every unmarried woman he came across would try to ensnare him and settle him down and force him into a routine. (Of course, he already lived his life to a precise and unalterable schedule – but it was *his* schedule.) He was a prime specimen of manhood, even now, when most other fellows of his years were getting round-shouldered and pot-bellied. He was sure that young girls had their eye on him wherever he went; he could hardly be missed, with his formal gait and forthright manner. Now, as he made his way towards

Belgravia, he retraced his more recent thoughts on the subject.

First off, he wasn't getting old or incapable. A ten-mile run, daily at dawn, saw to that. But over the last few years, since returning from India, he'd become conscious of a sort of emptiness in his life. Not in a damn fool sentimental kind of way; but he was starting to imagine what married life might be like, and the arrival of Mrs Chater in London had magnified these imaginings. He hadn't seen her in a few years and his mental picture of her was cloudy. Hadn't been paying her much notice at the time, he supposed. Thing was, she was passably attractive, and financially appealing. She wrote novels, so she'd be indoors most of the time, which was all to the good because he'd be outdoors most of the time. Best of all, although she was a bit of a bore going on about her books and plots and characters and stuff, she was not the passionate sort of woman. In the three summers he'd been up at Shillinghurst he'd never seen so much as a pat on the shoulder pass between Mrs Chater and her husband. This much relieved the Colonel. He wanted none of that sort of business. The type of marriage he envisioned involved separate beds, light conversation over the breakfast table, the occasional spot of entertaining, and perhaps a very occasional drive out to the country, if she fancied it. Also, he liked the sound of this spacious townhouse referred to in the notice of arrival she'd posted to him. Might make for a handy base.

His thoughts were pulled firmly back to the present as, just after the car turned into Belgrave Road, three extraordinary things happened one after the other. The road lurched to one side; the motor was knocked about as if by the hand of God; and a young chap was suddenly right in front of the bonnet. The Colonel's lightning-quick reflexes had him wrenching on the handbrake, and a collision was just avoided. The front wheels of the car clunked up onto the pavement and the engine cut out.

Well now. The road couldn't have moved, and he was the

finest motorist in the land, so the only explanation was that the young fool had wandered into his path. Yes, that must be right. He blinked in the strong sunlight, stood up, and shouted at the boy, 'You young idiot! Are you trying to get yourself killed?'

The recipient of his wrath had been knocked to the ground and was picking himself up. He was a slender chap, dressed in Oxford bags and a jacket. Was probably half tight. The Colonel stared at him with open dismay. The clothes were bad enough, but the flowing blond hair was worse. What was London coming to?

The youngster dusted himself down. Dash it, his nails were painted! 'I was thrown into the road, as a matter of fact,' he said haughtily. 'Local seismic activity. Quite minor, fortunately.'

The Colonel looked him up and down, and swallowed hard. He felt as if the world had taken another lurch. This feller was a young girl! His jaw dropped open.

'Are you all right?' asked the girl. Even spoke like a sahib! She came closer, staring directly into his eyes. He had wrestled a Bengal tiger single-handed without fear but her stare almost caused him to swoon. She looked about. 'I didn't realise there was tectonic shift of that intensity in this continent. Still, never mind.' She nodded good day to him, turned and walked off, holding what looked like a small cigarette case out in front of her. She appeared to have totally forgotten him.

The Colonel knew he could never forget her. His heart had melted into a sticky, pumping ball of goo. As he watched her slender, boyish, betrousered figure heading off along, the pavement the securities of his character, fifty-eight years in the making, crumbled.

Quickly he restarted the engine, swung the motor about and drew level with her at a courteous distance. 'Excuse me, er, miss,' he called. 'Feel bad for shouting and all that. Want to take a lift?'

'No, thank you very much,' she replied and turned her head away. Dash it, she was *wonderfully* feminine!

The Colonel struggled to control himself. To her, he meant nothing. It was damned unfair. He longed to leap from the motor à la George Clarke and make some despairing romantic gesture, but he couldn't.

Instead, he decided to try and forget the whole thing, and carried on up the road towards...

Towards blasted Felicia Chater, who could never compare.

Left behind in the TARDIS, K-9 was experiencing a fierce internal conflict. He had passed the time by sorting through data stored in the space-time craft's log, and put his protective function on standby. It would not be quietened for long, however, and was now advising the central decision-making cortex of his brain – the part that organics sometimes mistook for a personality – that it was his duty to check the external environment and, if necessary, track his master and mistress and give assistance.

His tail probe wagged with worry when the external sensors of the TARDIS console reported a recent increase in seismic activity. This, together with the signs of time pollution noted earlier by Romana, increased his concern. He turned from the console and sent a signal that tripped the door control. 'Prerogative of this unit to apply independent reason,' he announced. 'Seventy-eight per cent probability that Doctor Master will require additional input.'

He whirred through the door of the TARDIS and out into the street, where he described a full circle, his variety of appendages glowing, twitching and throbbing. His tracking sensors locked on to the distinctive alpha wave pattern of the Doctor and he trundled off. 'Coming, Master.'

His emergence onto the main thoroughfare was marked by incredulous stares from passers-by. 'No cause for alarm,' he assured them. 'This unit is non-hostile.'

Julia had cuffed Porteous behind the ear with the butt of her revolver, and had been bundling him into Woodrow's car when the tremor struck. She was thrown back on the pavement, from which she witnessed the terrifying ripple that passed along the upper storeys of the nearest building. At that moment the sun had seemed to flare up like a comet. Driven by duty, Julia had picked herself up, thrown Porteous into the car, and driven off.

In one way the tremor had been fortuitous, throwing the city traffic askew and enabling her to race through Central London unchallenged. She gradually reduced her speed as she travelled eastward into more sparsely peopled streets.

Woodrow's directions took her to the cramped docklands of Wapping, where it seemed a small army of men was working to unload the many cargoes travelling up the Thames. Even on a day of such cloying heat the river was flat and umber. The tremor hadn't bothered these men, Julia thought, as she passed a group pushing huge crates along on large wooden trolleys. Whatever their class, the English made it their business not to be impressed for too long by anything.

The warehouse was on the fringes of the area. It was large, taking one side of a street to itself, and faced a similar but derelict building. Two things about it impressed themselves upon Julia. One, there was an absolute silence to the place; every other corner of the area was alive with cries and shouted orders and the camaraderie of working men, backed by the hoots of incoming ships. Two, the windows were black as pitch, the scorching sun simply not reflected on their panes.

In an unsettling way, just like earlier at Stackhouse's residence, the big wooden doors of the warehouse were thrown open before she had time to get out and knock for admittance. She waved her thanks to the thin, grey-overalled men who had opened the doors for her. The gesture was not returned.

The car passed through the doors, and was swallowed up by the blackness. Julia's throat tightened and she took a hand from the wheel. For a few seconds, as the car rolled forward, this limbo seemed all-enveloping. A horrible sense of isolation washed over her. Then a yellow light cracked the darkness open, revealing what lay beyond.

The first thing she noticed was the presence of the pervading odour. The warehouse's interior stretched ahead of her for several hundred yards. It was brightly lit by three large arc lamps positioned in a triangle around the walls. The high ceiling was inlaid with an inverted pattern of old-fashioned grappling hooks and wheel-and-pulley mechanisms, but there were no crates, boxes or packing cases down below. The work being conducted here was nothing so mundane.

At the centre of the space was a long curved device made of a green non-reflective metal, into which were built an array of knobs and switches and several large circular screens across which coloured patterns whirled and sparkled. The device crackled with energy. It was supported by a network of metal piping, and this was still under construction. New pipes were being soldered into shape on rudimentary lathes and work benches lined against a wall, then inserted into the gantry-style array. The noise coming from the lathes was terrific, causing Julia to cover her ears from its sharpness as she stepped from the car.

Woodrow was beside her suddenly, showing again his irritating habit of lurching from shadows. His dishevelled appearance was made even more ragged by the harsh light of the lamps, giving him an aura of dust-motes. 'I know what you're thinking,' he said with inappropriate eagerness. He waved a finger about in a vaguely circular motion. 'One of Mr Stackhouse's inventions. Keeps any sound or light from coming in or out. Magical, really.' His eyes were circled by sore red patches and he was shaking, just perceptibly. 'Mr Stackhouse will be here soon, very soon.' He peered over her shoulder, anxiously twisting his fingers. 'You've brought him? Porteous?'

'Of course.'

She walked back to the car and indicated the supine form of the scientist. His box-like hat was secured to his head by a ribbon tied under his chin. Woodrow nodded and exhaled deeply. His shoulders sagged with relief.

'You said you would explain all of this,' said Julia. 'Well? What is this place?' She gestured to the crackling machine. 'And what is that?'

Woodrow backed away from her slowly. She noticed that he kept looking nervously over his shoulder. 'Not yet, not now,' he whispered. 'This place…' He shuddered, then snapped, 'Oh, you don't understand.'

She reached forward and took him by the shoulders. The fabric of his jacket was moist with fear. 'Tell me. You will tell me.'

'I can't talk,' Woodrow whispered. 'Look at them. Look at them!' He extended a bony index finger and pointed to the men working at the lathes and benches on the far side of the warehouse.

Julia had not given them more than a glance. All workers were the same, and she'd assumed these had been hired by Stackhouse from a local exchange and set to the task in hand. Another glance was enough to tell her that never had she been more wrong.

There were twenty of them, each man dressed in tattered and stained grey rags. Their faces were blackened with grease and dirt, and she recognised in their features something of Orlick's blankness of expression. All were disfigured, some more than others. One of them loped along dragging a broken leg; another's forearm was gashed along its length, the wound besmirched with dried blood. They worked slowly and industriously, showing no sign of discomfort. And they, like Stackhouse and Orlick, were surrounded by a curling vapour, the source of the awful smell.

Julia was again filled with a creeping sense of unreality. She turned back to Woodrow. 'Who… Who are they?'

He put his head in his hands and swallowed convulsively. To

her astonishment, he smiled slightly. 'They are the dead, Miss Orlostro. The walking dead.'

The Doctor pounded down the street back to Aldwych, deep in thought. The tremor had been a small one, some minor plate slippage, probably, but he couldn't help feeling there had to be a connection between it and the other business of the time pollution. Added to that was the remarkable coincidence that the quake had struck just after he had witnessed the kidnapping of the world's leading seismologist. Whatever was going on, the holiday was definitely off. He looked around; the people of London had taken the tremor in their stride, as might have been expected. There didn't seem to be any serious injuries or much damage to property.

Another concern was weighing on his mind. Going back to fetch K-9 from the TARDIS was an admission of defeat. The robot dog wasn't going to let him hear the end of this one.

To his considerable surprise, when he turned into Aldwych he saw K-9 trundling past St Catherine's House, startling a crowd of office workers. His first reaction was one of relief, which he hurriedly covered with a stern expression. 'What are you doing wandering the streets? I thought I told you to wait in the TARDIS!'

'Reasoning circuits caused override of this order,' K-9 said sniffily. 'Charge of wandering refuted.' He motored forward and looked up eagerly. 'Orders, Master.'

'I've half a mind to send you straight back,' the Doctor grumbled, in truth much relieved at having saved face. 'Still, now you're here you might as well make yourself useful.'

K-9 beeped and clicked. 'Your reaction not understood, Master. Suggest you were returning to the TARDIS to summon this unit.'

'Never mind that,' said the Doctor, crouching to address his pet. 'I've got a couple of little jobs for you. How are you on seismology?'

64

K-9's ear sensors swivelled. 'Please clarify?'

'Earthquakes, tremors, you know.'

'Definition of seismology unnecessary.'

'Well?'

'Query not understood, Master.'

The Doctor sighed. 'Are there any seismological records in that memory bank of yours?'

'Affirmative, Master.'

'June 1930, southern England?'

After a couple of seconds K-9 reported, 'No activity recorded, Master. However, my own observation conflicts. Minor tremor noted in this vicinity at 17:47 hours today.'

The Doctor nodded grimly. 'So, either the records are wrong—'

'Probability of error less than point five per cent, Master.'

'Or –' the Doctor clamped his hand over K-9's muzzle – 'the seismic disturbance was caused by somebody or something alien to this time continuum.' He removed his hand.

K-9 beeped. 'Highly likely connection with time pollution noted by Mistress Romana, Master.'

'Well, of course,' the Doctor snapped. 'You really like to spell things out, don't you?'

'It is not in my function to advise on grammatical sequences,' said K-9.

The Doctor unfolded a newspaper he had bought at a nearby kiosk, which he had folded over at a particular page. He tapped a report and showed it to K-9. 'How about this? Reports of minor earthquakes in California and along the Pacific basin.'

'Not recorded, Master,' said K-9. 'Probability of influence from time pollution rises to ninety-eight per cent. Suggest tracing and investigation of trans-temporal signal.'

'It's still transmitting?'

'Affirmative.'

The Doctor chewed on a thumbnail and sat back on the

pavement slightly. 'Yes, but how are we going to trace it? I gave my signal locator to Romana, and I don't want to move the TARDIS if I can help it.'

K-9's eyescreen flashed red. 'This unit is capable of tracing signal, Master.' His tail probe wagged. 'Ready.'

The Doctor frowned. 'Hold on. I don't remember fitting you with a locator facility.'

'Facility appended by this unit, Master.'

The Doctor laughed. 'You've been bettering yourself?'

'Affirmative.' He revved his motor impatiently. 'Ready, Master.'

'Wait a moment, wait a moment.' The Doctor brought forward his other purchase of the afternoon, a sturdy wicker basket with a door of wire mesh. 'Ever seen one of these?'

'Negative, Master.'

The Doctor unhinged the door. 'Never mind. In you pop.'

'Query use of this conveyance, Master,' K-9 said suspiciously.

'We don't want you attracting attention, do we?' He patted K-9 on the head. 'Go on, in with you.'

Reluctantly K-9 backed into the basket. 'This environment is unsuitable.'

The Doctor lifted him up and set off along the street again. 'Go on, then, get guiding,' he urged K-9.

The dog's voice came from the basket. 'Continue in a westerly direction, Master.'

The Doctor walked on.

'Westerly, Master,' K-9 repeated emphatically.

'What? Ah, yes, of course.' He turned around and prepared to cross the road. 'You know, K-9, it's a good thing I found you when I did. I can't see you making it over a busy thoroughfare, and the zebra crossing's still a few years away, of course.'

K-9 made a series of confused electronic sounds. 'Zebra: fast-running striped African mammal. Relevance to tracking of time signal, zero.'

'Oh, shut up, K-9,' said the Doctor.

The interminable wailing from next door continued. Sure now that it would be screeching its way through dinner, Felicia was considering her options. To call off the meal would be to send bad signals to the Colonel. He thought of himself as a lion of a man, and would surely take cancellation as a sign of weak-minded dithering. On the other hand, if she made a show of soldiering on while that ghastly howl went on and on she might appear mannish and insensitive. It was getting close to six. What should she do?

She dressed and applied her toilet, then descended to the drawing room, where sweet Rufusa had curled up with her head under a cushion to protect her long ears from the noise. Felicia sat at her typewriter, slid her spectacles onto her nose, inserted a fresh sheet of foolscap, lit a cigarette, and knocked out an inconsequential paragraph about nothing very much at all. *Undaunted* was the word that came into her head as the tapping of the keys made a pattering counterpoint to the invading howl. Undaunted was how she would appear as the Colonel was introduced. Indefatigable and self-sufficient. That would certainly impress him, without making her look too strong willed. And it would remind him of her artistic nature, which she was sure he found fascinating. Most did. What else might arouse his interest and serve as a lead for conversation? Ah, yes, her new course of exercises. She took the lama's book from the shelf and arranged it on top of the piano, where it looked casually discarded. Then she nipped back to the typewriter, with only moments to spare when there came a military rap on the front door.

Tebbutt entered. 'Colonel Radlett, madam.'

He entered, and there was a brief silence as they reacquainted themselves with each other. Felicia sighed inwardly. In the flesh, the Colonel was not the energetic and muscular man her memory painted him, but more of a strutting chicken in his plus fours and checkered cap, with his driving gloves clenched tight in one hand. Moreover, he looked as if he'd had a great shock, and there was a slight quiver in his legs. He nodded formally. Felicia felt bored already. 'Good evening, Mrs Chater. Er… Welcome to London, delighted to see you.' The words tumbled out automatically. His mind was clearly elsewhere.

'And so good to see you once again, Colonel,' she said, rising from the typewriter and sweeping off her spectacles. Bereft of their precision, Felicia's eyes swept more approvingly over her guest. He wasn't too ridiculous, she supposed. A peacock? She waved a hand. 'I must apologise for this dreadful row.'

The Colonel blinked. 'Eh? What? Row?'

Was he deaf? 'It's coming from next door and there's nothing I can do to stop it.'

'Next door, eh?' He tilted his head. 'Ah, yes. Right you are. Next door.'

She gestured to her typewriter. 'I was sure that I should feel drained after the drive down, and yet I find myself drawn to work.' She shrugged hopelessly. 'These new surroundings are filling me with new ideas, I suppose.' The Colonel looked blank, so she went on. 'I've just revised the final draft of *Three Bags Full*, you know. It follows on from *Have You Any Wool*. You'll remember I was working on that the summer before last, in dear Shillinghurst.' He remained blank. 'I have to say I'm rather pleased with it. I've developed the character of Inspector Cawston quite considerably.' She narrowed her eyes. 'Colonel, are you feeling all right?'

The direct question seemed to bring him out of his trance. 'What? All right? Yes, yes, quite all right, Mrs Chater.'

'Do please take a seat,' she said, gesturing him to the chair from which he would have a clear line of sight to the piano lid and the book of Tibetan exercises. He sat. There was another silence.

The Colonel's mouth opened and closed a few times, goldfish-like. Felicia smiled indulgently. 'Fine weather we've been having, what?' he said at length.

'Superb,' said Felicia. 'Do you know, just a few minutes ago, I was sure I felt the earth shake just a little.' She pressed a hand to her temple, displaying that in spite of her undaunted front she was still a woman. 'It must be that horrible noise from next door playing tricks on me. Still, we mustn't let these things get the better of us.'

For the first time the Colonel showed signs of animation. 'Could be. Didn't feel anything myself. Of course, a man's senses are sharpened in the jungle, Mrs Chater.'

She decided to feign polite interest. He was bound to see the book in a moment, and from there she could steer the conversation back to herself and her work and show him what a fascinating person she was and what a scintillating wife she would make. 'Oh really?'

'Oh yes,' he said, sitting forward in his chair. 'I recall once I was leading my battalion through the jungle at Chota-Hakri, fifteen miles from the nearest way-station. We'd drunk our last drop of clean water and were hemmed in every way but one. No choice but to push on. Suddenly there was a fearsome growling through the trees. The thick shrubbery made a kind of dense, dripping canopy of green over our heads, and I held my rifle at the ready, alert to any movement. The raw scent of human fear was in the air.'

Felicia concealed a yawn. She had forgotten how tedious the man could be.

Stackhouse climbed with difficulty from the back of his car, supporting himself with a silver-topped cane. His emerald eyes turned around the warehouse, taking in the activities of the workers and the warbling of the machine. Slowly he tottered towards Julia and Woodrow, his shambling walk emphasising the deathly pallor of his skin. Julia felt a powerful urge to cross herself, but remained calm as her new paymaster nodded at the sight of Porteous. The scientist had not yet regained consciousness and was slumped on a wooden chair facing the strange central apparatus.

'You have done well,' Stackhouse wheezed. 'You will be rewarded soon.'

Julia nodded. 'You mentioned a further matter.'

'In time, in time,' said Stackhouse. He edged closer to Porteous and laid a grey hand on his twitching brow. Julia's eyes flicked to the warehouse exit; Orlick stood before the doors, dark and broad-shouldered, killing any hope of escape.

One of the workers shuffled forward. The tip of a broken bone protruded from his shoulder, and his arm was twisted into three sections like the branch of a wind-beaten oak. 'Construction of the first project is almost complete,' he reported. 'The tests have proceeded satisfactorily.'

'What of the second project?' asked Stackhouse. He gestured to the far side of the warehouse, where a smaller team of workers were grouped over a large saucer-shaped object.

'The power source container is stabilised. Work on the cerebral links is continuing.' The grey creature, for Julia could see that it was not a man, added, 'Nourishment is needed. More nourishment is needed.' One of its bulging grey eyeballs swivelled in its socket and fixed her with a hungry stare. Julia shivered. She heard Woodrow, who was standing behind her, whimper involuntarily. 'More nourishment,' the creature repeated.

'It will be sent,' said Stackhouse. He turned to Orlick. 'Call Fortnum's. Double the order for the morning delivery.'

Orlick bowed his head. 'Yes, sir.'

The creature clicked its teeth and smacked its puffed lips together. 'We would prefer humans as a source of nourishment, sir,' it said.

Stackhouse growled. 'Be silent. You know that we must not draw their attention at this stage.'

'Sir, we hunger—'

'Return to your work!'

The creature hissed, tore its gaze away from Julia, and stalked away.

Porteous groaned. 'What in God's name—' He sat up and looked around him. 'Who the blazes are you?'

Julia remembered her orders. She stepped forward and pressed the revolver against Porteous's cheek. 'Quiet.'

Porteous started to cough. 'That smell!' he spluttered. 'Reeks like a line of pigs strung up at butchering time.' He caught sight of Stackhouse and raised a hand to cover his mouth. 'What the—'

'Listen,' said Stackhouse. He raised a finger and pointed to the central device. 'You recognise this?'

'Can't say I do.' Porteous moved to rise again and Julia slammed him back down in his chair. 'Looks like a big radio transmitter.'

'It is a sonic stimulator,' said Stackhouse. 'Its purpose is to increase pressure at selected points along this planet's crust.'

'And I'm Prince Leopold.' Porteous turned to Julia and pushed her gun arm away. 'Will you stop poking me? I think I'd better fetch a constable. There's a place for people like you, it's called the nuthouse.'

'Keep still.' Julia flicked back the safety catch on the revolver and placed the tip of the gun between Porteous's eyes. 'You will listen to Mr Stackhouse.'

'I'm not going to listen to any of you crackpots,' said Porteous, quite undaunted. 'Now, I—'

To Julia's surprise it was Woodrow who dealt with the situation. He stepped into Porteous's line of sight and produced a plain brown envelope from his inside pocket. 'Porteous,' he said. 'Do you recognise this residence?' He took a small photograph from the envelope. 'Well?'

'Well, it's my home,' said Porteous, looking cowed for the first time.

Woodrow showed another photograph. 'And this is your rose garden, isn't it?' He licked his lips. 'Isn't it?'

'Yes.' Porteous slumped in the chair.

'I have a colleague standing by,' Woodrow went on, 'and all I have to do is cable him using a special code word, and…'

Porteous shook his head. 'No, no. It's taken me the best part of thirty years to build that garden up. You can't—'

'It's entirely in your hands,' said Woodrow, tucking the photographs away. 'If you obey Mr Stackhouse, well, there won't be any problem, will there?'

Porteous turned back to Stackhouse. 'What do you want me to do?' He nodded to the machine. 'All that electric stuff. I don't recognise any of it.'

'Even a primitive such as yourself will learn the rudiments with ease,' said Stackhouse. 'When you are fully conversant with the operation of the stimulator, it will be your task to program it for maximum effect.'

Porteous shook his head again. 'Listen, I just don't understand you.'

Stackhouse leered into his captive's face. 'You are the only human with the knowledge I need,' he said. 'You will program the stimulator to destroy the world.'

The Colonel attacked his grilled roe as if it were the last food left on Earth. This had the advantage for Felicia that his mouth was more or less blocked, saving her from yet more of his reminiscences of India. Wrestling the Bengal tiger, the toothless soothsayer of Poonam, the punka-wallah that had saved him from a poison-tipped dart… She paid attention to one sentence in every four, and mouthed an encouragement whenever she thought it necessary. As she ate, she considered him. He wasn't so bad, she decided. Quite a catch, really.

Probably he was nervous and not used to talking to ladies. And most importantly, one knew he was there. So many of her friends' husbands were drear and reserved, if not henpecked. As Mrs Felicia Radlett – no, as Mrs Felicia Chater-Radlett – she would be able to impress with her choice of such a firm and handsome spouse. He'd be out all day golfing or shooting or whatever silly thing it was he did, and she could work uninterrupted. And he'd be handy about the house, and if she arranged her invitations carefully his tendency to ramble could be contained. Best of all, he was not the kind of man to demand caresses. She smiled. It would all work out superbly. All he had to do was propose.

'Eh? And what do you say to that?' he barked across the table. His voice wasn't that bad. Quite pleasant, really. Loud but firm. *Resonant* – that was the word.

'I'm sorry,' she said, nibbling on a corner of toast. 'I do beg your pardon?'

'I said, amazing how it turned out, with them asking me to be viceroy?'

She giggled. 'Oh, indeed, yes. What a turn-out, who'd have thought it.'

The Colonel gave another of his short barking laughs. Could become endearing, those laughs. What was his Christian name, Felicia wondered. Edward, or William, or something? She imagined a pet name. Silly Willie, or Steady Teddy, perhaps. ''Course I turned the offer down,' he said. 'Couldn't bear the thought of being sat behind a bally desk all day, signing this and docketing that. Oh no.'

'Of course not.' Felicia smiled sweetly. 'Although I seem to spend most of my time seated at a lonely desk.'

'Yes, writing your books and all that.' The Colonel looked uneasy. 'I recall a chap—'

'But I suppose it's the life for me,' Felicia cut in swiftly, pretending that she hadn't heard that menacing opener. It was time to bring herself and her fascinating career back into the dialogue. 'Even on a day as fraught as this one, my work beckons. The Inspector seems to call me to him, you know.'

The Colonel frowned and grunted. 'What with that blooming noise, I wonder how you keep your concentration up. Of course, once when I—'

'But I mustn't let it put me off,' said Felicia. That moustache would have to go, and the way he had of sweeping what remained of his hair over his head, but otherwise he was perfectly adequate. She went on. 'In fact, a challenge is what we all need once in every while, don't you think? I certainly believe it peps one up to have a spot of trouble, nothing too dreadful of course, but there again, it can be most invigorating to the character to—'

She was interrupted, but not by the Colonel. Tebbutt had opened the window of the upstairs dining room to let in the fine evening air, and through it there came a discordant wavering voice.

'I'm such a silly when the moon comes out,' the voice sang raggedly. 'I hardly seem to know what I'm about…'

'What's that row?' asked the Colonel. 'Almost worse than that wireless or whatever it is.'

Felicia, very put out by the disturbance – and just when she was making some headway! – crossed to the window and looked out into the twilight. The square garden below was empty but for a male figure moving in a zigzag between the benches. 'Moon, moon, aggravating moon –' the figure struck a dramatic pose and staggered on – 'pom, pom, pom…' He moved closer, and Felicia knew, just *knew*, he was her troublesome next-door neighbour. 'It's him, that Closed!' she told the Colonel.

'Closed? Eh? What?' he asked. 'Close the window?'

Felicia heaved the window up further and stuck out her head. As the figure came closer she saw that he was nattily dressed, if somewhat dishevelled. 'I say,' she called. 'I say! I say!'

The figure stopped and looked up. 'A funny thing happened

to me on my way here tonight… Who's that?' he said in a squeaky voice. 'Who goes there, eh?' Felicia saw that he carried an unusually shaped canvas bag.

'Are you Mr Closed?' she bellowed in Elizabethan tones.

He stepped into a pool of light cast by a street lamp and craned his head upward. 'Who is it that asks?'

'I am your neighbour,' Felicia called down, picturing herself addressing Raleigh. His face was blank. 'Your new neighbour.' She looked again at his face, her anger slightly lessened by her curiosity. He had a sensitive and gently rounded face; although at present flushed a light pink, it promised a certain artistic quality. His eyes were like shiny black buttons, and glittered in the dusk like those of an owl.

He squinted up at her and raised a juddering finger. 'That house is supposed to be empty, isn't it? Always thought it was empty; chap moved out a couple of months ago.'

'Until today,' she replied. He still looked blank. 'I moved in. Today.'

'Oh, good,' he said, and there was an odd silence. Felicia took note of the trim grey moustache that sat neatly on his upper lip. It made him look rather smart.

The odd silence continued.

She remembered that she was supposed to be angry about something, that indeed she had been angry about something until a few moments ago. What was it? She struggled desperately to recall her purpose in coming to the window. The odd silence dragged on and on and she blinked and found that she could not draw her eyes away from his. It wasn't a complete silence, of course, because there was that continuing drone from next door. Ah, yes. She'd been angry about that. 'I'm very angry about that noise, Mr Closed,' she said sweetly.

He frowned. 'Oh. Terribly sorry. Won't do it again.'

Felicia felt more lost than ever. 'Eh? Do what again?'

'Er, sing,' he called back.

'No, no. Not that noise, the noise coming from inside your house.'

He nodded. 'Ah, that noise.' He waved a hand vaguely in the air, and seemed to notice the high-pitched tone for the first time. 'Sorry. I'll see to it right away. Won't bother you again. Er, nice to have met you.' He moved as if to tip his hat, but he wasn't wearing one, and he returned his hand to his pocket, embarrassed. 'Bye bye.' He staggered towards his front door.

'Bye bye,' called Felicia. She found herself on the point of asking if they would meet again, but fortunately the words caught in her throat. That would have been both a forward and an extremely stupid question to ask of one's next-door neighbour. She pulled herself back in through the window, and turned to face the table.

The Colonel sat there, rigidity personified, his plate empty but for a circle of fishbones. Felicia blinked in the soft radiance from the dining room's lamp. Suddenly everything took on a vivid outline. Each object became more real and definite.

'Hmm.' The Colonel grunted, clicking his teeth in a quite disgusting way. 'Sorted that out, did you?'

Felicia nodded absently. 'Yes, yes.' To her own ears her voice sounded weak and distant now, and there was another sound smothering it – her thudding heartbeat.

'Well,' said the Colonel, 'it's always best to lay down the law, you know, let 'em see who's calling the shots. People think they can get away with almost anything. There was one time I remember, would have been, what, coming on for twenty years ago now, I suppose, I was in Bangalore and I was billeted with this other young chap, name of Bentley, I think, anyway there we were…'

Felicia stared at him, repulsed. He was old, tedious, and physically revolting; he was in her house and, worse, she had let him in. Now, with thoughts of Mr Closed filling her head, she found she could not remember why.

*

As she neared the signal's source, Romana found it more difficult to keep to the right direction. A few frustrating minutes passed in which it seemed that every street she turned into would lead her further from her ultimate destination. But the early evening was clear and beautiful, and she found herself rather enjoying the scents of rose and vanilla wafting from the area's large and well-tended lawns.

Then she heard it, faintly at first, an electronic note that spiralled and warbled wildly over the high rooftops of a nearby square. A quick glance at the locator confirmed her suspicions; the indicator dial was spinning frenziedly around the circular index.

Quickly, Romana found her bearings in relation to the house that seemed to be the source of the signal, and made her way around to the front entrance. A man was walking up to the front door. He carried a canvas bag in one hand, and was fumbling in the pockets of his jacket and cursing under his breath. She pulled herself back into the partial shelter offered by one of the trees that punctuated the sides of the square and considered. He looked harmless enough – but that was the sort of mistake the Doctor was always making. On the other hand, this seemed the ideal opportunity, literally, to get her foot in the door. She watched as he found his key and struggled to insert it in the lock. Deciding that anybody that couldn't manage to open their front door was unlikely to pose an intergalactic threat, Romana shrugged and advanced.

'You're twisting it the wrong way, you know,' she said helpfully.

'Thank you,' he replied fussily. From the disorder of his hair, and the flush of his skin, she supposed he had been drinking. 'But I really don't need anybody to tell...' He trailed off and looked her up and down. 'Who the blazes are you?'

Romana assumed her sternest expression. Instead of answering his question she leant forward and said, 'What do you know about the restricted flow of time-warmed chronon particles?'

The effect on him was immediate. A look of horror passed over his face, and he leapt into action, wrenching open the door and trying to throw himself through. The attempt was a total botch.

Romana grabbed him by the scruff of the neck and hauled him upright. His eyes met hers and there was terror in them. 'Well?'

'I – I don't know what you mean, miss,' he stammered. 'Er, I have to—' He swallowed rapidly and shuffled in her grasp. 'If you don't unhand me, I'll go straight to the police, I warn you. I am a private citizen going about my private business!' As he spoke he seemed to crumple, and his shoulders shook convulsively.

Romana couldn't help taking pity on him. 'Do you have any idea of the dangers of operating a primitive time corridor?' she asked, more softly.

He closed his eyes and muttered, 'Oh dear, oh dear, I knew something like this would happen one day.' Then he pushed the front door wide open, shuffled out of her grip, and said, 'I suppose I'd better invite you in, hadn't I?'

Julia watched as Porteous made himself familiar with the device Stackhouse had referred to as the sonic stimulator. The scientist's hands played over the banks of controls hesitantly at first, then with steadily increasing vigour as its properties became apparent. One of the panels inset on the device's fascia displayed a flattened image, in colour, of the Earth's surface with the coastlines picked out in red; another flashed with row upon row of faintly iridescent numbers that changed at intervals. The machine was evidently cruel and powerful and she kept her distance from it.

Stackhouse and Orlick loomed over Porteous as he worked, occasionally explaining the function of a certain fitting in their laboured way. At length the scientist turned to face them, and when he next spoke it was with an air of suppressed relish. 'You were telling the truth, sir. And you've got it all mapped out. My theories are proved. When those fools up at Edinburgh see this… Incredible. You could tune it to any point in the Earth's crust.'

'That is the purpose of the device,' Stackhouse said patiently.

Porteous scratched his chin through tangled tufts of beard. 'You may be daft, but you've got to see what you've got here.' He shook his head and swept out a hand over the machine. 'I mean, it's just fantastic. This kaboodle could earn you millions.'

'Mr Stackhouse already has millions,' Orlick said. 'And the stimulator is not for sale. You must program it as instructed.'

Porteous frowned and looked over at Julia and Woodrow, searching for any small sign of comradeship from his fellow humans. Julia kept her face still and her revolver level, and Woodrow turned his pallid face to the ground. 'Er, well, I thought that was just you joking,' said Porteous.

Stackhouse raised a stiff arm. 'You see how it can be done?'

'Well, I think so. Just a matter of training a beam from here using these –' Porteous tapped a set of black painted toggles – 'on any set of fault lines and then shaking them up right and proper. I'm not rightly certain about the workings of it, but that's about right, isn't it? It's you that's been shaking things up in the Pacific, am I right?'

'Yes,' said Stackhouse. 'But the tests are now over. You will begin work at once. You will calculate the fastest possible way of causing maximum devastation, and program the stimulator accordingly.'

Porteous nodded. 'I see. And you blackmail the world, eh? Got soldiers and a secret militia and Lord-knows-what lined up out of sight just waiting for the order to take over?'

'No,' said Stackhouse. His voice hardened and he came closer to Porteous. 'Begin immediately. This talking is pointless.'

'You're really serious, aren't you?' said Porteous, pulling his face back and wrinkling his nose. 'You really mean all of this?'

'Begin!' Stackhouse barked. The vapour that covered him swirled and seethed as if agitated. 'Total destruction of this planet must be achieved in the next three days. There must be no delays. My slaves will be watching you at all times.' He shuffled to face Orlick. 'It is almost night. We must return to the house. I must dine.'

Orlick bowed awkwardly. 'Yes, sir. I'll ready the motor.' He slouched off back to the vehicle.

Before he followed, Stackhouse turned to Woodrow and said curtly, 'Make sure Miss Orlostro understands the importance of discretion.'

The mouse-like stranger's home was a chaos of unique and useless objects, and Romana picked her way around a tuba, a suit of armour and a set of antique pistols among the many possessions scattered like toys along the length of the hall. Inside the house the signal's wail was more grating than ever, and she was forced to shout to make herself heard. 'Can't you switch that off?'

He shouted something back; she couldn't tell what, so she followed him into a spacious room on the left. This was also filled with junk. Its main feature was a dusty piano upon which stacks of papers were piled high in a precarious fashion. The heavy curtains were drawn and the stranger flicked on an electric light and proceeded to heave aside a chaise longue from its place by the fire. 'Would you mind lending a hand?' he called to Romana. 'It's underneath – the receiver.'

Together they moved the furnishing. The stranger tugged at a square of the carpet underneath, and Romana caught a glimpse of a metallic surface and a row of blinking red lights. He flicked a switch, and at last the signal was cut off.

The consequent silence was dense and charged with emotion.

The stranger looked at Romana wistfully, and there was a gleam of wetness in his eye. 'Well?' he said finally. 'What's to become of me, then? Which especially gruesome punishment have you got lined up?'

'I didn't come here to punish you.' She decided to adopt a friendlier approach. 'I'd better introduce myself. Romana.'

'Percy. Percy Closed.' They shook hands. 'But then, I suppose you already know that.' He blew his nose on a silk handkerchief and motioned for her to sit down. 'So. I'm being taken back, am I? Is that it?' He pressed the palms of his hands together and exhaled deeply. 'Always thought things here were too good to last. Can you give me time to pack a few things? Nothing big, just some knick-knacks, souvenirs, is that allowed?'

'I don't think you understand,' said Romana. 'I picked up that signal on my equipment and came for a look.'

He seemed to perk up at her words. 'But – But, er, you're not, er, local?'

'Not from this time period. In fact I'm not actually from Earth at all.' She leant closer to him. 'Mr Closed, why don't you tell me exactly what you're doing here in London?'

The last of the daylight had faded. Stackhouse looked from the car up to a sky in which the first stars were emerging. 'Soon,' he told himself. 'Very soon.' He allowed the thoughts flashing through the consciousness of this rotund body – the primary host, home to the core – to centre on the imminent destruction of the planet and the deaths of its idiotic natives. He pictured the feast to come. Sustenance would be necessary for the journey to follow.

Suddenly something cut across his thoughts. He sensed danger. 'Orlick,' he croaked. 'Stop the car. Immediately.'

When the vehicle had stopped, Stackhouse concentrated. He could barely feel it at the fringe of his consciousness, a vague and yet vigorous intelligence that was unlike that of any

Earth human. It was part of the core's function to maintain a constant vigil along the extra-sensory wavelengths. Many humans possessed a latent telepathic ability, but what he sensed now, although unfocused, was far stronger than that irrelevant babble.

'Do you feel that, Orlick?' he asked his valet.

'I can feel something, sir,' Orlick replied falteringly.

Stackhouse sat back against the padded upholstery of the Rolls. 'Orlick, you will sustain the primary host while the core investigates. I will locate and destroy this alien more quickly in my dissociated form.'

'Yes, sir.' Orlick slumped back from the wheel and his eyes closed. The vapour surrounding him billowed and a small colourless cloud detached itself and settled over Stackhouse. A moment later Stackhouse's body convulsed and fell forward grotesquely, and a second after that a much larger cloud streamed upward, puffs of gas emerging from his nostrils and from the cuffs of his shirt.

The dissociated core exulted in its freedom from the primary host. The demands of maintaining the myriad functions of an organic body were forgotten as it passed out of the car and into the night, the trace of the alien much clearer now. It was no longer Stackhouse, for a while at least. It was the will of Zodaal.

And Zodaal showed no mercy to any that dared oppose him.

Percy passed the girl Romana a cup of tea. 'There you are, my dear. Sure you wouldn't care for a drop of something stronger?' He gestured to the open flaps of his well-stocked drinks cabinet.

'No, thank you,' said Romana. 'Now, you were saying about this Bureau of yours.'

Percy sighed. In the last hour his life had been overturned, all the little certainties of the past few years dissolved in instants. He wasn't sure what to make of the newcomer; her good manners and charming smile he couldn't help taking to, but if she wasn't from back there, who was she? 'You've got the details wrong, you know,' he said with a slightly superior air.

'I'm sorry?'

'Your garb. Spot on for the period but you happen to be the wrong sex. They have rather strict rules about that sort of thing here.' He stirred his own tea. 'And the hair's far too long, of course. Your people can't have researched at all thoroughly. One can't simply turn up and expect to blend in like a lizard on a leaf, you know.'

'I didn't,' she replied. 'And I haven't got any people. I'm travelling with a friend called the Doctor.' She angled her pretty head slightly. 'What system are you using, Mr Closed? Chronon field oscillation?'

'Ah.' Percy coughed and stared at his shoes. 'Well, miss. I'm afraid to admit I don't really know. Not my place, rather. I leave all the technical stuff to the boffins back at the Bureau. And besides, the time corridor's not exactly ours, anyway. The Bureau, er, sort of stumbled upon it, in fact, and somehow got it open. Somebody else's old tunnel, leading from there to here. One way only. We couldn't go back along it, even if we wanted.'

Romana nodded. 'I see. And in your time what you've been doing is illegal?'

Percy nodded. 'Like all unauthorised time travel. It's dashed unfair. All we want is a bit of peace in our twilight years. Is that too much to ask? I was hired by the Bureau to act as their agent here, a position I've held for twelve years. There are fourteen others in the Circle now, all of them screened by the Bureau before being sent along. They pay a fee and then pass into my care. We're very discreet and we follow strict rules. No high technology, no interbreeding, that sort of thing. We're doing nobody the slightest harm.' He shuffled. 'And if I may make so bold, young lady, what gives you the right to lecture me on the morals of coming here?'

'I'm more worried about how you came here,' said Romana,

finishing her tea and setting the cup to one side. 'The time corridor you've opened up could collapse at any moment and wreak havoc on the temporal continuum. I'm sorry, but it'll have to be closed down as soon as possible.'

'Well, we could sit here and argue for hours about—' A thought struck Percy as he was reaching glumly for the teapot. 'Hold on, my dear. You said you were just passing through here in your, er, time machine thingy?'

Romana nodded. 'It was purely by chance that we picked up that signal.'

'And about when did you first notice it?'

'When we arrived. At about half past three.'

'Well, then, that's very strange.' Percy passed her a plate of buttered crumpets. 'It means the signal was sounding before you turned up. I assumed the Bureau were calling to warn me about you. Seems they can't have been. I wonder what they meant by it?'

'Well, why don't you check the message?' asked Romana.

'Good idea,' said Percy, setting down his cup of tea.

'Left, Master,' came K-9's tinny voice from his basket.

The Doctor had attracted some intrigued glances on his journey to Belgravia, a journey that had been lengthened by K-9's inability to navigate accurately through the winding streets. It was now almost dark.

The Doctor was whistling to keep up his spirits. 'Still getting the signal, boy?'

'Negative, Master. Transmission has been curtailed. I am continuing to guide you to the site of the receiver.'

'Ah. Any sign of Romana?'

K-9 beeped. 'Her heartsbeats are near, Master.'

'Ah, good. I wonder if she's got herself locked up or gassed or anything. She might have fallen down a hole, of course.' He looked around at the elegant white stonework of the houses.

'Look at those porches, K-9. Good old Sir Thomas Cubitt.'

'Correction. Sir Thomas Cubitt is dead, Master.'

'Well, maybe, but not when I knew him. He had a hand in most of the buildings around here, you know.'

'Not understood, Master. My memory contains portrait of Sir Thomas Cubitt showing only two hands.'

The Doctor wasn't listening. 'And cellars. Nobody could do a cellar like Cubitt, and wonderful window frames…'

Zodaal's concentration was soon rewarded. He sensed the alien's powerful mind and was wary of its many facets and concealed depths. Such a creature could not be allowed to live. Alone of Zodaal's many facets, the core had the power to kill.

He sped through the air, ignoring the particles of grime in his path (the residue of the human natives' disregard for their world's biosphere), his shapeless form hissing and crackling, his thoughts consumed by his deadly purpose.

In the light from a street lamp the Doctor made out the smart black letters of a street sign. 'Ranelagh Square. This must be the place, eh, K-9?'

'Affirmative, Master. Mistress Romana is located in a house on the far side of the square.'

The Doctor let himself into the railed-off garden in the middle of the square, taking care to close the gate after him. Neatly trimmed hedges were arranged in a circular pattern around wooden benches, lending a pleasing sense of symmetry to the scene.

'Master,' K-9 said suddenly. 'My sensors indicate the presence of radmium in local air.'

'What? Radmium? Don't be silly, K-9. Radmium's found only in the core of a double-spiralled star, and there isn't one in this entire galaxy. I think I should wash your sensors out.'

'Caution, Master. Re-check confirms presence of radmium in

its gaseous form. Cloud of radmium nearing.' His voice went up in pitch. 'Danger, Master, danger!'

The Doctor sniffed. Now it had been pointed out he could smell something. 'Nonsense, K-9. It's probably manure blowing eastwards. There are still a few farms in London, you know.'

'Negative, Master. Radmium detected. Imperative that—'

The Doctor never got to hear what K-9 said next. In a matter of seconds he was knocked off his feet by what he could only describe to himself as a tenacious and obstructive smell. It assailed his nostrils and invaded his mind, and he sensed a fearsome and evil intelligence at its core. The basket fell from his hand and he heard a muffled cry and a metallic crash from K-9 as he hit the ground.

The assault continued. The Doctor pressed his hands to his temples and opened his mouth in a soundless scream as he was forced to his knees.

Strangest of all, as he was strangled by the vapour the Doctor seemed to hear a peal of mocking laughter.

PART TWO

4
THE ULTIMATE OBSCENITY

The Colonel was sharing with Mrs Chater his experiences in Bellialonga. The woman seemed to be enjoying it. Only to be expected. She couldn't have had much excitement in that poky village, and it would do her some good to learn about life lived to the fullest, no doubt. She had a distracting habit of pressing the flat of her hand over her mouth every minute or so – peculiar gesture – and as his narrative continued her eyes became as dull and lifeless as marbles. Some of his stories had that effect, he knew – seemed almost to mesmerise people.

'… and sat before the rude hut was the ancient hermit, arms and legs like sticks, all in rags, and I never saw such a light in anyone's eye. Clasped tightly to his chest was a wooden idol with the most fearful expression. As yet he hadn't caught sight of me, concealed as I was in the vegetation, so I stole slowly forward…' He liked to lose himself in his memories – it improved the telling – and at this juncture it was usual to find himself back in '95 at Astmetagaga, creeping from cover, sweat pouring over his brow to run in tiny rivulets down his nose. This time was different; the dirt-encrusted hermit was replaced in his imagination by a slender young woman of regal bearing, with flowing blonde hair and a level blue gaze. '… I stole slowly forward, and I… and I…' He blinked. 'Er, where was I, Mrs Chater?'

'Colonel,' she said, rising, 'too delightful of you to recount your memoir, but I simply cannot presume to trouble you further. You must find it a drain to provide so vivid and detailed an account.'

What did she mean by that? He studied her for a moment, and she held his stare. Now the row from next door had been cut off and only the tick of the corner clock broke the silence. She wasn't an unattractive woman, he supposed, but there was a lack of vigour about her. He'd provided probably the best evening's conversation to be had in all London, and she'd showed next to no reaction at all. And now she seemed to be asking him to go.

'Ah. Suppose it must be getting late,' he said, draining his glass and setting it down with a definite thump. 'Lose all sense of time on occasion. Well.' Better make a dignified retreat. The Colonel, now he thought about it, couldn't wait to be off. Women were strange creatures. Other chaps' wives were all right, but on their own, no two ways, women were odd. Wouldn't try this sort of thing again for a while. Best to go home and tidy his medals and go to bed – seemed more natural. 'Well.' He stood up and tried to think of what to say next.

The window was still open, and through it there came the sounds of another disturbance. A lot of shouting, seemed to be. 'What in heaven can that be now?' He looked out. In the middle of the square below a tall figure was whirling about from side to side, and crying out. 'I say. Feller down there. Looks like he's having a fit.'

Mrs Chater joined him at the window. The shouting continued. 'Goodness me, I think you're right. What should we do?'

That was the sort of question the Colonel liked to hear. If action, direct physical action, should ever be needed, he was the man to be counted on. 'Well,' he told Mrs Chater. 'I'll get out there and see what help I can give.' He pounded out of the room, his spirits lifted. A good dose of crisis was the best tonic for doubts.

*

Percy scratched his head and puzzled over the sequence of short, angry bursts of static coming from the receiver. 'It's a repeated message,' he told Romana. 'But I can't make head nor tail of it.'

Romana was standing over him, a notepad in one hand and a fountain pen in the other, looking a bit like a secretary. 'You use a code, between you and the Bureau?'

'Well, yes,' he replied, shaking his head at the confused hissing coming from the small speaker. 'It's very hard to communicate down a time corridor, you know, so we have to use a simple alternating cipher. Sort of like Morse. But this…' He gestured helplessly at the receiver. 'It's all garbled, messed up. As if something's deliberately blocking the message.'

Romana seemed to be lost in thought. 'You've had no trouble of this kind before?'

Percy shook his head. 'I last had word from the Bureau just over a year ago. Yes, May '29. Everything seemed all right then.' He noted her troubled expression, and asked, 'What are you worrying about?'

'Oh, a technical point,' she said haughtily. 'In simple terms, if the message is being blocked, that suggests a block in the corridor. And any kind of block would lead to rapid decay. Perhaps that's what they're trying to tell you.'

'Really? Oh lawks. Cut off totally.' He yawned and stretched, turning off the signal with a flick of a switch. 'I don't really want to think about that sort of thing before turning in. I'm about ready to retire,' he told Romana. 'Not getting any younger.'

She sat upright in an armchair in the cluttered drawing room, appearing as unruffled as ever. She had the patient air of a statue. 'I'll sit up if you don't mind, Mr Closed.'

'Mm, yes, for your doctor friend.' He hovered at the door. 'You do suppose that he's coming along, don't you?'

'Well, unless he's been captured or attacked or fallen down a hole.' Percy gave her a confused look. 'That sort of thing tends to happen to him, I'm afraid.'

'Really, does it? A very active life you both must lead.' Percy continued to hover. 'Er, I do hope you won't consider it a presumption, if I should venture to enquire, that is to say, er…'

'What?'

'It seems only fair. I've given fair explanation of myself. So, you and your doctor friend. Where exactly do you come from?'

Romana frowned. 'Nowhere very exciting.'

'I see.' There was a pause. 'Am I to infer that's the only answer I'm going to get?'

'Perhaps you haven't asked the right question.'

Percy was halfway to formulating a reply to that when there was a muffled shout from outside. 'Who can that be at this hour?' he said. 'People have no consideration nowadays.'

Romana shot up from her chair. 'The Doctor!'

With the lithe grace of a panther, the Colonel shot into the garden and examined the centre of this noisome activity. Closer up, he saw that the victim of the fit wore a long, old-fashioned coat, the sort of garment he remembered his father turned out in on wintry days, and a dangerously lengthy woollen scarf of many colours. Chap had a mass of curly brown hair and eyes as big as golf balls. A painter, the Colonel supposed, one of these artistic types. Prone to afflictions of the mind; not enough physical drill.

'Now, steady on, man,' he shouted, running up. 'Get a grip of your – what the dickens—' The Colonel clutched his nose and doubled up, coughing. The painter was covered in a thin mist that seemed to glow a sickly green in the lamplight, and the stench coming off it was appalling. Bad fruit, something like, but many times more pungent. Could almost be poisonous. His eyes watered and he found himself falling lengthways along a wooden bench.

He coughed and spluttered, and straightened in an attempt to make out the scene as a clatter of footsteps sounded. Two figures appeared from the dark; a balding man in a gaudy shirt and flapping linen trousers, and – And… and her, the wonderful girl with the flowing blonde hair. And she was going to find him laid out like this! No!

The Colonel pulled himself up, wheezing. 'Now, hold on, keep calm, I have everything under control,' was what he meant to say, but the stench overpowered him and he fell over instead.

He lay on the ground, and a blush started to burn his cheeks. He heard the girl shouting 'Doctor! Doctor!' and another voice, something like that of a showtime puppet, which said, 'Danger, Mistress! Presence of radmium! This unit unable to assist!'

It was time to restore order. With a mighty effort, the Colonel lifted himself up, coughed out as much of the poison as he could, and assessed the situation. The painter was now on his knees, his eyelids closed but fluttering; the wonderful girl was fiddling with the catch on a dog basket, of all things; and the other man had his head in his hands and was swaying from side to side in sheer terror. 'Nobody think of lighting a match,' the Colonel told them. 'Gas can be highly dangerous.' It was all he could think of to say.

Suddenly, with a rush of displaced air that ruffled what remained of his hair, the green cloud was gone. It seemed to lift itself entirely from the painter and disappear over the trees, spitting and seething like hot oil as it did so. It carried the dreadful stench along with it, and after the chorus of shouts and cries the abrupt silence that followed its passage was overwhelming.

He leapt forward, seizing his chance. 'Best not to move him, miss,' he told the girl, who was hunched over the supine form of the painter. 'I'll put matters in hand. Send for a doctor.'

'He is a doctor,' she said, without even looking up at him. She cradled the painter's head and addressed the dog basket. 'How is he, K-9?'

That high-pitched voice came from the basket, and the Colonel felt the world shifting around him. 'Life signs constant,

Mistress. However, the Doctor Master has withdrawn his outer consciousness as a defence.'

The foppish man took one of the Doctor's arms. 'Oh dear. Shall we get him inside, then? What was that thing? Looked like a great cloud to me.'

Although the question hadn't been addressed to him, it was the Colonel who answered. 'Some pocket of chemical gas drifting over from a factory, I shouldn't wonder. Public hazard.' Even as he spoke he realised there had not been the slightest breath of wind all day.

The others ignored him, and carried the unconscious painter away.

Felicia was captivated by the dramatic scene played out in the square. It was Mr Closed that held her attention; his daring manner of dress pleased her greatly, and the panicky windmilling motion of his arms as he battled his way through that cloud of whatever-it-was she found most endearing. She'd never come across people like Mr Closed and his friends before. They all looked so wonderfully artistic, so very London. The poor chap who'd had the fit could well be a painter, and the flowing blond hair of the young lad in the Oxford trousers was daring in the extreme. She would make their acquaintance post-haste. They were plainly her sort of people. She pictured herself at unconventional parties mixing with the demimonde, where she would at last get the chance to unleash her experimental poetry. Perhaps she would even be introduced to socialists! How different it would be from Shillinghurst; how distant that parochial world now seemed, and how far beneath her!

'Oh, what a time we are going to have here,' she told Rufusa, who had sprung up to the window ledge at the first sign of the commotion. They watched together as Mr Closed led his associates away, and the Colonel, who had made a silly ass of himself by wobbling about and toppling over like that, tidied himself, waved stiffly up at her, and made his way back to the house.

'Odd lot, that,' he said upon his return. 'Didn't seem quite the right sort, you know.'

Felicia flashed him an icy smile, full of her new-found Bohemian contempt for the mundane. 'Really, Colonel? All a lot of fuss over nothing, probably. And was it really necessary for you to go tearing out like that? In my experience I've found that, in general, people are perfectly able to handle their own affairs.'

He gave an awkward shuffle. 'Just doing what I thought best. Anyway. Better be off.'

Felicia turned back to the open window. 'Good evening, Colonel. Tebbutt will show you out.'

Zodaal shrieked through the night sky over London, his thoughts blotted out by rage at his victim's triumph. The mind of the alien – he had sensed how it knew itself, as Doctor – had been too strong, erecting a barrier around itself and somehow equalling the ferocity of the attack in its defence. Only by concentrating himself totally on the destruction of his opponent could Zodaal have triumphed, and that would have lessened the binding energy with which he sustained his core, making him as powerless as his lesser selves. How he longed for renewed corporeal existence. Very soon, he reminded himself, all would be restored to him.

His fury was such that he could not ignore it. There were many humans out of their houses at this hour, although most were congregated in alehouses and picture palaces. All he needed was one human, a solitary specimen on which to pour out his loathing for their entire pathetic species and its petty concerns.

Such a human was easy to locate. Zodaal found him wandering drunkenly down an alley. His mind was empty and soured by drink. How the humans loved to debase themselves. Zodaal reminded himself he would shortly be ridding the universe of the corrupting taint of humanity.

He swooped without warning, enfolding the human in his suffocating grip. The beast's struggles brought him pleasure, and he savoured its final attempts to escape as he compressed himself into its body and crushed its feeble frame limb by limb. He extruded parts of himself and licked the vital juices from the brain.

Only partially sated, Zodaal removed himself, letting the skin-stripped and whitened bones of his victim fall to the cobbled street with a clatter. He steadied himself, orientated his senses, and crackled through the air on the way back to the form of Stackhouse.

It was hard to know what to make of the Doctor. He was an enormous hulk of a man, and Percy was not a habitual lifter of any weight greater than that of a generously filled cocktail glass. Romana acquitted herself well on that score, supporting her comatose colleague if not with ease then with admirable pluck. She dragged him back into the house, along the clear path through the hall and into the drawing room. Percy followed, carrying what seemed to be a squawking dog basket. He didn't want to look inside.

Romana settled the Doctor on the chaise longue and slapped his face lightly. 'He's gone into a state of sensory withdrawal.'

'Burn a feather under his nose?' Percy suggested. 'I've a bottle of salts.' He looked dubiously around at the accumulated mess. 'Somewhere, I think.'

'Don't worry. It might not be safe to wake him.' She stood up and sighed. 'The shock of the attack might have knocked him out for hours.'

Percy frowned. 'Attack? How do you mean? It looked more like a touch of the heebie-jeebies. Frightful odour.' He looked over the Doctor's apparel. 'He's got the clothing wrong as well. What a mish-mash.'

The dog basket squawked again. 'Mistress. Request release from this conveyance.'

'Sorry, K-9.' Romana unhinged the metal grille of the basket and a sort of metal box whirred out, beeping and flashing. 'How are you feeling?'

'Function unimpeded,' the box reported. It swivelled to face Percy and a menacing stub protruded from what seemed to be its nose. 'Identify yourself

'This is Percy, K-9,' said Romana. 'A friend.'

'Input accepted, Mistress.' The box retracted its weapon attachment and, astonishingly, nodded to him. 'Greetings, friend Percy.'

Percy waved feebly back. 'Greetings, er... K-9?' Hurriedly he brought his hand down. 'That is totally out of context,' he told Romana. 'Hundreds of years. It's a...' He couldn't bring himself to say the word.

'Computer,' said Romana.

'Ssh,' cried Percy, waving frantically for her to keep her voice down. 'You can't say a word like that here, not now.'

'Why? Nobody's listening.'

Percy shuddered. 'That is hardly the point. You really have very little idea of how to go about this sort of thing, for all your high-minded talk.' He knelt to inspect K-9. 'What does it do?'

Romana shrugged. 'Ask him.'

Percy felt foolish talking to a machine after so many years in the early twentieth century. 'Hello, K-9. How do you do?'

'Unspecific. Define "do",' it replied.

'Oh no,' said Percy. 'Er, what is your function?'

The computer's disc-shaped ears swivelled. 'Function is to assist and protect the Doctor Master and Mistress Romana. Abilities include data retrieval, defensive action and extrapolation from sensory input.'

'No tricks, though? Leaping through a burning hoop and all of that?'

'I am not equipped with leaping mechanisms.'

Percy rocked on his haunches and tittered. 'What fun. I suppose that you'll be able to tell us exactly what happened to your master over there, then?'

'The Doctor Master was attacked by a cloud of bonded radmium, friend Percy,' said K-9.

Romana looked up from her vigil over the Doctor. 'Radmium? That's impossible, K-9.'

Percy was starting to get confused. 'Er, why is it impossible?'

Romana shrugged and ran a hand through her hair. 'Well, for one thing, radmium's formed only at the cores of double-spiralled stars. And there aren't any of those in this whole galaxy.'

'That's what I said,' an unfamiliar voice boomed. Percy jumped. The Doctor had sat bolt upright. It looked as if he'd had an electrical shock. Every curl of his hair might have been statically charged.

'Are you all right?' asked Romana.

'Perfectly, perfectly.' He leapt from the chaise longue and walked up and down. 'Yes, everything's in working order, more or less.'

Percy felt he ought to say something. 'You went into a sort of mystic trance.'

'No, I withdrew to my subconscious. Learnt that trick a long while ago.' He held up one hand, fluttered his eyelids, and said in his deeply resonant voice, 'Ohm.'

'Yes, this is my home,' said Percy.

'Not 'ome, *ohm*,' said the Doctor, his eyes opening wide. 'It's a sort of meditation. Now what's all this rot about radmium?'

Romana stepped forward. 'Well, K-9 seems to think you were attacked by it. There was certainly something out there, the odour was overwhelming.'

The Doctor rubbed his chin. 'How very interesting. I can't say I've ever been attacked by a smell bef—' He broke off suddenly and slapped a hand over his mouth.

'What's the matter?'

'I've just realised,' he whispered.

'What have you just realised?'

'You've forgotten the introductions, Romana. We'll have to give you some lessons in etiquette.' He gave Percy a toothy grin. 'I'm the Doctor. Who are you?'

For a short while following the departure of Stackhouse and Orlick, Julia kept a silent watch over Porteous. She came to realise that her caution was unnecessary; the scientist had taken to his task with enthusiasm, and confined his efforts to further study of the sonic stimulator. As he babbled on under his breath, comparing one set of dials and levers with another, Julia beckoned Woodrow to her side. 'I want answers.'

He demonstrated one of the sudden spasms to which he was prone. To Julia he appeared always to be on the verge of vomiting. 'I think I know only half the truth. And even that is too horrible.' His eyes filled with a ghastly fire. 'Do you really want to know? Will you thank me for telling you?'

Julia nodded. He made a gesture indicating that she should follow him away from the workers, and into an area shaded by a quirk in the roof. 'I've a small office not far from here,' he said eventually. 'About eight months ago I received a summons to Mr Stackhouse's home in Blackheath. That surprised me considerably. My base of clients was composed in the main of gentlemen of much lesser position. I drove up and saw what you did – a splendid property in a woeful state. Stackhouse had dismissed every one of his servants but Orlick, and cut all links with his business and family. I gather he was taken ill some months before and had never fully recovered his health.' He mopped his brow. 'Back then, you know, I thought he was only insane, I did not fully understand…'

'Continue,' said Julia.

'He required me to sell off the contents of his residence

as speedily as possible. I had arranged such auctions before. Within a month I had raised millions. What comforted me, what kept my fear and doubt at bay, was his agreement to pay me a ludicrous figure for my services. There was a plenitude of mysteries about the man, and as you are aware even to look upon him is to invite terror, but I thought foolishly that I would soon be about other work, and that this business was a spot of luck. The dangers of associating with a madman are forgotten when one stands to benefit. But his business with me was not yet concluded. He had me rent this warehouse, and through my office ordered vast quantities of certain chemicals and metals, which were delivered here. Then…

'Then came the order which was to reveal the full horror of his condition. He sent me out to the countryside, into Essex, one night early this year. A few miles outside Colchester, where a gang of men were at work, building houses. I was to arrange an accident. I sawed through a link of chain, and a tackle carrying shoring timber crashed down, killing the men.'

Julia bristled.

Woodrow gave a short mocking laugh. 'You still believe in honour, do you? That there is a code to these things, you of all people believe that? Ha! Money is the only order, the agency through which good and bad men arrange their works. I won't deny I felt guilt, and it might have consumed me if I hadn't seen what happened then. Stackhouse and Orlick were there, at the site. Before the echo of the crash had died away I sensed their presence – you can always tell from that foul air that surrounds them. And then, I heard a voice. In my mind. I'd never heard anything like it before and I pray I never will again. It sounded like a slab being pushed aside from some ancient sepulchre. It whispered words I shall never forget. "Know the will of Zodaal!" Pure evil… and then…

'I watched as the dead men pushed themselves up from the wreckage, some without their limbs. All were imbued with unnatural strength. Covered in blood and dust, they staggered towards Stackhouse and he welcomed them and loaded them aboard a waiting van. They were away before the police arrived, and so was I. I had never known such fear. I had seen the dead rise! I tore through the streets back to my home, but Orlick was waiting for me and he led me here, my spirit broken. Stackhouse had set his slaves to work, building strange machines that in turn would build further machines. His army of dead worked ceaselessly, each of them with his own job, and as the days passed I saw them become greyer and stiffer and ever more lifeless; and that was how I came to know – Stackhouse himself is one of the zombies, Miss Orlostro. He needed me to conduct his business with the outside world, just as he needs Porteous now. His slaves are efficient, but slow.'

While Woodrow's narrative unfolded, Julia's gaze turned frequently to the shambling, grey-faced workers. Her mind was whirling with a mixture of reactions; incredulity and horror were uppermost. She pointed to the second group working on the far side of the warehouse. 'And those? What are they doing?'

'The second project. I don't know what that is.' Woodrow edged closer to her. 'But he means to do it. To destroy the world. And I don't see anything could prevent him. You've felt its power.' He chuckled. 'The slaves work without tiring, you see, so long as they're fed regularly. And do you know what they eat, Miss Orlostro? Shall I tell you that – the ultimate obscenity?' His voice cracked and his eyes rolled madly. 'They feed on brains, you know. From animals, yes, but you heard them talking. Stackhouse has promised them. As the Earth is eaten by flame, he will allow them to feast. They will dine on human brains!'

The Doctor refused the offer of a drink and listened in silence as Percy, for the second time that evening, explained the business of the Bureau. His overpowering cheerfulness seemed to subside as the story came to its end, and he fixed Percy with a reproving stare.

'I can't honestly fathom the reason for all of this fuss,' Percy stammered, much put out by that glare. What right did the man have to frown at people like that? 'I've been here twelve years and had no problems at all. As for the portal to the time corridor, it's well out of the way and in good order.'

The Doctor nodded curtly. 'And you look after the rest of the Circle?'

'Yes. I have money in investments, and some in land, and a little in Roumanian oil, and from that I distribute an allowance. We have a monthly meeting here in London. I attended one such gathering this afternoon.'

Romana was flicking through a copy of his handbook. '"It is impolite to ask for a second serving of soup. Don't be in a precipitate hurry to get to a chair. Don't be cold and distant, or on the other hand be gushing and effusive. Don't use hair oil or pomades."'

He snatched it from her protectively. 'My own observations. I was here for a full year before the first of the others came through, sorting everything out. They're a super bunch, really, the nicest people you could hope to meet. And all very discreet. None of the locals suspects. Chuck it, I have to ask again, where's the harm?'

'The harm, Mr Closed,' said the Doctor, getting to his feet and glaring again, this time out of the window at the empty lamp-lit square, 'lies in treating this century as a sort of retirement home.'

'Well, we're all aware of the risks,' Percy replied. 'But for the moment, London's much the safest place on the planet to be. Everything's in hand for the near future. I've taken up leases on some charming villas for us in the Lake District, well in time for the second...' He looked about nervously, out of habit, and whispered, 'The second you-know-what.'

The Doctor sat at Percy's piano and absently fingered a couple of scales. 'All the trappings are fine. The danger comes from using somebody else's old equipment.'

'Somebody else's very badly designed equipment,' put in Romana.

'As you keep saying,' Percy fumed.

The Doctor glared in his direction again. 'Which must have something to do with that cloud of radmium, and that signal of yours.'

Romana nodded. 'You think the Bureau were trying to warn Percy about the cloud?'

'Possibly. It might also be connected with that blockage you discovered.'

'Would you mind not talking about me as if I wasn't here?' asked Percy.

He was ignored. The Doctor fished a folded copy of *The Times* from his pocket and handed it to Romana. 'Another thing. Have a look at this.' He tapped a particular column. 'You felt that tremor earlier?'

She nodded.

'Completely the wrong time and place for knocks of that sort. What's more, a couple of hours ago I witnessed a kidnap, and the victim was the country's foremost authority on geophysics. If the country but knew.'

They both turned to glare at Percy. Even K-9's eyescreen appeared to glow more fiercely.

'So this is all suddenly my fault?' he protested. 'Everything here was fine this morning. Until you lot turned up.'

'Master,' said K-9. Percy jumped. He didn't like the way the blooming thing had of speaking when it hadn't been spoken to. 'Suggest limitation of further time pollution by implementing shutdown of time corridor.'

'Well, of course,' the Doctor snapped. 'In fact, I thought I might give you that job, K-9.'

The dog's tail wagged. 'Master. My cartographic record of the United Kingdom indicates Nutchurch is located sixty-two miles from Central London. At my average speed it would take me three and a half weeks to complete the journey, exclusive of recharge time.'

The Doctor shook his head. 'K-9, you are occasionally very dim. You'll be taking the train, won't you, along with Romana.'

Romana looked surprised. 'It's the first I've heard about it.'

'Well, I've only just said it.' He patted her on the shoulder. 'The sea air will do you good after being cooped up in the TARDIS.'

'And what are you going to do in the meantime?'

He pointed to his massive hook of a nose. 'Me? I shall be doing some serious sniffing, of sorts.'

Percy stood up. 'Wait a minute. Let me set this out. You're going to close up the corridor?'

The Doctor nodded as if it were the most obvious thing. 'It's just too dangerous, I'm afraid. Anything might slip through, and probably has.' He came closer to Percy, smiled, and whispered, 'Do you think I could trouble you for a hammer and nails?'

5

PURSUED BY ORLICK

The sky over London turned from white to eggshell blue. A circular shaft of the dawn's light cut through the grime-coated circular window of the small attic room. Stackhouse, now repossessed by the core of Zodaal, sat in his chair, deep in contemplation, the green vapour shifting about his still form. His anger at the continued existence of the Doctor lingered. It was essential that all opposition be eliminated.

Orlick's heavy tread sounded, and the door creaked open. The valet stood on the threshold, carrying a silver tray upon which was a freshly prepared meal. 'Know the will of Zodaal!' he said. 'Breakfast is served, sir. A terrine of lamb's brain.'

Stackhouse hissed. 'Your need is greater. You will consume it.'

Orlick bowed. 'Yes, sir.'

'I have breakfasted already,' said Stackhouse. 'And from a far more succulent creature.' His hands curled over the arms of his chair. 'Still… not enough. Only the death of this alien intruder the Doctor will sate my hunger.'

There was a short silence. Orlick's eyes flickered momentarily. 'My orders for today, sir?'

Stackhouse's reply could almost have been a monologue. 'This Doctor must have travelled here through the time corridor, from the future of Earth. Already he conspires with the dastard Closed. Or perhaps he is one of the race that left the corridor here, on this planet. It must be sealed, sealed now, to prevent the arrival of any more such operatives.' He pointed to Orlick. 'You must do this.'

Orlick frowned. 'Sir, I cannot leave you here.' He gestured to himself, holding the flat of his palm over his chest, and said, 'I am the secondary host. My function is to protect the core.'

'And to obey its commands,' snapped Stackhouse. 'Zodaal is threatened, Orlick, in his entirety. The corridor must be sealed, and only the secondary host has both the understanding and the mobility to perform this task. Remember, there are powerful defence shields built into the portal. And I can protect myself well enough.'

Orlick nodded stiffly. 'Very well, sir. I will take the Daimler down to Nutchurch immediately and attend to it.' He turned to leave the attic room, and then a thought seemed to occur to him and he turned. 'What of the alien already here, in London? This Doctor?'

Stackhouse's glowing eyes flashed. 'The core has considered this also. I know his whereabouts. And he will not be able to force aside a bullet using the power of his mind.'

The Doctor positioned the uncurled hook of a twisted coat hanger into a socket and stepped back proudly to inspect his night's work. 'Ersh erbert shet shen?' he asked K-9.

'Clarify, Master,' the dog requested.

The Doctor spat the nails from his mouth into one hand and waved his hammer vaguely in the air with the other. 'I said, how about that, then? Not bad, is it?'

K-9 examined his master's handiwork and nodded. 'Monitor system sufficient. Advice given by this unit on its construction invaluable,' he added primly.

The Doctor patted his head. 'Well, of course. You didn't think I was going to try and take all the credit, did you? Now, what can we use for a referential coil, I wonder?' He looked around keenly.

The door of the drawing room opened suddenly and a

woman dressed in a maid's uniform entered, carrying a feather duster. She squeaked when she saw the Doctor and K-9 hunched over the small wooden table upon which the monitor rested. The Doctor gave her a friendly wave. 'Hello, there.'

The woman caught her breath. 'Oh. You're a friend of Mr Percy?'

The Doctor shook his head. 'Well, not yet, not really, but I'm sure I will be. Don't worry, there's no oil on the cloth.' He leant forward quickly and plucked the feather duster from her hand. 'I hope you don't mind?'

She seemed unsure how to reply, and was on the point of retreating when Percy entered, in a silk dressing gown, and laid a gentle hand on her shoulder. 'Martha, my dear. As you see, I have some guests. Er, an extra two breakfasts, please, if you would.' She nodded, rather bewildered, and withdrew. Percy advanced on the Doctor and K-9, scratching his head and yawning. 'What have you been up to all night? I've hardly slept, what with all this worry and you two banging away down here.'

'This,' said the Doctor, indicating his new invention, now replete with the feather duster at its centre, 'is a seismic monitoring system.'

Percy gave the monitor a sceptical glance. 'It's just a lot of my cutlery and things, tied up with piano wire.' He peered at the Doctor. 'Are you feeling all right?'

'It's a seismic monitoring system,' the Doctor repeated sternly. 'If whoever-it-is starts doing whatever-they-do to this planet's tectonic plates again, this –' he tapped a small read-out screen – 'will tell us exactly wherever-they-are.' He crossed his fingers. 'Probably.'

Percy remained doubtful. 'How the blue blazes could you make something like that from a lot of junk?'

The Doctor tapped his own temples. 'Well, all it took was a bit of know-how. And a bit of K-9.' He addressed the dog. 'You didn't mind giving up your compensator for a while, did you?'

'Without the compensator, the monitor would be useless, Master,' said K-9.

Romana entered, her eyes widening as she took in the Doctor's efforts. 'Well done,' she said. 'But wouldn't it have been better to connect the compensator directly to whatever you're using for shorting?'

The Doctor grunted. 'If you've only come down to carp, why don't you just go back to bed?'

'I haven't been to bed, actually.' She passed the Doctor a small notebook, every page filled with mathematical symbols. 'I've been trying to decode the message from the Bureau, well, what little we have to go on.'

'Ah. Discover anything?' asked the Doctor, scanning her notes.

'I'm afraid not. Even in the 46-character cipher of Percy's time there was too much missing to make any sense from it, and before you ask I've tried every other permutation.' She smiled at Percy. 'Good morning.'

'Didn't either of you go to sleep?' he said despairingly. 'You seem so active it's almost indecent. Spare a thought for me. When you get to my age you won't feel so inclined to go dashing about like this.'

'I'm twice your age,' Romana said lightly. 'You said you were going to draw me a map. From the station at Nutchurch.'

Percy looked blank for a moment. 'A map? Oh yes, of course, here we are.' He handed her a folded piece of paper from a pocket of his dressing gown. 'You'll find the place quite easily if you just follow the curve of the bay along the cliffs. It's set back, tucked away between two outcrops of rock, and not far from a small farm. A kind of red metal door. You can't miss it.'

'Thank you. And from there it's just a matter of fusing the controls. K-9?'

The dog twitched its probes and trundled to her side. 'Mistress.'

'Better get back in your basket.' His snout fell and his eyescreen reddened resentfully. 'You know it's for the best, K-9.' The dog did as he was bid.

'Off so soon?' asked Percy. 'I've asked Martha to cook you up a breakfast.'

'No time for that, I'm afraid,' said Romana, lifting the dog basket. 'Our train leaves in an hour, according to your timetable. I'll meet you back here, then, Doctor.'

He was engrossed in his monitor device and did not look up. 'Yes, yes, goodbye,' he muttered abstractedly. He tweaked the angle of the coat hanger. Then, suddenly, he shot upright and bellowed, 'Romana!'

She turned. 'Yes?'

He held up a thumb. 'Good luck. And take care.'

She smiled and departed.

As soon as she had gone, the Doctor stretched out one of his long arms and fiddled with the controls at the foot of the screen cannibalised from K-9. Instantly the coat hanger started to spin of its own accord. He sat back and rubbed his hands together. 'There! Magnificent.'

Percy crept closer to the device. 'It's operating, then?'

The Doctor nodded. 'Well, it should do. It'll give us a lead, anyway.' He scratched his chin. 'Did you say something about breakfast?'

Orlick loaded the explosive into the boot of the Daimler. Shortly after the will of Zodaal had arrived in this primitive time period, it had considered the destruction of the time corridor. After a certain amount of internal debate, it was decided to leave the system operational for fear of drawing the attention of the Circle. Orlick himself had pondered the wisdom of the move, although it was not his place, as secondary host, to express doubts. So it was with a sense of troubled satisfaction that he began the drive to Nutchurch.

*

Percy finished his breakfast and studied the Doctor, who had spurned Martha's excellent cooking in favour of poring over the morning newspaper. His large eyes seemed to scan the columns of print at incredible speed, and Percy got the impression that he was absorbing every piece of information in the search for a link to their current predicament.

Percy dabbed at his lips with a napkin and coughed politely. 'Doctor, your breakfast will be going cold.'

'You have it, then.' He pushed the plate over.

Percy forced down a belch. 'I've already eaten both my own and Romana's.'

'Then throw it to the birds. This weather must be very confusing for them, and the roughage'll do them good.' He hunched forward suddenly and tapped at the paper. 'Here we are. More minor seismic activity, this time in Japan.' He broke off and sat for a moment staring blankly at nothing. 'Their set-up must be awesomely powerful. I wonder why they don't use it to greater effect?'

'Whose set-up?' asked Percy. 'This cloud, or whatever the heck it is?' He remained doubtful about the Doctor's apparent fit in the square the night before. 'Why, for heaven's sake, would a cloud want to set off earthquakes in the first place? Peculiar thing for a cloud to be up to, if you ask me. Why can't it just settle for raining like all the other clouds?'

The Doctor shrugged. 'Perhaps the cloud is a weapon of some sort. Or maybe part of a composite identity. Yes, that would make sense.' He raised a hand and punctuated his delivery with small precise movements. Percy was rather taken aback by his sudden seriousness. 'Directed by a controlling intelligence, most probably whoever it is that's been using your time corridor. I once saw something similar on Vybeslows VII, capable of – Ah.' Something else in the paper had caught his eye. 'The body of Mr Thomas Joyce, an unemployed labourer, was discovered just before midnight a short distance from his Lambeth home.' The

Doctor's face became even more sombre.

Percy felt his throat run dry. 'So?'

'The body was identified from his clothing... Witnesses claimed that Joyce had been stripped utterly of his flesh... Police say there is no evidence of foul play, and are working on the theory that Joyce may have fallen into a pool of acid.' The Doctor grunted. 'Ran foul of our cloud, rather. That's what it intended for me.'

Percy gulped and squirmed in his chair. 'Disgusting. Are you sure?'

'Quite sure.'

'You attract unpleasant company, it seems,' said Percy.

The Doctor slammed the flat of his palm on the tablecloth, causing the assorted crockery and cutlery to jump with a clatter. He fixed Percy with another glare and said savagely, 'You attracted this thing here with your meddling. You can't treat time like an omnibus, stepping on and off wherever you like.'

Percy had had enough of this stranger lecturing him on what he could and could not do. 'Balderdash,' he said, with as much gravity as he could muster. 'At least I and the Circle have made the effort to join in and settle down. We don't go blundering around waving gadgets all over the place. I'm fully aware of my responsibilities.'

'Are you?' The Doctor leant back and added curtly, 'I don't think you have the slightest idea.'

Fortunately for Percy this dialogue was interrupted by the entrance of Martha, who carried a small violet envelope. 'This has arrived for you, Mr Percy.'

'Really? Who can it be from?' He took the envelope and opened it, aware as he read the handwritten card inside of the Doctor's distracted gaze burning on him. 'Gracious me. It's from the woman next door.' He squinted at the rather grand signature at the base of the card. 'Mrs Felicia Chater. Widowed, in brackets.'

The Doctor sprang from his chair. 'How interesting. I don't think I've ever met anyone in brackets.'

'No, no, she's put the word "widowed" in brackets,' said Percy, then registered the toothy grin spreading over the Doctor's face. 'I say, you're chaffing me, aren't you?'

'What does she want?' asked the Doctor.

'Ah. Well, she says sorry for shouting at me last night – oh yes, I think she was a bit put out by the signal whistling on as it did – and would I and my friends like to join her for a few rubbers of mid-morning bridge.' He put the card back in the envelope. 'Well, another time, perhaps.'

'Why another time?' asked the Doctor.

'Well, with all this cloud kerfuffle—'

The Doctor waved a dismissive hand. 'I haven't played bridge since that time with Cleopatra. She was such a ditherer, kept revoking when she should have been slamming.'

Percy frowned. 'Oh yes. And what about responsibility?'

'Well,' said the Doctor, 'it can wait, can't it?'

The Colonel had not slept well. Not given to nightmares, he was disturbed when, upon closing his eyes, a parade of horrific images passed through his mind. He saw sun-bleached temples disgorging insurrectionists brandishing cruelly serrated knives; he saw old colleagues and friends strung up on stockades; he saw every beast of the night pouring from the cover of the jungle with one almighty charge; and, worst of all, he saw her, the beautiful one, stern, haughty and imperious in her jacket and scarf, watching over the carnage with an expression of total indifference. Three times he had woken in a sweat, the masculine oak panels of his bedroom providing some respite from his feverish thoughts. Yes, in fact it was rather like being in a fever. He recalled a bout of malaria, on his first trip into the jungle, the dazzling green of the high treetops spinning in his vision, and shuddered.

Only one thing for it. As soon as he thought it polite, the Colonel rose, breakfasted, and set off for the car with his clubs slung over his shoulder, this morning's run forgotten. Day off couldn't hurt – muscles weren't going to seize up. He desired relief from his desperate state, and only one person could provide it. Damn stupid time of life for a man to get smitten like this, but counting in his favour were his great experience and strong character. He'd show the girl a few things a young chap couldn't, and charm her away from the artistic set she seemed to have fallen in with.

With this aim in mind, he drove in the direction of Belgravia, fixing his story along the way. Wanted to check if everything was all right with that poor fellow in the long scarf. Neighbourly duty. Shocking affair. Anything he could do to help, she must not hesitate to ask. That sort of thing. Drop a few hints about the military life. Bound to impress. He'd probably get invited in and offered tea. Drop of milk, no sugar and no biscuits, thank you. Then fascinate her, capture her heart, take her for a drive, it was another superb day, not to be wasted. Perhaps a picnic. Glory of nature. Then he'd propose, she'd sigh, they'd join hands, and – and then there she was, for real, just like yesterday, crossing the road, carrying that dog basket. The Colonel was almost overwhelmed by the sudden vicinity of his heart's desire, and his hands dropped from the wheel for a second. Then he composed himself, coughed, slowed the car, and honked his horn. She looked up, and he waved. 'Good morning, miss.'

She looked up, brushing a strand of hair from her face. 'Oh, hello.'

The Colonel stopped the car but kept the engine running. 'Just going over your way. How's that fellow with the scarf?'

'He's fine, thank you,' she replied. There was an admirably determined set to her features, as if she was about to start off on a grand campaign. What a woman.

He couldn't think of anything else to say. 'Off to the vet, what?'

She smiled. The Colonel's heart leapt. She had smiled – at

him! 'No, I've got to catch a train. Excuse me.' She walked off.

The Colonel reversed the car, following her. 'Miss? Miss?'

'Yes?'

'Can I offer you a lift?'

She frowned. 'You're travelling in the wrong direction.'

'Nothing to prevent me turning about, is there? Where are you headed?'

'A place called Nutchurch,' she said. 'And if I don't set off soon I'll miss my train.'

The Colonel kept pace with her. 'Miss. To be frank, I've no appointments today. Rather at a loss for something to do, truth be told. Nutchurch, that's a little spot along from Worthing, isn't it?' He patted the leather of the passenger seat with one of his big hands. 'I say, why not travel in comfort? Train's dirty and unreliable. This time of year the crowds'll be swarming. I'll get you there in no time and have a day by the sea into the bargain.'

She seemed to study him, and looked between him and the dog basket. Most likely thought she could set the beast upon him if his conduct slipped. Not that it would. He was a gentleman. 'Quicker than the train?'

He nodded enthusiastically. 'Like lightning, really.'

'Thank you.' She swung open the door and climbed in, settling the basket on the back seat. 'Shall we be off, then?'

The Colonel was staggered. She had accepted his offer. Marvellous! He put out his hand. 'Pleased to meet you. George Radlett, Colonel of His Majesty's Army, formerly in India.' He found it difficult not to salute; there was something noble about her.

'Romanadvoratrelundar,' she replied. 'It's easier to call me Romana.'

'Ah, Spanish blood, eh?' said the Colonel. Already he was floundering for something to say. What were women interested in? 'Lived in London for long?' was the best he could come up with.

'We'd better get started, hadn't we?'

'Ah, yes, yes, of course.' They drove on, and the Colonel's knees started to knock together. This feeling was unbearable. He wanted to know all about this mysterious woman, to the tiniest detail. Very peculiar; he couldn't recall ever being especially interested in another person before. Worst of all he was struck dumb. He longed to start talking about parades or inspections or troop movements but had a feeling that would be a great mistake. 'Er, fine day, isn't it?'

She nodded. 'I suppose this vehicle is powered by crude fuel injection through a combustion system. For an Earth artefact it's quite well designed.'

The Colonel didn't understand – young people had a language all of their own nowadays – and so he concentrated on finding the best way out of London.

Julia spent the night awake. Woodrow had retired to his home shortly after midnight, leaving her to stand guard over Porteous, who now lay slumped in his chair, snoring loudly and muttering gibberish to himself every so often. In the darkened warehouse, curtained from the outer world, there was little sense of time, and Julia was able to count the passing hours only from her wristwatch. The zombies had no need to rest, and continued their tireless work on what Stackhouse had called the second project, paying her no attention at all. A strange calmness settled on her, disturbed only by her curiosity as to the nature of their toil. Her mind raced along familiar paths. She had no doubt that Woodrow had told the truth. The folklore of her own land was replete with tales of revenants stirring from the grave. With equal certainty she felt there was another, deeper and more fantastical truth beyond the first. Another look at the stimulator confirmed that belief. For why should the undead, with all of their supernatural power, have need of such a purely mechanical contraption?

Shortly after nine, finding that she could no longer keep her urge to pry under control, she walked calmly across to the far side of the warehouse and the second project, wrinkling her nose at the horrendous vapour covering the workers. On closer inspection, the saucer-shaped unit appeared larger – at least twenty feet by twelve – and its pale yellow surface shimmered and glistened unnaturally like a patch of spilt petrol. The entirety of its upper half had been thrown back on a hinge mechanism. Inside was a cushioned man-shaped outline surrounded by more of the technicalities beloved of Stackhouse, to which the zombie workers fixed additions at intervals. Attached to the head of the empty form was a crown-shaped object composed of strands of twinkling golden wire, meshed around a globe of pale blue glass. It was hard to believe that any of the lumbering workers could have fashioned such an intricate design.

Julia flinched as one of the workers raised his head and said, 'Keep away. Keep away.' His rotted black teeth and grotesquely lolling dark purple tongue repulsed her. He pointed a stubby finger to the stimulator, and the sleeping Porteous. 'Return.'

She obeyed hurriedly, recalling Woodrow's warning about the workers' preferred diet.

As she walked back to the stimulator, a telephone bell rang. In these surroundings the sound was made weird. She searched for the source, and saw the leader of the slaves lifting a receiver from its cradle in a darkened corner. 'Can I help you?' it gurgled. Then he held out the receiver to Julia. 'It's for you.'

She took it. Stackhouse's voice echoed hollowly. 'You,' it said. 'Miss Orlostro.'

Julia was unbowed. 'Yes?'

'I have another task for you.' Was there a hint of suppressed anger in his usually level tone of address? 'Listen closely.'

The day was turning out to be even more glorious than its predecessor. The Colonel had a natural feel for the road, and the directional instincts of a carrier pigeon. Didn't care for maps and the like, better to trust to his instincts, they never failed. Now he was thundering along the narrow and almost deserted country roads leading south, concentrating on the drive mainly because he couldn't think of much to say to the lovely Romana. The greenery, each leaf picked out in sharp detail by the climbing sun, shot by, and a heat haze washed over the horizon.

'That dog of yours is a quiet one,' he observed. 'Doesn't it bark?'

She shook her head, her long blonde hair blowing in the air disturbed by their passing. 'He's very well trained.'

'Ah, I see. What's his pedigree, then?'

'I've never really thought about it.'

'Ah.' Strange answer. 'Haven't entered him, then – Crufts or anything? No. Any relatives in Nutchurch?'

'No. This is more of a business trip.'

'Yes, yes.' The Colonel snapped his fingers. 'Got it. You're going to try and sell a few pictures, of that painter fellow's?' She looked blank. 'Painter fellow. With that long scarf.'

'We're not artists,' was the sum of her reply. She spoke correctly, but the Colonel couldn't help noting her rudeness. If only there was some way of getting through to her and knocking through the barriers between them. She must find him attractive, after all. He tried to remember what other chaps said about women but it was difficult; he'd never listened to those parts of their conversation – considered it a tad dull. The awful silence continued.

It was broken by that high-pitched voice he'd heard in the square the night before. 'Mistress,' it squeaked. 'Danger. Radmium detected.'

The interruption came as such a shock that the Colonel nearly crashed the car into an approaching hedge. 'What was that? Nearly leapt out of my skin.' He looked over at Romana suspiciously. 'Ah. Think I have it now, by jiminy. Throwing your voice, are you? Clever. Knew a chap once with the same talent, he used to…' He became aware that she wasn't paying him attention; instead, she had half-turned in the passenger seat to address the dog basket.

'Oh no,' she said. 'Concentration?'

'Variable,' the voice replied. 'Analysis of sensor readings indicates radmium source is moving nearer in relation to this vehicle, Mistress. Suggest evasive strategy.'

The Colonel chuckled and, as they had just turned onto a long and empty stretch of the road, removed his hands from the wheel and clapped. 'Really good show. On the seafront, eh? Amusing the kids? Romana and her talking dog. Could almost be coming from the basket. Inspired. Strange way to earn a living, but—'

The basket spoke again. 'Radmium source now less than one Earth mile proximity, Mistress.'

The Colonel shook his head. 'Don't think much of the script, though. Goes over my head. Can't think what kiddies'd make of it. If I were you I'd stick to the traditional routines, get it to ask for a bone, that sort of thing.'

'Be quiet!' Romana roared at him.

The Colonel was struck dumb. Girl certainly had a brass neck!

She reached back and unhinged the grille of the basket, and a moment later something that looked rather like an upturned tin bath with ears and a tail darted out. For a puppet it was damned strange; didn't even really look like a dog. He started to wonder exactly what he'd got himself into.

The sliver of Zodaal's will contained by the secondary host was startled from its handling of the Daimler by a momentary twinge of psychic interference. Orlick's rotted grey hands, strips of flesh hanging in tatters from the finger bones, clenched the wheel more tightly as the emotional reaction passed through his gaseous master. The myriad of extra-sensory impressions formulated by the natives of Earth were mostly parochial and unimportant; this was something entirely different, more akin to the startling power Mr Stackhouse had noted the night before. An alien intelligence was near.

He sensed its presence again, felt its fear. But this was not fear as experienced by a human. This creature's reactions were based on a similar but much more advanced and experienced scale of responses. This creature's perspective was infinitely wider, perhaps even wider than Zodaal himself could perceive. And its thoughts stretched backwards and forwards along the web of time. It was another agent, and it had to be destroyed.

Orlick closed one eyelid. He had to concentrate, see through the eyes of his enemy. The secondary host's merit was its physical strength, and it was unsuited for telepathic tracing. Gradually an image formed: the empty country road; an open-topped car; a red-faced man in plus fours; some kind of computer. Not far away, ahead on this road.

He put his foot down hard on the Daimler's accelerator pedal and reached inside his topcoat for his revolver.

'Can you make this thing go any faster?' Romana shouted to the Colonel over the roar of the engine.

'Blessed if I can think of any reason why I should want to,' he snapped back. 'Impudent request. I think we should stop at the next pub and get you a glass of water, young lady.'

'We're being followed,' she said urgently. 'We must go faster.' There was a dangerous glint in her eye. The Colonel recognised it. He'd seen men crack before. Didn't suppose a woman would be all that different. 'Please, Colonel, this is desperately urgent. Our lives are at risk!'

Must be the heat. The poor girl. Didn't know what she was saying. He checked in the mirror. Road was clear apart from a black Daimler. Fellow was spurting up a bit fast. 'Just you sit there and talk to your, er –' he gestured to the dog-shaped thing – 'your friend, what? Soon have you somewhere nice and calm.'

'Hostile gaining, Mistress,' said the dog. 'Speed imperative!'

The Colonel couldn't help shaking his head admiringly, 'How *do* you do it, eh? And get it to move like that? Trick wires or something, eh? Remember when I was stationed at Futipur-Sekri, back in '99, I—'

Then a bullet shot through the air.

The Colonel pulled his head down. 'What the—' He glanced over his shoulder at the Daimler. Its driver was leaning half in and half out of the door, one hand on the wheel, the other coolly taking aim and preparing to fire once more. 'Put that weapon down!' the Colonel cried. 'This is a public highway!'

The Daimler driver fired another couple of shots. Both went wild, in large part because of the Colonel's delayed shock reaction which sent the car veering all over the road. He turned a corner and picked up speed. 'Blooming hell,' he shouted, forgetting there was a lady present. 'What's he playing at?'

'Attacking us!' said Romana, lifting her head. 'K-9!'

'Ready to return fire, Mistress,' the dog replied. 'Reconfiguring in aggression mode.'

The Colonel was vaguely aware of the metal dog turning about so that its snout faced their pursuer, who had now taken the corner and was firing again. 'Keep your head down, dear!' he called. 'He's picked the wrong man for a fight.' At last he had an opportunity to display his manly strengths. The problem was, his only armaments at present were a set of golf clubs and he couldn't think of a way to employ them against their opponent.

There was a sudden flash of bright red light, which he saw reflected in the mirror, and which seemed to come from the dog's snout. It left a sizzling smell, something like batteries, in the air. Whatever it was, it went over the top of the Daimler, and succeeded only in blasting away a section of hedgerow, which went up with a mighty whoomp and a sheet of flame.

"Pon my soul!" exclaimed the Colonel.

'Oh, K-9!' called Romana. 'What a terrible shot!'

'Difficult to orientate between fast-moving vehicles, Mistress,' the dog replied.

Despite the seriousness of the situation, the Colonel found himself chording. 'I say, K-9, eh? That's his rank, is it? Ha ha, very funny, that.'

'Keep your eyes on the road!' Romana screamed up at him. Another bullet whizzed between them.

K-9, whatever he was, let off a second of his bright red flashes.

The Doctor sat hunched over his monitor apparatus. The coat hanger gave a slight twitch. 'Hmm,' he mused, rubbing his chin thoughtfully. 'Probably just an aftershock, that.'

Percy stuck his head around the kitchen door. 'Doctor?'

'Yes?'

'I was just thinking.'

The Doctor put his ear to the coat hanger and twisted it slightly. 'That's better.' He looked up at Percy. 'What have you been thinking?'

'Mrs Chater's invitation.' He curled the card between his finger and thumb. 'She'll be expecting three of us.'

The Doctor turned back to the monitor, not really listening. 'Hmm,' he said again. 'If only I had a tri-cyclical wave inverter.'

'Well, it'll quite likely throw her numbers out, won't it,' said Percy, 'if only the two of us turn up on her doorstep? So I was wondering, should I perhaps call a friend, do you think? To stand in for Romana. Would seem polite, wouldn't it? I could give Harriet Kipps a call now, I'm sure she'll be free. What do you say?'

'Or perhaps a metonymic synference, size three, of course,' said the Doctor, scratching his head. 'Eh? Sorry? Well, call whoever you like.'

'All right, then,' said Percy, and withdrew. After closing the door, Percy put his ear to its varnished surface; the Doctor's bass murmurs continued. Ha! Let the self-important ninny play with his coat hangers!

He nipped across to where the telephone stood on an oak stand and put through a call to Harriet Kipps. The ringing tone trilled in his ear, once, twice, a third time. 'Come along, dear Harriet, come along!' he whispered to the mouthpiece, casting a glance over his shoulder at the living room door. At last there was a crackle and then Harriet: 'Hello?'

'Listen, Harriet, it's ickle I—'

'Percy! And so soon! How sore is your darling head, I wonder?'

'Never mind my head,' he hissed. 'Listen. Something's cropped up.'

'Oh.' And after a pause: 'That rotten signal?'

'Something like that. I can't talk freely. It's up to you. Ring round the Circle, tell them all to wait for my orders.'

She gasped. 'Darling Percival, how can I be expected—'

'And you'll have to do it pronto.'

'Percy, you sound in the most terrible lather.'

'It's not like that,' he protested. 'My dear, you must know I wouldn't ask so much of you without good reason. Please, do as I say. I'll flash you later, by transceiver, it's the only way.' The drawing room door opened behind him. He raised his voice. 'Never mind, then, Harriet dear. Goodbye.' He replaced the receiver. 'Couldn't make it, not to worry.'

The Doctor stood in the doorway, a finger pointing in his direction. 'Closed,' he said.

Percy's throat ran dry. 'Yes?'

'You're very keen on authenticity, aren't you?' the Doctor asked, his head angled slightly. 'So why "Closed"?'

Percy relaxed. 'A simple error on my part. Well, I had to pick a name before I came here, didn't I? So the others could find their way to me when they arrived. I wanted something desperately ordinary, so I fished out an old photograph of clerks at work in a bank, with their names on little boards in front of them. The only male was sat before a little board that said, er...'

The Doctor chuckled.

Percy sighed. 'Well, how was I to know? By the time I realised, it was far too late. Wondered why everyone kept looking at me oddly. All my papers had been sorted out, you see, in that name. Fortunately my lease on this place was simply made out for Mr P Closed. Hence Percy. A sight better than Position, though. I didn't care for being called Position in the slightest.'

'Well, it's a name,' said the Doctor, shrugging. He pointed over his shoulder. 'What I really came out here to tell you was that it's working.'

Percy swallowed. 'So we can expect more earthquakes?'

'Somebody, somewhere definitely can.'

Woodrow hadn't slept for five months, at least not with the unthinking ease that typified the condition. Terror had burned itself into his eyes, and to close them was to invite a whole host of unspeakable horrors into his drifting unconscious – a monstrous melange of the vileness that he had observed, the vileness that he had been responsible for, and the vileness that the deepest reaches of his idling imagination threatened to unlock in sympathy. He lay curled in his sweat-soaked sheets in the tiny bedroom above his office, which was grey and dismal even in the scorching summer sunlight, its wallpaper hanging in mouldy strips and a variety of insect life infesting its corners. One of Woodrow's limp white hands lolled over the side of his mattress and hung over the remains of his supper, a hunk of cheese on a piece of rough bread.

Surrounding the bed, in knee-high piles, were bundles of five-pound notes.

There were footsteps, clumping up the stairs. Measured and unhurried. Not Orlick, then. Woodrow whimpered and raised the filthy coverlet over his chin. Why couldn't he be left alone?

A knock at the door. He ignored it. Julia Orlostro entered, looking as calm and impassive as she had yesterday on meeting Stackhouse. 'What do you want?' He backed away, pushing the top half of his body against the headboard. 'Go away, can't you? Keep away from me!'

She stepped forward and grasped him by the shoulders, her sharp painted nails digging at his flesh. 'Control yourself. And listen to me.'

'No, no.' He tried to break away from her grip but she was too strong and he collapsed sideways on the bed. 'What do you want here? Keep away, keep away.'

'Woodrow, listen to me. We must talk. About Stackhouse, his plans. You must listen to me.'

He shivered. 'Are you mad? They could be anywhere, listening to all that we say… They are the dead, the dead!' He began to sob.

She slapped him across the jaw, savagely. 'Be quiet, and pay attention.'

Woodrow almost appreciated the sensation. Such a human, earthly punishment. Faintly he tasted the iron in his own blood. 'What… Why have you come here?'

'Listen, Woodrow.' Her temper inflamed, Julia's accent became more pronounced. It was a measure of Woodrow's loss of humanity that only now did he come to appreciate her great beauty. 'Stackhouse has spoken to me. This morning. With new orders. He has told me to go to a certain address, at which I am to kill a man called the Doctor. I am then to call him and report my success.' She frowned. 'This Doctor. Is he known to you?' Woodrow stayed silent. 'You do not trust me. Woodrow, I am living, the same as you, a human being.'

He laughed dryly. 'Yes. But were you ever to be trusted?'

She gripped his shoulders again. 'Think. Why does Stackhouse want this Doctor man dead? Because he fears him; he is some kind of enemy.'

The sense behind her words penetrated Woodrow's brain for the first time. Hope surged through his thin frame. 'An enemy?'

Julia nodded. 'I suggest this. I will bring the Doctor here, and we will discuss our terms. If he can destroy Stackhouse, all of this –' she gestured at the stacks of notes – 'will be as nothing. You heard what Porteous said. The stimulator machine, it is worth millions. With Stackhouse out of our way, it can all be ours, Woodrow.'

'But we know nothing of this Doctor,' Woodrow pointed out, trying to calm himself. 'For all that we know, he might be worse than Stackhouse.'

'Then you must see the logic in my plan of bringing him here,' said Julia. 'We cannot let our chance pass by.'

NUTCHURCH 3 read the sign at the junction, barely glimpsed by the Colonel as he wrenched on the wheel and the Hispano-Suiza turned gracefully. In the wing mirror the Daimler was still visible, in spite of the distance he'd attempted to put between them. It was strange the way the driver kept going like that. Hadn't even stopped to reload, just kept going with one hand on the wheel. Determined, whoever he might be.

'It's no use,' said Romana. 'We're getting close to the town.' Indeed, a couple of other vehicles had already swerved by. 'We can't risk getting into a more populated area.'

'Apologies, Mistress,' said K-9. 'Defensive capability unsuited for this situation.'

'There's only one option left, then,' said Romana. 'Concentrate your fire, K-9. Lance function. Aim for the engine.'

'Warning, Mistress. Narrow beam lance function unreliable at this distance.'

'It's too late to worry about that.' The Daimler driver fired another couple of shots. 'Now, K-9!'

The Colonel didn't like the sound of that. He turned slightly in his seat. 'Excuse me, my dear,' he began, 'but I think it's high time you offered some sort of expla—'

A sizzling bolt of light shot from K-9's snout. The car shook from side to side and the Colonel lost his grip on the wheel. His vision blurred momentarily – it was a bit like a sudden desert dawn – and he was nearly thrown forward over the bonnet. He heard the engine stall and splutter.

Very quickly he gathered his wits, rubbed at his streaming eyes, ascertained that he was still in one piece and that the car was essentially undamaged, and turned to inspect his fellow passenger. Romana was fanning herself from a cloud of smoke that drifted from the wreck of the Daimler. K-9 was thankfully inert but its poise somehow suggested smugness. 'Pursuing vehicle rendered inoperative,' he said. 'It must have contained a quantity of high explosive.'

'Well done, K-9,' said Romana.

The Colonel squinted through the clearing smoke. 'I'll be jiggered,' he said as the smouldering skeletal frame of the Daimler became clear. 'Packs quite a punch, your K-9.' A thought struck him and he blinked at his fellow passenger. 'I say. What did you do to upset the man so much?'

'Nothing at all,' she said briskly. 'K-9, how's the radmium level?'

The dog made a rapid series of clicks something akin to a faulty ticket machine. 'Radmium concentration in this vicinity remains high. Suggest relocate to place of safety.'

Romana turned to the Colonel. He stared blankly back at her. 'We're still in danger.'

He coughed. 'My dear, the enemy has gone up in smoke. What we ought to do is call the police.'

'I'll try to explain,' she said, 'on the way. Please, Colonel, we've got to get away from here.' She indicated the road ahead, the beginning of the long track that led down to Nutchurch.

Mr Closed and his friends were shown in, and as the introductions were made Felicia's senses were sent spinning by the artistic thrill of the occasion. The painter in the scarf was apparently known as the Doctor, and possessed a marvellously resonant voice and an exciting lack of formality. The Doctor!

How thrilling! Not even a proper name! He probably spent all his time in artists' salons in Paris, and hardly ever did any real work at all. Dabbed a few pastels on canvas and drank absinthe in the shady hostelries of Montmartre. Again she studied Percy. He was even more inspiring at closer proximity. What a luscious lack of swagger in his mouse-like shuffles, sighs and giggles, and what wit and delicacy in his conversation – a world apart from that dreadful old bore the Colonel.

'Hope you don't mind me bringing the Doctor along,' he said.

'Not at all.' Felicia surveyed the painter's outfit, and congratulated herself on dressing down for the occasion, as casual elegance seemed *de rigueur* for this set. 'Tell me, how did you come to make each other's acquaintance?'

Percival, as Felicia already liked to think of him, waved a hand evasively. 'Oh, we met, around and about. As one does, you know.'

Felicia, who had no desire to be thought of as prying, or ignorant of the workings of the capital's aesthetic underbelly, nodded vigorously. 'Oh, of course, yes.' Secretly she dreaded what might happen if they were to start talking about galleries and the like and she was obliged to contribute, because in truth she knew nothing of modern art or literature, which were far outside her own sphere. She was aching for somebody to ask her about something familiar, and to that end had left her piano open, with the book of Tibetan exercises on top, and arranged her typewriter, with a half-filled page peeking out, so that it might be easily seen from the card table.

It looked as if the snare was going to work. The Doctor, who had been sniffing about the room with interest, turned at the piano. 'Mrs Chater,' he said, pointing, 'you have a superb Georgian tankard.'

What a very conventional thing for an artist to remark upon, thought Felicia. No doubt it was some sort of conversational bluff. She nodded. 'It was my late husband's.'

'Ah,' said the Doctor. He peered at the book of exercises and flipped through with an increasingly amused expression. 'This looks painful.'

Felicia smiled through gritted teeth. Informality was one thing, rudeness quite another. 'The esteemed lama Sherpabavahsa knows what is best for the human body in the modern age, I am sure, Doctor.' She gave a graceful twirl, taking care as she did to catch Percy's eye. 'Since taking the course I have become supple as a girl.'

'Really? Perhaps you're doing something wrong.' He put the book down and turned his attention to the typewriter. His manner was starting to get on Felicia's nerves. Clearly he was the kind of man who assumed he could dominate wherever he went. He squinted to read from her typescript. '"Inspector Cawston pushed aside the drapes and saw the foot of the missing man, poking from the half-open trunk, spattered with droplets of fresh blood..."' He looked at her quizzically. 'What was spattered with droplets of fresh blood, the Inspector, the foot or the trunk?'

Felicia sighed. 'The foot.'

'Hmm. Watch your participles.' He grinned suddenly, and the grin was so wide and toothy and gleaming that Felicia felt oddly transported. It was as if he'd sensed her frostiness and had chosen to dispel it in a moment. In two seconds her impression of him changed entirely.

She was brought down to earth by Percy, whose exploration of the drinks trolley had been curtailed abruptly at the Doctor's reading. 'I say,' he said, appearing to notice her for the first time. 'Of course! What a perfect idiot I've been! Mrs Chater, Inspector Cawston! *The* Inspector Cawston?'

Felicia, exulting inwardly, tried to look demure. 'Why, yes.'

'Phillip Cawston, of Scotland Yard?'

'The same.' It was all she could do to stop herself curtseying.

'But,' he spluttered, 'but, I've read them all! *Along Came a*

Spider, And Frightened Miss Muffet Away, Have You Any Wool, your entire oeuvre!'

'How nice to meet a reader,' Felicia said.

'More than that!' Percy's eyes travelled up and down, as if to check that she was really there. 'An admirer. The Inspector's adventures have captivated me from the very start.' His eyes lighted on the typewriter. 'No! And to think you are working on the next, only yards from my own home. It's too thrilling.'

'Of course it feels all very everyday to me,' said Felicia, glowing.

'Sat at this very seat!' Percy ran his manicured fingers over the woodwork. 'On this pretty little cushion!' He giggled and clapped his hands together. 'Wonderful. Now, tell me, how do you get your ideas?'

'Well, I'm really not at all sure about that,' said Felicia. In Shillinghurst this sort of enquiry had mostly evinced short shrift, but here in London, under the gaze of the salacious demimonde, it gave her enormous pleasure to prevaricate grandly in this fashion. 'They just sort of pop into my head, you know, in much the same way that the Doctor's paintings must come to him.'

The Doctor's curly head perked up. 'Eh? Paintings?'

'Oh.' Felicia gestured to his coat and scarf. 'I assumed…'

The Doctor shook his head. 'I'm afraid not. Well, not for some time. 1749, I think it was.'

Felicia didn't know what to say to that, and so simply nodded. 1749 was probably the address of an obscure, invitation-only German gallery. 'So, er, what do you do, Doctor?'

He frowned. 'Me? What do I do?' The question seemed to take him aback. 'Well, in general, I fight monsters.'

'I see.' Felicia grinned back at him. 'A philosopher.'

'Well, occasionally.'

'Never mind about him,' said Percy, shooing the Doctor away and stepping closer to Felicia. 'Let's talk Cawston. That sequence in the last book, when he was being chased over the Scottish moors by the Belgian spies in the bi-plane…'

Felicia tipped her head. 'I recall it, yes.'

'How exciting. Unputdownable.'

Felicia beamed. Percy beamed back. A golden aura seemed to enfold both of them, fading the rest of the world out. And in that moment, in an unspoken, madcap, breathless way, she knew. And he knew she knew. And she knew he knew she knew. They knew. They were in love.

With the crash of shattering glass, Julia entered the house in Ranelagh Square. It had been a matter of ease to scale the garden wall and enter through the drawing-room window. It was the kind of thing she could do in her sleep, and a welcome change from the baffling requests of the previous day.

She had seen no signs of activity through the windows on her approach. It would be best to lie in wait until this mysterious Doctor returned, and then take him swiftly and by surprise. Until then she could make a study of his effects. In outward aspect the house had seemed no different from that of any other Englishman. A piece of modern sculpture sat on the table top, its centrepiece a twisted coat hanger. Julia's heart leapt as she saw the piece of paper tacked to the edge of the table. In black capitals was written:

DEAR ROMANA

POPPED NEXT DOOR, BACK SOON, DON'T TOUCH ANYTHING, DON'T LET THE DOG TOUCH ANYTHING

DOCTOR

She picked up the note and smiled. 'Excellent.'

The card game seemed to pass in a haze. Felicia and Percy dropped tricks as easily as the Doctor picked them up. The world, thought Felicia, existed only for herself and her lover.

'I'm sure I really should have lost with that last hand,' said the Doctor, writing down the latest set of scores with a stub of pencil. 'Shall I deal?'

There was no reply. Felicia found that she almost couldn't speak. And she knew Percy felt the same.

'Er, shall I deal?' repeated the Doctor.

'Yes, yes, of course,' Percy said abstractedly.

The Doctor performed an elaborate, concertina-style shuffle that in more ordinary circumstances would have impressed Felicia. At this moment she doubted if anything would ever impress her again. The trivialities of life seemed to have disappeared. All she could do was look into the deep black eyes of her beloved. Such secrets they promised!

'I'll deal, shall I?' asked the Doctor, and without waiting for a reply, commenced to do so.

'Hold on, hold on,' Percy said abruptly, pulling his eyes away from Felicia's with what she knew must have been a mighty effort. 'What's the time now?'

'Just gone noon,' said the Doctor. 'Hmm. I wonder how Romana's getting on?'

'Ah.' Percy rubbed his chin. 'Another stifling day. Hardly the weather to be sitting indoors. I say, before we press on, would either of you mind if I just shuffled out for a moment? Just to take the air, you know.'

The Doctor grunted and continued shuffling. Felicia smiled indulgently. 'Why, of course, Mr Closed. Shall I walk with you?'

His eyebrows shot up. 'Er, er, no thank you, Mrs Chater. I'll only be gone a second. My chest, you see.' He straightened his collar. 'In a moment, then. Please excuse me.' He backed out of the room.

Felicia sighed.

Very odd, thought Percy as he scurried back home and through the front door, the way in which his new neighbour kept staring at him. He was terribly impressed by her work, but in person she seemed almost soft in the head. How curious. But then, someone with a reputation was almost bound to disappoint.

He made his way along to the drawing room and fished his canvas bag from beneath the table. He thought he remembered the Doctor pinning a note there for Romana. Wasn't there now. Still, no time to waste bothering about them. He had to organise the Circle, fight back. Well, not *fight* back, exactly. Take a stand. Safety in numbers. The transceiver rested beneath his knitting, just as it always had. He twisted the activator, and waited for the response signals to flicker on. Alerted by Harriet, the others would be waiting for him to give them their instructions. The corridor had to be kept open. With the directions he'd given her, Romana would be delayed for hours, and if just one of the Circle could get to the hut before her and trip the defence shield, the mechanism would be safe from tamperers. Then it would be a simple matter of packing the Doctor and Romana off. After all, they had no right to criticise. As for this cloud and earthquake business, well, they could sort it out for themselves. So far it had shown interest only in the Doctor, after all.

Three things occurred to Percy in swift succession.

Firstly, the transceiver wasn't working. Secondly, there was a cool summer breeze blowing across the back of his neck, which was coming from a broken window. Thirdly, a statuesquely beautiful woman dressed all in black was standing behind him, brandishing a heavy black pistol. Before he could react to any of those three things with more than a startled squeak, she had swung the butt of the weapon down on his head.

6

ESCAPE THROUGH TIME

Stackhouse waited for news in his darkened attic room. His links to the lesser manifestations of Zodaal's will on Earth were tenuous, but he could sense the smooth continuance of work at the warehouse. The foolish Porteous continued his programming of the machine, working eagerly, copying reams of notes from the displays onto his notepad and muttering to himself. Unlike most others of his race he seemed unperturbed by the presence of the slaves of Zodaal. Perhaps, Stackhouse reasoned, he was filled with the detached zeal of scientists the universe over, a quality he recognised in himself. Whatever the case, Porteous had been the best choice. If he continued to work at his current speed the program could start running by tonight.

His meditations were interrupted by the ringing of the telephone bell. He reached for the mouthpiece. 'Stackhouse.'

'It's done,' said the voice of Woodrow. 'The Doctor is dead.'

'There was no resistance?'

A slight pause. 'No. She found him, as you said, in Ranelagh Square. Put a couple of bullets into him. Says it was simple.'

'Good,' said Stackhouse. 'I will expect you here at the usual hour. Bring her with you.'

'Yes, sir.' He broke the connection.

A gurgling noise came from Stackhouse's throat, and a line of black drool trickled over his cold dead chin. For a moment his eyes glowed a much fiercer green. 'You lie,' he whispered. 'I sense the living mind of the alien Doctor. Distant but present. Idiots. You will soon learn the folly of daring to oppose the will of Zodaal.'

The girl's best efforts to explain herself had left the Colonel in a state of sheer bafflement. If her account hadn't been lent some weight by all the hoo-ha on the road he'd have asked for directions to the nearest asylum and driven her directly there. Trouble was, her tale had the ring of truth to it. Actually quite romantic, he thought, being chased by these foreigners or whoever they were, with their poison gas, and this vital escape route on the coast that had, at all costs, to be shut down.

'I say,' he remarked as the car roared along, 'this is all rather thrilling. Pressure on a young lady must be tremendous, living the life you do. Least you've got old K-9 to look after you.'

The metal dog beeped proudly.

Romana smiled and unfolded a piece of paper from her top pocket. 'These are our directions to the escape route.'

The Colonel was lost in reflection. 'If we do the business here today, I dare say there's a chance of honours, you know. Quirk I've missed out previously, really. Service of this kind'll be sure to lead to some decoration.'

'I don't think so, Colonel,' said Romana. She leant across and whispered in his ear. 'This affair is of the highest secrecy. No details can be made public.'

The Colonel's picture of a life divided between royal garden parties and state functions was rudely shattered. 'What, top secret? Can't breathe a word?'

'I'm afraid so.'

'Ah.' He matched her smile with the best of his own. 'I'm on to you, you know, young lady. You haven't fooled old George Radlett.'

She bristled. 'What do you mean?'

'Oh, the accent's very good, and the general poise is passable. But I see through the disguise.' He nodded over his shoulder at K-9. 'The dog's death ray, all this talk of spies and poison gas. This jazzy talk of yours. You're not one of us, are you?'

She narrowed her eyes. 'I'm not?'

He chuckled. 'You're in the employ of Mr Hoover, I'll wager. Secret espionage work, above even the ears of our government. Daring, though, to send a girl like you on a mission like this. Just as well you ran into me.'

She frowned. 'As I recall, you ran into me.'

'Ah!' The Colonel beamed as the bewildering events of the last day began, at last, to fall into a cogent scheme. 'I see now! All planned, was it? Your lot have been vetting me, have they? Best man for the job, and all that? Thought they'd pair us up? Splendid!' He put his foot down on the pedal to express his glee, giving a couple of passing pedestrians a moment's alarm.

Romana smiled sweetly. 'I'm sure I don't know what you mean, Colonel.'

'Ha ha. Got you now, what?' The car turned from the rough track that trailed over the hills and into one of the three long streets of the village. Already the Colonel could taste the brine blowing in from the beach; the sea itself was a strip of deep blue against the turquoise sky. It was hard to credit such a locality with events of international import, but he knew better than to rest for a second to enjoy the sight. 'Which way now then, my dear?'

Romana studied the map. 'Down to the beach. Then we'll have to proceed on foot, travelling right for about a mile.'

The sergeant had been biking up to Mrs Timberlake's cottage, on the outskirts of the parish, and was looking forward to one of the widow's bacon sandwiches and a mug of sweet tea when the resounding blast from over the hill reached his ears. He arrived at the scene ten minutes later, guided by the pall of black smoke smudging the clear sky, to find the fire service already in attendance. Water jetted in a high arc from the firemen's hose, and as it passed the front of the wreck the hideously twisted skeleton of the driver was picked out, his blackened bones emitting curls of hissing vapour.

The sergeant, the silver buttons of his starched dark blue uniform glinting in the summer sunshine, brought his bicycle to a halt and stepped off. 'What the devil's happened here, then, Bill?' he enquired of the fireman directing the dousing. Bill Hopkins, a baker by trade, looked pale and drawn.

'Engine caught fire, looks like,' he replied. He shook his yellow-helmeted head at the general unfairness of life. 'Poor beggar didn't stand an earthly.' He mopped his brow as a wave of heat washed over them. 'Leastwise, he can't have known much about it. Went up in seconds, must have.'

The sergeant touched the brim of his helmet as a mark of respect. 'Big car, though, ain't it? Like the one that brings the judge to Hove assizes. Someone important's gone up in there, Bill, you see if I'm wrong.'

At this point there was a brief ripple of consternation among the men manning the hose, and they staggered back, resembling for a second a tug-of-war team gaining ground. There were shouts and cries.

Bill Hopkins came forward. 'What's going on there, you lads?'

One of them pointed, and in a quavering young voice said, 'It's that poor fellow, Mr Hopkins, sir. I swear he moved!'

'Don't be daft, lad. Put that fire out!' He turned to the sergeant and rolled his eyes. 'The 'maginations some have got round here. Must be all this bright and heat.' To his underlings he said, 'Come on, back to it!'

They remained still, as if mesmerised, their gazes fixed on the still, skeletal shape in the car.

Hopkins snarled. 'What's got into you lads, eh? Your wives could put that out in half the time!'

Still there was no movement in response.

The sergeant took his arm, and pointed. 'Dear O Lord! Bill, they're right! He *is* moving!' He stood transfixed, tantalised, as the grey ghoul, without flesh, its frame worn half to powder, its eye sockets pulsing faintly green, stood slowly, its movements accompanied by a series of scrapes and clicks. Slowly it clambered from the smouldering vehicle, swinging one leg over the buckled door. Then it raised a hand, like a messenger of death, and beckoned to the nearest firefighter, the youngest man.

He backed off, crossing himself.

It tottered after him.

The sergeant swore under his breath. He had never before known what it meant to be paralysed with terror; his whole body shook uncontrollably at the sight of the monster stalking towards the young man, who remained hypnotised, unable to run despite the imprecations of his fellows.

The gap between hunter and prey closed.

The skeleton struck, clamping its claw-like hands to the sides of the young man's head. There was a hideous crunching sound, like a cabbage being sliced in half. The victim sank to his knees, gave a blood-freezing scream, and the monster lowered its mouth hungrily.

In the second that followed, the sergeant realised that he was the man all others were looking towards. He had to take the lead. Without thinking, he sprang boldly into action, hefted up the nozzle end of the abandoned hose, and directed the jet in the monster's face. The water struck the creature squarely and it toppled, hitting the road with a nauseating crunch. The young man's body fell in a heap, a bright red pool expanding about his head.

There was a resounding silence.

The sergeant was the first to move. He kept the jet of water on the monster and advanced slowly. Around him, most of the other men, freed from the trance, were fleeing.

The monster's jaw was caked in fresh blood. There was brain tissue in the still-twitching mouth of the skull. The sergeant closed his eyes and whimpered.

The monster struck, lunging up at him with macabre grace. Its stench overwhelmed him before he had time to register its claw piercing his chest and reaching up through the tight coil of his intestines to squeeze the life from his heart. His consciousness receded on a red wave of horror, and a voice infused with an oozing, unutterable hatred, whispered in his mind, *Know the will of Zodaal!*

It was obvious, thought Felicia, why nobody seemed to call the Doctor anything but the Doctor. He was overpoweringly witty and clever and mysterious, and she must be sure to acquaint herself with his philosophical works on her next trip to a bookshop. On previous excursions, she had swept past the philosophy section at Stoneham's without giving it a glance, but now she considered it her duty to become more high-minded and modern. As Felicia Chater-Closed, she would doubtless be required to engage in wide-ranging conversation on many abstract topics. Perhaps she might even give Cawston a fascination for the metaphysical in his current plot, and elevate her fiction to an altogether weightier plain. Her mind raced with the possibilities.

She became aware that the Doctor, who had tired of shuffling the pack of cards, was teasing Rufusa with a cocktail sausage. If anyone at Shillinghurst had behaved in so vulgar a manner at table she would have brought down the full weight of her wrath; but one had to make a certain allowance for the ingenuous whims of the aesthete.

'There you are, boy,' said the Doctor.

'Girl,' corrected Felicia.

'Girl,' said the Doctor. The dog, unused to such games, sprang for the sausage, wolfed it down, and begged for another. The Doctor provided it, but wagged a finger at her large, pleading eyes. 'This can't go on forever, you know. There are only so many chipolatas in the universe.'

Felicia decided it was polite to mention Percy's continued absence. 'Mr Closed has been gone rather a while, Doctor.'

He nodded. 'He's fighting the inevitable.'

Felicia was thrilled. 'You think so? You noticed, did you?'

The Doctor threw Rufusa another sausage. 'Noticed? Noticed what?'

Normally Felicia would have been reluctant to give vent to her deepest emotions, but something in the Doctor's childlike manner inspired frankness. 'Why, Doctor, don't be coy. The bond between myself and Mr Closed.'

'Eh?'

'Our bond.' She leant forward. 'A bond of the heart, Doctor.'

The Doctor looked rather confused, and opened and closed his mouth a couple of times. At last he said, 'But you've only just met. I mean, I'm not really an expert on these things, but don't you think you're jumping the gun a bit?'

Felicia waved a hand vaguely, in a gesture she hoped would convey a girlish, helpless quality. 'We are each of us in thrall to destiny, Doctor. Man must have his mate. That is a philosophy nobody can deny.' She tapped her chin curiously. 'Then to what inevitable do you refer?'

'Oh, well.' The Doctor shrugged, riffled in his pocket, and threw two silver-blue, bullet-shaped objects onto the table. 'I removed the power packs on his transceiver, last night. He won't be able to get up to any tricks until I give them back.' Noting Felicia's interest in the objects he returned them to his pocket. 'Not that it should concern you, anyway.' He glanced at the clock on the dining room wall. 'You're right, though. He went out half an hour ago.'

'Thirty-eight minutes ago exactly,' sighed Felicia.

'Tell you what, I'll go and see if he's all right.' The Doctor stood. Rufusa yelped, and he stayed her with a single admonishing glance and a movement of the hand. Such extraordinary authority. 'Won't be a couple of ticks.' A little sadly he examined his score sheet. 'Shame about the game.'

Felicia stood also. 'I'm rather concerned myself. I insist on coming along.'

The Doctor looked at her doubtfully. 'I'm sure it's nothing.'

'Well, then,' said Felicia brightly, leading the way out.

The front door of Percy's house was locked. To Felicia's astonishment, the Doctor opened it with a most unusual key, a sort of chunky metal pencil that throbbed in his hand and seemed to stir the air faintly. She quelled her amazement – these were probably all the rage and she didn't wish to appear a hick – and waited as the catch sprang and the door opened. The hallway was a scene of utter chaos, with all sorts of possessions scattered in disarray.

She shrieked. 'Oh no! A burglary!'

'I don't think so,' said the Doctor. 'It's always like this.'

Felicia covered her faux pas with a giggle, and reminded herself not to judge these bright, modern people by the standards of Shillinghurst. She followed the Doctor through the hall and into the drawing room, reflecting as she did so that the reformation of Percy's untidiness would be first on her list of priorities after their wedding. On the table was a heap of faintly crackling junk which she knew better than to comment upon; it might turn out to be a prize-winning sculpture from 1749.

'Hello, what's gone on here?' The Doctor fussed over the sculpture, and his face fell as he tweaked at a bent coat hanger that came off in his hand. 'A whole night's work, ruined. What did he think he was – ah.' He indicated the window facing the garden; a pane had been shattered, from the outside, leaving small shards of glass that crunched under his booted feet. He put a hand to his tangle of curls. 'I think you were right first time.'

Felicia gasped. 'A burglary?'

'More of a kidnap, I think. Look.' He knelt and indicated a trail of small bright red spots on the carpet. 'Blood.' He dabbed it on a fingertip and sniffed. 'Definitely Percy's. Higher level of immuno-agents than anyone from this time period.'

'Blood!' Felicia swooned. 'Oh dear! Oh no!' Her voice rose in pitch. 'Murder!'

The Doctor caught her and lowered her into a chair. 'Don't be silly,' he said brusquely. 'Of course it isn't murder. You need a body for murder.' He looked around. 'Now then. That canvas bag of his has gone, and so has my note to Romana. Of course, he might have faked all of this, but… No, how could he have smashed the window like that? And he's not the sort of man who can stomach the sight of blood, particularly his own.' He nodded. 'Definitely an outside job.'

Now she knew Mr Closed was alive, if not in the most agreeable position, Felicia began to feel a quiver of excitement in her heart. 'What a thrill. This is the sort of thing one writes about, not that one gets involved in.'

The Doctor regarded her levelly. 'You aren't involved, not really.'

Felicia put a hand to her brow. 'Doctor, we are talking of dear Mr Closed. Who could want to kidnap him? It's too terrible. And just when I felt sure of…' She trailed off, somewhat embarrassed. 'Oughtn't we to call the police?'

'No. We'd only be wasting our time.' He stared out at the garden and straightened. 'My deductive powers are far greater, and—'

He was interrupted by the ringing of the house's telephone bell.

'A ransom!' said Felicia.

Fortunately there was an extension to the dining room, and the Doctor leapt for the mouthpiece. 'Hello?' He checked the dialling plate. 'Belgravia 623.'

Felicia heard a woman's voice. 'Percy? Percy, is that you? It's Harriet.' There was an urgent, worried tone to the voice.

'Er, he can't come to the phone at the moment,' said the Doctor. 'Can I help you?'

The caller clicked off.

The Colonel knew Nutchurch only by repute – lads with shell-shock and the like were often packed off here for a spot of peace – and as he strolled along the beach he came to see that the modern world, so long excluded, had at last caught up with the place. A horde of bathers were basking in the sunshine, many of the women in quite indecent costumes, and ice cream stalls had been set up every few yards. On his way back through the deckchairs, carrying rations for the waiting Romana, he stumbled past a small but noisy group of youngsters, who were gathered around a gramophone. It was honking out some nonsense about the midnight choo-choo leaving for Alabam, and not a lot else. 'Bland, soulless dancing music,' he observed to his companion. 'No words or tune, just a lot of repetitive drumming. Insult to the ear.' Then he remembered her origins, and added politely, 'Suppose it's what the young'uns prefer over the water, though.'

'Oh, I prefer the sub-mediant consonance of the singing mountains of Parazzapel,' Romana replied absently, her eyes flicking between the coastal waters and her map.

'Yes, of course,' mumbled the Colonel, not wanting to look out of touch. 'Wonderful melodies.' He passed her a bottle. 'Ginger pop. Should perk you up after the upset on the road.'

'Thank you.' She put the bottle in her pocket and frowned. 'Colonel. These directions can't be right.' She pointed right, towards the line of sand hills, which not much further along the curve of the bay elongated steeply to form a rocky and clearly impassable bulwark. At this distance it was difficult to make an accurate judgement, but the beach appeared to peter out in the rocks rather nearer than half a mile along the shoreline. 'The detail in the map is totally different.' Her shoulders slumped. 'I should have known.'

The Colonel's eyes darted about. 'What, you mean we've been tricked? Your contact's let us down? Then we could be ambushed at any moment.' He slid a golf club from the bag slung over his shoulder and waved it menacingly. 'The enemy could be anywhere.'

A passing toddler, a white brick of ice cream clutched in his hand, laughed at the sight.

Romana sighed. 'I don't think so.' She crumpled up the map and threw it into a nearby litterbin. 'Just petty spite on Percy's part.'

'Hypothesis likely, Mistress,' said K-9.

Romana addressed the basket. 'Is there any way you can trace the entrance to the time corridor, K-9?'

The dog clicked and whistled. 'Negative, Mistress. Source of time-warmed chronon particles is near but my sensors are unable to specify on directional basis. Suggest divergence of party.'

Romana shook her head. 'No, we have to stick together.' She kicked the sand in frustration. 'We'll just have to look around until we find it.'

Not an adventurer by inclination, this was the first occasion Percy had been coshed by an assailant, and his first thought upon waking was to wonder why he was not tucked up snugly between stiffly starched sheets, and to conclude that whatever he'd been about the previous night had been sufficiently dubious to warrant obscurity in some dark fold of his memory. Then there was the question of the dark green stain – the first thing he saw when his eyes finally flickered open. The stain, spread across the panes of a dirty, broken window, was not the sort of decoration he would credit to the home of any acquaintance. Still more disquieting was the position of his hands, or, as he soon came to appreciate, the way in which his hands had been positioned. Keen to attend to a scratch on his nose, Percy moved to raise a finger – and found that his hands were tied securely together behind his back. He was slumped on a rickety wooden chair in a flea-infested room that, incredibly, was knee deep in bundles of five-pound notes. It was altogether too bizarre.

He attempted to shuffle about in the chair for a better look at his surroundings, and found that his bonds were tied too tightly to allow much movement at all. The heat in here was intense; afternoon sunlight poked through the stained windows, so he could only have been out a couple of hours at most. Recent events flashed before his mind, and his search for blame focused on the Doctor. Let him be slapped severely if that interfering fool was not the reason for his current predicament. It was unjust for a decent, public-spirited citizen such as himself to be dragged into these sorts of misdemeanours.

A slow, menacing tread reverberated through the creaking floorboards, and Percy shivered, then reprimanded himself. Was he going to submit to these scarifying tactics or fight back? After a moment's hesitation he realised that he had no choice. He was terrified.

A door opened behind him, and quite suddenly there was a man before him. He looked half mad and half starved, and was carrying a glass filled with water and a filthy sponge. Before he could speak – and his expression on seeing his captive awake was unreadable – Percy stammered, 'Er, I – I'd offer you money to set me free, but you seem to have rather a lot of it already.' There was no reply. 'That is, I suppose it may seem a lot, but perhaps you'd like some more, and I do have, I mean, I may have – Oh, lawks, I think I'd better shut up, hadn't I?' As he spoke, Percy's hands twitched reflexively in their bonds in an unconscious action. He was searching for his bag. He'd had it with him back at the house, hadn't he? The last moments before the attack were lost somewhere in his pounding head.

Without talking, the stranger leant over and applied the soaking sponge to Percy's forehead. Up close he wasn't so threatening, simply mad and smelly. Probably best to act polite. 'Old fellow, I wonder if you could tell me what I'm doing here?' Aware that his request could be mistaken for a demand he appended hurriedly, 'Not that this is a particularly horrid place, I'm sure it's, er, delightful. What I mean to say is that I'd like to know where I am, generally, so that I can work out where I want to go next, but there again I've no desire to rush away, oh…' He shrugged. Despite everything, the warm water was soothing on his brow. 'You know.'

A second stranger entered the room, and her footsteps were anything but furtive. She stood before Percy, expensively dressed in black, an opal at her neck, her hair pushed back to reveal her high forehead. Her striking attractiveness was rather too forward for Percy's tastes. There was something (he squirmed at the thought of the word) *sexual* about her beauty. Something familiar, also. He struggled to place her face but could not. Somebody in the papers? Possibly. Nobody in society, though; he would have recognised anybody mentioned in the columns instantly.

'We have to talk with you,' she said. Ah, Italian. Percy had spent a pleasant week in that country in the summer of '25, and so accustomed was he to the processes of formal conversation that he had to bite his tongue to stop himself mentioning it.

Instead he said, 'The usual custom in this country is to send in your card and wait to be admitted. A blow to the head is considered rather gauche.' It was devastatingly witty, but there was nobody around to appreciate it.

She held something up. 'You've been looking for this, yes?'

Gracious, it was the transceiver! Percy's eyebrows shot up. 'I really think you ought to put that down,' he said. Then, remembering himself: 'I mean, whatever it is, it might be terribly dangerous, mightn't it?'

She twirled it between her hands like a baton. 'You must know. It belongs to you.'

'To me? No, no, never set eyes on that before.' He felt a sudden urge to cry. Life had been a perfect dream until yesterday; why did things always have to be spoiled?

'So,' the woman drawled, 'you would not worry if I was to do this…' Her painted fingernails lingered over the activator buttons.

Percy tried to leap from the chair. 'No, madam! The power packs in there might overload if you…' He slumped back. 'Blow. I've shot myself with my own gun rather, haven't I?'

For the first time her shabby accomplice spoke, and he was English enough. 'This is taking too long,' he said, reaching for something inside his jacket. 'We can't waste any more time. What if *they* should come here and find us with him?' The thing in his hand dazzled Percy for a second, and it took him a couple of seconds to recognise it as a knife.

'Aah! Ah, no! Police! Murder!' he yelled.

The man sprang, pulling Percy's head back savagely and bringing the serrated blade of the knife to his throat. He moved with a terrible casualness, as if this was as commonplace a situation as opening one's post or taking a morning stroll. 'Keep quiet and still,' he whispered.

'I won't move,' whispered Percy.

'This is ridiculous,' the man snorted. 'How can Stackhouse consider this idiot a threat? There are dozens like him across London.'

'He conceals his intelligence,' replied the woman.

'No, I don't,' gasped Percy. The name Stackhouse rattled around his brain. Of course, the biscuit magnate, proprietor of Zanzibar cracknels, whom he'd met on the train to Nutchurch. Surely he couldn't have offended the fellow that much? 'Please.

What do you want?'

The woman held up the transceiver again. 'I want to know how you came by machinery such as this, Doctor.'

Percy momentarily forgot the knife poised at his throat. 'What did you say? Oh, good heavens! I'm not the –' he remembered there was a lady present – 'the flipping Doctor!'

The view from the sand hills was superb. The Colonel stood atop a promontory, filling his lungs with the all-pervading brine. In the distance a tiny sailing boat was passing, its single white sail billowing in the gentle breeze. From this distance even the noisy crowds on the beach seemed as much a part of the natural order as the circling gulls, the spray glistening on the grass, and the pacific suck of the waves on the shore.

He heard movement behind him and turned. Romana and K-9 were approaching, both with doleful expressions. Silly, really; how could the face of a metal dog convey emotion? He waved to them manfully. 'No joy, then?'

'We must have been about a mile into the hills, and there's nothing,' Romana reported. 'I'm starting to wonder if sending us down here was a ploy.'

K-9 whirred. 'Negative, Mistress. Portal is near.'

She sank down on crossed legs. 'Yes, so you keep saying.' The implication was obvious, and the dog's tail drooped sadly. 'Sorry, K-9. I didn't mean to be rude.'

'Apology noted,' K-9 said sniffily. He added, 'Query your acceptance of directions from suspicious humanoid friend Percy.'

'All right, K-9, there's no need for us to bite each other's heads off,' she snapped back.

He burbled in confusion. 'I did not suggest such an action, Mistress.'

The Colonel decided they both needed bucking up. 'This whatsit we're searching for…'

'Yes?'

'It could look like anything at all, really? I mean, it's probably disguised? And isolated?'

Romana looked hopeful. 'Yes. They wouldn't put it anywhere that someone might just wander into.'

'Ah.' He cracked his knuckles and scratched his head. 'Sorry, my dear. Come up blank myself.' He gestured seawards. 'Nothing down there but a lot of pebbles.' He peered at the bottle top sticking out of her trouser pocket. 'You haven't touched your ginger pop, my dear.'

She offered it to him. 'Thanks, but you have it.'

'Ah.' He took a couple of swigs. 'Funny thing. So peaceful here. Looking back I can hardly believe somebody was taking pots at us this morning. Dash it, I still say it's unfair to put a filly like you through all of this, good though you are. You ought to spend more time with girls of your own age.'

She smiled. 'There aren't any girls of my age.'

Whatever the Colonel's reply might have been, it was halted by an urgent buzzing from K-9. 'Mistress. Radmium detected. Concentration is approaching.'

The Colonel scanned the horizon in all directions. 'That Radmium blighter? Survived, did he?'

Romana sprang to her feet. 'How far, K-9?'

He bleeped and ticked. 'I cannot specify, Mistress, but my sensors indicate that he is coming closer. Suggest evasive action.' His head dropped. 'Regret I may be unable to supply adequate defence.'

'We'd better get under cover,' said Romana, looking about. 'But where? We can't risk going back towards the village.'

'True enough,' agreed the Colonel. 'Innocent lives not to be endangered. I suggest that bathing-hut, down there.' He pointed over the promontory. 'John Radmium won't think of looking for us in there, and it's well hidden from view.'

'What bathing-hut?' asked Romana.

'In a little cove just down there. Noticed it on my way along. Odd place to build a thing like that, miles from the beach, and right in the path of the tide.'

Romana fixed him with an expression that he could not decipher. 'Come on!' she shouted and set off at a cracking pace, K-9 trundling behind her. The Colonel shrugged and followed.

Evie Tisdall was gripped by terror. It was bad enough to be sagging off from the bakery, abandoning Mrs Jeapes on what was sure to be one of the busiest afternoons of the year. On top of that, here she was out on the dunes with Norman. He led her by the hand to a small patch of grass which was concealed from view behind a high pile of rocks.

'Oh, Norman,' she said as she sat, 'I still can't help feeling sour at coming out here.'

'Don't worry,' he said. 'It's such a fine day. Better to be outdoors, eh?' He gave her hand a comforting squeeze.

'What if anybody sees us, though?' she said, looking nervously around. On this perfectly still day the sound of the crowd of bathers came clearly from the beach. 'What if somebody tells my mum I'm out here? Mrs Jeapes'd skin me if she found out.'

'Nobody's going to see us,' Norman said confidently, placing a hand on her shoulder. 'Nobody ever comes out here, do they? Don't worry.' His words and his hand soothed her, and she leant back against the pile of stones. She couldn't recall a day as hot as this, without a trace of breeze.

Norman brought his lips to hers. 'Oh, we shouldn't, Norman,' she attempted to say, but the protest was halted by his caress. She lay back on the sand, the bakery, her mother and the Nutchurch crowds forgotten. Norman had a way like that, of making her forget things.

A few moments of forgetfulness passed.

Then Evie's nose crinkled and she pulled herself from Norman's grasping grip. 'Ugh, what's that smell? It's foul.'

'What smell?' Norman said angrily. 'I can't – Hey, you're right, what a pong. Like bad veg.' He poked his head up from their hideaway. 'It's terrible. I can't see nobody.'

Evie knelt up by his side and scanned the horizon. Between the long grass to their left she saw movement. 'Norman,' she whispered, 'there is somebody, somebody over there.'

'Ruddy Peeping Tom, I expect,' said Norman, standing. 'I'll give him a right thrashing.'

Evie caught his arm as the grasses parted, and a familiar blue-uniformed shape appeared, staggering oddly. 'Norman, no! It's Sergeant Edwards!'

'The dirty blighter,' said Norman. 'What's he doing out here, then?' They watched as the policeman emerged fully into the clearing. Evie blinked. The smell was getting worse, and the sergeant seemed to be covered in rings of bright green steam.

'He's come to fetch us back,' she said, wringing her hands. 'Oh, Norman, Mrs Jeapes'll give me the boot after this.'

The policeman stopped at the centre of the clearing, then turned his head slowly until he was looking straight at them. Evie gasped. His eyes were glowing bright green.

'Oh, Norman, Norman…' she whispered, unable to look away or to move.

Sergeant Edwards smiled, revealing a set of blackened teeth. Then he came for them, hands outstretched.

'But why would anybody want to kidnap poor Mr Closed?' Felicia asked suddenly. She stood contemplating her neighbour's broken window. In the last few minutes, the Doctor, refusing all offers of help and stamping firmly on her renewed plea for police aid, had busied himself with his collection of metal scraps. As far as she was able to tell, he was trying to put the riot of rubbish back into some sort of order. 'Tell me, he's not involved in anything – well, anything Bolshevistic?'

'No, no,' the Doctor grunted as he coiled a section of wire.

'Nothing like that. In fact, although I hate to sound immodest, I think his kidnapper was after me.'

'After you?' gulped Felicia. She felt hardly able to keep up with the pace of events. 'And are you, er…'

He shook his head. 'No.'

'But why would anybody want to kidnap you, then, Doctor? What makes you so much more attractive a target?'

'Oh, this and that.' He cut a piece of wire with his teeth. 'They tried to kill me last night.'

Felicia recalled. 'You mean the gas?'

He nodded. 'When that didn't work perhaps they thought to try a subtler approach.'

'Forgive me,' said Felicia. 'You don't seem particularly bothered about all of this.'

'Well,' he said airily, 'somebody tries to kill me about twice a day, in general.'

'Really,' Felicia heard herself observe faintly. The surreal elements of the situation seemed to be piling up. 'How quaint. You ought to have a policeman at your side, like Mr MacDonald.'

'Oh, I don't need a policeman.' He looked up suddenly. 'Have you got a car?'

She nodded.

'Can I borrow it?'

Such was her confidence in him that she almost assented. 'May I ask why, Doctor?'

'Well, you see, I think Mr Closed was grabbed by people I can locate using this.' He nodded to the chaotic wire sculpture. 'And that means I stand a good chance of finding Percy. Well?'

Felicia stood. 'I'll go back home, ring for Tebbutt, and tell her to bring out the fly.'

'No need,' said the Doctor. 'I'm an excellent driver.'

A narrow, overgrown path allowed the Colonel, Romana and K-9 access from the cliff top down to the small cove and the bathing-hut. The Colonel was out of his depth again, and watched with bemused interest as his companions examined the structure's wooden door.

'Can you open it, K-9?' asked Romana urgently.

A slender red metal wire with a small sort of suction cup at one end emerged from the metal dog's head and quivered over the doorknob. 'Electrical voltage defence system. Surface is bound by encoded seal, Mistress.'

'Well, can you break the code?'

'Affirmative. Computing release sequence,' said K-9. There was a pause. 'Continuing to compute release sequence.'

Romana looked anxiously over her shoulder. 'Hurry up, K-9. The radmium cloud could get here at any moment.'

'Calculating at optimum speed,' said K-9.

The Colonel was baffled. 'I say.' He pointed to the hut. 'You want to open the door?'

'Yes,' said Romana angrily, looking past him again.

'Well, how about me giving it a good kick, then?' He rattled the doorknob. 'Yes, locked tight. Well bolted. Still, might as well give it a go.' He rubbed his hands together and took a few paces back. 'Better take a run-up. Good thing I'm still in fair condition. Knew it was a good idea to keep in trim. You can never tell when a crisis might strike.'

Romana shook her head and put a hand on his sleeve. 'There's no point, Colonel. That door will open only to a particular coded signal. Which K-9 is trying to work out.'

'I see,' said the Colonel, more confused than ever. 'Seems an awful lot of fuss to go to just for a—' His nostrils quivered. 'Hang about. Think I just caught a whiff of that gas of theirs.' He looked up, but the cliff edge was deserted. 'Can't see anyone.'

Romana swallowed. 'K-9, check for radmium.'

'Source is nearing, Mistress,' he reported. 'However, I have ascertained the sequence for opening this door. Defence mechanisms checked.' He motored back from the hut with a satisfied beep. A couple of seconds passed.

'Well, open it,' urged Romana.

At her order a distorted chatter of sounds issued from K-9's voicebox, setting up a net of vibrations.

'Sounds like a swarm of dratted locusts,' said the Colonel, covering his ears.

'How long is this going to take?' asked Romana.

'Estimate three minutes fourteen seconds, Mistress,' said K-9. 'Core of the fastening device has been designed to repel forced entry.'

The bad smell was getting stronger now. The Colonel followed Romana's upward gaze but there was no sign of their pursuer. 'Can't see the fellow. Could be hiding, I suppose, ready to pounce.'

Romana turned to face him. 'Colonel, you don't have to be involved in all this. You can still get away.'

The Colonel's face dropped. 'My dear girl, we're all in this together. I can't leave you here at the mercy of these foreigners. Now, I might not understand what's going on with that blessed hut, but I do know that I've as much right as you to defend this land. More right, in fact. And if anarchists and Belgians and the like are plotting to bring down the flag, I tell you there's nobody better suited to routing them—'

'Colonel,' Romana interrupted. 'Look.' She pointed.

Scrambling unsteadily down the path towards them was a blue-uniformed, blue-helmeted figure. He was covered by a cloud of that malodorous green gas. 'Heck!' the Colonel exclaimed. He waved at the policeman. 'Officer! Watch out for that gas! Try and get clear!'

'It's too late,' said Romana. 'Look at his eyes.'

The policeman came nearer, his booted feet crashing through the thick gorse at the foot of the cliff. The Colonel backed away; the man's eyes were fierce orbs of bright green light, and his terrifyingly blank expression was offset by his thin grey lips, which were curled upward in a parody of a smile. A trickle of blood dripped from his chin.

'Damn it,' said the Colonel. 'I think he's been got at.'

The secondary host advanced towards his prey, guided by the sharp trace of the alien mind. This new form was more suitable than Orlick, younger and with stronger musculature, flesh stretched taut against the frame of bone. He saw his opponents through a misty green film as patches of moving redness. The female was the greatest danger. Her intention was clear. She planned to open the corridor and bring through more such as herself and the Doctor. This could not be permitted.

Another consideration drove him on. Like the core, he was unable to survive for longer than a few minutes in dissociated form, and had been driven by necessity to claim this new human body. Sustenance was an essential part of the conversion process. The brains of the young humans had not been enough. More cerebral tissue was needed to stabilise his new shape.

He planned his feast. The brain of the alien female first. Then the brain of the human male.

The Colonel brandished his golf club threateningly. 'Hop it, go on!' he shouted at the approaching policeman. 'This is a size five, and I'm not afraid to use it!' He backed away over the large pebbles, almost overpowered by the smell, and was suddenly aware there were only two ways to escape the cove – the path, blocked by the enemy, and the sea. 'I shouldn't worry, my dear,' he told Romana. 'I don't think he's armed. What's more, this gas seems to have slowed him up.'

'He doesn't need a weapon,' said Romana, pulling the Colonel back towards the hut. 'And don't let him get near you.'

'Oh, I'm not afraid,' said the Colonel, truthfully. This was the sort of adventure he'd been missing since his retirement. 'Just let him get near me, and I'll show him who's boss.'

The policeman came closer, taking slow but measured strides towards them. Up close, his eyes were even more alarming. That green light was putrescent like moss, its brightness evil and unnatural, yet somehow beguiling. Why should he try to run from power like that? It was pointless. The thing was stronger than him. It was going to kill him. There was no point in struggling.

'Sorry, Romana, my dear,' he heard himself say. His muscles unwound and his eyes glazed over. 'Sorry…'

The club fell from his grip and clattered, end over end, on the pebbles. The noise startled the Colonel, and he dragged his eyes from the creature. Its hypnotic spell broken, he saw it for what it was, a monster.

He turned away. 'My goodness, it nearly had me there,' he said.

K-9 chirruped and said, 'Portal open, Mistress.'

The door of the bathing-hut swung smoothly open, with a crackle of yellow sparks.

'Colonel!' shrieked Romana.

A cold, dead hand curled around the Colonel's neck and pulled him backwards. He spluttered and struggled, trying to crouch and then use his assailant's own strength to throw him forward. But the monster would not let him go. Its grip was strong and oddly careful. Through his failing senses he glimpsed Romana, thumping at its arm with the golf club and calling for help from K-9. Then it lifted him off his feet and tossed him aside like a bag of rubbish.

His senses spinning, he lifted up his head. The events that followed seemed to occur in a blur, as if he was watching from behind a piece of muslin. He saw K-9 turning from the hut, bursts of red fire spurting from his muzzle and slicing at the ghoul, ripping bloody holes across the front of its uniform. Each hit delayed it, but for every step backward it took two forward. Romana was standing in the doorway of the bathing-hut, dividing her attention between the battle and… and something else. The Colonel had no words for it.

The hut's interior should have been a darkened cubbyhole, with a row of hooks, perhaps a wooden bench. It was not. The bulk of the space was taken up by a tall white column covered in strange markings and symbols. He watched as Romana took a slender silver torch from her pocket and applied it to the side of the column. A small panel clicked open, revealing a tangled web of sparkling golden filaments. 'I suppose I've got no choice,' said Romana. She plunged her hand into the mass of strands and tugged.

Straight away a rushing wind came from the hut, knocking both Romana and the policeman to the ground. K-9 was blown off his tracks but the Colonel managed to stay upright. A second later, to the accompaniment of a roaring noise that was even more powerful than the wind, the front of the column dissolved in a shower of golden sparks, and was replaced by something that seemed to defy reality.

It was a jagged-edged hole in the world. Inside was a pattern of dancing light, which spun and twisted, red and then green, and then yellow; then a shifting purple pattern like an inverted ribcage; then a dark tunnel formed from opposing strips of bright blue, which opened out suddenly into a whirling vortex, its core a ball of white fire. The Colonel felt that he could stare into that fire for eternity, and that the fire, somehow, was eternity.

The policeman pulled himself up. He spoke, his words slurring. 'You cannot escape. Nobody can resist Zodaal. Surrender your brains.'

'Mistress, orders!' K-9 bleated.

'How safe is this portal, K-9?' Romana cried, pulling herself up. She steadied herself on the swinging door of the hut. Her hair was blown by the ferocious winds roaring from the vortex.

'Unprotected use of portal inadvisable, Mistress. Eighty-three per cent probability of dissolution along temporal plane.'

The Colonel shook his head to clear it and pushed himself to his feet. There was nothing but confusion before his eyes now. The ghoul was nearly upon Romana. He had to save her.

'Well, what about our chances of getting away from him?' she asked.

'Ninety-seven per cent probability of your death, Mistress,' K-9 replied, sounding distraught. 'I am — sorry, Mistress.' His head dropped.

The policeman lunged.

Romana leapt back into the vortex. 'I'll have to take my chance. Goodbye, K—' Her words were snatched away by the roaring wind as she was pulled backwards, then was sent tumbling over and over down the tunnel, vanishing in less than a second, sucked into the white core.

'No!' screeched the policeman. He clawed at the air frantically, apparently unwilling to follow. Then he turned to face the Colonel. 'But there is still you.' He shambled forward, eyes glowing fiercely, his misshapen form silhouetted against the whirling vortex. His mouth dropped open and he raised his hands, the fingers extended.

'I must follow the Mistress,' said K-9. 'But this unit is not protected against temporal stress. Advise!'

'Well, I could do with a spot of help!' cried the Colonel. The stench from the ghoul was close to overpowering him again. He saw its grey fingers inching closer.

Then it stumbled backward, groaning, a beam of light from K-9's muzzle transfixing it through the heart.

'Suggest your escape through the portal, Colonel,' said K-9. 'Hurry. My power is depleted. I cannot… hold him for long…'

'Righto.' The Colonel pushed the policeman aside and, without thinking, raced towards the vortex. One thing he'd never been was a coward. And no, he didn't know what was going on. But the girl Romana needed his help, and that was all that mattered.

157

He leapt through the hole. Immediately he wished he'd taken his chances with the zombie.

The coloured pattern absorbed him, and he was sent spinning crazily out of the world…

… and into quite another sort of place entirely.

PART THREE

7
THE DOMAIN OF ZODAAL

Woodrow climbed the bare staircase slowly, heart thudding, eyes bulging with fright. The setting evinced all his half-formed doubts about Julia's scheme. Here, with the stench of death and decay on all sides, it seemed to him that nothing could be concealed from the gaze of his master. What if he confessed that the Doctor was alive, and told Stackhouse that Julia had forced him to lie? The thought died instantly. The vile, brain-eating monster would take the barest hint of treachery as an excuse to indulge its hunger. And, he reminded himself desperately, there was still time for the real Doctor to triumph and by some means save them all. He abandoned that line of thought as, with a heavy tread, he stepped onto the top landing. The eerie green glow seeped from the open door at the far end, coupled with the hideous stentorian breaths of the king of the undead. He took a deep breath and took the last few steps of his agonised journey.

As ever, Stackhouse sat in his high-backed chair, his face turned to the shadows. Without moving he said simply, 'Woodrow.'

'I'm here, sir.' There was an ominous silence. Woodrow hesitated on the threshold, convinced that his master had already divined his secret in some extraordinary and unnatural way. Trying to keep his voice neutral, he asked, 'All is well at Jasmine Street?'

'Woodrow,' Stackhouse repeated. 'Come closer.'

It took all of Woodrow's remaining strength of will to hold his ground. 'Sir, I don't understand.'

'Approach.' Stackhouse's manner was unreadable. 'You will approach.'

Woodrow obeyed, inching towards the chair. Stackhouse remained still as death, the patterns in the gas cloud that surrounded him curling and reforming constantly.

His eyes opened, their glow fiercer than ever, the pupils completely obscured by the field of pulsing energy within. Woodrow screamed once and sank to his knees as if in supplication. His hands sprang up automatically in a gesture of prayer and he babbled, 'No, sir, it wasn't me that lied to you, she forced me, it was all her idea, I tried to stop her, I…' The words simply dried on his throat as a thick tendril of the vapour reached out like a living thing, divided in three, and invaded his open mouth and his nostrils. He felt as if three long, sharp knives had been driven into his head. Desperately he tried to pull away, but his body was locked fast and his limbs refused to respond.

'The Doctor is still alive,' Stackhouse said. 'I can sense the power of his living mind, undimmed.' He moved slightly in his chair, extending one of his short legs and kicking Woodrow's frozen body over onto the hard wooden boards. 'I should have known better than to trust a living human. Your kind squirm and wriggle over this world like maggots infesting a rotting carcass. Soon the great feast will clear the Earth before its immersion in cleansing fire. But for now…' He leant over, using the end of his cane to prod at the whimpering Woodrow's stiffened form. 'My plans are nearing completion. I have no further need of a human agent.' He took Woodrow's head almost tenderly between the thick, grey fingers of his outstretched arm. 'No further need.'

'No, sir,' begged Woodrow, 'please, no, don't, don't…'

Stackhouse's fingers tightened on his skull. 'You think I would choose to dine on your brain? Out of the question. As you have shown, it lacks the vitality essential in a dish worthy of the core.' He gave Woodrow's head a single, casual twist. Woodrow heard his own neck breaking. 'No,' continued Stackhouse. 'While Orlick is away, your form may be of value. There is enough of me to spare to create one more slave.'

Woodrow screamed for the final time.

The secondary host battled against the energy beam directed by the alien computer. Each ruby-red bolt was less powerful than the last, and slowly but surely the metal beast was being forced back towards the shimmering vortex of the open portal.

'Retreat, retreat,' it whined.

The host snarled. 'You are powerless.'

The beast fell silent. The red glow of its eyescreen dipped momentarily as it hovered on the fringes of the vortex. Then it emitted a sequence of howls, bleeps and clicks. Some sort of coded sequence? It was not the place of the secondary host to know such things. Then the beast pulled itself back quickly, and section by section, tail first, it was swallowed up by the shrieking void. At the same time the door of the bathing-hut started to swing to.

The host roared with anger and frustration and threw himself forward, but the door had already closed. Between the foot of the door and the lintel the myriad patterns of light started to fade, and second by second the whirling pattern was eaten away, until the central node of the vortex was all that remained. Then, with a grating thud, it closed. His enemies had escaped him. Still, the portal was damaged beyond repair. No more agents would arrive this way.

He lurched closer, stretching out one hand to the door.

If he had given the matter some thought, he might have expected the surge of static energy that burst from the portal's emergency shields. It knocked him back across the pebbles, his arms and legs jolted straight out. As he staggered back his frame began to dissolve. He felt no pain, only anger. There were no humans in the vicinity, no host to flee to!

He separated himself from the disintegrated form of the policeman, hung suspended for a few moments, then dispersed forever into the air.

The first thing Romana saw was blueness. Her head was clear, although she had sustained a couple of knocks and bruises, and she was lying in a heap against a high blue wall. Her eyes followed it up, and up, to where it met a blue ceiling. Not very inspiring.

Slowly she turned her head to make a fuller investigation of her new surroundings. The vortex had deposited her in what looked like an antechamber or airlock, a small room, decorated all in blue, with one low-lintelled door facing her. There was no furniture of any kind. Apart from her, the only other thing about was a battered-looking Colonel Radlett. He was still out, but a swift check of his life signs confirmed his continued health. Romana felt relieved. She had grown rather fond of him.

The door appeared to be locked tight, and her automatic response was halted by a sudden flash of remembrance. 'Oh, K-9,' she breathed. 'I'm sorry, too. What's the Doctor going to say?'

'Inadvisable to predict Doctor Master's speech patterns,' a familiar voice said, apparently from thin air.

Romana clapped her hands together. 'K-9, you're safe! Where are you?'

'Behind this door, Mistress,' he said. 'Do you wish me to open it?'

'Yes,' she cried, exasperated but much relieved. Life without K-9 had been hard to contemplate.

The door slid open smoothly, and K-9 motored through. Romana knelt down to examine him. 'You've taken a few dents, haven't you?'

'This unit protected against dents,' he replied. 'Structural integrity unimpaired.' He turned a quarter circle, wagging his tail as if in concern. 'Anomaly in logical extrapolation of events, Mistress.'

'I know,' she said, standing up and looking about the small room again. 'Unshielded, undirected travel through a time corridor. None of us should have survived it. And where is this place, anyway?'

'Insufficient data, Mistress,' said K-9. 'Suggest exploratory mission.' He turned towards the door.

'So,' said Percy as he came to the end of his tale, 'I know only a fraction more about the Doctor and company than you do yourself.' He twiddled his thumbs mournfully. 'You know, yesterday I was having such a good time of it.' He looked up at Julia, who stood staring silently through the mucky window. Where had he seen that face before? Something aristocratic about it, he felt sure. The kind of hardness that rich people, very rich and powerful people far outside the aspirant circles of café society in which he moved, often had. 'Er, do you believe me, then?'

She pursed her lips and tapped one end of the transceiver against her open palm. 'Stackhouse has a piece of machinery,' she said slowly. A note of contrition had crept into her voice. 'He calls it a sonic stimulator. When I looked upon it, a kind of coldness swept over me. It's unnatural. This is the same.'

'Well, not really,' Percy pointed out. 'If you could nip back, say, a couple of hundred years, well, a wireless would cause the same sort of storm, wouldn't it?'

Julia picked up his bag and put the transceiver back inside. 'You've seen the future?'

'Yes, of course I have.' Percy waggled his fingers meaningfully. 'Do you think I can go now?'

She ignored him. 'Then you are living proof that Stackhouse must fail in his plan.'

'Doesn't quite work like that, I'm afraid,' Percy said a little guiltily. 'In fact, the way it's been explained to me, well…' He trailed off as the full consequences of his actions dawned on him. 'Oh heck. It could be all my fault. The end of the world. Lummy. How in heaven's name have I managed that?'

Julia didn't appear to be listening to him. Her attention had shifted back to the bag, from which she produced several balls of wool, a pair of knitting needles tangled up in a half completed tea cosy, and a few crumpled sheets of music. 'Why did you come to our time?' she asked as she set the objects down. 'What can these things mean to you?'

Percy sighed. 'A reasonable standard of civilisation, a spot of peace and quiet. A more innocent age. Supposedly.'

'London in this day, quiet and innocent?'

'I did say supposedly. And you should see what it'll be like where I come from. I say, you couldn't…' He flexed his fingers again and assumed a hopeful expression.

Her attention had again been taken by something in the bag. Percy was slightly confused. He didn't think there was anything else in it. Then he saw the object clasped in Julia's hand and immediately he backed away from her across the room, the legs of his chair prison dragging against the rough wooden boards, a cry of alarm springing involuntarily from his lips.

'What's wrong?' she asked.

'I'd put that down carefully if I were you,' said Percy. 'It might start going.'

She frowned. 'Another machine?'

'It's a…' Percy slumped further in the chair. Today it seemed he couldn't keep his mouth shut. 'It's a flying-box.'

Julia examined the small object, and ran her fingers along its smooth sides where small glowing buttons were inset in a wave pattern. 'It flies, by itself?'

Percy fretted. 'I really shouldn't be telling you all this.'

'Tell me!'

'I really don't like it when you raise your voice like that.'
He waved his hands once more. 'I don't suppose there's any
chance…'

She closed the distance between them and held the box
aloft. Its gleaming facets made a contrast with the murkiness
of Woodrow's room, and Percy found himself backing away
again. He felt as if the future was chasing him. Oh, why couldn't
everything be all right again?

'How does it work?' Julia demanded.

'Well, I'm not certain about the mechanical principles,' he
babbled. 'But, put simply, it can lift you into the air – up a short
distance, anyway. It makes for easier travel.'

'You all use these, then, in the future?'

'Well, not all of us, no.' He decided to make a last attempt to
have himself freed. 'My hands. Please?'

She turned the box over in her hands. The coloured lights
from its activator switches played over her face, which was alive
with curiosity.

The large, dead, grey hand of Stackhouse fastened on Woodrow's
shoulder. 'What is the one true purpose?'

Woodrow rose from his kneeling position. His eyelids
fluttered. When they opened fully it was to reveal twin points
of luminous green light. He cleared his throat once. The sound
was like a pipe being unblocked. When he spoke it was in a
thick, creaking voice quite unlike his own. 'To serve Zodaal,' he
said.

'Good.' Stackhouse removed his hand. 'Listen to me. Reach
into the memory cells of your host form.'

'I can see the memory of this host,' Woodrow said falteringly.
'Recall is clouded by fear.'

'Search,' Stackhouse commanded. 'Search for the plan to
deceive me.'

Woodrow stiffened and his fists clenched convulsively. 'Miss

167

Orlostro is holding the Doctor, in the rooms above my offices. I am to return there when I can.'

Stackhouse lifted his hand. 'You will keep that appointment, Woodrow.'

Matters didn't seem at all correct to the Colonel when he regained consciousness. 'Must have had a knock on the head,' he reasoned, checking his scalp for bumps. 'Terrible sore throat.' A blurred female face appeared. 'Ah, nurse. Glass of water, please.'

Instead of going to fetch one, she placed her arm around his shoulders and propped him up gently. It occurred to him to wonder why he was in hospital. His condition was tip-top. There must have been an accident. It seemed as if his throat was burning. 'Glass of water, please,' he repeated. 'I'm very dry.'

'Loss of fluid,' she said. 'An inevitable side effect.'

The day's frantic and incomprehensible events came crashing back into the Colonel's mind and he shot upright. 'Good Lord!' he exclaimed. 'Romana!'

'Yes, now just relax,' she advised.

'But the beach, and the hut, and that policeman. We soon saw to him, didn't we? Rotten b—' He blinked and tried to take in his surroundings. 'My goodness. Where's this, then?'

It seemed to the Colonel that he was inside an upturned dome-like structure some seventy feet in circumference. The walls curved gently to an apex, a circular opening from which shone a thin beam of effulgent light, illuminating the entire scene. The predominant colour was a cool turquoise, and the claustral ambience was enhanced by a noise like the faint tinkling of Indian bells of prayer. Set at irregular intervals along the base of the dome were tall, wide pillars, with fixtures of glowing sculpted glass mounted on their fronts. Some of these had a kind of elaborate pattern inscribed on them in gold. The metal dog was moving around the pillars in turn, sniffing each as he went with his dangling red probe.

A shocking thought struck the Colonel. 'I say,' he said, clutching at Romana's sleeve. 'We're not… up there, are we?'

'Up where?'

'You know, my dear. Up above the clouds. Gone to meet our maker.' He looked about nervously. 'He's not around, is he?'

'Oh no, Colonel.' Romana helped him to his feet and gestured casually around as if the place was no stranger than Piccadilly. 'I can't be certain, but I think we're aboard some kind of space capsule.'

'Space capsule, eh? What's that, then?' asked the Colonel.

Romana sighed. 'A space capsule. For travelling between the stars. You should be familiar with the concept, if not the practice. There must be science-fictional structures in your culture by now.'

The Colonel shook his head. 'Do you mean –' he searched for the right words – 'this is like some sort of aeroplane?'

'I suppose so.'

'For going off to the moon?'

'I suppose you could go to the moon if you felt like it.'

'Hmm. If you fancied a jig with the man in the moon, eh? Must say, doesn't look like one.' Feeling steadier now, he went for a look around the dome. 'More like being up in a Zeppelin. Very grand, I must say. Oh dear, this whole lark is all a bit high flying.'

K-9 had completed his round of inspection. 'Mistress,' he said, turning to face Romana. 'Your hypothesis is confirmed. These instruments are flight regulators.'

Romana ran her hand along the glass front of one of the pillars. 'Then what kind of system are they regulating? There must be a power source.'

'My analysis suggests the power source is absent,' replied K-9. Anticipating a rejoinder he went on, 'Life-supporting environment is active, yes, but I suggest this is being drawn from a small residual supply.'

Romana turned her head from side to side. 'If the power

source failed, perhaps that's why this thing got stuck here.'

'That hut,' the Colonel said suddenly.

Romana knelt to address K-9. 'Is there any chance of achieving a transition back to the portal?'

K-9's head fell. 'Available data suggests probability of successfully effecting a reverse is less than eleven per cent, Mistress.'

'That hut,' the Colonel said again.

'What about it?'

'We stepped through it, into those lights…'

'And ended up here.' Romana made a defeated gesture with one hand. 'The thing's stuck here, halfway along the corridor.' She snapped her fingers. 'Of course. The shadow that was blocking Percy's signal. We're inside it.'

The Colonel fingered the strands of his moustache ruefully. 'Now, let's not lose ourselves in all this technical hocus pocus, shall we? Won't get us anywhere.'

'Nothing's going to get us anywhere,' said Romana. 'Don't you see, Colonel? We're trapped here. Wedged in time.'

'As a matter of fact, I don't see at all,' said the Colonel. It was time he put some sense back into the proceedings. 'But, you know, there's no use in moping, my dear. We must set about getting ourselves out of here. Can't be all that difficult.' He strode over to the side of the dome and rapped on it with his knuckles. There was a hollow clanging sound. 'There you are. These walls can't be too thick. We can use one of these free-standing objects as a battering ram and knock our way out.'

Romana gave him a hard stare and turned her back on him. K-9 at her heels, she walked slowly off through a low opening in the far side of the dome.

The Colonel felt slightly disappointed with her. It went to show that the training her people got wasn't up to scratch. Lack of spirit. He'd soon have them all out of here. By applying half his weight against its side, he was able to push one of the pillars, inch by inch, towards the wall. It was a darn sight heavier than it looked, and he found himself looking around the dome for something to use as leverage. The place was empty.

He heard a scrape and a click from behind him.

When he turned it was to see that a cake-slice-shaped section of the dome's wall had slid apart. There. He wasn't at all sure how he'd managed that but at least it was done. Something to be proud of. 'Romana, dear!' he called. 'K-9! Something to show you!'

Without waiting, he stepped through the gap in the wall. A much dimmer yellow light revealed a small oblong room that was cluttered with all kinds of esoteric paraphernalia, the bulk of it resting atop a long table something like a trestle. In contrast to the air of tranquillity in the dome, the inner room radiated a sense of menace, like some terrible murder had happened here. The clutter was inert, a mass of twisting strips of metal and arrangements of switches and levers. 'Looks like the work of a madman,' the Colonel told Romana as she joined him. 'Once saw an old hermit up in the hills who'd flipped his lid and sat twisting strips of bamboo all day. Bit like this.'

'You must have triggered a locking device,' said Romana. She crossed to the table and poked tentatively at a lump of tangled flex. 'This reminds me of one of the Doctor's lash-ups.'

K-9 swept his probe across the scene. 'Function of this assemblage uncertain. Components analogous to recognised patterns include molecular scatterformer and a high-width beam device calibrated to reduction setting. Origins of this technology unknown.'

'Don't start all that blether again,' said the Colonel stiffly. 'Now, what's all this over here, then?' He crossed to a plate of frosted glass in one wall. All that rubbish on the table ended up with a long thick cable that trailed over the floor and then passed through a series of holes drilled into the glass. By squinting and taking a step back he could discern a man-shaped figure, standing upright, on the other side. 'There's our culprit. Looks as if he's taking a nap.' He knelt and weighed the trailing cables in one hand. 'I wonder what'd happen if I gave these a yank? Might wake him up.'

Romana took the cables from his hand. 'Don't touch anything, please,' she said haughtily. 'You have no understanding of what's going on here.'

The Colonel bristled. 'I don't like your tone, young lady. I don't care who you're working for, you'll show some respect. Now then.' He turned back to the plate of glass, his cheeks burning red. 'Let's have this open, and get a serious, sensible explanation for what's going on.' He hammered on the plate. 'Hello. You in there, I say. Open up. I want a word with you.'

To his own surprise the glass opened outward, with a faint hiss like air leaking from a tyre. The recess within was occupied by a slanted bier on which rested a tall cowled figure, its face hidden beneath its hood. The Colonel would have been slightly unnerved if he'd been thinner of blood, but he'd seen far worse sights. 'Right,' he said. 'Now, first off, we'd like an apology. Myself and this young lady have been…'

The sentence died away as the hood fell back. He drew away, alarmed by what lay beneath. In shape it resembled the skull of a wolf. It was as big as a medicine ball, with two rows of rotted yellow teeth that must have been terrifyingly sharp. Its large rounded sockets were black and empty.

'Dead as mutton. Thing gives me the willies,' the Colonel told Romana. 'Odd thing to do, stand it up like that. Some rite or something, I'll be bound. Blooming foreigners. Huns, I'll be bound. Slippery lot.' He tutted and shook his head. 'The beast must have been huge.'

'It wasn't a beast,' said Romana slowly. She reached forward and drew the hood forward over the creature's head again with a kind of reverence. 'I think it was the owner of this ship.'

'Bipedal humanoid with lupine characteristics,' K-9

volunteered. 'Species unknown. Enlarged cranial elevation suggests highly developed intelligence.'

'Poor blighter must have starved,' said the Colonel. 'Ghastly way to go.'

'My analysis,' said K-9 sniffily, 'indicates that this being died from the extraction of moisture. Thus the body appears decayed. In this sterile environment real decay would be impossible.'

'Wait a moment,' said Romana, tapping her chin with the tip of one finger. 'K-9, did you say that one of those components was a molecular scatterformer?'

'Negative, Mistress.'

'I'm sure you did, I blooming well heard you,' the Colonel put in.

'Negative. I said "Components analogous to recognised patterns include a molecular scatterformer."'

'Don't split hairs, dog,' said the Colonel.

'I am not programmed for barbering,' said K-9.

'Be quiet, the pair of you.' Romana picked up one of the boxes resting on the table. 'This is it. Normally this would be used by miners, to extract certain elements in their gaseous form for easier processing. But in conjunction with all of this…' She gestured to the rest of the jumble. 'I think it was used to convert and extract a gaseous layer from that body, which was then bonded with radmium.'

The Colonel was appalled. 'Torture? Probably up against the Boer, then.'

'No,' said Romana definitely. 'I think whoever he was went willingly.'

To Percy's infinite relief, his bonds were at last loosed. 'Well,' he said, rolling his arms in a windmill motion, 'that's probably done my circulation no good at all. Well, I think I ought to—' He broke off. Julia was now covering him with a compact black revolver. 'Oh heck.'

She gestured to the door. 'Downstairs.'

Percy fumed. 'Now, really. I don't know how you go about things in your country, but here in England if we make an agreement we stick to it. It's called playing the game.'

Julia jabbed him with the tip of the weapon. 'I said downstairs.'

They clumped down the narrow wooden staircase, Percy muttering as they did. The rooms below were in a similar state to those of the upper floor. Julia led him through a small, bare office and into the building's main consulting room, which was dirty, dusty and empty. Next to a ledger on the counter was a telephone. Julia indicated it and said, 'Call the Doctor. I want him here.'

'Oh, good.' Percy was taken by surprise but much relieved. 'Listen, if you've decided to fall in with us, there's no point sticking that thing into me, is there?'

'Nothing is decided yet,' she replied. 'Now, call him.'

Percy lifted the mouthpiece and asked the operator for his own home.

Felicia watched with interest as the Doctor ran his hands over the steering wheel of her tourer. 'This takes me back,' he said, giving the horn a squeeze.

'It's a brand-new model, Doctor,' Felicia pointed out.

'I know,' he replied. 'Do you know, I seem to recall once being terribly interested in automobiles. Can't think why.' He fired the engine. 'Still, as long as it gets us where we want to go.'

'But we don't know where we want to go yet,' Felicia pointed out. 'This expedition does seem rather haphazard.'

The Doctor waved her objection away. 'That's what old Hannibal said, and he had a herd of temperamental elephants to deal with.'

Just as he reached forward to release the handbrake, a shrill ringing came from behind the closed door of Percy's house. Felicia clutched the Doctor's arm. 'I say, might that be our mysterious caller once again?'

The Doctor had already vaulted over the side of the car, without bothering to open the door, and was bounding up the steps to the house. A moment's work with his special key admitted him and he thudded through the hall. Felicia trailed behind at a more stately pace.

'Hello, Percival Closed's residence, who wants him?' the Doctor demanded into the mouthpiece.

As she reached the top of the stairs Felicia heard Percy's voice coming clearly from the earpiece. Such musical tones. The poor lamb sounded so frightened. 'Doctor! Thank heaven for that. Listen, I can't chat for long.'

'I was afraid you were going to say that,' said the Doctor. 'You're lucky, we were just on our way out.'

'Out?' Percy said, sounding outraged. 'While I'm trussed up here you were planning to go out? Very nice, I must say. Where were you thinking of spending the afternoon, Bloomingdale's? Or perhaps tea at the Ritz?'

'Get to the point,' said the Doctor.

'There's a gun at my head, I can't stay on the line for very long,' Percy went on. Felicia gave a startled shriek. 'What was that?' Percy asked.

'Just Mrs Chater, squeaking,' said the Doctor. 'Go on.'

'Ah, righto. Still there, is she? Er, where was I?'

'You can't chat for long, there's a gun at your head,' the Doctor prompted.

'So there is. Er, yes, well, my captor, as it were, would like the pleasure of your acquaintance, Doctor.'

'How very charming of him,' said the Doctor. 'At our last meeting he tried to kill me.'

'Eh? No, it's somebody else. Listen, I'll have to explain it all to you when you get here. Come to number, er, 15 Haverstock Row. Er, right away.'

Felicia was overcome by worry and leant over the mouthpiece.

'Mr Closed,' she burst out, 'are you all right? You poor man, how are they treating you?'

'Oh, all right for now,' he replied. 'Just get over here, all right? Look, I have to go.'

'Wait a moment,' the Doctor said urgently. 'Pardon me for saying so, but this sounds awfully like it could be a trap.' He waited for a reply. Instead there was a click and then a droning purr as the call was broken off. The Doctor put the phone back on the hook and stepped back. 'I don't like it when people hang up like that when you ask them if it's a trap.'

'Haverstock Row,' Felicia mused. 'I can't say I've heard of the place. But I've a street map in the car.'

The Doctor was already thudding back down the hallway.

Romana stood chin in hand, deep in thought, at the centre of the domed section of the capsule. K-9 whirred around at her feet, his tail wagging slowly, light indicators on his manual operation keyboard twinkling as he combed his data banks for any useful morsel of information.

'There must be some way to escape,' said Romana desperately. 'That creature got out, didn't it?'

'By reducing itself to a gaseous state, Mistress,' said K-9.

'Yes, I've been thinking about that.' Romana shivered at the thought and sat down, crossing her legs. K-9 sensed the change in her mood and came to her side. 'It used radmium to keep itself whole, then somehow funnelled itself out through the time corridor to Nutchurch. But why would anybody on a space flight be carrying a stock of radmium?'

'Probable link to power source, Mistress,' K-9 pointed out. 'Suggest this craft was powered by the core of a double-spiralled black star.'

Romana swallowed as the enormity of this conclusion dawned on her. 'Then no wonder it ended up here. Still, none of this helps us. We're still trapped.'

'Affirmative, Mistress.'

The Colonel was having no more of this obfuscation. He strode about the inner chamber, taking time to examine the various wall hangings and whatnot, and fitting it all into a logical pattern. 'I reckon I've got it,' he told himself. 'When we looked into that hut what we saw was some sort of optical trick, cooked up by our opponents. They knocked us on the head and lugged us down here. Of course, this is obviously a submarine used by the spies.' He chortled happily and rubbed his hands together. 'Yes, that's it, George, old boy. A sub.'

He was on the point of going through to inform Romana of his reasoning when something stopped him in his tracks.

Somebody whispered, distinctly.

He whipped around, but the chamber was still empty.

'Eh? Who's that? Who goes there, eh? Show yourself.' It felt rather daft to address the silence.

Then the silence was broken. At first so faintly he couldn't be certain he wasn't imagining it, the Colonel became aware of a sound akin to the flow of a brook, or was it more like tall grass blowing in a light breeze? A second later it spoke to him.

'... *error in core*... *separation*... *recover*... *must recover core power*...' The sound rushed off into nothingness.

He backed away. The chamber was exactly the same as before and the ghastly form on the bier remained still in death.

The voice came again. '... *transference must be attained*... *the bond must be*... *strong*... *the will of Zodaal*...'

The Colonel opened his mouth with the intention of calling for Romana, hovered hesitantly, then closed it again, firmly. He was damned if he was going to let her boss him about again. Perfectly able to deal with the crisis himself. 'Now, come along,' he told the voice. 'Don't hide yourself away in this cowardly fashion. Step out and let's discuss our terms. You may have fooled the young lady but you haven't fooled me. I'm made of

177

stronger stuff. Will of iron. I was picked for this job, you know. So, let's talk.'

'... *release the will of Zodaal... you must release... Zodaal must be complete...*'

'What are you jabbering on about now?' The Colonel strode briskly around the chamber, peering in every corner for a likely hiding place. 'You can't conceal yourself for ever, you know, my friend. I'm not afraid, you know.'

'... *the containment jar... you must destroy the containment jar...*'

The Colonel halted where the voice was strongest. It seemed to be coming from the section of wall behind those glass bottles. He tapped the wall. 'I say, I know you're in there.'

'... *you must help us... Zodaal must be complete... the jar... destroy it...*' The voice had an urgent desperate quality. Sounded a bit soft but the fellow was definitely an Englishman. Probably another captive, then.

'Don't worry,' he whispered. 'I'm coming to get you, old man. You hang on in there, I'll have you out in no time.' Couldn't see any lock or concealed catch or anything. Perhaps it was hidden behind the row of bottles. They were affixed to the wall by metal brackets, and looked as if they could easily be slid out. Carefully he removed the first, intending to put it down on the table.

The bottle jerked in his hand. It had looked empty, but now it had clouded with a swirling green vapour. '... *yes... release us... we must emerge... the will of Zodaal...*'

The Colonel felt the sides of the glass rippling and bulging in his hand as whatever was inside struggled to get out.

The world seemed to spin about him. Everything seemed too big for his head, too much to fit in comfortably. It was the same feeling he'd had when he'd seen those youths on the beach with their hateful gramophone, whenever he saw new things that didn't appear to make sense, but amplified to an unbearable level. Worse than that, it was a kind of fear. And fear was an emotion he'd never entertained until today.

As all this rushed through his head, he fumbled with the bottle and it slipped through his fingers.

K-9's snout raised abruptly and his eyescreen flashed in alarm. 'Mistress,' he bleated, already turning for the inner chamber, 'radmium detected in low concentration.'

Romana followed him. 'That creature must have followed us.'

'Negative. There has been no breach of this vessel.'

Romana ducked through the open door and froze with horror. The air throbbed with alien vibrations. Long jagged shards of glass lay on the ground. A cloud of foul-smelling green mist had formed around the Colonel, who stood stiffly upright, his eyes glittering, his face rigid with terror.

'Sorry, my dear,' he gasped, 'I've let us down rather.'

The whispering mist cloud seemed to react to his words, and seething and crackling it descended on his immobile form.

8

'I Must Feed
on Your Brain'

In the dry, close atmosphere of the consulting rooms, Percy sat with his elbows resting on the counter, staring plaintively at the still hands of a dead clock. He was thinking about time, and the horrible trick it had played on him, leaving him stranded in an age many hundreds of years prior to his birth. The implications of this temporal mix-up whizzed round and round in his head, making it ache; for surely if he was to die now along with Earth and all its inhabitants, he would thus never be born. It followed he would not take up his position with the Bureau, and so would not travel back in the first place, and therefore all was at rights, the world safe from his disastrous influence. That didn't seem logical, either. The whole affair was *too* complicated.

Julia was pacing the floorboards, revolver in hand. There was no point in trying to make conversation. She was the sort who could talk only of weighty and important things, he could tell, which meant they were really poles apart. Chances were high she'd make a good pal for the Doctor, though, and together perhaps they could sort out the mess.

These thoughts were still occupying his mind when he heard a motor drawing up outside. 'This'll be him, all right,' he said. 'Please don't shoot him, will you? I really do think he's our best shot at trumping Stackhouse.'

'Be quiet,' Julia warned. She strode swiftly over to him and lashed out with the upturned palm of her free hand, dazing him. He was lifted from his chair by his collar and made to stand in the centre of the room; before he had stumbled more than a couple of paces he felt the cold metal of her revolver against his temple again. 'Don't move or try to break free,' she whispered as they heard approaching footsteps. 'I can kill you very easily.'

'For the hundredth time,' he whispered back through gritted teeth, 'I don't have the slightest intention of running off. I make it a habit not to run for anything.'

'Quiet.' She brushed the point of the pistol across his temple.

The footsteps, measured and slow, with an odd metronomic quality, came closer. Percy was puzzled. He couldn't picture the Doctor dragging his feet along like that, especially in the light of the zest with which he'd conducted their telephone conversation. A shadow, sharply cast by the late afternoon's sunlight, was thrown across the dusty pane of the door. At the same time, a sensation familiar to Percy began to encroach. His nostrils quivered as the obnoxious whiff grew stronger, and he was about to let out a cry when the door was pushed inward and off its hinges. It fell with a resounding clatter, raising small clouds of dust. Silhouetted in the empty frame of the doorway was Woodrow.

Slowly he stepped forward, and a square shaft of sunlight from one of the office's higher windows caught his pale face full on, revealing as it passed his marbled eyes and frozen expression. Percy had no remaining doubts. 'Oh, flip,' he muttered. 'Horrible.' As he spoke he was distantly aware of Julia withdrawing the gun from his side and readying herself to fire.

The ghoul opened its mouth, showing a set of blackened teeth and a bloated tongue like one half of a rotted peach. 'You,' it uttered, raising one arm in a pointing gesture, 'I have come for you.'

'Oh no, not again,' said Percy despairingly. His legs shook and he tried desperately to calculate his chances of making it to the door if he tried to make a run around the thing. It was slow moving, for sure, but also it didn't half pack a punch. 'What does everyone want with me?'

Woodrow made a dismissive sound. 'You are of no matter.' His white finger, from which flakes of dead skin were already falling, their descent lit by the sunlight, was now pointing directly at Julia. 'You are needed. You are to come with me.'

In reply, she cried, 'Get down!', pushed Percy forward so he collapsed onto his knees, and fired three times at the heart of her former ally. Three bullet holes appeared in his shirt front, and the smell of cordite mixed with the odour of the green mist, but still he came on.

'You are needed,' he repeated, stretching his arms out. 'You are to come with me. Your brain is needed.'

Romana had never felt so helpless. The Colonel's prostrate body, now completely swathed in the mist, lay at her feet, while K-9 twittered and bleeped, searching his data banks in a last-ditch effort to find a way to remedy the situation. 'Colonel!' she cried desperately. 'Try and fight it!'

Astonishingly his mouth opened, and he gasped. 'Can't seem… to think straight…'

Then, without warning, K-9 shot forward into the mist cloud, his protuberances quivering with power. 'Reconfiguring,' he squeaked in a higher-pitched voice than usual. 'Recon-Reconfiguring – Activating full energy potential –' A wash of static overwhelmed his voicebox, and Romana felt a ripple of electricity pass over her body with a faint crackle.

'K-9, what are you doing?' she demanded. There was no reply, nor could there be. For as the dog was swallowed up by the cloud, its questing tendrils withdrew from the Colonel and surrounded him, seeking access to his inner circuitry through the hinged slats that ran along his base. His inspection panel, on which his name was printed, sprang open and the mist entered him. Romana watched with a mounting sense of terror. K-9 had taken a gamble, and probably saved the life of the Colonel, but the cost had been tremendous. Moreover, their enemy now had access to a vast data store and a potentially deadly laser weapon.

Quickly she dragged the Colonel up by the arm and away from K-9, who sat immobile and throbbing quietly, covered in the vapour, emitting all kinds of curious and unfamiliar squawks.

'What the—' The Colonel broke off, spluttering. 'That gas again. Revolting stuff.'

'Oh, K-9, what have you done?' Romana lamented.

The dog's eyescreen flickered, then went out, then returned, its colour now a sickly green.

'What's up with him?' asked the Colonel. 'Tad off colour.'

'He's sacrificed himself,' she replied, unable to keep the bitterness from her voice. 'To save you.'

'Well, I shouldn't worry, you can always get another one,' the Colonel said. 'Can't you?'

K-9 coughed three times. In a slightly less formal speech pattern, and slightly more sybaritic tone than previously, he said, 'This is a very strange host to find oneself in. An artificial intelligence of staggering virtuosity.'

'Who are you?' asked Romana.

'Well, at present, to all intents and purposes, I am your dear friend K-9,' came the reply. 'K-9?' There was a chuckle. 'Your idea?'

'No,' said Romana, still wary.

'No, it wasn't, was it? The creator of the original model had K-9 registered as a data patent on, let me see, October the third 4998.' It gave a pleased burble. 'Droll. Yes, I like that. Simple but striking.'

There was a brief electronic bleep, similar to the call sign of a radio conversation, and to her immense relief Romana heard

K-9's familiar tinny voice state, 'Nomenclature of this unit irrelevant.'

'I say,' the Colonel broke in, 'the little blighter's all right. He's still in there. Well done, old chap!'

'Naturally,' K-9 said. 'Purpose of reconfiguring was to provide more attractive outlet for gaseous creature attempting invasion of your body. The death of a human in this circumstance is certain, but my brain possesses alternator interfaces for use by visiting intelligences.'

'Then what is it, K-9?' Romana pressed him. 'What kind of intelligence?'

The signal sounded again, and the voice of the visitor spoke. 'It's all right to ask me, you know. I can speak for myself.' There was a pause, and he continued, 'I am Zodaal.'

The Doctor's nose, thought Felicia, was a quite remarkable instrument. Its sensitivity matched its prodigiousness, for as he turned the motor rather roughly around the winding twists of the narrow backstreets – but always with regard to the vehicle – he gave a couple of strong sniffs, and remarked, 'We must be getting close. I smell radmium.'

Not sure what he meant, Felicia commented, 'You're more likely to smell rotting fishheads here, Doctor. It's a most unsavoury area.' She looked disdainfully at the rows of slums, the cramped yards and washing lines across which massive, dull-eyed women were pegging bundles of filthy clothing. 'These people obviously don't take the slightest pride in their homes. It's just the sort of place you'd expect to find a ruthless gang of kidnappers. Mr Closed must be undergoing hell.'

The Doctor wrenched the wheel once more, and Felicia had to clutch the door on her side to keep herself upright. 'Hah! Haverstock Row. Here we are.'

The street was short and unexceptional – a couple of darkened houses with boarded-up windows sandwiching a shabby, dilapidated building, above the door of which was a sign that, in peeling letters, read MESSRS SOLICITORS WOODROW, WOODROW & SPENCE.

'That's the place,' said the Doctor. He brought the car screeching to a halt and vaulted over the side in that infuriatingly exuberant way of his. 'We're not a moment too soon by the look of things.' He gestured to a large black car that stood, with its door open, outside the solicitors' office. It might once have been a splendid vehicle, Felicia observed as she stepped from her own motor at a more demure pace, but now it was dented and scratched. Most of the damage looked recent. And now there was most definitely an unpleasant addition to the air.

She was about to remark on this to the Doctor when he leapt through the front doorway of the offices. There didn't appear to be a door at all, which she supposed was typical of common people's disregard for their own property. With a small sigh, she followed. It occurred to her that she ought, at this point, to be feeling more scared than she was; there again, she was a characterful sort, and the Doctor's marvellous air of confidence was starting to rub off on her.

Her courage was severely challenged by the sight that met her eyes inside the office. At first the scene was so crowded and confusing that it appeared to her bewildered gaze merely as a large blur of action, sound and colour, but such was the gravitas of the events unfolding that it resolved itself with a sudden clarity. Besides herself and the Doctor, there were three people in the dingy room: Mr Closed, looking somewhat battered and shocked but still charming; a tall black-haired woman waving a pistol; and a shambling, unshaven fellow, lurching towards them. He was undoubtedly the source of the overpowering smell, which almost caused her to gag. Some sort of vagrant, in all likelihood. 'Goodness me, what—' she started to say, but then the man turned round and she saw his glowing green eyes and misshapen upper body, and was struck dumb.

He spoke falteringly, addressing the Doctor. 'You. I can sense the... power of your... mind.'

'How very kind,' the Doctor said lightly. He kept his distance, and Felicia noted the distracted movements of his fingers as he rearranged his scarf.

'You are the one... known as the Doctor...' said the vagrant, tottering towards him.

'And I claim my five pounds,' Felicia heard Percy say bitterly.

'Yes, I am,' the Doctor replied. 'As so often seems to be the case in my social dealings, you have me at a disadvantage. I don't believe we've been introduced.'

The creature – for it was not, Felicia now knew, a man – edged nearer to him. 'You are to be... destroyed.'

The Doctor hooked his thumbs underneath a coil of his scarf and said boldly, 'Says who?'

'Zodaal must feed... on your brain...' It raised its hands, and to her disgust Felicia saw that its fingernails were long and sharp, like talons.

'I hope you don't mind me pointing it out, but you've got holes in your shirt,' said the Doctor casually. 'I'm sure I've got a darning needle if you'd like to borrow it. After all, you can't go around eating people's brains wearing a shirt with holes in it, can you?'

The foreign woman spoke. Her voice was marvellously husky and resonant. 'I pumped three bullets into it.'

'This form is impervious to bullets,' the creature crowed.

The Doctor humphed. 'I had a nasty feeling you were going to say that.' He sniffed testily, as if noticing the awful odour for the first time. 'There's a terrible smell of pickled cabbage in here, I think someone ought to open a window.'

'What are you?' the monster gurgled, lunging ever nearer.

Felicia cast her eyes about for any object that might be used against it. If Inspector Cawston had been present at this point, she wondered, what might he have done? In any case, the room was bare and dusty, and the sole ammunition was stacks of legal papers piled on the counter and a row of rickety chairs. A disused grate, caked in layers of soot, was set into one wall, and it was at its side that Felicia saw a very useful-looking object. A poker lay on top of an empty coal sack. In a split second, with a decisive air that surprised her when she came to think on it afterwards, she leapt under the monster's outstretched arm and grabbed the poker. She steadied herself and turned to confront her opponent, aware suddenly of the weight of the weapon and her own feebleness of frame.

The beast seemed to consider her of small import and continued to advance on the Doctor. 'What are you?' it asked again. 'Why did you use… the time portal?'

'I haven't used any time portal,' he replied, 'at least not lately. Look, er, don't you think we could sit down and talk this over sensibly?'

Felicia studied the back of the monster's head, the matted strands of greasy black hair, and then looked down at the poker clenched in her hand. She was caught in an agony of indecision. Cawston would have struck by now, but then he had never had cause to battle an opponent so strong. What if he wasn't felled by the first blow? She couldn't picture herself bludgeoning him to death.

'For heaven's sake, woman!' Percy urged her. 'Don't stand there!'

His manful exclamation settled her inner debate, for she could not be seen to falter in his company, and she raised the poker to shoulder height. In the same moment the Doctor made a swift movement, throwing the loop of his scarf around the monster's neck like a lasso. It snarled and bucked, its arms flailed, and it was free again. The Doctor overbalanced and toppled over heavily on his back. He was now a sitting target for the looming zombie.

'Now, now!' shrieked Percy, flapping his arms.

Felicia struck, thinking as she did that attempting to bludgeon a man's head was a most undignified thing to be doing on a summer afternoon. Perhaps it was this distraction, or maybe it was her lack of confidence in her own strength, but the blow was not a heavy one, and the poker seemed to bounce harmlessly off the back of the zombie's head.

'Give it a whack, don't just tap it!' said Percy.

'I'm not accustomed to brawling in public,' Felicia snapped. Her half-hearted attack had succeeded only in drawing the monster's attention away from the Doctor and onto her. It swivelled on its heels and glared greenly into her eyes. Instantly she felt her will to oppose it lessening in strength, and her grip on the poker weakened. The world about her seemed to fade out as it stalked towards her, its claws now reaching for her throat, its blackened mouth gaping.

The trouble with this Zodaal fellow, decided the Colonel, was that now he'd got started he wouldn't, or plain couldn't, shut himself up. There was a wireless-type gizmo at work, throwing the man's voice into K-9, although what it had to do with all the poison gas lark he couldn't fathom. Today there simply didn't appear to be enough time to stop and think.

'But we're suspended along a time corridor,' Romana was saying. 'How did this ship get here?'

'Not really a ship, in truth,' said Zodaal. 'In your vernacular – let me just have a look through K-9's memory – yes, I believe you'd call it a propelled warper capsule.'

The Colonel groaned. 'Not all this malarkey again. You'll blind each other with science at this rate.'

Romana simply ignored his interruption. 'Zodaal, what were you warping with? Not a grey interchange?' She lowered her voice significantly on these last words.

'I'm afraid so. My home world, Phryxus, is very distant from Earth, somewhere in the region your descendants, Colonel, will one day call NGC4258.'

'Don't give me all that blether,' said the Colonel.

'Go on,' Romana urged.

'Soon after we Phryxians began the expansion of our influence through space, we discovered a most unusual neighbour in the locality. A colossal grey interchange, equivalent in size to – let me just check, let's see – yes, forty million times the size of Sol.'

'I've studied that star,' said Romana. 'Its collapse in relative date 365509 led to the destruction of four developed civilisations in your galaxy.' She emphasised her words with a heavy kind of pity, like someone bringing bad news in an opera. The Colonel could just about follow this, and couldn't understand how anyone could get upset about something so distant and unfamiliar. 'Your planet was fortunate.'

'Indeed,' said Zodaal. 'We came to prominence many millions of years afterwards. Our society became what you call a technocracy, and our specialists became more and more intrigued by the power of the interchange. An investigatory programme was set up, and a process theorised by which matter from the grey field might be harnessed and inverted, using radmium as a bonding agent. The radmium was easy enough to harvest. The stellar activity in the region is famously volatile.'

'Did your people realise,' asked Romana, 'how dangerous it is to interfere with active matter from a grey interchange?'

'I believe they do now,' said Zodaal bitterly. 'It took my folly to show them that.'

'How?'

'I too was a scientist, but I specialised in other fields. My prime concern was to fashion control mechanisms in the minds of lesser anthropomorphs. The elders of Phryxus considered my studies unethical, and forbade me to continue. When I refused to release my specimens, I was imprisoned. The righteous idiots should have executed me then. I escaped – and they tried to cover up my flight, hide it from the public. But I devised a glorious means to strike back at them!'

Romana nodded. 'Hijack the capsule.'

'Right under their olfactory vents, yes. I saw it as my life's greatest triumph. I worked on every detail, industriously. Using gravity wave suppressors the scientists had created a stable zone, where robotic workers, some the size of small moons themselves, fashioned the starstuff to their bidding. It was the culmination of Phryxian civilisation, a means to unlock the door to functional intergalactic travel.'

'It was a hollow sham,' Romana said hotly. The Colonel felt ever more out of his depth. Why would anybody get themselves steamed up about all of this high-falutin' claptrap? 'The calculations could never have allowed for unpredictable shifts in the decay rate of the radmium bond.'

'I know that now,' said Zodaal. 'But I thought I could do it. The capsule was prepared, a date for the test flight set, and I attacked. The crowds all cheered as the craft slipped its moorings and the power links were activated. My army of followers set to, killing the pilot and installing me in his place. I broadcast a final message to Phryxus, exulting in my triumph. And I...' His voice faltered momentarily. 'I wept for my own success. The capsule was programmed to travel outside the galaxy through the interchange. Instead, as you know, the drives locked and the power source turned inside out. The capsule was dragged into the time core before emergency cooling could be attained, and I found myself here, clinging to the protection of a primitive time corridor as a clot fastens to the wall of an artery.'

Romana looked around the capsule, and there was a new kind of respect in her eyes, the Colonel noted. 'Your shields withstood magnitudes of temporal force?'

'They were designed to. Much good it did me. When I saw the barrenness of my predicament, how I wished they had not. An existence here, trapped and alone, was worse than any physical torment. I—'

He was interrupted by a bleep, followed by K-9: 'Entity

Zodaal, your use of the poetical section of my phraseology bank is unnecessary. Please keep to the facts.'

The Colonel laughed. 'Good dog, ha! You sound like my old English master.'

Romana examined some of the apparatus jumbled up on the table. 'So you set about trying to free yourself?'

'Yes,' said Zodaal. 'With the last useful energy reserves, I worked ceaselessly to effect my escape. The presence of this capsule served to decay the structure of the corridor. I knew it was impossible to enter the corridor in my organic form, and so I concentrated on transubstantiating myself. I had read widely on radmium, and knew that in its gaseous state it could be used as a carrier of life essence. I worked to achieve the transfer of my own self, my pure will to survive, into this form, to be beamed out into the corridor through a chronon funnel, and from there back into the corporeal universe. And I was successful.'

'Now, hold on,' the Colonel said, raising a polite finger. 'Obviously you didn't. My friend, you're still here.'

K-9's head elevated a fraction. 'As my host here would say, Colonel, negative. I'm afraid to say the process worked, exactly as I'd hoped.'

'But you're still in here, man,' the Colonel said exasperatedly. 'You'll have to square up to it.'

Romana shook her head. 'Then what did we see, back in Nutchurch?'

The Colonel shrugged. 'I don't know, his hoppo or something.' He put the flat of his hand to his forehead. 'Why does all this have to be so damn complicated?'

'It isn't, really,' said Zodaal. 'From my studies of this process, I saw how, once transferred, my essence could be divided. This solved my qualms instantly.'

'What qualms?' Romana asked.

When Zodaal replied, he spoke with cautious courtesy. 'The radmium bond is unstable, as you have noted. And as a gas it would have been nearly impossible to influence events to guarantee my continued existence. I knew that the only way to survive would be to consume the life force of living hosts at the end of the corridor. And I see from K-9's memory bank that this indeed has occurred. Oh my.'

'But how did you achieve separation?'

'That device on the edge of the table' – Romana picked up a circular contraption, like the top half of a child's spinning top – 'is a hyperozoic filter. I connected it to the extraction equipment, and used it to remove from my new gaseous state all traces of that which was unnecessary to my purpose. All blocks to my ruthlessness. The doubts and fears that had restrained me in the past. My qualms, you might say.'

K-9 took over the narration. 'Mistress. The fragment of Zodaal siphoned into the container and left behind here is composed of characteristics such as humour, wonder and imagination.'

'Dash it all,' said the Colonel. 'You can't mean to say the fellow just shook off his sense of humour and threw it away like an old coat?'

'Syllogism is parochial but essentially correct,' said K-9.

In the year since his arrival on Earth, Zodaal had grown accustomed to Orlick's constant presence. The valet had proved himself an excellent subject for the secondary host, and when it became clear that he was not going to return on schedule, and there had very likely been an accident, Zodaal's level of aggression was raised, for without his personal guardian he was virtually defenceless. Shortly after he had dispatched his new slave, Woodrow, Zodaal made the decision to vacate his house. With the stimulator almost ready, there was no longer any need for its employment as a retreat. Moving slowly, without the supporting arm of his servant, he trudged down the wooden staircase and climbed aboard the second car. The mechanical details of its operation were rudimentary, and soon he was driving to the warehouse, conscious all the while of the increasing heat and the stifling pressure. Whereas at the first outbreak of the stimulator's effects the humans had rejoiced, now, after a week's drought, many were dripping with sweat and appeared uncomfortable. Zodaal allowed himself a moment's relish as he contemplated the additional torments they were soon to face.

In the warehouse he found Porteous slumped back in his chair, his eyes red-rimmed, his bow tie dangling loosely. Before him the stimulator was ablaze with life. Each of its indicators glowed a deep fiery orange, and its holographic representation of the planet's fault lines, picked out by dotted markers, were complete.

He rested a hand on Porteous's shoulder to wake him. 'Excellent work, Professor. The stimulator is ready to be activated.'

Porteous shook himself free. 'You madman! I can't believe what I've done. This device is obscene. A monstrous perversion of science. I beg you, whoever or whatever you might be, don't use it!' He leapt up and grabbed Stackhouse by his moulding lapels. 'You must stop this insanity!'

Zodaal sent him crashing to the floor with a casual flick of the wrist. 'Strange. You have a fine scientific brain. You see further than most of these humans. And yet you possess the deluded scruples common to your species.' He grunted. 'It is better to abandon these, as I have done.'

He strode by the supine Porteous to examine progress on the second project. The leader of the slave workers broke off from his work. 'Sir. The final connections are about to be made. When the organic component is installed, we can –' it paused and licked its lips, from which a string of black drool oozed – 'begin the feast.'

'The feast will begin when I say it is to begin,' Zodaal reminded him. 'Safety factors must be considered.' He turned to face the massive main entry gate of the warehouse. 'It shall be soon. The organic component will be delivered shortly.'

As Woodrow lifted his arms to swoop on Mrs Chater, Percy jammed his eyes shut tight. Immediately he felt ashamed of himself. If they were all going to die, or have their brains eaten or whatever, they ought to go down fighting. At least the Doctor had had a go. So, almost without giving it a thought, he opened his eyes, raced forward, grabbed the poker that had fallen from Mrs Chater's grip, and laid into her attacker, bringing the poker down again and again on the back of the brute's head. His own strength, cranked up by his fear, frightened him, and the results were horrific. Woodrow's skull caved in with a crunch on the third blow, but the stooped figure remained standing, whirling about from Mrs Chater to face him. Half of the face was missing, a collage of shattered bone, flesh and dried blood. The stench was coming off the man in waves, and Percy backed away, taking care all the while not to look into its one remaining glowing eye.

'Good show, Mr Closed!' Mrs Chater cried, clapping her hands together.

'This isn't a blasted cricket match, you know!' he shouted back as Woodrow advanced on him, gurgling thickly. He beat at its front a couple more times, but on the second stroke a grey hand reached up and wrested the poker away. It flew across the room and fell with a metallic clatter. 'Oh, Lord,' Percy muttered, aware that he was being backed into a corner. 'Oh hell. Help me, Doctor, somebody!' He squinted through the thick green vapour; was that shifting shape by the fireplace the Doctor, picking himself up?

By edging himself to one side of Woodrow, Percy got a clearer view of events, and the next flurry of action seemed to him like a series of tableaux. The Doctor, swaying slightly from the knock he'd taken, staggered over to where Julia stood, frozen with horror. 'Your gun,' he shouted, gesturing frantically with his outstretched hand. 'Give me your gun!'

'It's no use,' she protested. 'Not against these creatures!'

The Doctor seemed not to hear her. He grabbed the revolver and with a reassuringly expert manner clicked open the barrel to check his remaining shots.

'Shoot the thing!' Percy shrieked. 'It's almost got me!'

But the Doctor was doing something extraordinary again. With one movement he flicked on the light switch, which on this bright day had not much noticeable effect, then aimed the gun not at Woodrow but upward, at the bracket connecting the heavy lamp to the ceiling. He then shouted, 'Rather small beer, these humans, I'd have thought. I'm still waiting, you know.'

Instantly Woodrow responded to the taunt and twisted about, making a hideous angry hissing sound. Percy had never heard such a sound. It was like boiling water being poured onto a hive of bees.

The Doctor seemed quite unmoved, and stood wearing a mocking expression directly in the creature's new path. 'You might have more difficulty facing some real opposition, mightn't you?'

Woodrow snarled and lurched.

The Doctor pulled the trigger, there was a percussive ping, and the heavy lamp crashed down directly on Woodrow's head, felling the creature with a mighty crash. Immediately afterward, before any of them had time to react, a splutter of sparks burst around the twitching, hissing body. The big dome of the lamp's shattered fitting acted as a sort of prison for Woodrow, keeping it contained despite its frantic struggles. Its head had taken the force of the blow directly, and its neckbone appeared broken. Its lips juddered, and thick rivulets of a black oily substance gushed over its chin. Incredibly it seemed to be attempting to speak. 'Brains,' it grunted. 'More brains...'

Percy kept clear of the beast and nipped across the room to join the Doctor and Mrs Chater. The irritating woman laid a protective hand on his arm and said, 'Oh, dear Mr Closed, are you quite all right? This is all so terrible.'

Percy shook her off. 'Doctor, what the blazes are we to do?'

The Doctor was already engaged in another burst of frantic activity. He moved across the office in a blur, arms cartwheeling as he wrenched open the cupboards and cabinets that faced the counter. All that was revealed were more and more stacks of paper. 'We need something inflammable,' he shouted. 'The body must be destroyed utterly. And try not to let it kill you, that would just be exchanging one problem for another.' He kicked a cupboard door in frustration when it yielded nothing more than a set of cleaning materials. 'Didn't the man keep a drinks cabinet?'

'How about my transceiver?' asked Percy. 'That works electrically.' As he spoke he lurched across to where his canvas bag rested against the counter. He brought out the device and tossed it to the Doctor. 'Trouble is, it doesn't appear to be working.'

There was a stomach-turning crunch of rending metal as Woodrow made another, and this time more successful, attempt to overturn the frame trapping it. Its one rolling eye fixed on Julia, and again it spoke. 'You,' it spat. 'You must be… You…' One side of it jerked up with ferocious force, and the shackles binding it creaked and snapped at their joints.

Julia turned aside from its threats, looking sickened. Her hands fiddled with something at her belt, and for a moment Percy thought she was perhaps reaching for another weapon. Then he remembered. 'No!' he shouted over to her. 'You've no idea of how it's operated!' But there was a gleam of determination in her eye, and without answering she reached down to the flying-box and twisted the large knob on its front.

The effects were instant. Percy watched as she was lifted up like a balloon filled with helium. The Doctor looked up from the transceiver and shouted, 'What are you doing up there?'

Julia's reply was to turn her face away. It was plain she considered them good as dead, with the writhing, heaving mass in the centre of the room about to emerge once more. Without saying a word, she simply rose, flew over their heads, bringing her arms and legs into position instinctively, and disappeared through the door.

'How abrupt,' the Doctor observed. 'She needs to read your book, Percy.'

But the most definite reaction to Julia's flight came from the monster. It howled in protest, and shook itself free, finally overturning its cage with a thud that rattled the floorboards. The wooden slats of the ceiling splintered in response, and a shower of brick dust fell like sleet. Woodrow lurched to its feet with a movement that was anatomically impossible, using its crushed legs to lever itself up.

'Oh, crumbs,' said Percy, as it lurched closer to them.

'Doctor, dear, do something!' urged Mrs Chater.

The Doctor was fumbling in his pockets. 'Mrs Chater, those power packs I showed you. You remember, those batteries.'

'Yes, what about them?' she wailed. Woodrow pushed itself on, holding them in its mesmeric power. 'It's going to kill us!'

'Did I leave them on your table,' the Doctor continued, thoroughly uncowed, 'or did I remember to put them back in my – Ah!'

'What now?' gasped Percy, preparing to meet his doom.

'Ah, yes, I did!' The Doctor produced a couple of power packs from his coat pocket and jammed one of them into the cavity at the back of the transceiver. 'Now, let's see… there should be some way of…' His long fingers flicked across the buttons.

Woodrow was now only a matter of five feet from them, and had raised its shattered arms, one of which was now not much more than a twisted stump, ready to swoop on them. Percy felt its foul vapour clogging at the back of his throat, and his eyes watered. 'Brai… Brains…' it slurred.

'Nothing's happening,' said the Doctor, rattling the transceiver. 'It was working all right before.'

Percy summoned up the energy to shout, 'Have you put the pack back in the right way round?'

'Well, of course I have!' snapped the Doctor. 'At least, I think I did. Ah, no, you're right, I didn't.'

'Hurry, Doctor!' screamed Mrs Chater. Illogically – perhaps because separated though they were by centuries she was at least a member of his own species – Percy found himself clinging on to her. They were about to die, after all, so the gesture was unlikely to be misconstrued later.

The Doctor raised the transceiver, and let off a blast of electricity directly at Woodrow. The crackling beam hit the beast squarely between the eyes, and it reeled back, making a pathetic mewling sound. The Doctor gave it no quarter, and let off another blast. Woodrow toppled backward, tripped over the jagged-edged mess of the fallen lamp, and landed with his stomach pierced by a jutting prong.

'That's really too horrible,' observed Mrs Chater in the sudden silence. 'Is he quite dead, do you think?'

'No,' the Doctor said firmly. 'That's the trouble with zombies. It's very difficult to get them to admit their time's up.' Already the almost unrecognisable shape, charred black, was struggling to rise again. The Doctor twisted a dial at the base of the transceiver. 'Maximum discharge should see to it.' He set the device down gently on the floor. 'Time to be going, I think.'

'Hang on,' said Percy, astonished he was still alive but not above practical considerations, 'I might need that again.'

The Doctor shook his head. 'Well, then, we could always allow our friend here to break free and come after us.'

'Perhaps you're right, let's go,' said Percy. He was somewhat embarrassed to find himself still clinging to Mrs Chater, who was responding with a doe-eyed look that was most unsettling.

'I don't quite understand,' she said. 'What's going on?'

Percy dragged her to the door. 'That's a sort of bomb, er, on a timed fuse,' he said, pointing to the humming transceiver. 'We have about fifteen seconds to get clear.'

'Oh, how clever,' she said, and allowed him to guide her out.

The street outside was dazzlingly bright and real after the horrors of the last few minutes, and Percy was almost overcome by the sudden normality, enough to make him wonder if he'd imagined it all. The sight of the Doctor crouching behind a parked car with fingers jammed in ears was enough to reconvince him. He pulled Mrs Chater to safety and lowered his head.

The explosion was loud and shocking. His heart hammered in the aftermath, as a dull crump signified the collapse of the whole frontage of the line of buildings. When he raised enough gall to look up he saw the innards of Woodrow's offices exposed for one last time like the inside of a doll's house; then there came a sizzling crackle and a fireball sprang up from nowhere, expanding to turn to ashes what might have been left of their enemy's host form.

'What an afternoon!' said Mrs Chater, standing.

Already a hubbub was rising from the nearby streets, and a fire bell rang distantly. 'Hadn't we better clear off out of here?' Percy asked the Doctor.

The Doctor stood looking at the burning wreck of the building. Blackened strips of paper blew in a flurry of cinders from the upper storey, and from their size and shape Percy recognised them as the hoarded five-pound notes.

'You're looking particularly inscrutable,' Percy remarked.

'My guess is that without a link to one host, it can't pass to another,' the Doctor replied evenly. 'The essence of the thing is spread between several hosts. Very effective.' He turned to face Percy. 'The trouble is we're no further forward.'

Mrs Chater tutted. 'How can you say that, Doctor? We have our Mr Closed back with us.'

Percy hurriedly withdrew his arm from hers.

The Doctor nodded. 'But we're no nearer tracking down our real opponent.'

'Are we not?' Percy said with a superior air. 'What if I were to say I had some useful information to impart, eh?'

'I'd say impart it,' said the Doctor.

Nonplussed by all that talk, the Colonel had wandered out of the capsule's inner chamber, paying no heed to an entreaty from Romana not to handle anything without first consulting her, and had found another object of great interest back in the dome. One of its smooth sides had melted away, and transformed itself into a sort of upright well, a transparent circular frame in which water was undoubtedly whirlpooling. Now while that supported his suspicion that they were under the sea, there was something not right about it. The water was clear, for a start, and there was no sign of marine life. He'd never gone in for that sort of nonsense, but it was more like how one might imagine the interior of a gypsy's ball. There was no point of focus, nothing on which to catch the eye, although there were moments when he thought he'd caught a glimpse of a familiar scene. He rapped the glass with his knuckles and its bubbled surface rippled his faint reflection.

He heard Romana's voice, which sounded a bit angry. Girl was coming through into the dome, bringing the possessed dog with her. 'You knew there were sentient beings waiting at the end of the corridor, and that the only way for you to survive would be to kill them.'

'What was the alternative?' Zodaal answered. 'To die here, slowly? You cannot understand. The Phryxian legacy is a constantly self-renewing cell structure. I could have lived here, alone and without sustenance, for millennia, tucked in the fold of a collapsing temporal rift. The lives of a handful of humans are as dust when balanced against that of Zodaal the great. But then I was not without remorse.'

'Well, you are now,' Romana countered. 'The part of you running about on Earth definitely is.'

The Colonel coughed to gain their attention. 'I say. I've found some kind of porthole. There we are. Think we must be suspended in some kind of tank.'

K-9 trundled forward. 'Negative,' he said in his own voice. 'Device is temporal imaging device, focused on time corridor. I shall demonstrate.' His probe slid from his eyescreen, rested on the glass, and sent some sort of tingle. The Colonel leapt back quickly as the glass shimmered, and a picture postcard view of the front at Nutchurch swam into perfect clarity through the floating bubbles. 'This image is from the open end of the corridor.'

'Up top, I see,' said the Colonel, rubbing his chin thoughtfully. 'Dashed clever, however it's done. In living colour, too.'

'K-9,' asked Romana, 'is it possible to focus on the other end of the time corridor? The source?'

'Affirmative, Mistress.' There was a further tingle on the part of the dog's probe, and the image blurred and changed. When it reformed it showed an altogether dissimilar and quite bizarre vista, and the Colonel had to blink a couple of times to fit the whole picture in. What he thought he saw was a big city, rather like photographs he'd seen of New York but with many more and wider skyscraping buildings, all joined by gangways and clear glass tubes. Most of them were a dirty brown colour, and there were small dots flitting about like fleas. He squinted. 'Lord help us, those are people, flying about!' he exclaimed.

'You're looking at the future,' Romana informed him. 'That's Nutchurch, many years after your time.'

The Colonel's throat dried. 'Where's the bally sea, then?'

'Probably they built over it. The town was swallowed up by London, I imagine.'

'In relative Earth year 2415,' K-9 said unhelpfully. 'Redesignated district 406 akker Playa del Nuttingchapel.'

The Colonel felt his legs give way, and the next thing he knew he was lying in a heap on the floor. 'Gracious me,' he heard himself say. 'Gracious me, gracious me. What, everyone dead, me among 'em. Horrible.' Perhaps sensing his confusion, K-9 switched the image back to the Nutchurch he knew. 'I just want to get back there, that's all I know. Back home, and let the future sort its confounded self out.'

Romana slumped down at his side, and said sympathetically, 'I suppose we'll have to hope the Doctor might rescue us. He's better at rescuing people than anything else.'

Zodaal coughed in that disarmingly polite way of his. 'If I might interject?'

'What?'

'Well, I'm anxious to make amends for all the trouble my other half has caused, and I have a suggestion.'

'For Pete's sake, get to the point,' said the Colonel. 'Can you get us out of this jam or not?'

It was the voice of K-9 that replied. 'Mistress. The intelligence of Zodaal has examined my data banks, including references to Gallifreyan time travel theory.'

'Of course!' Romana leapt to her feet. 'The Equation of Rassilon! If we apply it to the apparatus here, and create a field of restricted wave-particle duality…'

'Probability of effective travel through time corridor rises to ninety-seven per cent,' K-9 completed for her. 'Suggest work begins at once.'

'Blackheath!' cried the Doctor, and with a tremendous swerve of the wheel he turned the car in the middle of a road which was patently not wide enough for the task. A courting couple taking in the early evening had their romantic ambience shattered, retreating in haste as with a colossal belch the vehicle shot off in the opposite direction. 'Why didn't you say earlier?'

'I've only just remembered,' spluttered Percy, who was

gripping the side of the car with whitened knuckles. 'Something old Godfrey Wyse, one of the Circle, said at our meeting yesterday. Stackhouse lives in –' the car lurched again and his stomach lurched correspondingly – 'a place at Blackheath. Dismissed all his staff, and was said to have gone barmy. Now we know why. Good God, do you think you should be tearing along like this?'

Mrs Chater spoke. 'My husband, my *late* husband, met Stackhouse at a charity dinner many years ago. I remember him saying how closely he resembled the face on the tins, and how sour a man he was.'

'My experience entirely,' agreed Percy. 'Very rude chap. He was got at, then, at Nutchurch?'

The Doctor nodded, and casually zipped up a side-street. He had an almost uncanny sense of direction. 'He must have stumbled upon your time corridor at the wrong moment. This creature fixed on the nearest living human as its host.'

Percy rubbed his chin. 'After Harriet came through, yes. We had a narrow shave. What was that name Woodrow used again? Zuda or something?'

'Zodaal,' said Mrs Chater. 'Definitely Zodaal.'

The Doctor took one hand off the wheel and slapped it on his forehead. 'Zodaal,' he said. 'Do I know that name, I wonder?'

'I certainly don't,' said Mrs Chater. 'Could be Hungarian.'

Percy heaved a sigh. He couldn't understand why this silly female was tagging along in the first place, and she plainly persisted in seeing it all in twentieth-century terms. It was impossible to vent his frustrations on the Doctor and she made a good target. 'For heaven's sake,' he said, 'we're talking about an alien creature, from another world. It's hardly going to post its notice of arrival in *Harpers & Queen*, is it?' Irritatingly she seemed to take his words as a joke, and tittered girlishly.

'Zodaal,' the Doctor mused. 'Zodaal, Zodaal…' He removed his other hand from the wheel and tapped the top of his head, as if to stimulate his memory. 'Zantos, Zastor, Zephon, Zeta Minor, Zeus, Zilda, Zoe, Zygons… No, no Zodaal. I've obviously never encountered him before, whoever he is.'

A large brick wall loomed directly in their path. 'Doctor!' yelled Percy.

Without changing his expression, the Doctor wrenched the wheel around again. 'Definitely no Zodaal. Well, whoever he is, we've got to stop him. You didn't happen to learn anything of his plans from that Italian woman?'

'As it happens, yes, a little,' said Percy. 'But I'm not sure I ought to tell you, unless you promise to pay more attention to the road.' Even as he spoke the car made an elaborate zigzag to overtake a couple of others.

'The road is immaterial,' said the Doctor. 'What about this plan?'

'Oh, all right, then. He plans to destroy the world, next Tuesday.'

'How vulgar,' said the Doctor. 'Nobody does anything of importance on a Tuesday, surely?'

It didn't help Percy's spirits that Mrs Chater found that hilarious. 'A rapier wit, Doctor!' she called over the engine's roar. 'When I get back home I simply must write that one up, with your permission, of course.'

Percy shook his head despairingly. 'Don't you understand? Chances are you aren't going to get back home. None of us are.' He mopped his brow. 'Feel that heat? It's getting worse all the time. The situation's hopeless, and what's more, we're driving right into the enemy camp. I don't know why I don't just get out of this car right now!'

They reached a T-junction at this point, and the Doctor put his foot down on the pedal, slipping narrowly through twin streams of fast-moving traffic. A clamour of horns sounded their passage.

'I don't know,' said Mrs Chater. 'I'm starting to find all of this rather fun, you know!'

'That's the spirit,' said the Doctor, straight faced.

At five hundred feet above London, the heat was no longer so stifling; the climate was cool and pleasant, and when she felt comfortable with the sensation, Julia brought her feet together and hovered, stationary over the dome of St Paul's. Her escape from Woodrow had been exhilarating at first, fear giving way to wonder at the marvellous steadiness of this strange method of transport. A couple of minutes and she was accustomed to the properties of the flying-box, which carried her in whichever direction she chose to face at a speed regulated by the dial on its front. By turning the dial slowly to its downward position she had learnt how to return to the ground when she wished; evidently, the box lowered its user gently and safely to terra firma like the hand of a god.

Now she stood suspended, her only company a flock of curious birds, looking down at the city's thrusting peaks, the palace of Westminster and its attendant regiment of tidy white streets and courts, the still, flat stretch of the Thames, the crush and tangle of the West End – each detail picked out with clarity by the giant twilight sun. The contrast with the terrors of the previous hours was marked, and she felt she could hang here for ever, drifting over the world.

Except that the world was under a sentence of death, and now the Doctor was dead only she was in a position to reverse it.

A row of twenty grimy windows appeared through the iron bars of the gate to the Stackhouse residence, each pane reflecting the deep orange twilight. Percy swallowed convulsively as he stepped from the car, glad to have the ground beneath his feet but dubious of the prospect of action. The Doctor and Mrs Chater, who seemed to be thick as thieves, were busy pushing open the gates. 'Look, is this really a good idea?' he pointed out. 'Wouldn't it be better to go in the back way?'

Mrs Chater shook a finger. 'I thought you were a follower of my friend Inspector Cawston.'

Percy frowned. 'What's he got to do with it?'

'The Inspector always approaches his foes directly: (a) because they won't be expecting such a bold move; and (b) because it shows his mettle in facing up to them.'

'My dear, this is life, not fiction,' said Percy.

She patted him on the head. 'You dear silly.'

With a shocking creak the gates swung open. The Doctor squinted keenly around the overgrown garden and pronounced, 'Well, the approaches appear unguarded. That means he's either being very confident, or he's scarpered.' He wetted and held up a finger. 'Something feels wrong.'

'Which something in particular?' asked Percy.

'If this is his base,' said the Doctor, 'it's awfully quiet. Particularly if there's a sonic disruptor device in operation.' He took a slender silver tube from his pocket and fiddled with some switches along its side.

'Oh,' said Mrs Chater. 'It's that key thing.'

The Doctor held it aloft and swept it over the length of the looming house. 'Very odd. No response at all.' Pocketing the device he strode on up the gravel approach. 'This place needs a good going over with some secateurs.'

'Oh, I do agree,' said Mrs Chater. 'It's too dreadful when people let their properties slip like this.'

Percy followed them, despairingly.

They made their way down the path without further let or hindrance, to find the large oak-panelled door of the house standing open. The house beyond was a hushed, dark, ugly place; its flooring was zigzagged by cracks, and it stank of dust, which left a gritty taste on the tongue.

'Surely,' said Percy, 'it can't have got awful like this in just a year?'

'Perhaps the alien presence leaves a trail of decay,' said the

Doctor. He put out a hand to the banister of the wide stairway and rubbed the collected dust between his fingers. 'Its gaseous container acts as a corrosive agent. Ah.' He pointed out several overlapping sets of footprints leading across to the staircase and up the steps. Confidently he started up the stairs.

In the failing light Percy noted Mrs Chater's sudden quietude and loss of confidence, and to his own surprise he found himself putting a reassuring hand on her shoulder. Or was the gesture merely to assuage his own misgivings? They followed the Doctor up several flights of rotted timber, each step sending vociferous account of their presence to any lurking enemy.

At last, having passed up a further set of steps, they came to a narrow corridor. A fading nursery pattern was discernible on the wallpaper, which hung in dry strips on either side. There were three doors along the passage; only the last was open, spilling from it a vague hint of fading daylight.

The Doctor patted his pockets, produced a candle, and asked, 'Either of you got any matches?'

Percy handed him a book and watched as he struck one and lit the candle. Then he put his finger to his lips and entered the far room. An unbearable silence followed, and Percy found himself clinging even tighter to his female companion. The seconds crawled by.

The candlelight flickered. Then the Doctor's voice: 'Good heavens!'

Mrs Chater gasped. In a quavering whisper Percy asked, 'Doctor? Doctor?' There was no reply. 'Cripes, what are you doing in there?'

The Doctor's big curly head popped around the door frame. 'The horse has bolted,' he said cheerfully. 'But look what I've found.' His hand swung up, holding a dust-coated canvas.

Percy sprang forward and took it. 'Good heavens!'

'That's what I said,' said the Doctor. 'Be careful.'

Felicia craned her head over Percy's shoulder. 'It's an Uccello

Martyrdom,' she exclaimed. 'But in such a wretched state.' Indeed there was a spreading patch of mould covering one corner. Percy reached out to test the canvas's integrity and it simply crumpled in half, releasing a cloud of dust.

'I told you to be careful,' said the Doctor. He withdrew his head, and Percy, after setting what remained of the painting down, followed him into the attic room. If he had been expecting a treasure trove he was disappointed. The dying sunlight that slanted through the one round window high up one wall, showed only two items of furniture; a small and heavily scarred antique table, of the sort with a hinged lid and a cavity for storing stuff, and a high-backed chair with a huge green powdery stain where its previous occupant had once sat.

'The lair of Zodaal, until quite recently,' said the Doctor. He examined the items on the table top: an old newspaper, a decanter and glasses, and a wooden box with a carved dragon design on its lid. This last item seemed to cause him the greatest interest.

Mrs Chater looked around the room. 'He's fled, then. But where to?'

'Well,' said the Doctor airily, 'in my experience, these scheming sort of people are very organised, and can't resist putting everything down on paper.' He strained to break the catch on the box.

'Ah,' said Mrs Chater knowingly. 'I see. We're on the hunt for clues, then, are we?' She took the Doctor's candle and cast its light around each darkened corner. 'Can't see anything that looks remotely clue-like.'

Percy observed the Doctor's struggle with the box. 'You think there's something in there?'

'I won't know until I've opened it, will I?' He applied extra pressure and a rasping click came from the box in response. 'But we must explore every avenue. Now, let's have a look.'

He set the box gently back down on the table and with an

outstretched finger lifted the lid a fraction.

A wisp of light green vapour curled out, and Percy smelt a familiar smell.

Immediately the Doctor tried to close the lid, but it was too late. The lid was pushed open from inside, swinging back on its hinge to reveal a sickening sight; a grey hand, severed at the wrist, animated by the green mist, its bloodless fingers flexing in a gross parody of a concert pianist's. A second later, and it sprang through the air.

Its target was the Doctor. He dodged, but it anticipated his move and clamped itself tightly about his throat, its thumb and index finger pressing down on either side of his neck. Reeling, he sank to his knees and brought up his own hands. But the hand's grip was immovable!

9
RETURN TO PERIL

'Damn!' said the Colonel. 'Mind what you're about, dog.'

K-9's ray cut off, and the two pieces of metal he was welding hissed and spattered around the Colonel's finger. 'It is necessary for you to aid my construction of this transfer device,' he said primly. 'Co-operation is essential.'

Satisfied that the metal surfaces had settled together, the Colonel lifted his scalded finger and wagged it. 'I don't mind mucking in. I mind where you point that snout of yours. Blazing about like that you could have my hand off.'

'My welding attachment is accurate to a beam width of point three millimetres,' said K-9. 'Your safety is assured. Please ready the fibral links for connection.'

The Colonel looked down doubtfully at the mass of wires and mechanical what-not at his side. 'Fibo links? Which are they again?'

'The looped strands,' said K-9.

'Ah, yes, this bundle of spaghetti.' He held them up and added, 'Now go carefully, won't you?'

In place of a reply K-9 simply swept his thin beam across the ends of the spaghetti, until it was fused to the central bulk of their apparatus, which as far as the Colonel could make out, was supposed to be getting them from… well, from wherever they were back to Nutchurch. Romana was occupied on the other side of the capsule's domed section, fiddling with pieces of Zodaal's machinery that spilled from one of the pillars. His first task for K-9 had been to link what she was up to with their own efforts by knotting a lot of cables together. He was glad of the chance to demonstrate his knotting skills, though it was hard to keep a clear head with that ghastly whiff coming off K-9 in waves. Occasionally Zodaal would come to the surface for some words of advice, but mostly he kept to the background, doing his calculations. It occurred to the Colonel that Zodaal's lot had got him into this grey hole doings in the first place by botching their sums, but he kept the thought to himself.

'If I'm right,' said Romana, stepping back from her work, 'the funnel is now set to transmit us down the corridor. Here's hoping, anyway.'

K-9 spoke with the voice of Zodaal. 'I have applied the Equation of Rassilon to the mathematical modelling of the corridor's suction force. The time suction should carry us through the fabric of the grey hole in a stable pocket of relational space.'

'One moment,' said the Colonel. 'What's all of this "we" business? I suppose we're taking you with us, are we, then?'

'You owe me your escape,' Zodaal pointed out politely.

'Then we're quits, old chap,' said the Colonel. 'You'd still be corked up in that flask if I hadn't come along.'

'And for your aid I am grateful. Still, I have no wish to remain trapped here, in this formless state.' K-9's eyescreen glowed greener for a moment. 'This outlet is good, but I shall need organic material if I am to survive for a longer period, "uncorked", as you say. I can find this on Earth, surely?'

The Colonel shook his head. 'All that zombie business? I'm afraid not. It's just not on.'

'There are many other sources of suitable material,' Zodaal said sweetly. 'You, Colonel, have eaten animal flesh.'

He gave a suspicious grunt. 'Long as that's all there is to it.

Suppose we can find you a cow or something.'

Romana came across. 'There's another reason for taking him with us.' The Colonel stared at her blankly. 'If we can reunite him with his other self, his personality will be complete. Then perhaps we can reason with him.'

The Colonel snapped his fingers. 'Of course. Put the halves back together and he'll see the error of his ways. Stop all of this unsporting walking dead palaver. Will it work?'

K-9 answered, 'I have already weighed the percentages. There is a seventy-eight per cent probability that re-establishing his full personality will alter the entity Zodaal's plans.'

'Not bad odds,' said the Colonel. He gestured to their work. 'Shall we be getting back, then? Sooner the better.'

'Ah,' said Zodaal. 'There is a problem.'

'What?'

'This outlet, this artificial intelligence, cannot sustain me for much longer. If I am to remain corporeal –' and here his voice darkened a shade – 'suitable organic material is needed.'

The Colonel coughed. 'Well, you're not getting it from me.'

Romana knelt to address the green eyescreen. It was odd, thought the Colonel, the difference the change of colour had wrought in K-9. Now he looked almost malevolent as he said, 'Nevertheless, such material is needed.' Almost slyly he added, 'Brain tissue could be synthesised using equipment in your TARDIS. But my hunger is strong, and time is short. I may dissolve.'

'There's an alternative,' said Romana. 'Your form is stable, contained in your flask, isn't it?'

'The flask is broken,' said Zodaal.

'This isn't.' Romana's hand delved into a pocket of her jacket and brought out the half-finished bottle of ginger beer. She tossed it to the Colonel. 'Drink up.' Then she turned back to Zodaal. 'Until we can get you back to your other self, how does this suit you?'

'What a good idea,' said Zodaal.

His tone was polite enough. But as the Colonel gulped down the last mouthfuls of fizz, he thought he sensed an air of menace behind the words.

Percy watched in a state of utter helplessness, filled with disgust at his own lack of pluck, as the Doctor tumbled over and over in an attempt to loosen the lock of the hand about his throat. Mrs Chater had at least made an effort to come to his aid, hitting the hand with the full weight of the wooden box that had contained it. All this was to no avail. The hand maintained its throttling attack.

Now the Doctor seemed to be trying to say something, or more accurately gasp something. 'Get – The chair – Window –' He broke off, choking. It looked as if he was trying to stand up again.

Mrs Chater moved, pushing the leather chair towards the window. For a moment Percy was baffled; then the logic of the scheme hit him like a splash of cold water between the eyes. Glad of the chance to prove himself he leapt up and felt for the catch on the window frame.

There was no catch.

'I can't get this ruddy window open,' he cried.

'Break the glass!' cried Mrs Chater.

It was strange, Percy thought, that as he took off his shoe and started battering at the unrelenting panes of glass, with Mrs Chater's shrieks and the Doctor's gasps assailing his ears, all he could really think of was how he was going to recount it one day to some incredulous audience.

The glass shattered and Percy found himself being lifted bodily from the chair by one of the Doctor's hands. The Doctor then took his place and with a tremendous effort, the muscles in his arms bulging through his thick woollen coat, he at last tore the grasping hand from his throat. It continued to flex its fingers in its spidery fashion as he tossed it out.

Immediately he sank down into the chair, rubbing his throat tenderly with one of his own hands. 'Extraordinary degree of control,' he said distinctly. 'I don't think it liked me. No brain to speak of. He must have programmed it for that single task.'

Percy looked about fearfully. 'There aren't any more of them about, are there?'

'I should hope not,' said the Doctor. 'It was probably left here to deal with passing priers. Rather good luck we found it.'

'I beg your pardon?' Percy spluttered.

'Well, nobody else would have stood a chance.' He paused. 'Isn't anybody going to ask me if I'm all right?'

Mrs Chater clapped her hands together. 'Well done, Percy.'

He frowned slightly at this – he couldn't recall giving her permission to address him by his first name – but his pleasure at being congratulated banished any lesser concerns. 'Well, it had to be done, so I did it,' he ended up saying.

'Yes, I'm all right, thank you very much for asking,' the Doctor said resentfully, then sprang up, having made another of his sudden recoveries. 'Now, let's have a look in that table.'

Percy gulped. 'Do you really think that's wise?'

The Doctor shook his head. 'No. But this place is our only lead. We may have to turn the whole house upside down.'

'Somebody will have to,' said Mrs Chater. 'Such chaos. I say, that hand will be prowling about outside, won't it? What say we hunt it down and force it to speak.'

The Doctor grinned. 'In sign language?'

Percy gripped the Doctor's arm. 'There may be another hand. I mean, they most often come in pairs, don't they?'

But the Doctor had already swung up the table top. The small octagonal cavity inside contained a musty manila file, titled in faded ink. It might have been a hundred years old. The Doctor opened it up carefully. 'Ah. A chit.'

'A what?' asked Mrs Chater.

The Doctor held up a small scrap of paper. 'For work rendered by Messrs Solicitors Albert Woodrow, Woodrow and Spence.' He flicked through the file. 'The poor fellow must have started his business with Stackhouse without realising what it was he was getting into. Treated it like any other job. Typical solicitor. Produces acres of paperwork and charges you for that on top.'

Percy took out another invoice and examined it. 'I'm not sure about that. Ten thousand guineas for arranging a poxy auction of contents? He saw Stackhouse coming. Then again, I don't suppose an alien would have much idea of going rates.'

'Dreadful. Stackhouse was well respected,' said Mrs Chater. 'And it came to this.' The Doctor was poring over another, larger, piece of paper. 'What have you got there?'

'This could be it,' he said. 'Notice of a leasehold agreement, signed by Stackhouse. 3 to 16 Jasmine Street, Wapping. And orders for the delivery of a smelting furnace and a large quantity of metals. I think we've got our man.'

'Well done,' said Mrs Chater. 'Wapping, you say? I've never been there.'

'I have,' said the Doctor. 'I think I remember a few shortcuts.'

'Oh dear,' said Percy.

'Shall we be off, then?' asked Mrs Chater gleefully. 'No time like the present.'

Together they set forth.

Percy's heart sank. Another address, another frantic race through the streets with the Doctor at the wheel, another confrontation with the forces of evil. There could be any number of hands – connected to bodies in all likelihood – waiting for them.

With a last regretful glance at the crumpled Uccello Martyrdom he followed.

The stubby fingers of Stackhouse's remaining hand curled around the silver knob of his cane in a gesture of impatience.

His slaves had now finished their work on the second project, and were grouped in one corner in an irregular grey huddle. They made no noise but for an occasional feral grunt or squeal, evidence of the struggle to contain their appetites. He shared the sharpness of their hunger, but he contained the reasoning core and knew it was essential to wait until all details were correct.

The slave leader lurched over. Tatters of blackened flesh hung from its skull, and it was now almost naked and stripped of skin. 'Sir,' it began, 'work is over. We must feast.'

Stackhouse flinched. 'We must wait for the final component. Return to your group.' He made a dismissive gesture with the flat of his hand.

The slave leader did not move away. Instead he raised his own arm and with an index finger worn down to a flake of bone pointed to Porteous. 'This one, sir. You don't need him. Please, sir.'

'Return to your group!' Stackhouse repeated fiercely.

The slave leader's features twisted in discontent, and it turned its back, then waddled drunkenly back to its darkly mumbling fellows.

Stackhouse stepped around Porteous's body and stood before the activation panel of the stimulator. His face was lit by the fiery display of the Earth's undersurface. He leant his cane on the machine's side and caressed the programming controls. 'It is perfect,' he told himself. 'The vibro-frequency lines are aligned, the power source screams its readiness.' He rested his head against the glass fascia and wallowed in the random rumble of the vibrations. 'Must I wait?' He looked down at the steadily winking program panel and his fingers lingered on the central activator – a thin red stylus mounted in a swivel mechanism. 'The program is ready, and the final component will arrive soon.' He considered, and was about to withdraw his hand from the controls when a fresh burst of resentful howls came from the slaves. The sound seemed to reverberate in his own soul, and he realised how desperately he required sustenance. There had been enough waiting. He would activate the program.

He swivelled the stylus.

The slaves clenched their fists and hissed their approval, breaking out of their huddle with skullish grins to face the stimulator, which had started to throb with regular blasts of power from its inner source, illuminating the warehouse with a cathedralesque blaze of whirling colour.

'Beautiful,' said Stackhouse. 'Beautiful. It begins!'

With an exultant hiss, the vapour forming Zodaal's better half withdrew from K-9, streamed briefly through the untrammelled air of the dome, and poured itself down in a typhoon shape through the neck of the bottle. The Colonel picked it up with care and screwed the top back on. 'Like a genie in a lamp,' he mused, peering at the small clouds forming inside. 'Relief to be rid of that smell, though.'

Romana was attending to the inert K-9. 'How are you?' she asked.

His head lifted minutely and he made a yawn-like motion with his head. At the same moment his eyescreen flashed on, back to its healthy red. 'Circuits now free of Zodaal's influence, Mistress,' he said. 'Suggest immediate reverse transference.'

The Colonel had been drilled on what was to happen next, and was standing ready when Romana pushed over the switch that set the whole transfer shebang going. Later, going over it in his mind, it was difficult to work out the following events in detail. Everything was a jumble. First there was a loud, splintering crack; then a wall of shadow appeared, washing over them; then he was lifted off his feet and sent spinning, tumbling over and over. It was quite like what had happened when they'd gone into that hut, except this time the process of travel was much smoother. There was a queer kind of pressure building up against his temples, and a hollow sensation at the pit of his stomach, but the Colonel was determined to keep his eyes open. He wasn't going to fall asleep on the job again. It was also of vital importance that he held on to the bottle.

The blackness was total, and empty, as if it had no start or finish, as if it wasn't truly a place at all. He marvelled at the nothingness but drew back from it at the same time, aware abruptly that although he could see, or thought he could see, there was no sensation, no sensation at all, in his body, not even an awareness that it existed. He felt very small, almost humbled.

Then the wall of darkness parted, split down its middle by a gathering typhoon of livid blue light. They started rushing towards it. Or perhaps it was rushing towards them, opening itself up to embrace them? This was like coming out of a railway-tunnel, he supposed. But there was no more time to think because the blue light crashed abruptly over him, and his senses whited out. He hung on doggedly to the bottle throughout as a screaming whistle, rising ever upward in its piercingness, threatened finally to overwhelm him.

And then there was shingle beneath his shoes, and a fat, warm blob of rain splished on his nose.

'Great heavens!' He was back in Nutchurch, back in that cove, the bottle still in his hand. He looked to his side and saw several things all at once: Romana and K-9, looking none the worse for the journey; the splintered remains of the bathing-hut, its electrical innards shattered in a pile of broken timber and crushed bricks; and a veritable shower of warm rain that was already turning to hail. The sky had darkened and was filled with clouds. From the beach came sounds of a great commotion as startled bathers who had lingered to watch the sunset raced off, semi-clothed, for more ordinary huts or for the guesthouses on the promenade. 'What a downpour, eh?' He put his hands on his hips and took great lungfuls of the brine. 'Relief to be back, I must say. And no sign of PC Radmium, either.' His memory of being inside that capsule was already starting to fade in contrast to the realities of Nutchurch, as if it hadn't happened at all, and he felt a great stirring of gratitude for his world and all its contents, good and bad.

'Observations, Mistress,' said K-9.

After looking the Colonel over, Romana said, 'Go ahead, K-9.'

'Irregular and unnatural climatic conditions,' he reported. 'Atmospheric changes and variations in pressure building.'

Romana hugged herself from a sudden blustery wind. 'Zodaal must have stepped up the seismic disruption.' She cast her eyes to the ground. 'I dared to hope the Doctor might have sorted him out.'

The Colonel's chivalrous instincts were awakened. 'Dear girl, I suppose you'd like my coat, eh?' He started to take it off.

She looked at him as if he was insane. 'We must get back to London with the bottle.' Something appeared to catch her eye, and she pointed over his shoulder. 'Look.'

He turned. Buffeted by the inrushing tide, less than fifty yards from their current position, floated a shapeless bundle of rags. A second glance revealed it to be the uniform of the policeman. 'He must have scarpered somewhere,' the Colonel reasoned.

'Negative,' said K-9. 'Emergency devices of portal disintegrated his structure. Electrical energy is fatal to chemically altered forms of possessed hosts of Zodaal.'

'That's useful to know,' said Romana. 'We must get back up to London.'

There was a fierce clap of thunder, and a few seconds later a blinding flash of lightning. The wind increased in intensity. It was almost like a grenade going off in your face, thought the Colonel. He struggled to make himself heard over the roar. 'We can't go driving in this!'

There was another wave of sound and fury, and great balls of ice started to descend, pattering off the pebbles of the little cove and making a rattling percussion off K-9's tin body. The Colonel blinked and shaded his eyes. Already it seemed to be growing darker. Through the murk he saw Romana, K-9 in her hands, scrambling up the rough path to the cliff top. The long grasses were swaying, blown flat by every other blast of the wind. He looked over his shoulder, out to sea, and glimpsed a small boat, no bigger than a tug, floundering in the raging waters. Then, seemingly out of nowhere, arose an almighty wave, about the size of a London street, and smashed it to pieces with a single crack like a whiplash.

He turned and scrabbled up the path after Romana, his shoes slipping in the track that was already turning to slithering mud.

It was when the rising moon was covered by smudges of cloud that Percy began to realise that something ghastly was taking place. There was a shocking pain on his brow, and a quick glance across the bucking car (the Doctor's driving had not improved) showed that Mrs Chater was undergoing a similar trial. Her features were pinched and she held the bridge of her nose between thumb and forefinger.

'I can feel one of my headaches coming,' she said. 'Sort of sweeping over me, in a wave.' The enthusiasm in her tone had lessened somewhat.

'Me too,' said Percy. The dark alleyways, narrow and twisting, of Wapping formed a louring backdrop to the latest stage of their endeavours. In the distance the arching cranes at the docks were dark against the day's afterglow, casting a grim horizon. 'There's something else, though. I feel a bit sick.'

'That'll be the atmospheric pressure increasing,' the Doctor called back from the driving seat. 'Our opponent has brought forward his plans, it appears.'

As he spoke an almost imperceptible fall of raindrops pattered on the upholstery.

Percy shivered. 'This is it, then? The end of the world?'

It was Mrs Chater who answered. 'Of course not. I have complete confidence in the good Doctor. He is more than a match for this cowardly gas.' She smiled. 'This is the funniest situation I have ever been in, and I am quite determined to enjoy it.'

Percy shook his bewildered head. 'You people are plainly quite, quite barmy.'

The Doctor held up an admonishing hand. 'This is it,' he said, pointing to a sign that in faded black letters read JASMINE STREET. He killed the engine and they stepped out into the road. It was silent; the nearest sounds were the plaintive hoots of horns at the docks. 'Well,' said the Doctor. 'When people are trying to blow up a planet they usually make more of a din about it.'

'Perhaps we've got the wrong place,' suggested Mrs Chater.

The Doctor shook his head. 'No, I feel sure...' He peered keenly along the darkened, boarded-up buildings along the street's length, then grinned broadly. 'The warehouse. Look at the windows.'

Percy squinted in the direction indicated and saw his point. All four rows of window panes had an odd, flat sheen. 'They're blacked out by something. Sound-proofing?'

'Something like it.' The Doctor made to hurry forward, then appeared to remember himself and stopped to address them. 'You both realise this could be appallingly dangerous?'

'Oh, yes,' Mrs Chater said happily.

'I have noticed,' Percy muttered with heavy sarcasm.

'I mean,' the Doctor continued, 'er, you could always wait in the car.'

Percy's reply was lost as Mrs Chater pulled herself upright with a fierce jerk, struck a noble attitude, and said, 'Not another word, Doctor. Mr Closed and I are your willing adjutants. To this villain I say, Never, sir! Wit and wisdom will have their way against the hollow shams of your magic, for what are we if we stand idly by while—'

'Yes, yes, I see,' the Doctor said hurriedly. 'Let's go, then.' He strode off.

Percy clattered over the cobbles after him. 'Hang on, we can hardly walk in through the front door.'

'Yes, we can,' he replied. 'We want to get captured, don't we?'

'No!' said Percy.

'Yes, we do. Getting captured is much the best way of reaching whoever's running the show.' He smiled. 'I have done this before, you know.' He and Mrs Chater continued their brisk clatter towards the big wooden doors of the warehouse.

'Well, I haven't,' Percy protested, 'and I don't care for it in the slightest. I feel bound to say that as a pastime walking head-on into a crowd of zombies ranks behind hammering a nail up one's nose while swimming in a crocodile-infested swamp!'

'Do hush, dear,' said Mrs Chater kindly.

They had now reached the doors. The Doctor whipped out his sonic device and swept its humming end over the wooden slats. 'There must be an alarm system,' he surmised, 'so with any luck they'll pick up this disruption.'

Mrs Chater nodded. 'I see. And come out and capture us?'

'There's a thin line between getting captured and getting killed,' said Percy, with small hope of being listened to. 'This is like a pig knocking politely at the door of an abattoir. They have tried to kill us twice in the last day.'

'Correction,' said the Doctor. 'They've tried to kill *me* three times in the last day. I suppose my average must be going up. You just happened to be in the way.'

'My point exactly,' said Percy.

He never got the chance to go on. The next moment the doors swung open from the inside, with a crash that had him almost jumping out of his shoes, and a filthy wave of the infernal vapour washed over them. Revealed behind the doors were two creatures more hideous than any he might have imagined, and he gazed at them with a kind of sickly fascination: at their grotesquely angled bones, with festered grey flesh remaining in ragged patches; at their lockjaw lips from which issued trickles of black drool; at their outstretched, grasping claws. It made him feel physically sick to look upon them. But worse was the noise they were making, like the cries of a beast in agony, drawn out and raucous. There was no doubt of their intention, and equally no doubt that the Doctor had been proved wrong, and fatally so. The possibility of flight was remote; Percy was paralysed with fear.

The monsters came for them, enfolding them with all their bony strength, and he fainted away.

The drive back to London was a nightmare. The upholstery was soaked by the time the Colonel got his party safely back to the car, and after putting the lid up they clambered in and got themselves wet through. The squall over the coast was worsening all the time, and the view of the village as they left was an alarming one, with waves of almost tropical size crashing against the meagre fortifications, and citizens and holidaymakers rushing about madly to protect their property. The car swerved about a bit as they got going on the uphill road, and the Colonel felt he would remember always the electric atmosphere of those moments, with Romana huddled over K-9, the scene lit from within by the metal dog's eyescreen and from without by frequent forks of lightning, and the hail hammering down on the canopy. He was glad of the turbulent conditions, for without the lightning flashes the way ahead would have been invisible. As it was, their outward journey was frustrated by obstacles: a fallen tree, which K-9 sawed through at Romana's urging, and attempts by several police vehicles to flag them down, which they ignored. The Colonel made a mental note to apologise to the constabulary at a less pressing moment.

Fortunately he was an expert motorist, and the weather cleared up as they neared London. He was able to weave neatly through the traffic with aplomb. They were back in the vicinity of Victoria by half past eight, tearing around its tight white corners. The Colonel congratulated himself. 'There you go,' he told Romana. 'I may not understand all of that dimensional doo-dah but I can take a corner, eh?'

Minutes later they pulled up in Ranelagh Square, and Romana was out of the passenger seat and through the front door of the house next to Mrs Chater's before the Colonel had unseated himself. K-9 beeped from the back. 'Request your assistance in exiting this automobile.'

The Colonel lifted him up – he was astonishingly light – and walked up the steps to the open door. As he went he looked up at Mrs Chater's house, and saw that no lights were shining from its windows. 'Woman's probably out boring some other chap to death,' he told himself. 'Serve him right. I'm well out of that.' He stepped into the vestibule of her neighbour, which was lit by a lamp in a Chinese-style shade and wallpapered a weak yellow. Of Romana there was no sign. 'I say,' he called. 'Romana? Where are you?'

There was only silence in reply. But, thought the Colonel, it was a kind of deliberate silence. In confirmation a timber creaked, from upstairs. 'Romana?' he called again, more softly.

'Caution,' said K-9. 'Hostiles detected. Evidence of high technology.'

The Colonel set him down on the hall carpet and started to climb the stairs, one by one, preparing himself for action. If his fair lady companion had been grabbed it was up to him to save her and restore at least some of his own crumpled dignity. He listened keenly as he ascended. From one of the first-floor rooms there came a muffled thump. He stepped onto the landing and crept up to the dining room door, which stood half open. There could be any number of brigands through there.

He was just about to burst in and prove his strength when something icy cold and metallic jabbed into his neck. He gasped and stood stock still, convinced that his time was up.

Then an unfamiliar, but cultured, voice said distinctly, 'This is a neutron-powered cutter, old man. If you move I shall fire it and take your head off. So I think it best that you don't.'

Julia hovered over Wapping, the fabric of her suit moistened by the long warm raindrops. The bright moonlight picked out the details of the bleak buildings below and the men – many of them dressed in oils – swarming aboard a newly arrived dredger and breaking out its heavy cargo. The change in weather had brought a dull ache up just above her eyebrows, and she had to concentrate hard to fix the position of Stackhouse's headquarters, and even harder to orientate her passage towards its solid bulk. Her mental processes were consumed entirely by her determination to defeat her former master. The crisis had stirred a heart she had long considered dead.

She alighted on the outer ledge of one of the highest rows of windows, which of course was totally impenetrable to any outsider's gaze, and sought for any join or crack that might allow access. The panes were secure in their iron frame, but the frame itself was flaking in places, and using all her strength she was able to bend one rusty metal length aside. Then she pulled out one of her cuffs, wrapped her fist up in it, and punched the exposed square of glass. Its shatter was swallowed up by the deafening rumble of the stimulator. She raised her elbow and knocked out the remaining panes of glass, then swung herself in. Her flying-box she kept active on its lowest setting, and she was supported on the very edge of the sill.

The view her height afforded was staggering. The stimulator was now incandescent, and surrounded by a haze of crackling forks of multicoloured energy that lit the rest of the warehouse. She had a singular sensation of looking down like a god on to the field at Armageddon. But on this field the dead were walking, the slaves now grouped in a slavering, screaming formation about three prostrate bodies. A sudden burst of argent light gave her the chance to identify them. One was Porteous, another was the man Closed, the third was the woman she'd glimpsed briefly at Woodrow's offices. Standing before this unholy gathering like a priest before his congregation was Stackhouse, looking as corpulent and proud and evil as ever. Standing at his side were two of the slaves, who were supporting between them the tall, eccentrically attired figure of the Doctor. He had survived, then. Until now.

The Doctor's senses returned and he tried to pull himself up, uncomfortably aware that he was held tight in the clenches of a couple of zombies. 'Do you mind letting go,' he asked the first, 'I've just had this coat cleaned and you'll ruin the crease on the arm.'

There was a malevolent gurgle from ahead. He registered the presence of his opponent, standing in a haze of green vapour, his grey face lit by fitful bursts of colour from the machine on the far side of the warehouse. 'Ah. You must be Mr Stackhouse.' He extended a hand but his offer was spurned. 'And this must be your seismic wave generator.'

Instead Stackhouse said, 'It is a sonic stimulator.'

The Doctor shrugged as best he was able. 'Let's not quibble. It's very big, I must say. You could go into the circus with that. Yes, I can see it now, roll up, roll up and see the great Zodaal and his amazing earthquake machine.' One of his captors let off a hiss of anger in his ear and tightened its grasp. 'On the other hand, you could settle for blowing the world to smithereens.'

Stackhouse edged closer to him, reaching out one of his short flabby arms and then running the back of his hand over the Doctor with rude curiosity. 'You are the Doctor. What manner of creature are you? What brought you here, to this planet in this time zone?'

'I don't think you'd believe me if I told you,' replied the Doctor. 'Er, do you mind if I ask a question? I've been wondering why you're planning to shake this planet apart. I mean, the human race can hardly pose a threat to you.'

'Of course they do not,' said Stackhouse slowly. 'The genus homo sapiens is an irritant animal, merely the means by which I shall achieve my goal.' He gestured back to the throbbing stimulator. 'The destruction of this backward ball of rock will release a gigantic outflow of energy.'

'Granted,' said the Doctor. 'But it won't be much use to you or your chums by then, will it? If you're going to go up in smoke with the rest of us.' He paused, and added meaningfully, 'Unless of course you were planning on being somewhere else when that happened.'

One of the zombies responded to his words and drooled onto the lapel of his coat. The Doctor reacted angrily and faced its green stare squarely. 'I wish you'd stop doing that. My dry cleaner will have a fit at this rate.'

'You talk like a human idiot,' said Stackhouse, 'but I sense that your words act as a screen to your alien intelligence.'

'Why, thank you,' said the Doctor. 'If I could reach my hat I'd put it on and raise it to you.'

'An intelligence that may be of use to me.' Stackhouse waddled over to a large blue saucer-shaped object that occupied a berth in one wall of his base. 'This is to be the means of my escape from Earth, Doctor.' He reached forward and rapped on its metallic lid with the top of his cane. Although there was no discernible hinge, the entire top half of the saucer flipped open and revealed a large human-shaped cavity, with clear spaces for arms, legs and head. The space for the head was lined with gold studs, which appeared to connect with a transparent canister, shaped like a horizontal elongated teardrop, that rested just above.

'I see,' said the Doctor, who had been dragged forward. 'You're going to climb in there and shoot off, then wait and collect all the energy in that, are you?'

'In one way you are correct,' replied Stackhouse, with a hint of relish behind his words. 'I will be travelling in the capsule, but in my dissociated, gaseous form, in there.' He indicated the glass teardrop. 'When the energy expended from the death throes of Earth is absorbed, I shall use it to refashion myself. This ghoulish existence is not my natural form, Doctor. Soon I will be whole again.'

The Doctor nodded grimly. 'You'll sacrifice an entire world and its people simply to stabilise yourself? That is rather selfish.'

'Yes. And when I have, I shall enter the body of my new host. The final, organic component of this flight vessel.' He came closer. 'I had hoped to use a human, of especially vigorous body and strength of mind. But she has eluded me.'

'I have a dreadful feeling I know what you're going to say next,' said the Doctor.

'Yes, Doctor,' replied Stackhouse. 'Your survival was the only error in my plan, and now even that has proved fortuitous. You will become the host for my essence! You shall know the will of Zodaal!'

The good humour drained abruptly from the Doctor's face.

PART FOUR

10

REUNIONS

It was a most perplexing set of circumstances. On being ushered through into the dining room of Closed's house, with the cold gun still held to his neck, the Colonel found Romana chatting brightly with two exceedingly queer women. One was a faded belle, mascara applied too heavily about the eyes (and of course he rarely noticed any detail of a woman's appearance unless it really stuck out), the other was a thin, bird-like creature with a pair of circular framed spectacles perched at the end of her nose. Both of them were carrying strange objects that were clearly weapons of some sort, shaped like ordinary pistols, perhaps a bit larger, but made of a strange metal and with an unearthly air to them. He snuck a glance down at the silvery tube pressed against his own person and noted the similarity. Then the bird-like woman waved an agitated hand and said, 'Godfrey, put that down. These people are friends of Percy's.'

His captor followed the order, and the Colonel turned to face him. Chap was old, with a big, round jocular face, the sort of person who seems always to be on the point of bursting into gales of laughter. He pumped the Colonel's hand and said, 'Dear me. Sorry about that. I'm a touch jumpy tonight, that's all.' He nodded to Romana. 'Wyse, Godfrey Wyse. Pleased to meet you. Where's young Closed got to, then?'

The faded belle coughed uncomfortably. 'It seems there's a

problem, Godders.' She faced Romana. 'Do go on, dear.'

Romana was about to resume whatever narrative the Colonel had interrupted but he put up his hand. 'Just a minute. Who are this lot?'

Her face fell. 'I can't manage two explanations at once. K-9 –' she addressed the dog, who had just entered the room – 'talk to the Colonel.'

'Please specify, Mistress.'

'Explain the situation to him, please.' She turned back to the gathering and started to talk about something so absurdly technical and overcomplicated that she might as well have been speaking Algerian.

K-9 motored off into a corner, flashing his lights to get the Colonel to follow. He wasn't at all keen on being shunted off with the dog, and under saner conditions would have made a protest, but such was the seriousness of Romana's expression that he obeyed.

K-9 said softly, 'Colonel. These people are temporal deviants.'

'Eh?' His brow furrowed. 'Ah, you mean anarchists? Dynamiters? Thought there was something fishy about 'em.'

'Negative. They are incorrectly located in time.'

The Colonel was more confused than ever. 'What, they're late for something?'

K-9's ears wiggled and he made an exasperated howl. 'I am reconfiguring my linguistic frame. Cross-referencing literature bank 1890 to 1945.' He beeped. 'Reconfiguration achieved.'

'Well?'

'These men and women are travellers in time, from the future. They are colleagues of our ally Mr Percival Closed.'

The Colonel rubbed his chin. 'Rummy. But I suppose I've no choice but to take your word for it. And what's with all the paraphernalia? The guns and stuff?'

'Their weaponry is also from the future, and uses death rays and artificial thunderbolts more powerful than any stick of dynamite.' He enounced the words with his usual flatness, which amused the Colonel.

'There,' he said, patting the dog on its tin head, 'you can talk sense if you really set your mind to it, what?'

K-9's head slumped.

'I don't like being knocked out,' said Percy as he struggled to open his eyes. 'It simply isn't me. If I wish to be unconscious I have a perfect right to decide when and where for myself.' He turned his pounding head and saw Mrs Chater, who was awake, and kneeling over a dishevelled-looking fellow who lay spark out on the grimy floor between them. They were inside a small and very dark anteroom, through which vibrations thrummed from the nearby stimulator device. A heavy metal door, covered in studs, blocked any hope of exit. But at least they were alive. Percy recalled his final few moments of consciousness and shuddered repeatedly. How on earth had they wriggled out of that one? 'Ugh,' he remarked, 'my hands are covered in smuts.'

'Do be a sweet and shut up,' said Mrs Chater. 'Come and lend a hand with this one.'

Percy levered himself up with a groan and examined their cellmate in more detail. The fellow was short, and his hair and beard were matted with grease and dirt. One wing of his spectacle frames had cracked, adding to his disorderly appearance. A tall felt hat was affixed to his head by a piece of string knotted under his chin. Percy applied his fingers to the task of untying it. 'Let's get this off him. Brain's overheated, probably. Who is he?'

'I've no idea,' said Mrs Chater brightly. 'Never seen him before in my life. When I came to, he was lying next to us. A funny little man, isn't he?'

'Hmm.' Percy thought back to the Doctor's report of that abduction in the teashop. 'This is quite possibly the crank that got kidnapped yesterday.' The thought prompted him to ask, 'Where's the Doctor got to?'

Mrs Chater shrugged sadly. 'He must be still up there, a prisoner of Stackhouse.'

Percy grunted and continued to fiddle with the knot. 'Or dead, more likely.'

'No!' Mrs Chater shook her head vigorously, her bell of hair swaying elegantly in accompaniment. She really was, thought Percy, astonishingly well-preserved. 'The Doctor is alive. Don't ask me how I know. I can tell. Call it a woman's intuition, if you like.'

It crossed Percy's mind to make a remark about deliberate denial of the facts, but something stopped him. For some reason he didn't want to scald her with his wit. Instead he concentrated on the knot, and with the nimble fingerwork of the experienced knitter he had it untied at last. But when he removed the hat, something extraordinary happened: a heavy metal contraption fell out.

'Heavens,' Percy observed. 'Brings out a whole new meaning to keeping it under your hat, eh?'

'How intriguing,' said Mrs Chater. 'But what is it?'

Percy examined the thing, aware that his companion had simply assumed that being a man he was better qualified for such matters. The central weight of it consisted of a sort of thick metal drum, like an old gramophone cylinder, that was fixed to a wooden base. Wound around the drum several times was a length of thin cardboard; this was designed to roll from the drum and through a slot to where a stylus wet with blue ink traced a jagged series of lines across it. On top of the drum was mounted a small, wildly spinning weather vane-type arrangement. He spoke hesitantly. 'It's a sort of atmospheric or seismic monitor, I think. Very elementary. Then, I suppose it would be. Dashed odd thing to put on one's head.'

Mrs Chater took it from him and tried to pull the paper out from around the drum. It wouldn't budge. 'It appears to be stuck.'

Percy pointed upward. 'Overwhelmed, I should think, by all this.'

Their fellow prisoner moved in response to their words, opening his mouth and muttering, '… kinetograph… my own design… it's mine… I'll show them…'

'Well, whatever it is, it's hardly of use to us,' said Percy gloomily.

'Not a bit of it,' said Mrs Chater. 'I thought you'd read my books, Percy. You can't have been paying much attention. Remember Inspector Cawston's words: "Always use whatever lies to hand."' She hefted the kinetograph up in one hand. 'A jolly fine weapon, I'd say. Bring this down on a ghoul's head and it'd be sure to knock it flying.'

The Doctor's zombie captors dragged him towards the waiting operating table. He put up a show of resistance, well aware that he could not escape from creatures of such strength, and that his chances of flight from the table were much higher. They manhandled him into place, with his arms and legs pulled out straight. Stackhouse waddled over and ran the tips of his fingers over a small panel, which released three steel clamps that clicked tight shut over the table.

The Doctor tried to hold up a finger. 'Er, excuse me, but isn't it usual at this point to offer the patient some sort of anaesthetic?'

Stackhouse grunted. 'It is not necessary.'

'Perhaps not from where you're standing,' said the Doctor. 'Look, when you start operating I'll be thrashing about in agony, won't I? You wouldn't want bloodstains all over your lovely base, would you?'

Stackhouse picked up a small slender tool and activated an attachment, a rotating metal star with four murderously sharp edges. 'My base is not lovely.'

'You take everything very literally, don't you, Zodaal?' the Doctor asked. 'It is Zodaal, isn't it? Interesting name. Where did you come by it, I wonder?'

'When your brain is linked to mine you will know all,' replied Stackhouse, replacing the cutter and testing another surgical appliance, this time a scissors-like device with several interlocking blades.

'No doubt,' said the Doctor, 'no doubt. But a fat lot of use it'll do me then.' He blinked. 'I don't think you'll like my brain, you know. I mean to say, wherever it is you come from, Zodaal, your brains must be very similar to the brains of these humans you despise. Am I right?'

'On Phryxus suitable cerebral tissues are selectively farmed from accelerated genetic material,' said Stackhouse.

'Phryxus!' The Doctor sat bolt upright, or tried to, succeeding only in bashing his head against one of the restraining straps. 'Ow! Er, where was I... Phryxus!'

'You have knowledge of my world?'

'Well, in an academic sense. I don't think I've ever actually been there. You have been around the houses, haven't you? Phryxus is billions of parsecs away.' He narrowed his eyes. 'Makes it even more likely, really.'

Stackhouse ignored him, concentrating instead on checking a tiny bone saw.

The Doctor coughed. 'I said it makes it even more likely, really.'

'Be quiet,' said Stackhouse. 'Nothing you say is of importance.'

'What?' The Doctor shuffled up on the table and sat up as far as he was able, resting the weight of his upper body on his elbows. 'Not important?'

Stackhouse waved his two slaves forward. 'Suppress him.'

The zombies loomed over the Doctor, stretching out their claws menacingly.

The Doctor held up a hand and bellowed, 'Wait! All I'm trying to point out is that my brain is very different from a human brain!'

The slaves hesitated and looked to Stackhouse for guidance.

He replaced the saw in its cavity and shuffled forward to confront the Doctor. 'What do you mean by this?'

'Well, it may not be compatible,' the Doctor babbled. 'I should hate for it to disappoint you.'

'How does it differ?' Stackhouse leant over him, and it was almost as if his glowing green gaze was boring through the Doctor's skull to examine what lay within. 'Speak the truth.'

'Well, for one thing,' said the Doctor, 'there's the arrangement of the lobes. Totally at odds. Then there's the cerebellum, the links to the nervous system. Not like a human brain at all. Rather tidier, in fact.' He pulled a face. 'So you see, I don't think you'd fit.'

Stackhouse put out a hand and cupped the base of the Doctor's head, then growled. 'No! This is...'

'A setback, I'd say,' said the Doctor.

'Be silent!' Stackhouse let his head fall and then paced around the table, his hands clasping and unclasping. 'Another organic component is needed. The three humans here, then. Porteous's mind is addled, tired. The female is spineless, backward. It must be Closed.' He nodded to the nearest slave. 'Bring him here.'

'Yes, sir.' With a last longing look at the Doctor the slave lurched away.

'Er, Zodaal?' asked the Doctor. 'If you don't want me, can I go?'

Zodaal replied with an abrupt sweep of the flat of his hand which caught the Doctor squarely under the jaw. 'I find your idiocy tiring.'

With difficulty the Doctor rubbed his chin. 'I can tell,' he said, dabbing at the bruise with his scarf.

Stackhouse shuffled away from the table, leaving the Doctor under the watchful eyes of the remaining zombie.

'Just you and me, then,' said the Doctor. He felt in his pockets and brought out a crumpled paper bag, and riffled through it. 'Hmm. No green ones left. An ill portent. Have to settle for a red one.' He popped it in his mouth, chewed, and waved the bag at his captor. 'I don't suppose you'd…?'

The creature snarled, and lashed its foul black tongue around its grey lips.

'No, I don't suppose you would.' He returned the bag to his pocket and chewed thoughtfully.

Over the zombie's shoulder he could see the Italian woman, hovering above the stimulator like a giant black bat, her eyes fixed on his. He gave her his most significant glance, and a moment later she had lifted up and away again.

For once, the Colonel was fairly sure he was following it all. Romana had cleared the dining room table and was poring over a map of London provided by the big chap, Wyse. The women, who were looking a mite fretful after all those explanations, were sitting nervously at the very edges of their armchairs. The Colonel decided to make himself useful by putting a brew on.

'Spot of tiffin will calm us all down,' he said, handing out the cups and readying the pot. 'Clear our heads for all the thinking.'

'Percy's an absolute clot, and that's a fact,' said the faded belle, who had been introduced to him as Mrs Chipperton. 'Fancy getting himself embroiled in all of this.' She weighed her metal gun in her hand and sighed. 'Good job you kept these handy, Harriet.'

Her companion nodded sadly and stirred the sugar in her tea. 'I know. Always better to be on the safe side. If I hadn't brought these along imagine the state we'd be in now. We'd have had to call on help from the –' she waved at the Colonel – 'sorry, the locals.'

'You may still have to.' The Colonel sipped his tea. 'I'll have you know, my good lady, the British army is the finest in the world. They'd soon have this business bang to rights.' He picked up one of their weapons. 'Very fancy, I daresay, but you don't win wars by being fancy. Discipline's what's needed, oh yes.'

K-9 piped up suddenly. He had been perched on a chair facing the window, against which long streaks of warm rain were starting to splutter. 'Mistress. Doctor Master is outside the range of my sensors. Also, interference from atmospheric disruption has reduced the efficacy of my tracking equipment.' His head sank low. 'Estimate this planet will succumb to excessive gravitational pressures within a period of four days.'

'It's all right, K-9,' replied Romana. 'Mr Wyse and I should have this ready again soon.' She slid the final addition to the device – a twisted coat hanger – into a socket, and instantly it started to hum with a curiously high pitch.

'I say.' The Colonel got up from his chair. 'You really think you can find the troublemakers with that?'

Wyse shot him another of those off-putting smiles. 'I should say. I was once an engineer, you know, dab hand with simple relational systems like this.'

'Oh yes?' said the Colonel suspiciously. The fellow was older than him. 'When was that? Long time ago, what?'

'No, no. A long time to come.' Wyse smiled as an opaque surface just under the coat hanger illuminated, and a series of weird symbols flashed across it. 'There we are, Romana, dear.'

Romana read off the symbols. 'Kappa eleven seventeen by six beta two.'

K-9 burbled happily. 'Wapping, Mistress.'

The Colonel knew his geography, and slammed down his thumb on the relevant section of the map. 'There we go. This time of night barely half an hour's drive.'

Harriet drained her teacup and stood. 'We'd best be off, then.' She took her gun back and swivelled a mechanism in the butt. 'Rescue the silly fool.'

'Wait,' said Romana, with a hint of the parade ground in her voice. For a brief moment a flicker of the attraction he had felt for her bloomed in the Colonel's breast. 'We can't rush in there without thinking.'

'Yes, I suppose we ought to have some sort of plan,' said Mrs

Chipperton. 'People generally have plans in this sort of situation, don't they?'

'We already have one,' said Romana. 'Colonel.'

He took his cue from her and produced his ginger pop bottle. 'We shall release this in the proximity of our enemy and foil his scheme.'

'And if we need you, we'll call,' said Romana. 'K-9 will send a signal that you can pick up on your transceiver, Mr Wyse.'

'Right you are,' said Wyse.

Romana turned to the Colonel. 'Do you know the way to Wapping?'

'Of course I know the way to Wapping,' he replied. He moved for the door. 'Best foot forward, then.'

'Mistress,' said K-9. 'I also know the way to Wapping. Please remove me from this chair.'

Although Mrs Chater had drilled him thoroughly in what was to follow, Percy felt his heart miss a beat when at last, after what felt like an eternity, the heavy bolts of the coal cellar door were driven back and the heavy metal oblong swung out on its hinges with a despairing creak. As it did, a patch of that fearful green glow spilled in with its ever-accompanying odour of rotting vegetables. Outlined was a skeletal figure, the most emaciated of the slaves he had seen yet.

Quick as lightning he stepped forward, right into the creature's path, raised both arms and yelled 'Boo!'

At the same moment Mrs Chater struck. She was standing behind the door on a scuttle, Porteous's kinetograph held in both hands. She struck with force, bringing the metal weight down directly on the back of the creature's neck. The result they had hoped for was achieved; the head was swept clean off and went bowling over and over into a far corner. There was no blood or gore, just a clean break, leaving only a jagged splint of upper spine protruding from the stump.

Mrs Chater immediately dashed for the open door, as had been decided. It had also been decided that Percy would follow her. Instead he stood still, transfixed by the horror of the blindly groping headless skeleton as it flailed about wildly. Its fingertips brushed his shoulder, leaving a black smudge on his shirt, and he was rooted to the spot.

'Run, Percy!' he heard Mrs Chater screaming, and he knew what he had to do. But his survival instinct had been overpowered by the walking nightmare standing before him, and seconds later its smouldering hands were upon him, drawing him to it with one savage lunge. He recoiled as it tightened its hold, raising one of its hands to his face. He had an odd sensation of being suspended, halfway between life and death.

The sound, when it came, was unbearably loud. A couple of pistol shots cracked in his ears and rebounded off the walls of the cellar. At first he thought he had been shot, but then the zombie's grip loosened, and then Mrs Chater had her hands all over him and was pulling him to a low-ceilinged passageway outside the cellar, and whatever was passing for safety in this zombie-infested warehouse on this disintegrating planet.

As his senses swam back into order he saw his rescuer, still immaculate, her silver pistol smoking. The flying-box gleamed at her waistband. 'Quick, you two,' she urged them, gesturing behind her along the passageway to a narrow flight of rising steps set against the wall. 'Get up there and get away. The doors are at the top of the steps.'

Still rather shocked by the gruesome nature of recent events, Percy and Mrs Chater were frozen.

'You must get away,' Julia continued. She added urgently, 'Stackhouse is coming for you.'

'Oh, damn it,' said Percy, spurred into action.

'Wait,' called Mrs Chater. 'What about him?' She pointed back to the cellar and the fallen form of the scientist.

'There is no time,' said Julia. She shook Mrs Chater by the shoulder. 'I said go!'

Mrs Chater caught up with Percy as he hurried up the steps. 'Really. These Continental types, always in such a blind rush, and so hot-tempered.' They turned a corner and emerged on to a small landing; the din of the stimulator was suddenly much clearer, and mixed up in it were the cries and groans of the starved slaves. Green light spilled from an open door on the next level. A sickening fear welled up in the pit of Percy's stomach and he ground to a halt. Mrs Chater wittered on, 'And what about the poor Doctor? We couldn't leave him behind.'

'Couldn't we?' Percy was sweating. 'It's his own lookout.' He wrung his slippery black hands together. 'We're all done for, anyway. Huh. Not much of a choice. Be gobbled up here or escape and have it done in the comfort of one's own home.' He whimpered. 'Damn this century!'

Mrs Chater appeared not to have heard him. 'The Doctor's the key to it all. He's bound to have a plan, you know.'

Percy shot her a withering glance, took a deep breath, muttered, 'Well, have at it, then,' and bolted up the steps, his shoes clattering. He burst through the open door at the top and found himself in the midst of a hellish scene. Such was the concentration of activity on the far side of the warehouse that his own appearance went unnoticed. There was Stackhouse, as portly and pompous as he recalled from that fateful railway journey but with the cold grey pallor of the undead; there was the stimulator, a spreading blaze of throbbing, thrumming machinery seeming almost to reach the roof, shrieking and throwing wild patterns of light about; there were the zombies, grouped close like ragged soldiers on parade; and there, next to a big saucer of some kind, was the Doctor, spark out on a surgeon's slab.

He pointed this last detail out to Mrs Chater as she joined him. 'If he's got a plan I'd say he's not making a very good fist of it.' The warehouse's big doors stood only a few feet away. 'Let's be off.'

She caught his shoulder. 'Percy, no! We must save our poor friend!'

'He looks past saving. Come along!' He dashed into the open and heaved at the gates; they swung open with a thunderous creak that would have instantly advertised his whereabouts had it not been for the row coming from the stimulator. He slipped through the gap into a deep abysm of blackness. It was as if he had suddenly gone stone-blind. Then, just as suddenly, and he never knew how, he was out in the street, in the middle of a raging thunderstorm, and was racing for cover under the awnings of one of the buildings opposite.

It was only when he got there, soaked through, and turned up his collar against the raging wind, that he realised Mrs Chater had not followed him.

Julia heaved up Porteous's body against the wall of the coal cellar. The shattered, smoking frame of the zombie twitched in the middle of the room, threatening to right itself at any moment. She shook the scientist awake. 'Listen to me, Porteous, listen to my voice.' She shook him again, and his eyelids raised like those of an aged lizard, revealing weary, bloodshot orbs. 'We have to stop the machine!'

He sagged against the wall. 'No way to… control it, it's… totally automatic…'

'We have to!' Julia was surprised by the passion in her words, and uncertain of its origins. All she knew for certain was that a deep sense of rage was building up inside her, an atavistic anger that anyone could try to destroy her entire world. 'How, Porteous?'

He shook his head, and a tear rolled down his cheek. 'Why did I do it?' he moaned. 'Why? For the sake of a bed of roses?'

Disgusted, she let him fall.

*

Felicia recalled girlish games of hide and seek as, bent almost double, she crabbed sideways across the warehouse floor to the Doctor. All of the villains were engrossed in their nefarious machine and her passage was more or less unobstructed, although she had a hairy moment when one of the walking dead lurched by on some errand. At last she reached the table where the Doctor rested, and popped up her head. 'Hello, Doctor, dear.'

'Felicia!' he whispered, angling his head up as far as he could against his straps. 'What are you doing here?' He sounded almost angry.

'Don't be such an ungrateful sauce. I've come to bear you away.' She looked over the array of fiddly-looking buttons and things ranged along the sides of the table. 'It's a good thing for you that I've been keeping up my exercise regime.'

'This is appallingly dangerous,' hissed the Doctor. 'Where's Percy?'

She sighed. 'Fled, I'm afraid. He is really too much a dear, but lacks the moral gumption. I'll have to see to that, won't I?' Her fingers brushed over a line of switches. 'Would it help if I press one of these?'

The Doctor pointed. 'That one. I think.'

Felicia did as bid and the metal straps restricting him shot back on hidden catches. The Doctor leapt up, patted her on the shoulder, then let out a despairing cry and struck his head with his hand.

'What is it, what is it?' asked Felicia frantically.

He turned her about, and she saw the answer.

The leader of the slaves was bearing down on them.

Percy shivered. The awning he had chosen as a shelter was useless, and raindrops pelted down on him as if to add the weight of nature to his rapidly plummeting sense of self-regard. He had left both the Doctor and Mrs Chater behind, some minutes ago now, and the warehouse doors had remained resolutely shut. They were trapped in there, possibly dead, and he would have to live out the remainder of his days, however few, in the knowledge that he had let them down. The sky was split by another peal of thunder, and he cursed his pathetic nature. If only he'd been born with the bravery of the Doctor or of Julia Orlostro – Julia Orlostro! The thought tripped a door in his memory, and her face flashed back in front of his eyes, this time from a picture page in a newspaper. Of course! He really should have seen it before. She was the Contessa di Straglione, the disowned heiress of a wealthy Italian family turned adventuress, variously rumoured to have been implicated in a whole host of plots. Nothing had been proven until a couple of years back when she'd been arrested for the cold-blooded killings of two accomplices who had tried to betray her. Her money had been seized, but she had fled before she could be brought to trial, causing the wildest sensation. It was widely supposed she had flown abroad. Now he had the answer to all the speculation, but nobody to tell it to.

'What are you doing there, you'll catch your death!' a familiar voice rang out.

He looked up, startled, as a group of figures appeared through the mists of the downpour, silhouetted in the flickering light of the streetlamps. Three of the newcomers were instantly familiar, and for a second his heart soared and his troubles were forgotten. 'Harriet!' he yelled, and ran out to welcome her. It was all he could do not to throw his arms around her. 'And you, Davina! And you, Godfrey!'

Wyse shook his big bald pink head. 'You've gone and landed yourself in it right and proper, haven't you?'

Despite his relief Percy felt a surge of irritation. 'There's no need to carp. We're beyond scoring points now, you know.'

Davina came forward and straightened his collar. 'Poor Percy, looking like a drowned rat.' There was something in her hand, a glint of metal.

He straightened up. 'Where did you get that thing?' he yelled, pointing it out. 'That's quite against the rules.'

'She got it from me, dear,' said Harriet, stepping forward and raising her own weapon. She wore an almost triumphal sneer. On a lady of this period's face it was as out of place as the gun. 'What do you intend to do about it? Dock my allowance?' She raised the barrel to his chin playfully.

'Funnily enough, I am rather glad to see it,' stammered Percy.

The rest of Harriet's party came into view, and Percy gulped when he saw the stern expression on Romana's face. K-9 trundled along at her feet, and there was an old buffer of military bearing tagging along too. 'You lied to us,' Romana said simply. 'We wasted time searching for the time corridor.'

'Blow the time corridor,' said Percy urgently. He jabbed a finger over at the warehouse. 'You're not going to believe what's going on over there.'

'A dissociated gaseous alien and his army of zombies are plotting to blow up the world,' said Romana.

'Perhaps you would,' said Percy.

'I suppose the Doctor's in there?'

He nodded. 'And not doing too well, I'm sorry to say.'

The military man coughed loudly. 'I say. All this chat is a waste of time. Shouldn't we get cracking?'

'I agree with the Colonel,' said Harriet, hefting up her weapon. 'We ought to get in there right off. This carries a tri-neutron charge, it could blow one of these zombies to the wind.'

Romana sighed, and Percy got the impression that she was retreading an old argument. 'We'll stick to what we agreed.' She looked over at the warehouse. 'K-9, are you ready?'

He whirred up. 'Affirmative, Mistress. Reconfiguring in offensive mode.'

The Colonel caught Romana's arm. 'Sure you don't need me in there, my dear?'

'If we need you, we'll call,' she said. 'Come on, K-9.'

They set off across the street.

Percy was baffled. 'What are they doing? They can't just walk in there.' He baulked at the memory of doing exactly that.

'They're armed, all right,' the Colonel reassured him. 'With a bottle of ginger pop.'

'You are fast becoming an irritant, Doctor,' said Stackhouse. 'And my slaves are hungry. Soon, as this planet begins to buckle and bend, they will emerge and begin their feast.' He smiled cruelly. 'Perhaps they deserve an aperitif.'

The Doctor and Felicia were surrounded on all sides by the mass of slaves. Some of the bolder zombies were reaching forward to prod and poke at their flesh.

'Say something, Doctor,' Felicia urged.

'You can't kill us,' the Doctor protested.

'Why not?' asked Stackhouse.

'Well, we're bound to be of some use, aren't we?'

Stackhouse came closer.

'I mean, we'd make good hostages.'

'No,' said Stackhouse. 'I have no need of hostages.' He signalled his drooling, stinking minions forward.

'Er, well in that case,' said the Doctor, 'er... well, I'm very clever, you know, I'm sure you could find a position for a man of my abilities. I could fix your gadgets when they broke down, and so forth.'

'My machinery is infallible,' said Stackhouse. 'And I am the most intelligent and capable being in the entire universe.'

'Ah.' The Doctor's face fell. 'Ah, well, that rather narrows my options, then, doesn't it?'

The slaves snapped their jaws and prepared to spring.

The Doctor held up a finger. 'Er, wait!'

'What now, Doctor?'

'I just wanted to point out that your intended host, Mr Closed, has flown the coop.'

Stackhouse looked about and grunted. 'No matter. There will be other suitable humans, and there is time left to me.' He lowered his voice and addressed his slaves. 'Kill him.' Then his smile grew ever more twisted. 'No, wait.'

The Doctor heaved a sigh of relief. 'I was hoping you'd say that.'

Stackhouse pointed to Felicia. 'Kill her first, so that the Doctor may learn the folly of opposition.'

The Doctor's face clouded and he lunged forward angrily, gripping Stackhouse by the lapels. 'No! You've made your point, Zodaal!'

Stackhouse threw him to the floor with a brush of the hand. 'Then I shall make it again.' He pointed to Felicia again. 'Devour her brain!'

Felicia backed away, desperate to keep her composure, but reflecting inwardly that matters had reached a pass where this might no longer be necessary. She threw back her head and screamed.

'Wait!'

An unfamiliar female voice, carrying a spirited conviction, rang out over the rumble of the stimulator. Immediately the zombies halted their progress, and turned as one with Stackhouse to face the newcomer. It was the Doctor's young friend in the Oxford bags, walking towards them across the warehouse floor with some sort of odd metal box whizzing about at her side.

The Doctor leapt up. 'Romana! Am I glad to see you, yes, I think I am. Evening, K-9.'

The box inclined its head. 'Evening, Master.'

Stackhouse advanced on the strangers. He put out his hand towards Romana. 'You,' he gasped. 'You are the same as the Doctor.'

'I hope not,' she said. She was bringing something from her pocket. Not a gun or grenade, as Felicia had hoped, but a small bottle. 'Let them go,' she demanded.

'You really are getting better as you go along,' the Doctor called over.

Stackhouse sneered. 'Foolish female. You have delivered yourself to oblivion. My slaves will feast on you also.'

As he spoke, the girl Romana was bringing the bottle up to head height. Felicia glimpsed curls of smoke inside and dared to hope again. There was clearly something in there. An answer to their dilemma?

Romana threw the bottle. It shattered immediately, releasing an astonishingly large patch of glowing green vapour, identical to that which she'd seen attacking the Doctor in the square the night before. The vapour swooped upwards, hissing and sizzling exultantly.

The effect on Stackhouse and his slaves was immediate and impressive. They backed away as if terrified, holding their arms up to their eyes and making kittenish, strangely pathetic sounds. The vapour cloud bellowed and descended upon them, its greenness splitting and invading their now rigid, desiccated forms.

The Doctor patted Felicia on the shoulder and leapt over to join Romana and the K-9 thing. 'Well done, you two,' he said happily, punching the air. 'I presume you've done something very clever.'

'Zodaal's personality was divided,' said Romana, smiling. 'We simply found the other half, and reunited him. He'll be a changed character.'

The Doctor's mood darkened. 'What?' His head whipped round to where Stackhouse stood, now coated in additional vapour. 'I hope you know what you're doing, Romana.'

'Probabilities have been computed, Master,' K-9 said.

Stackhouse jerked one arm up, and covered his face with the spread fingers. His slaves mimicked the motion, like a row of puppets moving in perfect unison.

The Doctor rubbed his chin. 'Well, something seems to have happened. Now, I think we'd better see about that—'

Stackhouse brought his hand down. His eyes were now glowing an even fiercer green, and his face was more animated than before, assuming a sardonic expression that looked for once like it belonged to a human face. 'Thank you, my good friends,' he said in a richly inflected voice. 'Thank you very much.'

'I don't like the sound of that,' the Doctor mumbled.

Romana stepped forward. 'Zodaal. You must turn off the stimulator immediately.'

He chuckled. 'Oh, no. No, I don't think that will be at all necessary. In fact I can already think of a way to accelerate the process.' He nodded to K-9. 'The input of your data bank has been quite a boon.'

Felicia ran to the Doctor's side. 'Pardon me, but did that plan work or didn't it?'

It was Stackhouse who answered her. 'Didn't.' He chuckled once more, and it sent a shiver right through her. 'Although it has made me see the funny side of all this.'

11
APOTHEOSIS

It was with a mixture of relief and apprehension that the Colonel greeted the bleeping signal from Wyse's pocket. He had been bursting to follow Romana, but now his resolve wavered at the prospect of facing their foe directly. The trouble was, Wyse and Closed were soft, drawing room fops, and the others – well, the others were women, dammit. What use would they be in open battle, even with their metal ray guns? 'Gung-ho, then,' he muttered, bracing himself, and setting his sights firmly on the big wooden doors of the warehouse. He turned to Harriet. 'You'd better show me how to let off one of those. Don't want it going off in my face.'

Harriet passed him the spare and coiled his hand around the butt. 'It's very simple. Just aim and fire.' Then she addressed her colleagues in polite but forthright tones, like a typing instructor. 'Right. Nothing for it, then.' She checked her watch. 'We'll go in in three. Fan out and aim for a wide sweep. Davina, you and Godders keep the ground free, I'll take out the leader.' They nodded and readied their weapons.

The Colonel coughed. 'Er, what shall I do?'

Harriet shrugged. 'Keep your head down and try to fry as many as you can of these creeps.'

The Colonel felt put out by her enthusiasm for the fray. Most unsightly in a woman. He frowned. 'Excuse me.'

'What?'

'Where you come from,' he said, trying to find the right words, 'are they all like you? I mean to say, I'm not trying to be rude, but…'

Mrs Chipperton answered. 'Yes, women can use guns. Everyone can.'

'Not strictly true,' said Closed, who was standing back, still shivering and dripping wet. 'I never could get the hang of it. And it was exactly because I couldn't that I came back here in the first place.'

The Colonel couldn't cope with weakness and cowardice from a man, no matter what age had produced him. 'Straighten up, man,' he growled. 'Romana is depending on us. In fact, the whole world's depending on us.'

Closed stuck out his tongue.

Harriet took off her glasses and stepped out into the street, her beige evening wear flowing gracefully around a body that seemed indecently lithe and active for a cultured woman. 'We're wasting time. Let's go.'

Stackhouse stood smiling in the flashing, whirling frenzy of colours glancing off the surfaces of his machine.

'And now I suppose you're going to kill us,' the Doctor said. 'I mean, that's what you were going to do, before my assistant's timely intervention.' He shot the cowed Romana an admonishing look.

Felicia tugged his coat sleeve. 'Don't go and remind him,' she hissed.

'I know what I'm doing,' he replied.

Still Stackhouse and his slaves did nothing.

'K-9, why aren't you firing?'

'Regret my defensive capability is ineffective against these hostiles, Master,' K-9 whispered. 'I can only delay them.'

'You need an upgrade,' the Doctor said.

Stackhouse sprang back to life, moving towards them with an agility that belied his bulk. 'Doctor. I see that I was wrong about you.'

The Doctor spread his arms wide. 'Well, I am basically a very warm and kind person.'

'I didn't mean that,' Stackhouse continued. 'I believed you to be one of Closed's people, one of the Circle.' His eyes narrowed. 'But now I see that you are a Time Lord.' He pointed to Romana. 'That you are both Time Lords.'

'What was in that bottle?' the Doctor hissed at Romana.

'I thought it would work,' she hissed back.

'You will instruct me in the operation of your TARDIS,' said Stackhouse. 'At last the power to traverse temporal barriers will be mine.'

The Doctor made a sceptical noise. 'You think the Time Lords will allow you to blunder around in my TARDIS?'

Stackhouse laughed. 'I know that the hierarchy of Gallifrey is weak and corrupt. I am sure an agreement can be reached.' He gestured to his slaves. 'I must assess my new knowledge. Take them all below. All but the computer. I have need of it.'

K-9 motored forward bravely. 'I will resist you, Zodaal.'

Stackhouse knelt down and patted him on the head. 'You forget, good dog. I have already dwelt within you. I can do so again.'

The Doctor's party were led away across the warehouse floor. 'Best to go quietly, K-9,' the Doctor called. Then he turned to Romana and whispered, 'You know, when you turned up just then, I got an idea of what it must feel like when I appear and rescue everyone.'

'Except you don't always get it right, either, do you, Doctor?' she replied tartly.

'Just quite right will do, I've found,' he told her. He smiled and patted her hand. 'To get something that badly wrong takes real talent. Well done.'

Julia had observed the exchange between Stackhouse and the Doctor, and used it as an opportunity to settle down behind the stimulator. This close to the power source the din was overwhelming, and she clapped her hands over her ears and struggled to retain her consciousness. Concentration was the best way, and so she focused her mind on the thick coiling cables leading into the machine's rear. If she could loosen them, somehow sabotage the machine for long enough to delay Stackhouse, at least… The metallic surfaces were scalding to the touch. This would take real determination.

She reached up for the lowest of the cables and started to tug, screaming as the pain travelled along her arm. She let go, and staggered back, losing her balance, her whole left side contorted with agony.

A booted foot appeared in her blurred field of vision. She looked up. One of the slaves, now grinning widely, was looming over her.

'Ah,' it breathed. 'The final component…'

Felicia sighed deeply as the heavy door of the coal cellar swung shut. 'This place is starting to be quite a home from home,' she said, and slumped to the floor. In the darkness she could just discern the crumpled form of the decapitated zombie lying next to her. 'Hello, old chap,' she greeted it. 'After all this rushing about I'm starting to feel pretty washed up myself.'

The Doctor and his friend Romana were not going to relax for a second, though. 'His other half, you say?' the Doctor was asking.

Romana nodded. 'The idea was that his better nature would make him reconsider.'

'And you fell for that?' The Doctor shook his head. 'Zodaal is a maniac. A very clever maniac, granted, but no matter what, a maniac. He dumped his spare parts for efficiency reasons, but now his plan's up and running why should it matter to him?

There are qualities in all of us we'd like to be rid of, I suppose.'

'Like insufferable smugness, for example,' said Romana.

'Oh no,' said the Doctor. 'I imagine that could come in very useful.' He grinned. 'Don't worry. It was a mistake nearly any fairly gullible person could have made.'

'Thank you.' She winced. 'Doctor, there's something else I think I ought to tell you.'

He looked over with a doubtful expression. 'Yes?'

She cast her eyes down. 'K-9 gave Zodaal the Equation of Rassilon.'

The Doctor's mood changed instantly. 'What?'

'The Equation of—'

He held up a hand. 'No, no, I heard you.'

Felicia was starting to get lost. 'An equation? I see, a sort of scientific formula?'

'No,' said the Doctor.

'Yes,' said Romana.

'Well,' said Felicia, 'what does it matter, anyway? If he's going to blow up the world, lock, stock and barrel, what use will a formula do him?'

The Doctor rubbed his chin; he seemed not to have heard her. 'Zodaal must already have a good working knowledge of stellar engineering. With that equation he'll have unlimited access to all time and space. And what's more he's got K-9, and the TARDIS...'

'And us,' pointed out Romana.

'... and me,' the Doctor concluded. 'He's got us over a barrel, rather.'

'You're forgetting something, Doctor,' said Felicia.

'Am I? I don't think I am.'

Felicia shook her head. 'Our dear friend Percy is still at large.'

The Doctor spluttered. 'Percy?' He angled his head to one side. 'Is that supposed to make me feel better?'

Romana spoke. 'She's got a point, Doctor. Percy and his

friends in the Circle are outside, and they're armed.'

Felicia clapped her hands together. 'Wonderful! I knew he was sure to sort everything out.'

The Doctor said nothing, but slid slowly to the floor next to the zombie corpse.

Zodaal extended a wisp of his new, stronger self, and probed the mind of the K-9 computer. Its unimpressive exterior seemed a calculated ploy on the Doctor's part, for its intelligence centres were staggeringly complex and advanced. There was even a defence mechanism, but he was able to sidestep that easily and penetrate the wafers that contained the creature's reasoning and memory store.

'Don't try to resist me, little K-9,' he whispered to it. 'Remember, I hold the lives of your master and mistress in the balance.'

'Im-Imperative,' K-9 stammered back. 'This unit is... protect... protec... Must disengage...'

Zodaal sensed a warning flash crackling between the memory wafers and blocked it. He chuckled. 'How touching. You were prepared to destroy yourself for them.'

'Function is to – Is to –' K-9's voice broke, and he emitted a fierce electronic growl.

'Now let me see,' said Zodaal. He familiarised himself with the system's recall triggers and reviewed the events of the previous hours: the dissipation of the secondary host, and the journey from the grey hole. As he did so a bewildering sequence of mathematical constants flashed before his awareness. 'Of course!' he cried, exulting in the new knowledge. 'Of course! So obvious! Only by treating the mass and density flow as irregular could a state of genuine flux be achieved!'

The section of awareness he had left in the body of Stackhouse recalled him urgently. With some reluctance he let the equation slip from his mind and flowed out of K-9, taking care to disable the dog's self-destruct mechanism and motive drive as he departed.

As Stackhouse he saw the leader of his slaves approaching. In its arms was draped the body of Julia Orlostro. 'Sir,' slurred the slave, 'the final component.'

Stackhouse clenched his fists. 'Superb. Everything is following my plan.' He moved forward and examined the body; the left arm was burnt and discoloured, but the frame remained strong. Tenderly he lifted the head. 'She is most suitable,' he whispered. 'We must install her immediately.' He pointed to the operating table, and the slave carried her across, its eyes flashing with glee.

K-9 watched them pass. Unable to move, and barely able to speak, he raised his head defiantly, and bleeped out his signal to the Circle another time. 'Colonel,' he whispered. 'Please… hurry…'

'Don't worry,' the Doctor told his cellmates. 'I've been in tighter corners than this.'

There was no word in reply from either of them. Even Felicia's enthusiasm and energy seemed to have dried up.

'There was that time with the Hypnotron,' continued the Doctor. 'Ha. Beat him. The Aquamen. Beat them. And then there was the Steel Octopus. Thought he had me licked, but of course he didn't know I've got a badge for knots.'

'Doctor,' whispered Romana.

'What?'

'If you're trying to cheer us up you're not succeeding.'

The Doctor huffed. 'Well, I—' He broke off suddenly. 'Romana, there's a hand on my knee!'

'Don't worry, it'll be that zombie. I knocked his block off, you know,' said Felicia.

'This hand has a pulse,' said the Doctor. He started shuffling about in the dark.

'How can you possibly feel somebody's pulse with your knee?' asked Felicia.

'My knees are very sensitive.' The Doctor succeeded in propping up the dazed body of Porteous. He jabbed a finger between the man's eyes and clicked his fingers beneath his nose. 'Come on, wake up, wake up.'

Romana felt for Porteous's heartbeat. 'He's suffered enormous trauma.'

'So have I.' The Doctor clicked his fingers again, and to Felicia the sound was sharper than a pistol shot. Porteous's eyes flickered open. 'I…' he gasped. 'I'm so… sorry…'

'He's gone nuts,' said Felicia sadly.

'Not necessarily.' The Doctor sucked a finger. 'Let me think. There must be a way to get him back to normality.' He clicked his fingers again. 'Of course!' Then he leant close to Porteous's ear and said loudly, 'That lettuce is perfectly healthy. I've never seen such a firm, green crispy lettuce!'

Porteous gave an enormous sneeze and bolted upright. 'Nonsense! That lettuce is rusty—' He broke off as he registered his new surroundings. 'Hey, what the heck – Oh no.'

'I'm afraid so,' said the Doctor. 'Hello, I'm the Doctor, this is Romana, that lady is Mrs Chater, and you've brought the end of the world a good few millennia nearer, and I hope you're going to be profuse in your apologies.'

But Porteous seemed almost not to be listening. Instead his hands had flown to his head and were scratching at his thick tangle of grey hair. 'Where is it?' he muttered. 'Where is it?'

The Doctor handed him his hat. 'There you are. Now, then—'

Porteous shook his head insistently. 'No, you don't understand. The kinetograph, I must have the kinetograph.'

Felicia was formulating the answer to his query when a most peculiar noise came from above, laid over the continuous rumble of the stimulator. In its staccato rhythm it might have been the sound of bullets, but it was higher in pitch and had an eerie, ethereal quality.

*

It was when he saw the doors of the warehouse open to reveal the veritable army of the undead, turning slowly in a horrible kind of unison as they sensed the invasion of their territory, that the Colonel's bubble of confusion, bluster and disbelief was at last punctured. He shook with the vigour of conflict, unknown to him for so many years, and he revelled in the swift responses of his mind and body. All that running and golf had kept him tip-top. Even the tremendous din booming out all over the place couldn't shake him. He raced forward, checking for areas of cover and convenient shadows.

Surprise was on their side. These chumps hadn't reckoned on their firepower. He watched as Harriet stopped, legs slightly apart, crouched like a cat, and trained her metal gun on the most advanced of their slavering enemies. She loosed off two shots, whizzing bullets of bright blue, reminiscent of K-9's death ray, which hit it smack on. It doubled up, clutching its chest; grotesquely it remained standing despite the gaping hole in its middle. A border of blackened entrails framed the large circular wound. Harriet fired once more, and this time the blue bullet sliced clean through the cadaver. It fell in two halves, its legs kicking and flailing uselessly. All this was over in moments, before he'd really had time to think about it.

And there was soon even less time to think. The other zombies advanced, arms outstretched, hissing angrily like bees beaten out of a hive. Harriet felled a couple more, while her colleagues ducked below and between her line of fire, letting off shots at random themselves, in an attempt to penetrate the main section of this sanctum. By far the best marksman of the group, Harriet used unfamiliar curses as she tried both to protect herself and clear a way for her friends. 'Colonel!' she cried. 'Don't just stand there! I need back-up!'

The Colonel suddenly became aware of his own inaction, caused in the main by his open-mouthed admiration of Harriet's skills. His heart was pumping furiously as he joined her in battle.

They stood almost back to back, and he raised his own gun and pressed the trigger button. The gun went off with a mighty jolt that would have pulled a weaker man's arm from its socket, and he watched in amazement as the bolt of blue light – he saw now that it contained no bullet – flew in a graceful arc before embedding itself in the throat of a looming zombie.

'Well done!' cried Harriet politely.

'I was aiming for its head,' the Colonel admitted. 'Still, not bad for a starter.' The creature seemed to hear him and lurched towards him, its jaw snapping. 'Your time's up, chum,' he told it, and this time succeeded in reaching his intended target. The head was knocked into the air like a football and sent spinning through the misty green clouds surrounding them.

There was no time to rest. The second wave were advancing, rather more cautiously, but it was hard to tell in this visibility – he couldn't see much further than five feet ahead – if Wyse or Mrs Chipperton had got through.

And then he felt another pang. There was no sign of Romana or of K-9 – and seeing as their plan had plainly failed, what had befallen them?

Stackhouse was readying the bone saw over Julia's head when the attack came. The sound of the high energy blasts caused him only irritation – a slight annoyance. Turning his head, he saw the small group of humans bursting through the far door, their gun arms raised, and the immediate response of his legion of slaves. 'Fools,' he muttered. 'They cannot hope to outmatch the slaves of Zodaal.' Then he returned to the matter in hand.

During the disturbance, Julia's eyes had opened. He recognised the look in her eye. 'Ah,' he crowed. 'At last, Contessa. The human reaction known as fear.'

She struggled against the restraining straps and her eyes flicked across to the whirring saw blade. 'What are you doing?'

He put out his hand to her temples and turned her head to

one side. With ghoulish relish he said, 'I'm searching for the right spot to make the first incision.' She cursed him in Italian. He shook his head. 'Yes, very good. Resisting to the last. That is why I selected you.'

She whimpered, 'But… But Woodrow—'

'Brought you to my attention, yes.' He brushed aside a fallen lock of her hair from the back of her neck. 'You are totally ruthless and unscrupulous, with a strong sense of self. The men you killed were your friends, but you would not suffer them to live.'

'One of them was my own brother,' she spat.

'Exactly. Yes, I knew you would return here and try to better me. You could not bear to see me win. Now you will take the ultimate honour.' He brandished a string of black connecting leads that led from the saucer to the table. 'When the Earth is destroyed, the kinetic potential of its death throes will be absorbed by my escape capsule. Then, through this link, my intelligence will overwhelm yours. I will become you.'

'And what of me?' she stuttered, shivering with terror.

'You will remain enslaved to the will of Zodaal for all eternity,' he cawed, throwing back his head and laughing manically.

Then he brought the saw to bear on her.

'Here it is,' said Felicia. She picked up the shattered remnants of the kinetograph, and passed them to the Doctor. 'I'm afraid it took rather a bashing, Mr Porteous.'

Porteous stared at the smashed components in the Doctor's hands, then put a hand to his brow and said, 'Ruined. I don't believe it. All ruined. Years of work.'

Romana asked, 'What exactly were you trying to do with it?'

Porteous huffed. His return to good health was startling; whatever trick the Doctor had pulled had definitely worked. 'I was collating figures, young lady,' he told her. 'To present to the Royal Society. They wouldn't have been able to ignore me then.' He picked out the weather vane piece from the crushed machine and held it up sadly. 'I had to keep the equipment on my person at all times, you see. To avoid hoaxers, or tamperers.' He gave a short, sharp laugh. 'How they all mocked. Well, they won't be able to now, will they? They'll see my theories were sound.'

The Doctor's face darkened. 'Oh yes, they'll see, all right. As their front gardens are swallowed up by streams of molten lava, I'm sure the first thing they'll say will be "Poor old Porteous was right all along." Rather a Pyrrhic victory, wouldn't you say?'

Porteous shuffled. 'I didn't think that madman up top would ever get away with it. I'm desperately ashamed.'

Felicia regarded him with disdain. 'All a bit late in the day now, rather.'

'Not necessarily,' said the Doctor, picking over the machine parts, and fiddling in his pocket.

Harriet and the Colonel had managed to beat back the zombies pace by pace. The monsters had soon seen the error of their aggressive advance, and held their ground by moving back slowly, only occasionally stepping into the metal guns' range of fire. It was a cowardly tactic, but it had slowed their defeat considerably. Counting in their opponents' advantage was the ethereal nature of the mist that animated them. For as soon as a zombie body had been blown to fragments, the green vapour simply merged into the cloud of its nearest remaining brother.

'They're trying to waste our ammunition,' the Colonel realised. It was hard to credit a zombie with strategic skill. He waved his gun over at Harriet. 'Don't know what they're up against, do they? These are everlasting, I'll bet.'

'I'm afraid not,' Harriet called back. 'In fact, my clip is almost empty. So is yours. So conserve your fire.'

'Oh heck.' The Colonel looked between his gun and the line of zombies that remained. There were about eight of them, ragged, blackened walking skeletons, each flexing its bony fingers and rolling its jaw hungrily, waiting for the moment to strike.

Perhaps things weren't going so well after all.

Stackhouse connected the last of the leads to the small plastic contact points he had drilled into Julia's forehead. The woman still wore an expression of great agony. He sneered into her sightless eyes. 'You inconvenienced me, Contessa. It is good that you should feel pain, now, at the beginning of our partnership. You will not be tempted to rebel again.'

'You are… evil…' she whispered.

'Still conscious, eh? Good. Such spirit.' A noise distracted him, and he turned to look at the stimulator. Two of the attacking humans, a male and a female, had broken through and were hammering frantically at the program controls. They appeared not to have taken notice of him. A fatal error.

'Idiots,' he muttered. 'The stimulator is protected.'

A moment later a brilliant flash lit up the room for one second. When it had passed, the bodies of the humans lay at the base of the machine.

The Doctor stepped back from his work on the kinetograph. 'There we are,' he said softly, pointing out the remaining power pack from Percy's transceiver, which he had inserted at the base of the coiled wiring. 'It might gain us some time, anyway.'

Romana shrugged. 'An electrical charge can come in very handy against a zombie. Not much use on this side of the door, though.'

'Hmm. Solid steel, several inches thick,' said the Doctor despairingly. He leant his head against the cellar door and blew out his cheeks. The screech of blaster fire echoed from above. 'I wish I knew what was going on up there.'

'But we do know,' Felicia said happily. 'Our cavalry have come. I knew Percy wouldn't let us down.'

'It's hardly a cavalry,' Romana said gloomily. 'And I wouldn't rely on Percy for anything.'

Suddenly, the heavy door swung open smoothly. The Doctor tensed, expecting to see Stackhouse or one of his slaves. Instead there was revealed an unexpected, but far more reassuring, presence.

'Hello,' he said. 'I got sick of waiting up there. Thought they might have chucked you in here again.'

'Percy, dear!' Felicia emerged from the cellar and threw her arms around him. 'You're right on time!'

The Doctor, the remnants of the kinetograph clutched to his chest, was already bounding up the narrow flight of steps outside. Romana and Porteous hurried in his wake.

Percy shook his head. 'All this dash, dash, dash. It can't be good for them.'

The Colonel's fears were confirmed when he pressed the trigger button of his gun and there was no corresponding burst of blue fire from the barrel. 'The devil take it, I'm out of bullets!' he called to Harriet.

'So am I,' she cried back.

The zombies sensed their fear, and started to creep slowly forward.

Something in Harriet's voice stirred the Colonel. He shucked off his jacket and strutted forward manfully. 'Well, come on, then,' he shouted at his enemies. He put up his fists. 'Let's do this sportingly, shall we? You see, you chaps, I'm an Englishman. And you should be very frightened of that. Because an Englishman may be many things, but he never lets a lady down!' The monsters encroached but the Colonel held firm. 'Put them up!'

All of a sudden a brown blur whipped by him, moving at one hell of a lick. It outmanoeuvred the startled zombies, weaving between them in a crazed slalom, with a cry of 'Excuse me, gentlemen!' It took the Colonel a couple of seconds to realise that it was a feller, and another couple to realise that it was Romana's doctor friend, the painter with the scarf. Then Romana herself zipped by in hot pursuit, dragging a tubby little chap by the hand. They dodged the zombies as if they simply weren't there.

The zombies turned their backs on the Colonel, who immediately collapsed.

Harriet raced to his side and clapped her hands to his head, then leant his head against her breast. 'How brave!' she cried, thrilled.

The Doctor skidded to a halt before Stackhouse, who stood triumphantly over his escape capsule. The slave leader was hunched over the saucer, securing its new occupant to the sensor links within. The Doctor's eyes clouded with disgust as he saw the whitened features of Julia Orlostro, and the thick black wires trailing from plastic sockets on her forehead to the empty bell jar above. 'You've been busy, I see,' he said.

Stackhouse whirled about from the stimulator. 'You again!'

The Doctor gave a cheery wave. 'Yes, me again.'

'Ah, what do you matter now?' said Stackhouse, waving his arm contemptuously. 'The equation is stored safely in my memory. Your TARDIS will survive the destruction of Earth, and I shall unlock its secrets with ease. My apotheosis is near! I shall return to Phryxus mere moments after I left, and wreak my vengeance!'

'They only locked you up,' the Doctor pointed out. 'They could have killed you.'

'Perhaps they should have,' he replied. 'I had killed enough of them in my bid for power. Still, why should I tell you this? You are unimportant, Doctor. An irrelevance.' A thick trail of slime fell from his mouth. 'And I am hungry. So hungry. As are my slaves. They demand nutrition.'

'That's always the problem with slaves,' said the Doctor. 'Pay or conditions, it's never enough.'

At Stackhouse's words the slave leader stepped forward. 'At last... the feast begins...' It indicated the bodies slumped at the foot of the stimulator. 'These brains, sir: may I dine?'

Stackhouse fixed the Doctor with a wicked grin and said, 'You may. I shall dine upon the brain of this Time Lord.' He hissed, exposing snapping, rotted, viscid teeth. 'Yes, I shall dine well…'

The Doctor backed away, towards the stimulator, uncomfortably aware of the zombies massed around him. He could see Romana and Porteous running up from the corner of his eye. 'Before you do that, Zodaal, perhaps you'd like to have a look at this.' He held up a long roll of squared paper from the kinetograph, and with a flick of the wrist it unrolled.

'What is this?' said Stackhouse, batting it aside.

'I really would advise you to look, Zodaal,' the Doctor continued. 'You see, Porteous has been recording seismic activity for a couple of years, and your little tests of that thing –' he gestured to the stimulator – 'had rather disappointing results. It can't do half of what you claim.'

'Lies, Doctor,' said Stackhouse, but he was looking with interest at the read-out. 'I read the reports!'

The Doctor shook his head. 'You can't believe everything you see in the papers, Zodaal.' He held out the strip of paper. 'See for yourself. You got your sums wrong, just as your lot did before, on Phryxus. I suggest you put in some practice.'

Stackhouse took it and started to read. 'What is this? It is meaningless!'

'Now!' cried the Doctor.

Romana sprang forward, holding out the live, spitting end of the unwound kinetograph cable. Stackhouse saw her and moved to check her motion, but as his arm flew up it came into contact with the electric current.

Its effect was immediate. He went rigid and staggered backwards, his emerald aura now suffused with a flickering, buzzing, shower of sparks. Patches of the thick dead flesh coating his jowls blackened and dissolved. His face and hair melted like a candle seen in a speeded-up film, and long skeins of grey flesh dripped from his fingers like wax. His innards were exposed as he thrashed crazily, his clothes frying away until he resembled nothing so much as a rotting joint of meat. At the same time every one of his slaves reeled and wailed, their animating vapour pouring from their mouths, ears and nostrils like steam.

The Doctor pulled his gaze away from the horrid spectacle and leapt over to the upturned saucer of the escape capsule. He moved to pull the connection cables from Julia's forehead, but then saw how they had been attached directly, and winced. His hand moved above her, in an agony of indecision. 'I was too late,' he said at last. 'I'm sorry.'

She spoke in an agonised whisper. 'My own fault… My own greed… Quick… in my jacket…' She nodded downward. 'I cannot… move…'

The Doctor reached down and felt inside her jacket. His fingers furled around the grips of a small silver pistol. He brought it out, looked down at her, and shook his head. 'I'm afraid I simply don't do that sort of thing.'

'Even…' she gasped. 'Even… to save… the world?'

He handed her the gun. 'The responsibility is yours.'

There was a sudden flurry of activity to his side. He looked up to see that Stackhouse's body had now almost totally dissolved, and the billowing green mass of the core was rising from it and rushing towards him. Seeing that her work was done, Romana dropped the cable and backed away with Porteous. At the same time, the slaves started to drop, falling one by one like the dead meat they in truth were. The vapour from their bodies swirled and coalesced, drifting towards the core and forming part of its great mass, until only the slave leader remained, fallen on his knees but looking up at the Doctor with fiercely glowing eyes.

'Fool!' he shrieked. 'Nothing can halt the apotheosis of Zodaal's eternal will! This planet is doomed!' That said, the body flopped like a puppet and the gas fled to join its greater mass.

The huge cloud hovered over them.

Romana clutched the Doctor's arm. 'What's it doing? Will it attack us?'

'It tried that once before, remember,' he told her. 'No, its priority now will be to rebottle itself and get away.'

His prediction was soon borne out. The cloud shifted until it was directly above the escape capsule. Then it assumed a funnel shape, and poured itself into the bell jar. The entire process took less than five seconds, and as soon as the cloud was safely stored, the top half of the saucer clamped down.

'What now?' asked Romana.

'I suggest we get down,' said the Doctor. He pulled her to the floor, on which Porteous had already bowed his head to mutter some kind of prayer.

Even as he spoke, the saucer started to vibrate and spin wildly. In less than half a minute it had attained its optimum momentum, and they lifted their heads as it zoomed upwards on a stream of hazy air, its anti-gravity motors sending it streaking up to the high roof of the warehouse. There was a splintering boom and it passed through the roof and up into the night sky.

Romana stood up. 'He got away.'

The Doctor shook his head. 'No, I don't think so.'

Julia felt the earth falling away beneath her. She could see nothing but the upper half of the padded escape capsule, and could hear nothing but the thrum of its power as it lifted her up. She thought of London, as she had seen it from the air, of the great mass of people down below, rich and poor alike. A hot tear trickled down her cheek.

She heard a voice of unutterable malignance, oozing with hatred, whisper, 'We will wait here, you and I, for the death of that pathetic planet. Then you will be mine.'

With unbearable effort, Julia raised her burnt arm and brought the tip of her pistol to a point directly between her eyes.

*

'Is there any way to switch that thing off?' the Doctor demanded of Porteous as he hustled him towards the still active sonic stimulator.

'The program panel's wired up, Doctor,' Romana called warningly. 'It's terribly interactive.' She had knelt to examine the bodies at the foot of the machine. 'They're alive, but it's protected.'

'Master, Mistress,' said a familiar tinny voice.

'I wondered where you'd got to,' the Doctor snapped. He looked about but there was no sign of K-9. 'Come and lend a hand, wherever you are.'

'This unit has been immobilised, Master,' said K-9. 'Request immediate carriage.' His eyescreen flashed from the shadows.

Romana lifted him up and brought him across. 'Doctor. We could channel the power from the security device through K-9.'

He grinned. 'You are suddenly full of good ideas. I've almost forgotten how useless you were earlier. Get him linked up.'

Within seconds, Romana had positioned K-9, muzzle forwards, against the stimulator's program panel. The moment he touched its surface a crackle of energy buzzed about his own antennae. 'Absorbing energy flow.'

The Doctor took this as his cue, and his fingers dived for the program panel, where they immediately collided with Romana's fingers. They locked eyes. 'I think I'd better do this, hadn't I?' he said.

She removed her hand.

The Doctor worked furiously at the keyboard. Schematic outlines of the continents and their shifting bases flashed over the main fascia in a blur. 'It'll take days to unravel all of this,' he said, shooting a venomous glance at Porteous. 'You really are too clever for your own good.' He shrugged and removed his hands. 'Of course, there is another way.'

'What's that?' asked Romana.

'I'm sure K-9 can guess,' said the Doctor.

'Reverse the fluctuations of the machine's power source,' said K-9.

Romana was appalled. 'But that could destroy this entire country!'

'If we leave it running it'll destroy the world,' said the Doctor. 'If we stop it now, chances are it'll take only the surrounding area with it.'

'How much of the surrounding area?'

He smirked. 'Well, I wouldn't stand there if I were you.' Then his hands returned to the program panel. 'Lend a paw, K-9.'

K-9 extended his probe. 'I am instructing the power source to close down, Master.'

Romana hurried away from them. Godfrey and Davina were just coming to their senses, and she ushered them and Porteous in the opposite direction, towards the doors. 'Come on, we've got to get out of here, all of us!' Through the clearing mist of battle, and over the fallen bodies of the slaves, she saw Harriet staggering up, supporting the Colonel. 'Get away!' she called, gesturing urgently. 'Get away!'

'What's going on now?' the Colonel demanded. 'What happened to all those zombie characters?'

'They're dead, Colonel,' said Romana, urging him back.

'Didn't seem to stop 'em before,' he grunted, sounding dismayed. 'Shame. I was about to give 'em what for, eh?' And to Romana's astonishment, and relief, he gave Harriet's waist a playful squeeze.

'Please, there's no time to talk,' she reminded them all. Then a thought struck her. 'Wait a moment. Where are Percy and Mrs Chater?'

The Colonel pricked up his ears. 'Chater? Felicia Chater? What's she doing mixed up in all this? Thought she was a right stay-at-home type.'

'Thank you, Colonel Radlett,' said the icy cool voice of Felicia, who appeared suddenly with her arm entwined around Percy's.

'But I'm quite capable of leaving the house without coming to harm.'

'Wish I could say the same,' said Percy.

There was a strange, uncomfortable moment in which everyone in the small group looked at everyone else trying to work out who was with whom and doing what.

'For the last time,' Romana bellowed at the top of her voice, 'move!'

'Critical state has been attained, Master,' K-9 reported. 'Suggest immediate evacuation.'

The Doctor looked up proudly from his work on the program panel. 'Well done, you. Well done me, come to that.' He leapt away from the stimulator, which had started to groan, loudly and alarmingly. As he strode briskly away he struck his chest and declaimed, 'And thus the whirligig of time brings in his revenges…'

'Master,' K-9 called urgently. 'I have been immobilised. Request your assistance!'

The Doctor doubled back at once and swept K-9 up in his arms. 'Did you think I'd forgotten?'

'Affirmative, Master,' spluttered K-9. 'Immediate evacuation required!'

The Doctor raced back off. The stimulator shook and bellowed, and the rotten bodies of Stackhouse and his slaves were immolated in the first wave of fire that burst from the raging machine. Over the final roar of the device, the Doctor's voice echoed back.

'Oh, the pity of it, K-9, the pity of it…'

Romana was overcome by worry as, from her position of supposed safety behind the Colonel's car, surrounded by her small entourage of fellow adventurers, she saw the blackened windows of Stackhouse's silent warehouse glow pink, then bulge, and then shatter outwards in a rapid series of tinkling percussions. For a second, she feared the worst – and then the Doctor bounded through the open doors, K-9 in his arms, a ridiculous grin on his face.

She ran out, grabbed him, and pulled him to the ground.

A moment later, a soundless explosion claimed the warehouse for itself, sucking the structure inwards with a gigantic inrush of sound and energy. When she lifted her head, it had simply disappeared.

'What about Zodaal?' she asked the Doctor.

'What about him?' he replied.

Zodaal waited inside the containment vessel. In his imagination he pictured the imminent destruction of Earth. Nothing could prevent it. His technology was infallible. Soon there would be enough energy to transfer, become whole again. To touch, to feel, to experience life as a living creature does. He was still weak after his flight from the Doctor, and the feast he had for so long anticipated had been denied him, but soon his vengeance would be visited on humanity.

And then he sensed a stillness, an emptiness about him. He concentrated the psychic talents of his core, and probed the mind of Julia Orlostro.

The mind was empty. Dead. The brain had been destroyed; she had destroyed her own brain. There was no outlet! He was trapped in the vessel, with not even the dying brain of a human to flee to! With not even the freedom to dissolve on the air! The vessel was strong, unbreakable from the inside. With no outlet, he might drift for millennia through the reaches of space – eternal, immortal, formless!

'I'm telling you,' Percy told the assembled company. 'That women in there was the Contessa di Straglione. The diamond-loving adventuress! To think she had a gun at my head!' He nodded to what remained of the warehouse. 'Must have perished in there. It's true what they say. A crime leads to its own detection.'

The Doctor was looking oddly at him. 'I think you have a lot to thank the Contessa for,' he said. 'She was the pivot of Zodaal's scheme. Without her, he'll just drift on and on.'

'Until somebody sets him free,' Romana pointed out.

'Not our problem,' said the Doctor. That said, he turned to face all of the people he and Romana had collected. It was still raining, but now the rain seemed somehow natural, and under the street lamps' glow the gathered faces seemed to shine with a new kind of hope.

'What now, then, Doctor?' asked the bedraggled Percy.

'Well, I don't know about you,' the Doctor replied. 'But I could strangle a cup of cocoa.'

The Colonel shook his head. 'Chap's clearly twisted,' he whispered to Harriet, who was resting her head on his shoulder.

12
AS WE WERE

The following afternoon, after everyone had had the chance to freshen themselves up and get some sleep, Felicia opened the doors of her new home to all of her exciting new friends. After all their exertions it was, she had decided, more than necessary, so that everyone could compare notes and stories, and also because she burned with curiosity. Percy had explained as best he could, and rather reluctantly, about the Circle, and said that, in the circumstances, although it was highly irregular, she could be considered for membership.

So now they were all gathered in her drawing room, a noisy bunch, knocking back cocktails and puffing on foreign cigarettes, and here she was at the very heart of it all, the hostess! So very different from the stuffy social occasions in Shillinghurst – how she had risen above all of that! Percy had brought his gramophone around from next door, and a jazzy modern melody was playing. The old Colonel had grumbled a bit about that at first, but his new-found friend, the demure Harriet, shushed him, and amazingly he caved in.

Percy was ensconced in her most comfortable chair, regaling the gathering. 'I'd never been so terrified in all my life,' he was saying, coming to the conclusion of his tale, 'as when that wretched zombie stalked into the coal cellar. But then dear Felicia –' and here he broke off to clasp her hand tightly – 'dear

Felicia struck, and knocked its head clean off!'

Everyone clapped, Felicia curtseyed politely, and Godfrey Wyse said, 'I suppose that's when your heart melted, Perce. You knew if you refused her you'd be next!' Everyone laughed.

Harriet was the next to speak. 'Really, I never took you for the marrying type, Percy.'

'Every man must one day hang up his vagabond shoes,' Percy said evasively. 'And I might say the same for you, Harriet, dear.'

Harriet giggled and clasped the Colonel's hand. 'Well, you might also say that I hadn't met quite the right chap until yesterday.'

'Quite right,' the Colonel boomed. 'These fancy fellows one sees about are no match for a bit of experience.'

'And the Colonel has the most super collection of rifles and other pieces,' Harriet enthused. 'He and I share a common passion.' Everyone sighed affectionately. 'Go on,' Harriet urged the Colonel, 'tell everyone what you were telling me earlier, that tale about coming across that tiger of yours.'

The Colonel made no show of reluctance. 'Well, there I was, you see, posted to the jungle near Futipur-Sekri, and as I trudged up the dry mullah-wallah…'

The jolly atmosphere lessened instantly, but everyone made a special effort to pay attention, for Harriet's sake. Felicia caught the eye of her beloved, and they shared a secret, significant look. And that look lifted Felicia's heart for a second, and made her feel a moment's charity for the entire company, yes, even for the tedious old Colonel. In the last few days she'd had an adventure and met a husband, and all had turned out right.

She waited for an opportune lull in the Colonel's narrative to cut across with, 'I think I'll check up on the Doctor and Romana. See if they've finished tinkering with that clockwork dog of theirs.' She rose.

Percy stood also. 'I shall join you, my dear.'

Harriet laughed. 'There, you see! She has you on a string, Percy!'

Felicia ignored the remark, smiled graciously, and filed through to the study with Percy in tow. Inside the small room they found a most extraordinary scene. K-9 was upended on the table, and while Romana probed about his exposed innards with a pair of pliers, the Doctor was hunched up next to the dog's upside-down head with *The Times* in one hand and a pencil in the other. 'What about this? "A speed restriction; Italian potter's hour"?' he was saying. 'Seven letters, something m something something something r something.'

'Amphora, Master,' said K-9.

'Eh?' said the Doctor. 'Amphora, what do you mean, amphora? How do you... Ah, yes, amphora, of course.' He scribbled in the solution. 'Amphora. You must be getting better.'

'His traction's running,' said Romana. With seemingly no effort she picked K-9 up and set him to rights. 'How's that, K-9?'

'Most satisfactory, Mistress,' said K-9, darting around the table to test his new fittings. 'Clue, Master.'

'All right, all right,' said the Doctor. 'How about "a cute little ratio", in six, with an s for the third?'

'Cosine,' said Romana and K-9 at the same time.

'Ha, yes, very clever,' said the Doctor.

Felicia coughed. 'Er, Doctor? Are you coming through?'

He looked baffled. 'Coming through what?'

'Coming through for cocktails and sandwiches,' Felicia said patiently.

The Doctor shuffled and looked uneasy. 'Well, I had a meal about a week ago, and I...'

Felicia stared at him accusingly.

'Oh, all right, then. Just the one.'

As they walked back to the drawing room, K-9 at their heels, Felicia asked Romana, 'Tell me, my dear, have you been presented?'

'I'm not sure,' said Romana. 'What with?'

'No, no, silly, presented,' said Felicia. 'You know, you ought to get out of those boys' clothes and into something more proper. I could have a word with my couturiers, a lovely pair of sisters who can turn their hands to anything. Oh, if I were your age, well, right now I'd be walking up and down Bond Street being noticed.'

'If you were my age—' Romana began, but the Doctor shushed her.

They returned to the drawing room to find Harriet waving a piece of paper and the company wearing a look of combined amusement and shock. 'You'll never guess,' she said, 'you'll simply never guess.'

'It's a telegram,' said Percy.

'Yes, but who do you think it's from?' cried Harriet.

'Well, we won't know until you tell us,' said Felicia.

'Listen,' said Harriet with a wicked gleam in her eye. She read aloud. ' "Dear All, stop, gone up to Edinburgh, stop, the world of science can go thump, stop, will marry on Tuesday, stop, no flowers, stop, Davina and Heath"!'

Percy's eyes nearly popped from his head. 'Old Chippers, taking up with that grubby little scientist! Who'd have thought it!'

'I suppose strange events make for a strong bond,' said Felicia. 'I say! Even Rufusa has found a mate, it appears!'

She pointed to where Rufusa was nuzzling up to the snout of K-9, who viewed the approach with metallic disdain. 'I am programmed to protect myself,' he said chirpily, and everyone laughed at that, too.

The merriment continued a few minutes more, and from Percy's point of view the world had never seemed a happier place. The bright sunshine was back, but it was an even, temperate, English sunshine. It was hard to believe that their arduous encounter with Zodaal had happened at all. There were only a couple of reminders of their ordeal: a tin of Stackhouse's biscuits on the table (he had reached for a Zanzibar cracknel but found it bitter), and a splendidly pompous paragraph cut out from the morning paper, in which several of Porteous's old colleagues in the meteorological sphere attempted to explain away the quirks in the climate of late. Now he had time to think and be grateful for the good the adventure had done him. His new wife was sure to keep him on a steadier keel, and he would cherish their companionship. They would take strolls, attend functions, and generally sneer at everybody else. After all, she was a famous novelist and he was a celebrated host. They would thrive on each other's reputations. What fun it was going to be!

His thoughts were drifting, aided by the smoky air, the babble of conversation, and the drink, but he was sober enough to pick out a fragment of conversation that passed between the Doctor and Romana.

'Six letters, a box that can be big or small, t something r something i something,' said the Doctor.

'Already?' asked Romana, a little sadly.

'Well, you were the one who didn't want to come here in the first place.'

'Please don't be smug, Doctor. I suppose we can't say goodbye?' She looked regretfully at the Colonel in particular.

'They'd never let us go,' replied the Doctor. 'And we shouldn't linger. Just in case the Black you-know-who should turn up. Do you know, I never got to take those books back. Never mind.' He picked up K-9's basket from the corner where it rested, and ushered his pet back in.

They slipped out in the hubbub, and nobody else noticed, being far too caught up watching the now red-faced Colonel leading Harriet around the room in an erratic *pas de deux*. K-9 trundled unobtrusively after them.

Percy slipped out in pursuit, and caught them in the hallway. 'Where are you three off to, then?'

Romana sighed. 'If only we knew.' She stuck out a hand.

'Goodbye, Percy. Give our regards to the others.'

Percy shook her hand. 'Ah, well. Toodle-pip and all that.' He addressed the Doctor. 'Er, I'll try not to do anything irresponsible in the future.'

The Doctor smiled. 'I think you already have,' he said with good humour, and then he, Romana and K-9 were gone, slipping through the front door into the dazzling June day.